Rusalka

by Agnieszka Kazmierczyk

PAPERBACK ISBN: 978-1-7353456-8-0
EPUB ISBN: 978-1-3937237-0-7

***

WRITTEN BY AGNIESZKA KAZMIERCZYK
PUBLISHED BY ROYAL HAWAIIAN PRESS
COVER ART BY DANIELA IVANOVA WITH PERMISSION
COVER DESIGN BY TYRONE ROSHANTHA
TRANSLATED BY RAFAL STACHOWSKY
PUBLISHING ASSISTANCE: DOROTA RESZKE

***

FOR MORE WORKS BY THIS AUTHOR, PLEASE VISIT:
WWW.ROYALHAWAIIANPRESS.COM

***

VERSION NUMBER 1.00

1

The news of the move fell on Wojtek unexpectedly like a flowerpot from the fourth floor. Had he not passed through enough in his sixteen years? It seemed to him that he could share his own experiences with at least a few of his weenie friends from school. Or maybe the trip should be a cure for the father? After all, for several years he has been talking about "lack of self-realization", "routine" and "unfulfilled youthful ideals". He always used to say that the years spent at the AGH University of Science and Technology in Krakow were the best in his life, and that not every student graduated from the power engineering department.

Antoni Stożyński had no luck in life. He grew up without a father. He was not a half-orphan, although he would have liked it sometimes. The mother's salary was barely enough to cover the basic bills - father drank his earnings regularly and consistently. After vodka, he was neither aggressive nor vulgar. His quiet, drunken existence, however, disturbed the peaceful life of Antek and his sister Kaśka. It was hard for him to focus on his studies, although he was an extremely talented student. He couldn't read in peace, and that was his favorite activity. Finally, he had to take over any "male" housework. That's why he became a great engineer in the future - not only in theory.

When he met Ewa, his fate changed. He was then a fresh graduate of a prestigious university, looking for a job. She, a fourth-year student of pedagogy at the nearby Pedagogical University - today's UP. During his studies, Antoni dreamed of building a modern power plant, and thus, brief student liaison was not in his head. Ewa changed his worldview. Love exploded suddenly, and its fruit, Wojtek, appeared a year and a half after the couple's first meeting at one of the events in the Olimp dormitory.

It might seem that two young people - without a job, with a child on the way - will fall into a kind of melancholy, because in the 1980s the word "depression" was not as fashionable as it is today. However, this did not happen. Antek got a job in Bielsk Podlaski in an oil refinery plant. Wojtek patiently waited for his mother to obtain a master's degree and only then decided to appear in her and father's world. Ewa did not part with the boy immediately, but she also started her professional career soon.

After the fat years, it's time for the lean ones. After a routine gynecological examination, Ewa had a tumor in the small pelvis. It seemed harmless, but the attending physician decided to perform laparoscopic removal of the unwanted foreign body. Ewa, carefree by nature, did not acknowledge that the excised tumor must be subjected to detailed histopathological examination, because it could turn out to be a malignant formation. She only heard that five days after the operation, she would return to her boys. It also happened.

Two weeks later the phone rang. Thirty-four-year-old Ewa, working at the Pedagogical and Psychological Clinic at that time, picked up the receiver, but did not know that this conversation would turn her whole life upside down.

Wojtek lost his mother when he turned thirteen. It coincided with the change of primary school into middle school, where he knew no one. Perhaps it was better, because he didn't feel like confiding in old buddies or making new friends. The text "lost my mother a few weeks ago" worked perfectly. The potential interlocutor turned on his heel and left Wojtek in the longed-for peace.

Now again for something. After three relatively quiet years, another change was preparing in the silly work of the next minister of education - the junior high school. And what kind.

But why Belarus? - he had been asking his father for several days. After all, they also have power plants in Poland. Except that the "old man" insisted and wouldn't let go. He mentioned something about an ideal moment. But what was this perfect moment supposed to be? Because his mother died and he couldn't deal with it? Because school was over and you could settle in during the summer holidays? Well, probably not because they have better schools in Belarus? Wojtek had been wondering about his father's motives for many days.

The fact was that Antoni Stożyński dreamed of a big case, and the construction of a wind farm in Nowogródek was a dream come true. Not to mention the fact that just the thought of something new gave him the strength to get out of bed in the morning. And Wojtek - yes, Wojtek was another reason.

2

Two weeks left until school graduation. The official farewell of the third grades, the presentation of awards and diplomas was terrifying. Wojtek was, in short, alienated. This is what his tutor, Mrs. Lisowska, told his father about him. What did it mean? That he didn't have a girlfriend, that he didn't drink at parties with his classmates, or that he wasn't smiling? And he hadn't been smiling since the first day of junior high school. He had no reasons.

It wasn't always like that. He had a happy family. His old folks were jealous of him. Because they downloaded the latest movies from the Internet, because they knew Rihanna's songs and took him on a wonderful holiday abroad every year. And not to some Egypt or any other Arab crap, but to Cuba, Sri Lanka, and Malediev. Yes, Wojtek did not lack money. But it wasn't them, contrary to what his buddies thought, that made him happy. You could always talk to your mother normally. Father trusted him immensely. And they always had time for him. Classmates were given two hundred zlotys instead of a family dinner, "so that they could buy themselves something nice" or a new laptop and did not bother when "adults work hard to pay the rent". Yes, his folks were cool. But life is not a fairy tale, it's a fucking reality - Wojtek thought.

When did he start cursing? I guess when mother said about the diagnosis, or a little later, when she took her first chemo.

He wasn't always like this. After all, that's not how they raised him. In primary school he had many friends, he experienced his first love. He was a top student, but also captain of the school football team. He talked a lot and his laughter was infectious. Even then, his mother claimed that his Slavic beauty would one day be appreciated by representatives of the opposite sex. Tall after his father, blonde after his mother. And those blue eyes... Some said they weren't blue, they were transparent. They have been compared to the eyes of Husky dogs or to the color of the Caribbean Sea. It made him laugh.

He has changed. Not only externally. It had started with a change of clothes, black clothes had started to dominate his wardrobe after his mother died, and now, three years later, he was still so - gray. He became rude, indifferent, nothing pleased him. Yes, he did report on every day to his father, but he could see that his interlocutor was staring as blankly as he himself. He read a lot, his father had a large bookcase. He left the football. He listened to music more often or sat in front of a computer. Antoni worked a lot and he didn't feel the need to talk to anyone else. After seeing the Suicide Room film, he also gave up visiting online chats. He also didn't use Facebook for a long time, although his friends from primary school tormented him with new messages and questions. He didn't know if it was concern or meddling.

On the one hand, the move terrified him, on the other, it gave rise to a strange and forgotten feeling of excitement - about the unknown. He opened his laptop and typed in a search engine: Belarus. He accessed Wikipedia, which he really hated. At the moment, however, he did not care. They were to live in a village in the Nowogródek County. Father was supposed to work in his capital - Nowogródek. The numbers were ruthless. Fifty-three thousand inhabitants. All over the county. There were twenty-five thousand of them in Bielsko - in one city. He omitted historical information, found something about the planned construction of a power plant. And finally, what he knew from school. Lake Świteź was nearby. He associated the betrayal of the shooter from Mickiewicz's piece only because their Polish teacher made a debate on this subject, it was even funny. The father promised to find him a good high school. His grades were decent, and he should have gotten somewhere easily. He has been learning Russian, as well as English and German, for ten years. Antoni always said that if the opportunity arose, they would leave. Mother did not mind, and because they wanted to be properly prepared, they learned three languages. So far, the holidays were beginning and Wojtek was to have a summer house at the famous lake at his disposal. If only I would not share the fate of the shooter, he thought, and smiled to himself. For the first time in... a long time.

3

Like almost every man, Wojtek hated packing. However, he assumed that he was leaving a certain stage of his life behind him in Bielsko, and thus, he would not take up any junk that had only sentimental and mental value. In fact, what surprised father, he put his things in one small suitcase. In addition to the clothes, there was a large photo of all three of them - from a time when they did not know yet that their happiness was about to end. In moments like this, when things ended, he always wished he had any siblings. It would be nice to have someone who is with you all the time, even when you're down or snarling at everyone. Unfortunately, the parents explained that they could not have more children because of some mother's problems. Later they intensified.

"You have everything?" Father called from the porch. "There is already a car, I would also like to move already, to unpack before dark."

"I'm going, I'm going..." Wojtek felt a strange feeling. He was never to come back home, which he associated with a warm childhood, boundless love and puppy years. He just sighed and ran down the stairs.

They spoke little on the way. Anyway, lately it has been difficult for them to get along at all. The mother topic was virtually nonexistent. And starting others did not come to Wojtek as easily and spontaneously as before with Ewa.

Antoni, on the other hand, thought that whatever he said would sound banal, old-fashioned and create an even greater wall, one that they would no longer be able to walk through or tear down. He didn't really know what his son was in his head right now, what he was thinking about, what his plans were, and whether Eve's death made any impression on him. He had never seen Wojtek cry, even at a funeral, he had to be comforted instead of a teenager. He expected rebellion, bouts of aggression, impudent behavior or depression, tears and all that post-funeral hysteria. None of these things came up. And that worried Antoni the most. Knowing that he would have to devote several hours a day to work, he found a large wooden house right by Lake Świteź. Perhaps Wojtek will rest there, collect his thoughts and take a break from the hustle and bustle. But won't he be bored to death?

They arrived there shortly after sunset. The town gave the impression that time had stopped here. Wojtek watched the emerging roofs of houses, and then city buildings. They did not differ much from those he knew from Poland. He did not feel the climate change, the breath of exoticism. In fact, it was just like home here. Or maybe it didn't matter to him and he did not pay attention to the obvious differences? He wanted to go to sleep and forget for a moment the pain of existence.

4

There were no blinds on the windows. In general, the apartment rented by father's company seemed very modern and - for a moment lacked a word - sterile. Yes, the white walls, glass stairs and metal handrails were definitely not conducive to creating the atmosphere of the warmth of a family fireplace. The apartment - that was what father used to call it, consisted of the downstairs, i.e. an open living room with a kitchen, a study, a bathroom and a toilet. Upstairs, they had two bedrooms and a large wardrobe. Mother would go crazy about it, Wojtek thought, but in a moment he pushed the thought away, replacing it with a question: What will we guys fill all these baskets, shelves, hangers with? He liked to dress well, preferably at a brand store, but he had never been a metrosexual armpit shaving cutter.

His bedroom was fine. A large bed, a desk and a table with two chairs. Everything is white with elements of black glass. He also liked the skylights, they let in a lot of light. And Wojtek needed light, because apart from reading, his first passion, he had one more - drawing. Not views, landscapes, but the dark faces of a man. His anger, fury, pain... He used only a black crayon or a pencil, and he did not show his scribbles to anyone, locking them in the proverbial drawer.

Father suggested a tour of the area and some hot snacks. Since there was no mother, they ate whatever they could. Most often, these were jar-filled meatballs or ready-made dishes from a nearby shop. They didn't really have any relatives. Father's side grandpa drank himself to death - Wojtek did not know exactly what it meant. Grandma died shortly after him, suffered a massive heart attack and did not survive the decisive next day. Aunt Kaśka, father's sister, went abroad because she met an Arab and there was no contact with her. Mother's parents, from what she said, hadn't been in touch with her. She paid for her studies herself, working in the evenings. They were also not interested in their daughter's wedding or the birth of a grandson. Even when Ewa was dying, they did not visit her in the hospital or hospice. He hated them, although he knew little about them. When asked about his grandparents, he said: "all died". There was only a sewn-on aunt, Monika. Mom's best friend and cousin. The crazy traveler who always made him laugh. Now they talked quite rarely, although she promised to visit them in Belarus, because she has a few points on her travel map to count there.

They entered the restaurant. It looked like the ones he had seen in Zakopane. Decorated in a traditional way. He could not read the menu, but his father recommended him a potato cake, and syrniki for dessert. In general, Antoni explained that Belarusian cuisine is based on potatoes, or rather potato mass, and various types of dumplings. Wojtek was not very interested in it. He knew he had to find a self-service market in which he will be able to buy semi-finished products.

"Today we will go to the lake. We will spend the entire afternoon together, we will see the area. From tomorrow, unfortunately, I will have to spend a lot of time reviewing projects and talking to investors. Don't be angry, we'll spend every weekend together any way you like." In Antoni's voice you could hear an attempt to explain himself and thus silence the remorse. He knew the boy had only him now, but he had to earn money to give him a decent life, education, and a future. He had no other choice.

"Fine. Are there any other houses? Anyone looking in there?" This time Wojtek did not just try to keep the conversation going, but for a moment he thought that maybe he would meet someone interesting.

"As far as I know, apart from our big house, there are two smaller ones. There is a lonely old woman in one of them, I am not sure about the other. You'll find out for yourself as soon as we get there."

"Cool," Wojtek replied, and in his head came the thought that it could not be worse. Not only he will land on a total crap, somewhere at the end of the civilized world, but his neighbor instead of an attractive, long-legged brunette will be a lonely old lady. But he had been trying to ward off bad thoughts for some time, so he stuck his teeth into the last bit of the syrnik cake and savoring the taste of the dessert.

5

After driving a car for an hour and a half, they reached the designated place. He even liked it because it was so... dark. It was only five o'clock, but this was where the darkness began. Wojtek did not know if it was the fault of the changed climate or the mist that was hovering over the lake. In the wooden house, his harbor, he left his backpack for the next two months and, without looking around, decided to go around the lake. It was surrounded by something like a shaft made of tangled roots. There was only a dense forest nearby. For a moment, Wojtek felt uncomfortable... But he is a man and he will not be afraid just because he spends his holidays at a campground in the forest. He wanted to check the color of Świteź's water, but there was little to see through the fog. All he saw was white. At that time, he did not know yet that it was a lobelia, which bloomed white in the summer months. He also had no idea that her flowers contained poisonous lobeline.

"Wojtek! Go home because the mists are about to get so thick you won't find your way!" Father alarmed.

The teenager humbly listened to the request, knowing that from tomorrow he would be the helm, sailor, and ship himself, and for most of the week no one would bother him with lessons.

"The refrigerator is full. You have vegetables, fruit, meat in the freezer, dairy products, drinks..." father enumerated standing by the open refrigerator, while Wojtek was already "enveloping" other rooms.

The cabin was single-level but large. There was a bathroom with a large bathtub, a toilet, a bedroom with three beds, a kitchen with a bar table and a large living room with a fireplace. Even though it was the end of June, it wasn't warm at all. There was dampness, though the house looked freshly restored.

"You have to know your old man's fine connections. "Antoni, noticing that the conversation about the provisions had failed the test, decided to change the subject.

"Yeah, where?" Wojtek replied with a slight irony, but half smiling, looking at his father.

"The cottage and the whole surrounding area are currently owned by the Belarusian authorities, which established a landscape reserve here. In the past, Świteź was privately owned, but they did not care for it well enough.

"How can I spend my vacation here, since it is a national park?" Wojtek was surprised.

"Hmm... Let's say that someone high-ranking wanted me to work for him, and I, in turn, really wanted my only fantastic son to have a vacation that others can dream of. And now everyone is happy." You could see the pride on Antoni's face.

Wojtek did not answer anything, but patted his father on the shoulder. However, this symbolic gesture was more important to both of them. Antoni felt appreciated for a moment, and his son realized that he was still very important to someone, although sometimes he had a different impression.

There was no television in the cottage, the internet only worked occasionally and with very little power. The phone only caught range when it was reclining on the porch. So there was nothing left for Stożyński but to take out the cards and play a rummy tournament. It was one of their many family traditions. In the past, Ewa took care of the entire setting. There was a table with the name of the tournament - each had a different name. So there was the Lenten tournament, the generations tournament, the birthday tournament, and so on. After the game was over, everyone received commemorative diplomas (printed on their home printer).

She would definitely call today's match: the men's tournament. They, in turn, treated it as a method to pass the time. After dinner, they quickly fell asleep, tired of the road, the move and the emotions that had been felt for the last few days.

6

When Wojtek woke up and looked at his watch, he couldn't believe it was almost noon. Before he stretched, he noticed a note left by his father: "You snored pretty good, so I didn't wake you up. I'll be here Friday night, if anything happens, call me. Dad."

"What would be going on here?" Wojtek shook his head and decided to make a plan for the rest of the day.

Outside the window the sun was shining quite intensely. The croaking of frogs and birds was also heard. Wojtek ate a quick breakfast (lunch?) and decided to get to know the neighbors. However, it was not as easy as it might seem. It took him about two hours to walk along the lake shore, and only then a tiny house emerged from the distance. Wojtek, although he was not very keen on a social chat, decided it would be good to have a friend nearby in case... in case something could happen.

Taking his time, he finally reached his destination. The scenery and the apartment itself reminded him of fairy tales read by his mother in her childhood. It looked like a crumbling cottage of the witch from Hansel and Gretel or a mud hut from a fairy tale about a golden fish. Outside, there were bunches of weeds which gave off quite a pleasant smell. A black cat was lying on the porch, which gave the landscape an even more mysterious and fairy-tale atmosphere.

Wojtek knocked on the door and after a while an old lady appeared, apparently the one father mentioned earlier.

"Good morning. I am Wojtek Stożyński and I will be your neighbor for the next eight weeks." In short, he introduced himself to a new friend.

The old woman did not seem surprised by the boy sight. She looked closely at him and invited him inside, gesturing with her hand. So Wojtek did not immediately hear her voice.

She was wearing a long, cornflower cotton dress. Her hair was white as yesterday's evening lake, and her face was marked with remnants of the past. It seemed to hide a secret, although Wojtek believes that all old people had it to themselves.

"You have very sad eyes," she finally began the conversation.

"There was a lot of gossip about you and your family in the area, even before you moved here. I do not listen to gossip, but it is easy to read from your face that something very bad has happened to you or someone close to you," she continued.

Wojtek felt a sudden discouragement towards the newly met person. He envisioned her as a long-lost grandmother who would receive him with open arms, serving him freshly baked cookies and hot milk. A grandmother who will not ask unnecessary questions, but will listen when necessary, hug him and not send back without wise life advice.

Now, however, he has lost all his enthusiasm. He saw the old gossipmonger who only dreamed of a new sensation. It was supposed to be a holiday attraction, a new entertainment for nearby people. A toy that will dispel the boredom of the coming summer days.

The woman sensed the sudden change that was taking place in the boy, and as if reading his mind, she said:

"No, I'm not a gossipmonger. Nor do I care if what they say is true. If you like, tell me your story yourself. My name is Olga and I was born eighty four years ago. My friends died long ago, and my family went to another city for bread. You don't replant old trees so I'm left alone here, but that's not a complaint. I was comfortable with my loneliness. Now the kids are back and live in a cottage on the other side of the lake. But I still feel lonely. Hmm... two lonely people far from the world. I think we have more in common than you might think." She turned and set a pot of water on the tiled stove.

Wojtek stood speechless. The tone of this woman, the timbre of her voice and the wisdom that emanated from those simple words that had just dropped to the floor, made him want to stay here longer.

She made herbal tea for him. They tried to talk. Russian mixed with Polish. However, the need to exchange opinions, experiences and feelings was so strong that the language barrier turned out to be a minor obstacle. Olga was known in the area as a herbalist or a healer. People who ceased to believe in saving actions of drugs or medicine were able to help them anymore.

The old woman did not refuse support and advice. In her little cupboard, she gathered paper bags, each with a label. There were dried poppies, coltsfoot, wormwood and much more. Each of them had its own unique properties. Wojtek did not immediately open up to a stranger. It was only when Olga began to reveal her secrets that he became more daring.

"I have three kids. I had five. I didn't get married for love. My lover was very poor. Parents did not want to hear about our joint plans. They found another candidate for a husband for me. Over time, I got used to this situation. I got my first pregnancy right after I got married, they were twins. They died in my womb. Then my daughter Svetlana and son Anatol were born. We lived peacefully, but after the Chernobyl disaster, the children decided to leave Świtez for some time. However, it was mainly associated with financial problems. Ivan, my husband, died at the age of sixty-seven. Then Svetlana wanted me to live with them in their new home, in a small town. I did not agree, then they returned." Apparently tired of the constant telling, Olga drank the herbal tea. "Enough about me. It's enough for the first meeting. You know, it's weird because I've never told anyone about these things before. You seem to be trustworthy," she added.

Wojtek was not bored with the stories of the old lady. On the contrary, he had not listened to anyone so great interest for a long time. He knew this was not the last meeting in a small cabin.

"Come on, now you tell me at least one story about your short life..." Olga encouraged.

The boy didn't know what to talk about. About the mother's illness, about her slow dying, about the deteriorating relationship with the father, about loneliness, a feeling of helplessness, the desire for love or the quick course of maturation. And again, as if by magic, Olga came with aid.

"Have you ever been in love?" She shifted the conversation to unsafe intimate tracks. She already knew that it would not be taken badly.

Wojtek smiled slightly and replied with disarming sincerity:

"And what does it mean to be in love? Probably if I were, I'd know the answer. Anyway, recently my head was occupied with other, slightly more serious matters." Despite his great desire, this statement did not sound as mature as it was in his head just before it was uttered.

"One thing is for sure: you will fall in love with this place. It is like me. From the outside, it looks gloomy and sad, but inside it hides many secrets..."

He didn't know what exactly the woman meant, but he had to agree with her - he was starting to like Belarus. And from today he knew that he would never be alone here again.

7

When he noticed the time, he thanked for the afternoon together and said goodbye to Olga. He also promised to visit her in the near future and encouraged to visit its modest premises. It was getting dark outside. The landscape was lit only by the moon, which was full today. Nevertheless, the teenager decided to walk a few more steps from the herbalist's house. After a quarter of an hour he noticed the stone. He came closer, and then his eyes saw the inscription:

Whoever you will be on the side of Nowogródek,
go for dark coniferous forest in Płużyn,
remember to keep your horses,
to watch the lake.

He did not know the quote, but it seemed hackneyed and not very poetic. He didn't turn back, though he knew if the darkness engulfed him, he wouldn't be able to back home. He didn't know the area and his orientation in the field was not that good. Suddenly, the boy's eyes saw a strange and unexpected phenomenon. A girl was sitting on a tree branch overhanging the lake. He could see her very clearly, she looked like she was "sunbathing" in the moonlight. He decided to come a little closer.

He tried to do it silently so as not to scare the lady. From a short distance, he could tell for certain that she was about his age. She combed hers beautiful long, wavy brown hair singing something in an unknown language.

Her complexion was flawless - the color of the walls in the apartment in Nowogródek. She wore a white blouse which reveal a flat stomach and a seaweed-colored mini skirt that made him fall in love with her long legs. He managed to notice a golden headband in her hair and huge deer eyes. The contemplation was interrupted by the arrival of a young man. However, arrival is a wrong word. The boy suddenly emerged from the water, making Wojtek feel quite complex. He could see every single or well-defined muscle and dark, thick hair. There was something strange in his eyes, but Wojtek did not see them clearly. They seemed to be completely white... He hid a little deeper into the bushes and at the same moment he heard a raised male voice, then a quick exchange, and finally something like a punch... a slap in the face... Boy didn't know what happened, because he hid behind the tree. He did not want to be accused of eavesdropping, much less of peeping. But now he stuck out the tip of his nose and saw that the girl was crying. Had the other hit her? Before he could answer that question to himself, the pair had vanished from sight. The teenager felt his heart beating faster, but at the same time he wanted to be home as soon as possible. The return journey took him several minutes. He decided to pay Olga a visit first thing in the morning.

8

He couldn't sleep at night. He kept the same image in front of his eyes. These were his private dreams, or maybe dreams after all? The picture was the beautiful girl he had seen yesterday. There was nobody next to her, except maybe Wojtek himself. He wondered at the moment if she was perfect or if she had stood in the right light? It wasn't just her godly body or the way she brushed her hair. A sad song she was humming, and finally this dramatic scene that Wojtek became a witness to. All this made it impossible for him to forget about her.

Morning has come. Tired and sincerely concerned, the teenager did not consider whether the time was right to pay a visit. Besides, old people don't sleep well, he thought. He put on yesterday's T-shirt and ran towards his new friend's house. The door was open, but no one was inside. There was only a note on the porch:

If you're reading this, it means my gut feeling was right. Nice that you came back. I knew we were gonna be friends. If you want, wait. O.

The strange news made Wojtek think that this day would be very successful. He went inside. The cabin consisted of a tiny bathroom, a kitchen that was not much bigger, and one room. He already got to know the kitchen yesterday. Tiled stove, sideboard, table and two chairs. Olga did not accept visitors too often.

He looked into the room. One wardrobe, a bed with a thick duvet, a bedside table and a bookcase. On the cupboard there are photos, probably of daughter and son when they were still children. And books, lots of books. He reached for the first of them. He didn't understand much, but thanks to the pictures he found that it was reading about herbs and their properties. He put it back in its place. The next one was similar, except that this time the pictures caused anxiety. Before he could flip the pages, he heard a familiar voice.

"Hello, boy!" Olga entered the room so suddenly that the book fell from Wojtek's hands. "Don't be afraid, it's just me." The old woman laughed.

"Who are these people in the pictures? Why do you need such reading? Are you interested in magic?" He asked.

"It's complicated. Sit down, let's talk over a good tea of freshly picked marigolds."

Olga started bustling around the kitchen and the boy watched her carefully. Rather, he expected that the eighty four old woman would read the Bible and say the Chaplet of Mercy, rather than keeping drawings of demons on the shelves or God knows what else.

"We are in a very specific place. You must have read Adam Mickiewicz's ballad about our lake at school. Do you remember? A sunken city, brave women and children who decided to die to preserve their honor and family pride." She looked at him for confirmation.

"No, we only read the story of the shooter and the virgin who put him to the test or something. I'm sorry..." He didn't want to disappoint her.

"Oh. I will put it briefly. Various legends and beliefs are associated with the lake. Mickiewicz described what the local people told him. There are so many stories that they were collected in the book you found on the shelf," she explained slowly and patiently.

"And you believe it? We are in the twenty-first century, and I thought no one was taking such superstition seriously anymore. Especially such a wise dudette, I mean a woman like you."

"You see, I've been living in the world for many years. And at Świteź I spent my whole life. Believe it or not, every legend is truthful, just like any rumor. But let's not talk about that anymore."

Such explanations were enough for Wojtek to see in Olga a thinking woman who is enormously rich in life experience. He allowed himself to be persuaded to eat borscht and cheebureka. And however it sounded, it tasted delicious.

They said their farewells at around five in the afternoon. Wojtek on purpose did not ask Olga about the possibility of swimming in the lake. He wondered what the answer might be. After all, they were in the national park. He knew he was doing wrong when he brought a towel and swimming trunks with him. The crystal-clear water, however, seemed to urge him to take a bath - at least that way he drowned out his remorse. What would the mother say? Great nature lover. The urge to cool down on this warm summer's day won with common sense.

The sun was going down. He felt a gentle chill as he plunged into the water. The surface of the lake did not move. He enjoyed every moment. Finally, he did not have to worry about the result of the gymnasium exam, graduation, choice of high school. He didn't think about whether he would meet his father's expectations, or whether he would be able to give him the happiness that the moments spent together with him... Now there was only him, the sound of the wind and the singing of birds. Suddenly, out of nowhere, a whirlpool of water appeared next to Wojtek. Even though the boy was a really good swimmer, he couldn't get out of it. He felt the water pulling him deeper and deeper, and though he tries and tries very hard, he was unable to break free. Within a moment, he was under water. It was not past two and he passed out...

9

He woke up in an unfamiliar place. Father was at the bedside, who apparently from exhaustion did not even notice that Wojtek opened his eyes. The boy was amazed at his legs sticking out from under the covers. There were circle-shaped purple-green marks around the ankles. Next to the father was an older, elegantly dressed man in a white coat. There was re-identification on their faces. At that moment, Wojtek's and Antoni's eyes met.

"God! Sonny! My darling son! I thought you already... How glad you woke up!" There were tears in the man's eyes, they were undoubtedly tears of joy. After a while, when the emotions slightly subsided, Stożyński remembered the presence of doctor Rachowicz, informing at the same time that he had been taking care of the boy for two weeks.

"Two weeks? How is it possible that I can't remember anything? Was I in a coma or what? I swam in the lake... How did I get here? After all, you were in Nowogródek?" The questions bombarded father, and Dr. Rachowicz, who knew a bit of the Polish language because his roots were in Poland, listened to them.

"Calm down, boy, you are still very weak," the doctor asked Wojtek. "Your dad will tell you everything. Just get your emotions under control. We don't want to lose you a second time," he explained.

The Stożyńskis had a long conversation with each other. Antoni told his son everything in turn. The boy slowly calmed down, which could be noticed by watching the appropriate indicators on the apparatus connected to the young organism.

"While I was working in the office, the phone rang. The ambulance was called. Someone informed that I had rented a house by the lake. Apparently, an emergency room worker in the handset heard a woman's voice calling to the lake in Belarusian, informing that something bad had happened. According to the account, the woman spoke her words through tears, so I got in the car and arrived as soon as possible. I saw you lying by the house, you were breathing but you were unconscious. The doctor and paramedic took you to the hospital." Antoni thought that this shortened version was enough for his son. At least now that he is tired and weak. He was wrong.

"You are not going to end this touching story this way." Wojtek was angry. "And where are the answers to the most important questions? Who was the woman? What did she look like? How had she carried my drowned body to the cabin? How did you know it was about me and you had to call an ambulance? Why do I have blue marks around my ankles?"

Father was silent. Not because he was trying to hide something. The reason was prosaic.

"No matter how much I want it, I cannot answer. The woman the hospital employee spoke to was probably young, so I was told, judging by my voice.

Doctors thought it was your girlfriend, but I corrected them. I have no idea who she could have been. I thought you would tell me this. After all, we haven't seen each other for a few days, so I assumed you met someone..."

"I met, I met Olga, an eighty-four-year-old woman, not a young, hysterical girl. Probably Olga called for help. Just how did she know? After all, her hut is far from the place where I swam, and second... Olga would not have brought me to our house. I don't understand anything..." Wojtek felt confused. Each hypothesis turned out to be highly unlikely. He could not find an explanation for the situation. "Okay, I don't know who the woman was. Perhaps the doctors have an idea where the marks at the ankles come from? It has probably already been investigated?"

"My son, together with Dr. Rachowicz, we came to the conclusion that you were swimming in someone's company. Then your companion began to sink and dragged you to the bottom of the lake with her. Such an explanation seemed to us the only logical one. Now, when you talk about bathing alone, it doesn't make any sense." Antoni was as surprised as his teenage son.

"No, I was definitely alone. Memory gaps show up later. I know I went there alone. Unless that girl..." He broke off. He didn't want to tell his father about it. After all, he didn't even know where and who she was from, she could only be there once.

"Which girl?" Antoni asked.

"No, nothing... Everything is confusing... When I was in a coma, I think I was dreaming about a girl." Father bought this version and did not ask unnecessary questions.

10

Several days passed before the doctors came to the conclusion that Wojtek's condition was stable. Then he was also released home. The father insisted that they spend some time together, but the boy knew that the whole project, which Antoni had coordinated from the very beginning, would suffer, treating him like his own child. Eventually they came to an agreement. The father will return to work, but Aunt Monika will come to visit the boy. And so she announced the visit, and the teenager could use some of the positive energy that always filled her.

Wojtek slept poorly for the last few days in the hospital and at home for the following days. A mysterious girl appeared in his dreams again. The dream began the same way: he could see her from a distance, she was perfect, she was tempting with her beauty. In her first dreams, right after the pseudo meeting, she smiled at him and followed him with her eyes. Now she was dragging him to the bottom of the lake. From those last dreams he woke up screaming.

"Monia! How good you came! But that you chose a boring cabin in such a mess instead of the exotic village of Indian somewhere in South America, I am surprised!" Wojtek has not laughed so heartily and sincerely for a long time.

"So funny! Do you have the nerve to mock your old aunt?" She threw, hugging the boy.

Monika was a forty-year-old short brown haired girl with a lot curly hair.

She did not look like her age, which was due to her good genes, proper diet and selected for hours "rejuvenating" outfits. She had no husband or children. She never dreamed of a family. She spent her youthful years with a backpack and a hat, traveling to the farthest corners of the world. Wojtek used to say: "We have our private Martyna Wojciechowska, who always comes back to us." The three of them have already seen photos from their last year's trip to Bolivia. She did not have time to share her impressions with Ewa. Even though five years have passed since then, Monika still hasn't forgiven herself for not being with her dying college friend. She could not break the contract she signed with the organization. But for sure? Maybe she should return their money and come to Poland. Holding her hand during chemo, supporting the guys... In any case, she won't turn back time. Now she has decided to do everything to make Ewa's son happy and spend a good time. Especially after this bizarre accident. She planned to stay two weeks, until the end of July, and use all her charm so that this time would not be lost for Wojtek.

"We have to plan our two weeks together. I do not include Antek in my plans, because he is constantly doing something, renovating and improving. What can you offer me from local attractions? Some savage Slavs? Threatening animals? Wild nature?" There was a slight smile on Monika's lips, and her eyes had a gleam that hadn't faded out since her student days.

"How can I tell you this so that it doesn't hurt so badly."

There is our house, a lake, nothing for a long time, then a little hut of the granny Olga, a forest, a forest, a forest, thickets and...

that would be it." Wojtek did not hide his irony. He liked to tease his aunt. He thought to himself that he wanted to be like her, that is, never to grow up. To have so much joy, spontaneity and ease. Now he knew it was impossible, at least not in his life.

"Do not talk! We need to find a guide to the area and read in the tourist attractions section what you can do here for two weeks." She wasn't baffled.

The next day, Monika and Wojtek went to Nowogródek, and there they found out about the upcoming festival. Fortunately, Monika was a polyglot and made contacts easily. Thanks to these features, combined with personal charm, the tourists were soon on the bus to Gródek.

"How is it called? I don't know if I want to participate in this. I don't like folk music..." Wojtek wanted to avoid it, but he realized that his aunt would be adamant.

"Are you crazy? The woman said that to be in Belarus in July and not to take part in Basowiszcza or Basowiszczach, ay, I do not know how to say it... at least to ignore such an event is a sin," she argued.

"Besides, it's an event organized by students, so firstly it can't be stiff and won't be popular, and secondly... you know how Aunt Monia likes students." The woman laughed outrageously.

So they went to Gródek, because it was near this city, in a forest clearing, that the Young Belarus Music Festival was to take place.

11

On the way, Wojtek told Monika about everything that had happened since arrival. About how he met old Olga, about an evening walk and a strange quarrel between two beautiful young people, and finally about his mysterious adventure with swimming in the lake. Monika listened patiently, and as she was a woman rich in experience and extremely bright, she quickly diagnosed:

"Dude, you fell in love at first sight! And don't even try to deny it, because you can see it, hear it and feel it. Now we just have to find her... What do you say?" She asked.

"Let me put it this way: like every woman, you exaggerate everything. However, I will not deny that it would be quite fun seeing the girl again. Just tell me, just out of curiosity, how are you going to track her down, since we know absolutely nothing about her..."

"It's very simple, after returning from the concert we will go to the place where you saw her in the evening. It may not be a perfect plan, but what's the harm to try? In the meantime, it would be nice if you forgot the dark haired girl for a moment and let your aunt enjoy life." Monika cut off the topic firmly.

For Wojtek, the last exchange of views was enough to make him happy. Monika was wrong, he was not in love, but for sure the girl intrigued him enough that the plan to finding her, and maybe starting a conversation, finding out something about her, was the number one goal for him right now.

He just has to survive this boring festival, and then he will start his detective mission with his partner - the penetrating Monia.

They arrived at the place, which is the famous Boryk clearing, around seven o'clock. It was impossible to miss it. Hundreds or even thousands of young people probably gathered here since morning. Some of them drank alcohol, some sang in groups to the accompaniment of guitars. They were all smiling and at first glance you could see that they were enjoying life to the fullest. Wojtek, this community resembled the Polish Woodstock Station Festival or Jarocin, which he knew only from television, but he had no doubts that the people gathered here do not differ from native rock fans.

Before he knew it, Monica was no longer in his sight. He started calling for her and he made a round around the stage to no avail. He tried to call her cellphone, but the noise made it almost impossible to hear the muffled sound of the phone. So he gave up, stating that he was the child left in her care and that her aunt would start to worry in some time.

In the meantime, he decided to look around. They all looked almost alike. They wore dark T-shirts with different names of rock and heavy metal bands, mostly long hair and black combat boots or yellow martens.

This style was a stranger to him, but Wojtek has always been extremely tolerant and open. This was what his parents taught him from childhood. So he answered greetings to him with a smile.

Suddenly, behind one of the tentatively pitched tents, he noticed a man who looked like the one from the lake. Although the memories associated with him were certainly not pleasant, Wojtek decided to follow him. He felt deep down that a stranger would lead him to the girl he'd been thinking so much about lately. He turned off the phone's sound so as not to be caught and discreetly followed the boy. They had been walking for a long time, and Wojtek felt more and more scared and lonely. As he was about to give up and return to the concert venue, if he could, he saw the face that had appeared so often in his dreams lately.

"Wodja!" The muscular bully cried out to the girl. She turned and Wojtek's doubts were dispelled.

Yes, it was her. Same long hair, same perfect figure... she looked like a ghost in a long white dress. So her name is Wodja, whatever that means.

After a short exchange, during which Wodja often used the word ondyn - maybe it was the boy's name - Wojtek realized that his potential rival was a violent and unpredictable man. He turned to the girl with a request, or perhaps an order. It was not hard to guess that she had no desire to do it. Ondyn - as Wojtek decided to call him - whistled on his toes and five long-haired boys came out from around the corner. Wodja tried to ask again, her eyes full of regret, but her companion was ruthless.

He gripped her hair, apparently tightly, for a cry of pain escaped from the girl's lips. Wojtek wanted to stop this brutal scene, but he realized that his frail sixteen-year-old body would not be able to cope with the muscleman and his five colleagues. So he stood, feeling like a last idiot, watching the events to come.

The six men and the woman started walking very briskly. Wojtek was one step away from them. He didn't know how much time had passed, but he felt that he was about to lose strength. When the group reached the lake, Wojtek breathed a sigh of relief. For he believed, and rightly so, that this was the end of the murderous journey. There was an exchange of views between a man and a woman again. The five long-haired men stood without a word. The teenager thought they must be pretty smashed or drunk. Imagine his astonishment when - as if on command - everyone jumped into the lake. Wojtek watched the course of events from a distance, but after a while he began to worry. None of the night swimmers came to the surface. The boy didn't know what to do... He was thrashing, hundreds of thoughts flashed through his head. They drowned... or someone drowned them... Wojtek decided to leave, finally explaining to himself that they probably came from a different side.

Returning to the clearing, he thought about the still fresh events. He didn't understand anything... Or maybe he was just over-sensitive, maybe he didn't know how to relax, or maybe since his mother died, he had perceived everything too darkly, even the innocent fun of his peers.

Monika, surrounded by a wreath of young men, did not even notice Wojtek's disappearance. It crossed her mind that maybe this poor sixteen-year-old would finally go crazy. She even hoped the boy would break some rules, get drunk, brawl, or maybe find him in the arms of some sexy doll. So she decided not to babysit him. If only he would not come close to Lake Wiejka, because his last contact with water was certainly not successful.

She glanced at her watch eloquently, like a responsible guardian, when he finally showed up. It worried her that his movements were nervous and his face pale.

"First of all: do you know what time it is? I was worried! Second, why do you look like you've seen a ghost? And third, don't you know what the cellphone is for?" She tried to feign bitterness and disappointment.

"First of all: I know what time it is and so far it hasn't bothered you. Second, I must tell you about what I saw. And frankly speaking, it's good that you have already got something stronger, because it will be hard to handle when sober. Thirdly, you cannot be reached, so you are a poor babysitter," commented Wojtek, not sparing his aunt.

They decided not to come back at the night, and they wouldn't have how anyway. They rented a room in a random house. Hosts didn't mind, quite the opposite - the festival night was one of the few occasions when it was possible there to get some extra money on the side.

In the morning they left for Nowogródek, and from there to the cottage. The story told by Wojtek did not make much of an impression on Monika. While the boy was convinced that the young people had drowned, his aunt perceived it more in terms of drunken antics, which, unfortunately, were alien to her charges.

12

The last days of July, ending Monika's stay in Belarus at the same time, passed lazily and rather unattractively from the 16-year-old's point of view. On weekends, the three of them visited the monuments: Mindaugas castle, the church where Adam Mickiewicz was baptized, the bard's manor, as well as synagogues and churches. Monika and Antoni talked a lot, recalled the most interesting stories in which the main character was always Ewa. Wojtek wondered many times why father had not decided to make a life for himself. It's been three years now. He was still not bad, he had a lot of money and a lot to offer. Women his age should find him attractive. The boy also thought about how it would be if his father and Monika... No, it couldn't work. She is a free bird type, he is a workaholic. She loves fun and good entertainment, he is rather calm. She is a traveler, unable to sit still, he is a typical homebody. And yet, as he looked at them now, he thought it would be fun to have her with him permanently.

Monika left on July 31st. Father took her to the platform, Wojtek said goodbye at the cottage. Suddenly it was quiet and empty. As if the remnants of life had evaporated with her suitcases.

Wojtek realized that he had not seen Olga for the past weeks. She must have thought he was offended or that he is bored with the company of an old lady.

He decided to fix it, because none of these reasons were real.

After the first weekend in August with his father, he went to visit Olga. On the way, he picked up a bouquet of flowers, thinking that in this way he would buy the old woman's favors again.

"Hello. You've been gone for a long time. Something bad happened, right?" She said in a calm voice, not taking her eyes off the crochet hook she was embroidering with.

Wojtek was overwhelmed with amazement, but after a while he convinced himself that the rumors about his miraculously saved life had reached here.

"It would be a lot to tell. As you surely know, I was swimming in a forbidden place and I was punished. Then my aunt visited me and I didn't really have a chance to come over for tea. But now I am and we can catch up, because I have all August at my disposal," he tried to make her laugh.

"Don't you know that Świteź is dangerous? You shouldn't bathe in it, not for nothing the state authorities have established a landscape park here. Don't tempt fate, boy..." The tone of her voice and the way she emphasized certain words terrified him.

"All right, all right. I understood, I learned a lesson, and the marks around my ankles will remind me of my mistake, because somehow they do not want to come off," he continued the story.

The old woman stepped closer and looked at the blue hoops around the boy's ankles.

Then she looked out the window and nodded. Wojtek felt more and more uncomfortable. He studied her face and figure as she stood in deep thought. He hadn't seen her in weeks, but she seemed different from the last time. She was as if uglier, her breasts were larger and drooping, and her body was covered with too much hair for a woman. How could he have missed it before? She was wearing a funny red cap today, probably for work in the garden, because a fern had stuck to it.

Coming to the conclusion that today's meeting was not likely to be a successful one, he said goodbye, making up an excuse for meeting his father, and left Olga quickly.

However, his intuition told him that he should watch a little old lady. He returned home, stocked up some sandwiches, and then settled into a comfortable position near the old woman's hut.

The following hours brought nothing new. Finally, just before sunset, Wojtek saw a figure approaching with a shopping bag full of shopping. It was definitely Wodja. His heart began to beat faster, he wanted to jump out of the bushes and ask Olga what it all meant. However, he quickly realized that he had not told her about meeting the secret girl. Or maybe they knew each other. Stupid! Instead of immediately revealing himself to the old woman, he was looking for a girl, sleeping in the bushes at night. Now he will surely get her address, phone number, and find out about her in general.

He waited patiently for Wodja to leave Olga's cottage. It was obvious that she came with the shopping - by the way, what a good heart she had... Hours passed and after eight o'clock Wojtek was already very impatient and hungry. So with pains of heart he gave up visiting again, he did not want to disturb the women in their women's matters.

13

The next day he was awakened by the doorbell. First since arrival. He rubbed his eyes and saw Olga standing on the stairs.

"Good morning, boy!" She noticed Wojtek. "I brought you dumplings for dinner, and if you let me in, we'll have the best kulaga in the world for tea," she encouraged.

"Hello! Wait a minute, because I left my keys somewhere... yyyyy... I got them. Invite. And this thing for k... smells awesome!" As he opened the door, his hand was reaching for the honey and blueberry dessert.

When they sat down at the slightly dusty table, Olga immediately played the role of the hostess. In the house, it was possible to see with the naked eye the absence of a woman's hand. Dust, curtains drawn, flowers wilted. The old woman restored its natural charm in no time. She made some tea and finally, a bit tired, sat down in the rattan chair.

Wojtek was watching her closely the whole time. She had the friendly expression on her face again, as when he had met her. There was no grimace on her... Was he hallucinating the last time, or was he ill-disposed to the surrounding reality?

"...another one."

"Sorry, I didn't hear what you said, I was thinking," he tried to explain and hoped she hadn't noticed his reflecting eyesight.

"I asked if you wanted more. You demolished the entire plate very quickly." She smiled kindly.

Wojtek did not want to wait a minute longer.

"After our last meeting, I was walking past your house in the evening. I thought you had a visitor, a beautiful young girl..." He tried to jump gently on the topic of interest to him. For a moment there was such an overwhelming silence that you could clearly hear the rustle of the grass surrounding the hut. "Something happened? I didn't want to be rude or nosy... I just..." Wojtek tried to get out of the awkward situation.

"No, it's okay. I'm already talking. You've probably seen Svetlana, my daughter, the old woman muttered at last."

Wojtek asked her to repeat it, because his Russian had told him that it was about a daughter, but it would be impossible. Olga is eighty-four and the lake girl is no more than eighteen. It didn't add up. He was even more surprised when the woman said a second time.

Olga, seeing the uncertainty and amazement on the speaker's face, began the story:

"I know what you are thinking: how can such an old woman be the mother of such a beautiful, young girl? I lied to you, I did not give birth to Svetlana or Anatol."

Wojtek listened with great concentration. Olga's last sentence influenced his attitude towards the woman. He already knew that he can not trust her and believe her.

The woman continued:

"Well, seventeen years ago I met Svetlana's mother, who lived in your wooden house. I watched how she take care of the baby right after giving birth, how she addressed it. I figured she wouldn't be able to cope with motherhood. She was conceited, thought only about herself and her needs. Then I decided that I would raise the girl." At this point she paused and reached for her cup of tea.

"What does it mean: I decided? You can't just decide to take child away. This is called kidnapping..." Wojtek was becoming more and more inquisitive.

"You see, fate was favorable to me, which cannot be said about the girl's mother. One day she went to the lake to wash her nappies. She knew she was not allowed. Even then, it was the area of the park. Exactly the same thing like your case happened to her. No, not exactly, because the whirlpool was dragged inside. Nobody heard her, nobody helped. This is how I became Svetlana's mother," she finished the story.

Wojtek felt that it was not all. Anyway, the whole story seemed to be a far-fetched for him. So he did not let go.

"And Anatol? You said you didn't gave birth him either. How did you become his mother? Where is he now? Is he seventeen too? I thought you had grown-up children, or maybe grandchildren as well, and here..." He broke all the lines between curiosity and inquisitiveness. It didn't matter to him, however, he wanted to know the truth. The only question is: what is true?

"Hmm... Svetlana lived with me, then left for work bored. She lost one year in school and doesn't want to lose another year. She will start high school education in September." She continued.

Wojtek forgot for a moment about the incredible fates of Olga's family. His ears were filled with news: he and Svetlana (whom the man from the lake called Wodja) would start learning at the same educational level in a few weeks. It was only necessary to find out what school Olga enrolled the girl to and... he did not want to blur this vision, but the firm tone of the old woman broke him from his waking dreams.

"Anatol, my son, is twenty years old. He was cursed by his parents, so I took him in. End of the story."

This time, Olga sounded quite credible. But what did the word "damned" mean? Abandoned? Beats? Sexually abused? You could guess for a long time these days. Wojtek was not that patient.

"I don't understand, but could you say more? Where is he now? Once I saw Svetlana with some boy. Maybe it's her brother?"

This was the second thought in the last hour that had filled him with optimism. So the muscleman isn't her boyfriend, he's her brother. It does not constitute any competition. It will only be necessary to teach him good manners, not to let him struggle with a woman, even if it is his sister.

"The kids live on the other side of the lake, I told you already, in a cabin similar to mine.

However, it is hidden behind numerous rushes, so it is not easy to spot. Anatol will no longer study, he will take care of his sister and old mother. As for his parents, I don't want to talk about it. What you have heard so far must be enough for you." She was firm, so Wojtek did not insist on revealing further details. For one interview, he had met enough of them.

Anyway, he was already a bit lost. He did not know if Svetlana had attended school before or studied at home. He did not understand whether she was away for work or bored. Each version of Olga's family story was different from the previous one. He stated that if the girl did not tell him about herself, he would never be sure of what had really happened in her life. And Anatol? This one was one big question mark at all. How did he get here? Where were his parents? Why does not want to learn, study? It's all strange...

"I have a request for you. Could you please talk to your father about Svetlana? He is a man of influence here. He sure has the best school for you. I would be grateful to you if you tried... if your dad... I mean a place in a good school for my daughter," she choked finally.

14

Wojtek spent the next weeks of August alone, thinking about a strange conversation with Olga. He did not disclose to his father the details of this acquaintance, and even less the bizarre secrets of the old lady and her "wards". However, he decided that the penultimate weekend before the start of the school year was the right time to start the talk. On the one hand, the presence of a beautiful girl who charmed him within a few moments, every day at school seemed like a dream come true, on the other hand, her whole story with her pathological mother and departure was not so much vague as disturbing.

Nevertheless, the desire to get to know the beauties from Świteź overcame all fears and Wojtek turned to Antoni:

"I know what it's going to sound like, but don't really think it's a big deal," he began quite awkwardly.

"Should I be afraid?" Father asked half-jokingly, but deep down he wasn't laughing at all.

"It's about a girl who..."

"Oh, it changes the form of things... As for the girl, son, I was afraid of this conversation, but since the time has come..." Antoni interrupted.

"Could you at least let me start, I think I can dream about finishing. I will close myself in a moment and you won't learn anything anymore," he blackmailed his father.

"What are you so touchy? Come on, I turn to hearing, but you will not miss the lecture on birds and bees. Mother always said that at some point in your life, as a father and a man, I will have to make you aware..."

Wojtek pretended not to hear this nonsense. He turned his eyes and made goofy faces until his father was done.

"I told you about an old lady who visits me often and cooks me delicious dinners, right?" Antoni just nodded, fearing that another interruption of the story with an unnecessary interruption would actually discourage Wojtek from confiding.

"Well, she is very poor and very good. It mean... she took in a girl seventeen years ago, whose mother died in a tragic accident, and has been looking after her since then. And this girl, her supposed daughter named Svetlana, has already missed a year, because she went somewhere there, and now she is to start high school, but they have no money for a good school and they thought that maybe you could do something..." He threw all the words at the speed of light.

"Done," his father said shortly.

"What? Just? Won't you ask me anything?" Wojtek did not believe it.

"You told me everything. You need to help good people. So much. You just need to give me the personal details of your friend and her babysitter over the phone this week. They will put them into the system. Your high school is full of people with the weirdest stories, teenagers from all backgrounds, corners of the world.

I think that you will not only gain a lot of knowledge there, but you will learn tolerance and respect for all otherness. I envy you very much," he concluded.

Regardless of the fact that his father's departure is still half an hour, Wojtek decided to share the good news with Olga as soon as possible. So he said goodbye to his old man, hugged him tightly and threw as he was leaving:

"Thank you again... I love you, Dad."

"I love you too, young man," Antoni replied.

This seemingly ordinary moment was very important to both men. When Ewa was alive, the word "I LOVE" was spoken in their home at least once a day. And it wasn't because it was appropriate, it was nice. It's just that all three of them had this inner need. They wanted their loved ones to have no doubts that regardless of differences of opinion, small quarrels at dinner or bad mood - at the end of the day someone would reassure them of their love, thus giving them a sense of security and inner peace. After the death of the mother, none of the gentlemen was eager to say the word. Firstly, the time of mourning was not conducive to this, secondly, it is more difficult for men to express themselves spontaneously about their feelings. Antoni was all the more pleased that today Wojtek came as naturally as when they were the three of them.

Someone had told him about six months ago that he would be friends with a woman sixty-eight years older him, he would have laughed in his face. Now, however, he felt that, despite many understatements on her part, Olga had become an integral part of his life. He regretfully thought about the coming autumn and his separation from Świteź and his friend. Lost in thought, he stood in front of the cabin door. It was opened by a girl who, though strange, was well known to him.

15

Wojtek was walking quickly towards the cottage he already knew well. He had traveled this path frequently in the past two months. If someone had told him about six months ago that he would be friends with a woman sixty-eight years older him, he would have laughed in his face. Now, however, he felt that, despite many understatements on her part, Olga had become an integral part of his life. He regretfully thought about the coming autumn and his separation from Świteź and his friend. Lost in thought, he stood in front of the cabin door. It was opened by a girl who, though strange, was well known to him.

"Hello, Wojtek. Finally, we get to know each other. I waited a long time for this moment," she spoke to him. And Wojtek could not get a word out of himself. He only stared at her tiny lips, huge eyes and shapely hands. "Are you done? If so, please come in. Mom was expecting you and prepared a sarburma. I hear you have a good appetite," she added, going inside.

In his mind, the first meeting with the dream girl was completely different. It was he who took the initiative, boasting that he would fulfill her dreams of an elite high school. It was he who invited her in, filling this moment with romantic quotes from the best literary works. All she had to do was stand, smile and smell beautiful to make this moment unique and unforgettable.

Now he knew that Svetlana was not a shy dreamer from a sentimental novel, but a teenager with a sharp tongue and fully aware of her charm "almost" woman.

"Boy, tell me what news you bring." Olga got straight to the point, wasting no time in greeting.

Wojtek now had a chance for rehabilitation, he wanted them to see him as a man of great influence.

"I did it," he said shortly.

"More like your father, you didn't have much to do," added Svetlana tartly.

"Svetlana! Keep your nerves in check! If it wasn't for him, you wouldn't have a chance to live a normal life!" Olga was angry.

"Normal life... what is it? He's just getting me school, not changing my life. But okay. Sorry. You could just say it in a different way," the girl replied.

Wojtek was slightly confused, but continued:

"Anyway, whatever my tone, we'll start in a week. The high school is supposedly a community of people of different origins, coming from different cultures, so it should be interesting. You just need to provide me with your details: a Belarusian identity document of the guardian or yours, telephone number, date of birth..."

There was silence. This surprised Wojtek, because writing a few pieces of information on a piece of paper could not be a problem.

"What is this information for?" Svetlana finally broke the silence.

"Well, I don't know, after all, in every school you give your data for writing a certificate, as if something happened to you..."

Imagine Wojtek's astonishment when the women suddenly switched from Russian to Belarusian, so that the conversation started without his participation. Judging by the facial expressions, gestures and raised voices, he concluded that something was bothering them in order to fully enjoy the news. He did not understand what or why. Finally, Olga sat down and spoke calmly to her daughter. Wojtek got scared because her gaze was so penetrating that Svetlana almost cried. Still, he didn't understand what was going on. The girl was nodding her head, as if she was reluctant to accept the offer made by her mother. There was only one word he understood from all the conversation: Anatol. Ultimately, it can be guessed that despite the teenager's great reluctance, she agreed.

"For when do you need this data?" Olga asked.

"Tomorrow is best, but I don't think a one-day skid will wipe out your chances. But I dont understand..."

"You don't have to understand everything, boy..." the woman interrupted him. "Now you better go. We are very grateful to you, you can always count on our help and care, like then..." She broke off.

"When?" Wojtek wanted to know what Olga was talking about.

"Listen? You must have misunderstood me. Goodbye."

Olga gestured to the door.

No, he was not wrong. He knew Russian well, and during his stay on the Świteź, he also trained himself. He had no doubt that the old woman had suggested that she had looked after him before. But when? At that moment he remembered his stay in the hospital and the information obtained from the doctor: a woman called an ambulance. He might have asked, but felt that if she wanted to, she would have told him herself. Since she hadn't said a word when he talked about his accident, it was better not to bring it up again. Olga was easily offended and discouraged. Or maybe... yes... so it was

Svetlana… or Anatol was the one who carried his body all the way to the wooden house. It would make sense now. Maybe he'll even make friends with this muscle guy... No, he has something like that in his eyes... - Thousands of thoughts circled in his head.

16

Wojtek was woken up by the doorbell again. He didn't have to think long. He knew it was Olga. He ran to the porch and saw only a storm of waves from behind a small curtain. He couldn't show himself like this. He had bad breath, messy hair, and pus in his eye. Shouting "wait," he ran to the bathroom, ate some toothpaste, brushed his hair back, and pulled on a T-shirt that covered the imperfections of his upper body.

When he finally opened it, he found a girl sitting on the stairs.

"You're worse than a woman. What can you do so long? It's not a date, you don't have to look perfect. I just brought you a piece of paper and I'm leaving," she said, still sitting with her back.

Wojtek could not decide whether the malice or the sadness was more audible in this statement.

"Give me that card." He resigned from his initial intention of making a sharp retort.

On the card were the words: Akwilina Dubrowski, Awgusta Dubrowski, and next to it, the phone number, identity document and address with the city of Nowogródek.

"What is this?" Wojtek did not hide his irritation. "It's a fake! You do not live in Nowogródek and, as far as I know, your name is not Akwilina!"

"Svetlana is my middle name. Akwilina is too... serious, so I don't use it. And in Nowogródek, under this one address, I lived for a while.

I do not want to write: live in a mud hut by the lake. They'd start pointing their fingers at me right away," she tried to explain, though it was awkward.

"Nonsense. A load of crap. Do I really look like such an idiot? You're insulting me right now. Either you tell the truth or forget about school." Wojtek did not give up.

"If you like me at least a little and you want me to learn, you will not ask unnecessary questions. You'll hear nothing more from me. At least not now. I don't know you enough to reveal pages of my life to you. You have to... you can trust me and help..."

At that moment, she appeared to Wojtek as beautiful and helpless. And as much as he wanted to pursue the topic, he simply had no conscience. Whatever Svetlana - Akwilina was hiding, one could actually wait for the discovery.

"I have to leave now, I will go to my father, because we were supposed to do some shopping for school anyway. I don't have any books, notebooks, or suitable clothes. I'll give him this card right away. And you have any money for the "school layette"?" He wanted it to sound so cool and casual, but it didn't work.

"I don't need your grace! I am not poor, I have enough to live on." She turned on her heel and walked briskly towards her home.

First, he wanted to keep her, apologize and finally let her know that she was wonderful, beautiful, and that her character make his heart beat faster and totally softens him...

But he didn't do anything. They had nine months of learning together, and if his plan comes into force... also traveling together to school, coming back, and therefore hours of talks...

17

To get to Nowogródek, counting from the moment you left the wooden house, you had to have about one and half an hour. Wojtek devoted these ninety minutes to composing a speech that would soften his father's heart and allow him to implement the plan. In his mind it was something like this: "The girl you got school is very poor, and you always said that you have to help others as much as possible. Well, I know that for the time of the school year I was supposed to live with you in your apartment in Nowogródek, but then Svetlana would have to go out on the bus from Świteź early in the morning, and then return alone in the evening. She is known to be a beautiful girl so it would be highly dangerous and risky to let her do this. So I thought that maybe she could take one of the rooms in the log cabin, and I could stay there... Together we could study and go to school...".

During the meeting with his father, only after a common shopping and created the right mood, more or less around lunchtime, Wojtek decided to present his vision. It sounded much less pathetic and less serious than the speech arranged on the bus. Father played for time, eating slowly the dessert he had ordered earlier. He needed not only to think carefully, but also to consider what Ewa would have done if she had been here with him.

He was convinced that she would say something like this: "Wojtek is already sixteen years old. Good thing he liked a girl. It's good that she is not a spoiled doll, but a well-mannered lady. Anyway, if we can help her... I know, I know, you're afraid that if they live in the same house... it's scary to think. But do you remember our youth? What is forbidden tastes better. Maybe if we trust him and give him a certain amount of independence, he will not want to disappoint us?". Yes, Ewa would definitely give him a chance. And even if he does something stupid... Well, you learn from your mistakes.

"Agreed," he could only say that much.

"Where's the talk? Prohibitions, orders, rules?" Wojtek could not believe that it was so easy, so he tried to find the bottom of this short answer.

"There will be none of these things. All I can say is: I love you and I trust you immensely. I guess your mother and I raised you to be a cool young guy. I believe that you will not disappoint me either..." There was emotion on the face of this serious man.

Although Wojtek did not like to show his feelings in public, because he considered it embarrassing on the one hand, and on the other a typical show, this time he made an exception. He walked over to his father and hugged him tightly. He also knew that he would not do anything that would hurt or upset Dad.

The same day they went shopping, which painfully reminded them of the approaching school. In connection with the decision about staying by the lake, they also had to order a car to transport the necessary furniture and other Wojtek's belongings.

There was no desk, lamp, chair or bookcases in the house. In the evening, all the equipment was already delivered. The only thing left to do was to order them out, but Wojtek wanted to wait for Svetlana with that.

18

He wanted to text her, but realized he didn't have her number. She didn't give it on the sheet of data either, there was probably only a number to the guardian, but Olga didn't have a phone number. How is it possible not to have a cell phone in the twenty-first century? It was rather unreal. By the way, he realized that he had been living without facebook, e-mail and messenger for two months. Half a year ago, he would not really have believed that it was still possible. He also rarely watched TV, mainly in the evenings at his father's.

So he went looking for the house of Svetlana and Anatol, to help her move things, if, of course, she agreed to his suggestion. Only now he realized that he had not yet succeeded, and it was too early to open a bottle of champagne. Or maybe she doesn't want to live with some newly met boyfriend? Or maybe she is very religious and would even consider it a sin? No, he had to succeed, he wouldn't put her in danger.

It took him about three hours to reach the other side of the lake. He searched the area very carefully, but nowhere he couldn't find any hut like that of Olga's. Ultimately, he decided to turn back and ask the old woman for the exact "address" of his daughter. He did not have to do this because he found Svetlana with her.

"I come with a proposal," he did not greet.

"Good morning. Yes, I'm fine. What about you?" Olga could make you feel like a moron at the beginning of the visit.

"Good morning. Sorry, but I'm looking forward to your response. I came up with a great plan, my father accepted it, now only you have to agree," he explained his uncultivated behavior.

"The plan is definitely brilliant." Svetlana started the conversation again with irritability. What was it about this girl that she could never rejoice or humbly listen to until the end of his speech?

Olga turned to the girl in her native language, most likely with a reprimand.-

"Okay, tell me, what did you come up with?" She asked in a changed tone.

Wojtek presented the proposal using only delicate words and apologetic expressions: he did not want to offend anyone, he did not want to abuse his trust, he absolutely did not try to argue with anyone's views, especially religious ones, he did not question educational methods..."

"Let me talk to my daughter in private, okay?" Olga finally interrupted the boy's considerations.

Wojtek humbly went out onto the porch, although he would not understand anything anyway. For the next half an hour he wondered about the landscape around him, he thought about how much his mother would like this place. Strange because he hasn't done this since he arrived. So much has happened. So much time and thought he was now devoting himself to that girl he still knew almost nothing about.

He didn't even notice when Svetlana sat down next to him. She seemed very serious, honestly, he had never seen her like this before. Well, maybe then at the lake, when she didn't feel that anyone was watching her.

"Wojtek, I am very grateful to you for what you do for me," she began.

"It's nothing, I just wanted to..." he interrupted, but this time she wanted to speak.

"Be quiet and let me say something this once." Boy nodded. "Olga, I mean mom, agreed. I can occupy one room, in return, she will cook our lunches every day and take care of us. If only I agree to such a lifestyle..." she sounded quite ambiguous, but Wojtek carefully wrote down all the questions in his head, not wanting to interrupt for the moment. "You see, I can't stay at your house overnight. At least for now. If Anatol knew... Anyway, I don't have such a possibility yet. I would love to spend time with you at school, do homework and study, but for the night... I'll just go out. Understand?" The story was supposed to end there.

Wojtek understood too well. Olga was a modern woman despite her eighty-four years, but there was also her brother. He looked uncompromising and, as he remembered, he was unpredictable. Probably Svetlana was afraid of his reaction to living with a boy who he did not even recognize. In fact, it was some solution.

He would walk her to her house for the night, her brother would be calm, and they would commute to school together in the morning. He was even a little impressed that the girl had her own rules. He didn't really understand what it was about: "I can't, for now." She probably meant it might take time, a closer look... or maybe she was waiting for her eighteenth birthday. Does not matter. He concluded:

"Let it be that way. We say: "win-win situation." This means everyone will be pleased with your solution. And that makes me happy."

"You don't even know how you make me happy." On Svetlana's face a sincere smile and a kind of... calm appeard. Blissful peace.

This sentence was enough for Wojtek to admit to himself that he has some feelings to this girl. And he realized that living together with her might very confuse him in his recently ordered, though not so ordinary, life.

19

The last week of August was spent by the teenagers carrying Svetlana's things to a wooden house. Wojtek was a bit surprised that all of them had already been transferred to Olga, but the women claimed that Anatol wanted to help and that it was his doing. All things - if you can say so - were quite specific due to their small number. An old-fashioned mirror, a hairbrush that looks like it was out of a costume movie, a small, slightly torn cupboard and few clothes. Only white tunics, shirts, airy dresses, pleated skirts. No jeans, leggings, T-shirts, hoodies. Zero cosmetics. He did not interfere. Svetlana's beauty definitely did not need any additional setting and care. And the clothes - girls from his junior high school used a word for this ancient way of dressing... ah... vintage. Maybe she was fan of it. Or maybe it's some folk. After all, she had been living in a secluded place for years, without the Internet or fashion magazines. It didn't matter to him.

Their first afternoon at the cottage was very busy. Wojtek helped to arrange the furniture in the room intended for Svetlana. It took what was superfluous. The girl also asked if she could make some changes, not big, rather decorative. He agreed without hesitation.

He stood and watched as she turned this ordinary place into what could be called home. In the middle of the kitchen table she put down a vase and put fresh flowers in it.

He didn't know what kind it was, but he immediately smelled their beautiful scent. On the kitchen eaves, she hung braids of garlic, and decorated the bar counter with pots of basil and thyme. In every free corner she hung bags with dried flowers. Before, he did not know what he missed most about this place, he saw it the moment she pinned the curtains in the windows. None of these things were new, much less expensive. However, all of them together introduced a cheerful and homely atmosphere to the wooden house. He was grateful to her, but he didn't want to say too much so as not to scare her. So he gave Svetlana a radiant smile.

Seeing the approval and joy in his eyes, she knew she had done well. She felt that Wojtek was a good and trustworthy man, so she wanted to tell him the truth all the more. But isn't it too early? Will it not scare him too much and... lose? So she chose silence, although she felt that soon she would not have any secrets from the boy. She believed that Wojtek would help her, that he would finally free her...

20

The school year had to start at last. They went together to its opening ceremony. The journey passed unexpectedly quickly. They sat down in one of the desk and watched their colleagues. The teacher seemed nice. Svetlana was most concerned that she would reveal her age to everyone, which would spark silly comments and taunts. However, Mrs. Marta was extremely tactful and did not mention it a word. Their class was extremely original. It counted several Poles, Czechs, and Germans, but there was also a Frenchman out of nowhere. Belarusians completed the whole. Most of the parents of the first graders worked in diplomacy, government institutions, or - like Wojtek's father - were engineers or rich investors. The teenagers did not intend to make new friends, and even more so to make friends, because having learned from experience, they knew that they would not stay here for longer. Svetlana and Wojtek were considered closely related – they still stuck together. Until one day in October, when an unpleasant - from Wojtek's point of view - situation took place.

During the long, twenty-minute break, Wojtek and Svetlana, as usual, ate lunch. They usually shared the same two-person table in the school cafeteria. Wojtek was happy about it, because he could have the girl only to himself, and he still had little company of her. Today theirs seat was taken.

So they sat down at a larger table and immediately got company. The German Alex joined them. Why did Wojtek hate him? Maybe it was because the girls called him "divine", maybe because of his relaxed manner, maybe because of the charm with which he had attracted teachers, or maybe because of that gleam in his eye that his companion seemed to notice now.

"Can I sit here?" He asked quite simply.

"Sure," Svetlana replied, not waiting for Wojtek's answer.

"It's been a month and I still don't know what your relationship is. There are rumors that you live together. Are you a cousin? Are you step-siblings? If you don't want to, you don't have to answer," he asked.

"If you must know, we are not related, we just live together." Wojtek who spoke these words was bursting with pride. Just for a while.

Svetlana has already corrected the last sentence:

"It's not like that... not at all. I live very far from school and Wojtek, at my mother's request, rented a room for me. Anyway, I only spend time in it until the evening, then I go back to myself. So the rumors are greatly exaggerated." She smiled.

Wojtek felt as if someone had stuck a knife straight into his heart. So all their conversations, all their travels together, laughter and tears, depending on the situation, were useless. He he was just renting her a room.

Nothing more. He looked in the direction of talking to each other, indeed, clearly flirting companions, and lost his appetite. He left the table, only throwing:

"See you on the bus."

21

They only met at the bus stop. Wojtek was walking at a quick pace and Svetlana, although she wanted so much, could not catch up with him. She felt he was insulted and knew that her words, though true, might offend him. So she decided to fix everything before it was too late. Especially since that puffy Alex did not make any impression on her. She didn't even like him. She just didn't want to be gossiped about, she preferred to give an explanation to this popular boy, pass it on and let everyone else leave her alone. Now she only had to explain it to her Wojtek, that is Wojtek.

"You are angry?" She asked, making that sweet face of hers that always acted on him when she needed something.

He didn't answer - not because he chose not to speak, but because he didn't know what to tell her now.

Svetlana did not give up, just waiting for them to sit next to each other on the bus. She was supposed to wait with it, but she thought it would be the best time to finally shed that burden. Only this way she could regain his trust.

"I've wanted to tell you this for a long time. But I had to convince myself that you wouldn't laugh at me and leave me. Now that you are very important someone in my life, when I know that I can trust you, the time has come.

Although it's not easy for me..." It sounded so dramatic and pleasant to his ear that Wojtek finally turned his head away from the window and looked into those big brown eyes.

"I will not interrupt you and whatever you say, know that you have me on your side. Always. I'm your friend." He wanted to encourage her.

"My story is sad, and I will understand correctly if I become repulsive to you. But I need your help not to be like that. Everything else can be changed."

Her words were unclear and, according to Wojtek, they did not add up.

"Everything starts with Olga, so I'll start my story with her... As a young woman she got married, her parents forced her to do so, because she did not love the man. However, she became pregnant and expecting twins..."

"But I know the story. She told me exactly the same." Wojtek could not stand it and interfered.

"And she told you she started bleeding and needed to save her children? And she added that neither she nor the children survived?" Svetlana asked impatiently.

"What are you talking about? How did she not survive it? Then who are you living with? Who was I talking to? Who cooks all these good dinners for me?" Wojtek once again did not understand anything.

"It's not Olga, but łojma..." Svetlana expected a series of questions, but saw only Wojtek's eyes waiting for answers, so she continued. "We live on Świteź Lake, it is a magical place. Olga when she felt the pain and saw blood, she already knew she was not going to get out of it alive, neither she nor her children.

These events took place a long time ago, when almost everyone knew the legends and spells related to the Slavic demons of nature. Olga was no exception. She had the lobelia flowers with her, you must have seen them during the full moon on the lake. They contain poison. If you feel that you are dying, you can say a spell and eat one flower. This is enough to poison your earthly life and gain non-mortality, unfortunately in the form of a demon."

Everything sounded so incredible that Wojtek did not know whether to interrupt the girl's nonsense or listen to the end and wait for a slightly more logical explanation... He chose the number two.

"Olga did just that. She lost her children, but gained a life herself. However, she was no longer a beautiful, young Olga, but just a łojma," continued the girl, although she noticed with regret that Wojtek did not understand.

"Who's that?" Wojtek decided to ask.

"Łojma is a forest demon that settles near water. It is extremely dangerous. It looks for new mothers and takes their children. All because the form of łojma is taken by pregnant women who died before giving birth. The longing for a child is so strong that it leads to kidnapping. Łojma looks like an old woman. When she is angry, her demonic qualities can be seen: hair and huge breasts. Otherwise you won't notice anything suspicious.

Now he knew the girl was telling the truth. So he wasn't hallucinating. It was Olga who changed depending on the mood. But is it all possible? But why would Svetlana make things up? He had to believe her. He wanted to believe her. So he listened carefully...

"So, your mother didn't die at all?" He dared to ask this difficult and probably very painful question.

"I can't remember it, I was a baby after all. However, I have the impression that Olga helped my mother die, and she chose me for her child. Unfortunately, I suppose the same happened to Anatol, but that's a separate story."

"I'm sorry. I'm very sorry. I just don't understand how I could help and... like you said... make a difference. Do you want to get away from her? No problem... Father, I'll ask him, he'll organize a school for us in Poland. You only need to have some documents..."

"It's not that simple, Wojtek... There is something else... but for now... let me finish this one thread before you get completely lost. Well, Olga is keeping a closed box somewhere in her house. My intuition tells me that there is something in it that is related to my origin, maybe my mother's name, and maybe even mine. I need to know. She also keeps a book about demons on a shelf. I need it to free myself from it, I also need a lobelia, but I will take care of it myself. I'll explain everything to you later. For now, our goal, if you will help me, will be to lure Olga out of the house and discover what she kept in front of me in mystery for the last seventeen years..."

He sensed that she wouldn't say anything more today. She was tired and excited at the same time. All the time he also had the impression that she expected his approval. He hugged her tightly against him and kissed her forehead. It meant more than a thousand words to her. He knew he had to help her, although he was not entirely sure if the whole story could be true. He had not yet believed in ghosts, ghouls, vampires and werewolves. He has always followed logic in his life. Time will tell. He couldn't lose anything. At least that's what he thought then.

22

The autumn days passed similarly to the previous ones. The only difference was that Svetlana and Wojtek had a plan, and Olga was no longer a nice old lady, but a creature who had done a lot of harm. Wojtek could not forget what his friend told him for a long time. But he knew that he couldn't show that something had changed in him. It would frustrate their elaborate preparations.

One afternoon, as was their custom thus far, they visited Olga. It was, however, a completely different afternoon. Svetlana began to complain of stomach problems at the beginning of her visit.

"You need to drink wormwood. This is the best medicine. It works immediately, the old woman advised."

"I know, but it hurts a lot and I don't know if it would be better to brew some fresh herb. Do you have one at home?" The girl was implementing her plan.

"Maybe you're right. Unfortunately, I only have one from last year. So we'll go right away to the clearing on the other side of the lake and bring some. Or I will go alone if you are in so much pain." Wojtek saw in Olga caring mother again. Maybe Svetlana was wrong? Olga was a demon, but apparently, she didn't lose all human reflexes. After all, Svetlana grew up to be a smart and healthy girl. He needed to know the truth.

"No, if we walk slowly, I'd rather accompany you. I must finally learn how to distinguish this herb."

"I will stay in front of the house and wait for you, I'm tired." Wojtek sounded quite convincing.

As soon as they left, the boy began searching. Fortunately, the cabin was not large, so he had fewer potential hiding places to search. He looked into the herb cupboard, the stove, under the bed. There was nothing suspicious. When he had almost given up, he walked over to the photos of Svetlana and Anatol. He picked up the frame with the girl's photo and then had an epiphany. The back part was strangely bulging. He decided to check it. He didn't have much time because he had wasted it on fruitless earlier work. He took out his phone and took pictures of a page torn from some newspaper that he couldn't read - everything was written in Belarusian. The second card-file contained personal data and, oddly enough, he could read it easily. He took a picture. Suddenly he heard Svetlana's eloquent moans. In a hurry, he hid the scraps in their original place. He had almost forgotten that Svetlana had asked him for a book that had scared him so much. He was afraid, because the lack of it would certainly not escape Olga's attention. However, he did as promised. The book was already under his wide sweatshirt.

"We are back! Weren't you too bored?" Svetlana was so natural that Olga could not guess anything.

"No, I think I fell asleep. I just woke up and went to look at your childhood photo. You were a sweet little one." He forced a smile on himself..

Olga did not even look at him, she immediately started preparing the potion. Svetlana hated wormwood, but she drank it down and then vomited. This performance was enough to remove any suspicion of a lie. After supper, the young people said goodbye and returned home on the pretext of having to do their homework. In fact, just a few steps behind Olga's hut, they started exchanging views.

"You found something?" Svetlana was impatient.

"Yes, but you have to translate it because I don't understand anything. However, let's not risk it and wait until we get home." Wojtek kept common sense, although it was not easy. At home, they quickly sat down at the table, having locked earlier door. Svetlana stared at the note and the press clipping for a long time. Finally she spoke:

"This is my real mother's story. And mine. It says here that a Polish woman in Belarus committed suicide by drowning in Świteź Lake. They also mention a child, a girl she probably took with her in an act of desperation. However, they mention that the child's body was not found. And that her fate is not fully known." She was silent for a moment, tears streaming down her cheeks. "You've already seen the rest, Anna Lach and probably her Polish address, right?" she asked.

"Yes. The street and house number as well as the city are given. I think it's your mother's data. We should find her family without much effort. If you only want.

Father will take advantage of his connections we can also try our via facebook." Wojtek was already planning the next steps.

"I cannot go away for more than a day, or rather half a day. Don't forget I have to go back to my house for the night," she suppressed his enthusiasm.

"Exactly. We haven't talked about it yet, and I think this is the right moment. Why do I take you to the other side of the lake every evening? Why can I never go into a hut that you didn't show me either? And why is it so important that you can't go looking for your own family, roots?" It was not the first time that he inundated his interlocutor with questions.

23

"I was hoping we would postpone this topic. Or maybe I didn't want to touch it at all. I thought I could deal with my curse on my own. I don't want to lie to you. In that case, sit down comfortably, because we are in for a long conversation, or rather my monologue."

On the one hand, Wojtek was glad that she trusted him, and on the other hand, the word "curse" made him fear and anxious. But there was no turning back.

"Łojma, or Olga is immortal. It may end its life by itself, or it may end its life by someone who knows magic and demons. Being immortal, she wanted her children, me and Anatol, to share her fate. When I was about five or six years old, she instructed us that if we ever drowned, we should catch and swallow the lobelia immediately. We did not know then why she repeated it so often. Until one summer afternoon. Łojma said it was very warm and we should go swimming. It was just after the full moon. When we were a bit from the shore, she shouted that it was not far to the center of the lake. We did not realize that we might run out of strength. However, it did. We shouted, asked for help. Łojma just stood there and reminded us of a lobelia. Finally, when we came to the surface less and less, we reached for the flower. I don't remember exactly, but it felt strange.

Then, I didn't know what she did to us yet. I found out when I had the first impression in the evening that when it strikes midnight, I'm suffocating on land and I have to jump into the water as soon as possible," she paused so that the boy could sort it all out.

Wojtek listened in amazement and still did not understand what Svetlana was. After all, they are not łojma, because her appearance did not indicate it. So who?

"Are you a mermaid? This you want to tell me? Are your fins showing off in the evening and you jump into the water?" It wasn't until he said it aloud that he saw how hellaciously it sounded.

"Mermaids only exist in fairy tales. I am wodja."

Now he remembered that was what the bully had called her when he watched them at the festival.

"What is wodja? And what is this her, this your curse?" He already knew the answer to the second question, but he wanted to know as much detail as possible.

"Wodjanicha, or wodja for short, means rusalka. It is the soul of a drowned girl, locked in a human body. We are inherently bad. We are to attract and kill. You must know that I did too. Over the years, I've learned how to control this murderous urge. The last time I killed a young man was three years ago." She noticed that the words make a great impression on Wojtek. However, it was not an impression in the positive sense of the word. Nevertheless, she decided to go on. "Some of us must spend winter in the lake. But Olga must have cast a spell on me because, as I mentioned, I choke on land at midnight every day and I have to enter the lake. That's why I can't stay with you. That's why you're not walking me back. I have no home," she broke off.

"And your brother? Anatol? Where he lives? Also in the lake? He is also wodja?"

"Anatol is undine," the word sounded familiar too, "my male counterpart. He, however, has no control over his lusts. He is extremely angry. He respects nothing and nobody. Even me and łojma. He drowns people. He takes money from them, which he uses for worldly entertainment. Anyway, he shares them with me and Olga. This is how we get money, for example for food. Undine often causes whirlpools for his own entertainment. Do you have any idea where your ankle marks come from?" She knows that the boy can stop listening to her at any moment and run away as far as possible.

24

Wojtek did not want to run anywhere. His feelings for Svetlana were even stronger. Right now, he would do anything to free her. He wanted to help her so much, even if he were to fight all the demons of the world, including Anatol.

"What do we have to do to get out of here? To find your family? So you don't lose your breath?" She already felt that he had forgiven her all shameful past.

"We need to find a spell in the book that will undo the spell. Once, one of the drowned women said that by recreating the situation, so by drowning, eating a lobelia and chanting a spell, it would be possible to regain human form. I don't know if it's true, but I have to try. Then you have to be with me and save me..."

Svetlana revealed everything to Wojtek. There were no more secrets between them, no understatements. She didn't know what this teenage boy was feeling and thinking when she finished her story. She didn't have to think about it too long.

"Well. Let me summarize. Olga is that evil demon who has consciously and willfully hurt you and your friend whom you call brother. You are an evil demon, not of your own free will, turned into a good one. There is also Anatol, or if you prefer undine, who is an evil demon and has not undergone any transformation, indeed, he wanted to kill me for entertainment. Is everything correct so far?" She was a little upset that he had simplified the story so much, but she nodded her head in agreement. "We must have a plan. All the smallest details must be settled, because what I hear is not going to be as easy as stealing a spellbook." He was right on that point.

They started by leafing through the book. They didn't know what to look for. Especially since the spells were written in a strange language. It was neither Russian nor Belarusian, but something like a combination of them. So they had to be guided mainly by symbols and drawings. Finally they found a print that interested them. It featured a young girl walking out of the lake smiling. There is a lobelia next to it. They were sure it was the spell. The first phase of the plan has been completed. Now it was time to wait for the full moon and then to get the rest of the details.

School life continued as before. Wojtek only wondered how Svetlana knew and knew so much, since, as he found out, she had not attended any school before.

"Olga did not want me to have contact with my peers. She was afraid that I might tell them our family secrets. Now, after seventeen years together, she is convinced of my loyalty, so she has agreed to an experiment with the lecture. I studied alone, at home. After all, there was nothing else to do. It was just me, Anatol and Olga. After a while, the company of books, especially historical and literature was much more attractive. Olga also took care of accounting tasks, brought various maps and a globe. I have always been interested in life outside the lake, which is probably why I have no major problems with my studies today. Besides physics and chemistry, of course, but you are good as my tutor." She was laughing. "Anatol didn't go to school either. Except that he lives a completely different life. While I try to keep the remnants of normalcy, I try hard to be like my peers, he is a demon in the full sense of the word. He lives from evening to evening. During the day he rests, and at night he goes hunting. He robs, murders, buries the bodies. He's got a moment of weakness sometimes when he's acting normally, but that's rare. I must admit, however, that clothes, furniture, food are his merit."

Wojtek was shocked. How can you destroy the life of two tiny people? After all, she could raise them, have them with her... but turn them into demons? Svetlana explained to him, however, that only in this way she could keep them forever. Old selfish.

25

Their peers treated them a bit like queers. Alex told nonsense about being a couple, but waiting "with it" to marriage and Svetlana doesn't spend the night in their nest. He was jealous, at the beginning of the school year he hoped that something would spark between him and Beauty, as most of the class called her. Faced with a complete defeat, he decided to at least separate potential candidates from candidates by inventing a few stories.

Wojtek and Svetlana did not bother at all. The school was just an addition to their real, complicated lives. And their overriding goal now was to bring the girl back to the world of the living. Each of their conversations started something like this: "Good. Let us say it again. It is full moon and the lobelias are beginning to bloom. You swim to the middle of the lake before midnight and tell Anatol that two bastards have entered the lake on the other side of the lake. He's drifting away. Olga is asleep. You say a spell and take the poison contained in the flower. And then I, your savior, come in. When you go down, I save you quickly. We reach the shore as two people. No demons. Olga does not learn anything as long as circumstances favor us. Then we return to Poland to find your family. Missed something?" Wojtek's plan seemed to be perfect in its simplicity. However, Svetlana was not that optimistic. She was afraid that something will go wrong. That undine would come back too early and hurt Wojtek. That's why she wanted to have Plan B.

"We must have some backup in case my enraged brother returns sooner than we would like. You have to find a spell or a way that will keep him away from us for a moment," she argued.

So they went back to browsing through the magic book. They found a drawing of a man with white eyes, with a horse and honey next to him. Svetlana collected only those words that resembled her native speech.

"It seems that the Slavs believed that you could offer a sacrifice in the form of a horse with a head anointed with honey to undine. The sunken booty was supposed to deprive the demon of its murderous instincts for a while," she explained, not being convinced herself of the correctness of her explanation.

The next full moon was to come just before the winter holidays, which is called winter break in Poland. It was cold and an additional obstacle for Wojtek and the success of their mission was the frozen lake. Svetlana, however, had an ice-hole at her disposal, which she used every day when she went to sleep. The problem of the horse remained, but Wojtek promised to solve it. Once again he had to lie to his father and again he was not disappointed with him, and the teenager's whim was fulfilled in the blink of an eye. So there was a horse, which even got its special location like a stable, there was a spell and a knight in shining armor. Only full moon was missing.

26

The first semester of their study together in high school has come to an end. Wojtek got the third and Svetlana the fifth best average in the class. The father was so pleased that he decided to surprise his son.

"Did I tell you that I'm proud of you?" He started one of their rare weekend conversations.

"Like... a thousand times?" Wojtek was ironic as usual.

"Come into your room and see what's on your bed." Antoni sounded intriguing.

"Tickets and voucher to Kenya... for the first week of break..." The son read without much enthusiasm.

"I thought that you and I deserve, firstly, an award, and secondly, rest. I do not even mention the strengthening of the father-son bond. You don't even know how happy I am... I have already taken a leave of absence, although it was not easy, I bought us oils and binoculars..."

Wojtek listened and he became more and more absent. Father was so happy, so excited... he was counting on him so much... and he would have to hurt him and how he explained it to him for no reason.

"Dad... I'm not going," Antoni interrupted his speech. There was silence. Eventually interrupted by father.

"I understand." As usual, the father was not angry and acknowledged the anguish caused by his son with one word. There was disappointment in his voice.

He could tell him the truth at the risk of being ridiculous. He could throw a fairy tale about the fact that he is in love and prefers to spend time with the girl whom - incidentally - his father liked, but he had lived with her for almost a year, so Antoni would not leave him alone. There was one more way out. He had to say something that would hurt his father so much that he would drop the topic and not repeat it for a very long time. It was the worst possible exit. In this situation, however, it seemed to be the only right one.

"I don't want to go with you. We haven't been spending much time together lately. You seem to be a stranger who suddenly wants to re-enter my life. But what for? Since I'm fine the way it is. I don't need any more time with you. I wouldn't even know what we're going to talk about for seven days. Sorry, but this is one of your sillier ideas. Now I'm sorry, I have my case. On your way out, steek the door. We'll talk in a week. Bye."

Antoni did not believe what he had just heard. Wojtek was not brought up this way. Or maybe the last years were hard to call upbringing? After all, he gave him everything the boy asked for. He found the best school for him, went all out to extend the rent of a lake house for the entire school year, put in a stove there, and recently even bought him a horse - which was a bizarre whim. From the beginning of his stay in Belarus, he helped his son as much as he could. No only to son. There was also his girlfriend. He likes her and treated her like a daughter. He helped her financially, paid extra, which Wojtek did not know about, equipped her with textbooks for her education. He gave her home. And now he's get suach a repay? Thrown: bye and no, I'm not going? Antoni was devastated. But he didn't want to discuss it, so he packed his things and left.

Wojtek could not calm down. Why he treated his father in this way? In the name of love? Just what love? He didn't even know what was really going on between him and Svetlana. They didn't even kiss. Then in the name of platonic love or friendship. But friendship is more important than your own father? This father! One he could always count on. One who never denied him anything. One who trusted him immensely. Wojtek felt terrible. However, he promised he would help. So he couldn't just leave her now. He had a plan: in the first week of the holiday, he would lift the curse on Svetlana, in the second, under the excuse of visiting friends, they would go to Poland. There was no time and place for the father in this plan. One day he will tell him everything, explain it somehow. And the father, as is the father, will forgive you.

27

The long-awaited full moon has arrived. So far, nothing has stood in the way of two young people. They only had one small incident behind them. Olga asked Svetlana one day if she had seen her book. However, she replied that she now has a lot of her own books and that she doesn't need that for anything. Olga believed.

"Let's repeat. At ten o'clock I sink my horse... By the way, it's a pity, but your life is of course the most important. At this time, you send Anatol to the other side and say the spell. Are you sure you can read them?" Wojtek panicked.

"Don't worry, we've practiced this a hundred times. Everything will be fine," Svetlana reassured him.

"Well. Remember that as soon as you pick up the lobelia, you scream out loud."

"I remember."

"Then we're going to the lake," he concluded. Svetlana did not know one more thing. Wojtek delved into the mysteries of the magic book. On the drawing of undine he found another one - apart from a horse and a barrel of honey. He did not know if the method given by the secret author was effective, but he decided to protect himself. He did not say anything to the girl, so as not to unnecessarily upset her.

Everything seemed to be going smoothly. Svetlana swam into the middle of the lake, told Anatol about the intruders on the other side, and got rid of him. She uttered a spell, screamed. When Wojtek was almost with her and he had her in his arms... he saw Anatol next to him. She did not have time to eat the lobelia.

"You thought you were smarter than me?" Undine said. "You thought you would bribe me with your horse? This only distracts me for a moment. You wanna steal my sister? Anyway, I can see that she is not her anymore," he continued, regardless of Wojtek walking away from him.

Suddenly, Wojtek felt a strong whirlwind that began to draw both him and Svetlana. He felt he didn't have the strength to keep going. Then he remembered that drawing from the book.

"I don't know if it's true, but apparently you can't see through your clear eyes during the day... I can help you... but take the vortex back." Wojtek has negotiated the terms of the truce.

The vortex stopped.

"You would have to have what I think. If you cheat, you can forget about wodja and your own life."

"You mean something like a modern artificial lens, right?"

"What I need is moon glass. You have it?" Ondyn was getting more and more impatient.

"I can have it," Wojtek was not bluffing.

Before he argued with his father, he told him that the old woman Olga suffers from cataracts, but that she is terrified of surgery and that only an artificial lens will help her see the world more clearly.

The father once again did not ask questions and agreed to buy the necessary thing. Now it would be good. But still had to wait for its execution...

Undine - Anatol let the teenagers swim to the shore. Svetlana was starting to wake up. Still waking up as wodja.

Anatol would not let them go any more. The moon was hiding slowly, and the sun appeared in its place.

They became hostages of undine. And he was not a reasonable or cooperative guardian. Fortunately, he gave in to hide the case from Olga. Wojtek promised that he would get the lenses that his father would receive in a few days as soon as possible. But now that their relationship was extremely strained, it might take longer than normal to bring them back.

"How many days will the full moon last?" Wojtek felt that he was plucked. He should have brought the lenses right away, but nature made the rules for this unequal fight.

"As every. Maximum three days. Will you make it? I'm afraid my brother won't be able to keep his mouth shut for long. Not only that - he will not let us go anywhere now. He will watch me like an eye in his head until he gets his ransom. Everything is gone!" Svetlana was confused.

Anatol raised his hands in a gesture of victory, he also pointed to his eye and the place where the watch was worn.

"Yes, I know, our time is running out. You don't need to remind me!" Svetlana shouted at him. "What's the plan? Do we have any?" She looked at Wojtek with pleading eyes.

"We need to get coverage, throw a trick, and get my father over here quickly."

"Will he come?" She asked.

"He never disappointed me. He won't do that now either." Wojtek said it, but he was not entirely convinced himself. After the last meeting, Antoni did not speak to him, did not write or call him. It was the first time they had remained silent for so long.

Antoni breathed a sigh of relief when he heard his son's voice on the phone. He claimed that it was stupid, that they should talk and that Olga needed these lenses very much, so it would be good if he could bring them with him. He canceled all the meetings scheduled for that day and went straight to the lake. On the way, he also visited an optician who undertook to hand over the ordered goods by phone. He thought about what he should say to his son, but everything sounded wrong. He decided to bet on honesty. It was always the best solution. He felt really hurt. Let the young know about it...

Anatol was warned that Stożyński would visit them. He was supposed to watch them closely from the side, and he knew they were planning to repeat the action of yesterday. All three feared Olga's sudden entry. Therefore, just before their father's arrival, Wojtek and Svetlana visited the old woman, always having their dangerous shadow behind them. They drank tea, they told about father and son quarrel. Wojtek even asked her for advice.

"You have to tell him the truth. Don't be ashamed of your feelings for Svetlana. Because I understand it's because of her you're not going?" Olga watched them and felt the tension. On the one hand, she blamed them on the Stożyński quarrel, on the other hand, she did not like Svetlana, who was absent.

"All right?" She threw at her. "You want to talk face to face?" she asked in Belarusian.

Svetlana replied that she felt something for the boy, and they both knew what happened to her. That she should have made it clear to him that there would be nothing between them - she used a language known only to them.

Wojtek felt uncomfortable, but he knew that Svetlana had to smooth the situation. He did not interfere. Olga advised that this conversation be transferred to another day. When they are alone. Svetlana nodded her head. Soon after, they left.

Antoni showed up late. They had little time. However, this time father was not an easy interlocutor. First, he wanted to be alone with his son. However - to Wojtek's surprise - Svetlana insisted on participating in the conversation as well. He did not object.

"I wanted to tell you at the outset that I feel sorry for what you told me last time."

"I know. The more so because for the first time I lied unashamedly..." Wojtek intrigued him and - what can say - worried even more. "I wanted to stay for Svetlana. Just like that. I fell in love.

Antoni looked at his son, at the girl. And he just nodded his head for a moment.

"No problem, but you could have said it right away..." They grabbed hands and then Antoni pulled Wojtek towards him.

"That's not the whole truth. Wojtek wanted to help me," she interjected.

"Yes, he helps you from the very beginning. I am proud of him." Antoni agreed with her.

"You don't understand. I am wodja. A girl who lives in the lake."

Antoni decided that his Russian was probably too weak. Or maybe she used some idiom.

"I have the curse of this place, of these people, that can only be taken off during a full moon, and that is now happening. That's why he didn't go with you, that's why he asked for a horse, that's why everything happened..." she said quickly and incoherently.

Antoni was beginning to think she was crazy, and Wojtek did not really know how to explain it all to this engineer who valued logic. Svetlana knew that the elder Stożyński would not go as easily as with the son. In a flash she moved from the chair to the far end of the room. It seemed to flow, not go.

Her form changed: her eyes seemed to turn into flickering eyes, blood ran to her nails... she still looked beautiful, but this time both men were terrified...

When she noticed this, she stopped immediately... Nobody said anything.

"Dad, go now. Leave your lenses on, sleep on with it."

"When you come back next time, it might be over," she said in an innocent voice, but a moment ago...

"Should I leave now? Now? When I am hallucinating? Or when what she says and shows is true? Should I leave you here with her? She deceived you, deceived you, and you are now under her influence!" For the first time Antoni bridled so much. He wanted to pack his son immediately and return to Poland.

"Do you have glass?" Anatol walked in. "The full moon is about to end."

"Who are you? Get out of here, I don't know what I'd do!" Antoni was fed up with third parties.

Then Anatol gave a show of strength. He knocked over Stożyński, showed his demonic gaze...

"Don't hurt him, but hold him here for a moment. We have to finish what we started. Then you will get a lens."

Svetlana and Wojtek ran towards the lake. Anatol stood hostage with his father. Antoni couldn't believe his eyes, and yet it all happened here and now. He had an evacuation plan in his head, but so far he had only one dream - to live this moonlit night.

"I jump into the water." Svetlana swam to the middle of the lake. Lying on her back, she spoke the words of the spell. She took the lobelia and stopped moving, falling to the bottom. Wojtek waited a moment, he noticed that his beloved puts a flower in her mouth... He swam over to her. She was falling to the bottom. He pulled her out. Anatol and father watched the entire scene. Wojtek turned her over on her side, water ran out of her mouth, but she was still unconscious. The boy started a rescue action. After a few minutes it was possible to say that it was successful.

Wojtek approached a nearby stone and took out a bag with two slides from behind it. He then instructed Anatol on how to use them - it was night so he had to take the boy's word for it. He let Svetlana go, but he did not fail to add:

"You'll be damned. Even if you come back to the world of the living, you are cursed, don't forget it. If you go away with him now, you'll never be happy again," he finished and plunged into the water.

The young people breathed a sigh of relief. Svetlana did it literally and figuratively. For the first time in time immemorial, she could breathe normally without being in a lake. It could only mean one thing. She was a normal girl again.

"It's too good to be true. You think I can just walk away now and look for my relatives?" She smiled at her tired companion.

Antoni watched the entire scene from the side and wiped away the tears of his sigh, though his mind still did not grasp everything that happened in the last few hours...

28

"Are you so naive? You thought I was going to let you go without saying goodbye?" Olga stood behind her, or rather a hairy, old, ugly woman with huge breasts and a demonic look.

They looked at each other and knew now that this long evening was not over for them yet. What could she want? And how could she actually stop them now? - Wojtek wondered, until he finally let it out:

"Svetlana, let's go. You've listened to her long enough and remained faithful. You are free." He believed his words.

"Not completely. Perhaps you can come in for tea and I will tell you everything..." the old woman insisted.

"We're not going anywhere! And if, as far as possible from this place!" Antoni was slowly losing his temper, he wanted to help these two.

"What else have you done to me?" The girl knew Olga wasn't bluffing. She knew her and her calmness. It no longer looked like łojma, so she had to have the upper hand.

"My dear, you've been with me for the last seventeen years. You may not have forgiven me for what I did, but you must admit that I took good care of you. Until he showed up." Here Olga showed Wojtek with her hand. "When I saw his goo-goo eyes, I knew he was going to get us in trouble. This was before you stole the magic book. So I've cast a new spell that will keep you close to Świteź until I take it off. If you prefer me to be more specific, I will add that it is not in your book. It is older than it. Thanks to it, Svetlana will be able to go no more than two kilometers from the lake. Of course, we can get along though..." She raised an eyebrow significantly.

"What do you want? You know my father can arrange everything for you." Antoni nodded as a sign that it was true. "Just say what! Do you want money? A better home? Do you want to go on vacation? I will arrange it, just give her a break!" Wojtek was screaming.

"See, I'm not bad to the core. I'm just very lonely. Of course, I was left with Anatol, but the man, especially undine, is not constant in his feelings, moreover, his impetuosity... I need to raise a new daughter, whom I can entrust with secrets and with whom I will spend my free time... until she grows up and betrays me like wojda!" There was disappointment in her voice, but also a coming hope.

"What exactly would we do?" Svetlana's joy was giving way to discouragement.

"It's very simple, my friends. You have to get a new daughter for me. Of course, a little one, preferably right after birth. Yes, so that I could raise her according to my own rules..."

"And then drown and ruin her life! Nasty old selfishness!" Wojtek couldn't stand it.

"I will not be angry. Let me just say you have a week. After this time, the spell takes on real power and nothing and no one will free Svetlana again. Good night! Sleep well." She turned and walked calmly in the direction of her hut.

29

She said clearly. They had a week. The last week of vacation to free Svetlana. For several days they wondered where to get the baby. After all, Olga was old, but not stupid. There was therefore no fraud involved. Antoni still couldn't understand what was happening here on Świteź Lake. He was afraid for his son, at the same time he had to go back to work. However, Wojtek will never agree to go with him. He had to come up with something quickly.

"Unless it's quite small and almost invisible." said Wojtek during one of their long conversations. Antoni was asleep.

"What do you mean? You know if we try to cheat her, she'll never leave me alone. We have to be smarter than her." Svetlana was very pessimistic this time.

"Do you remember when I told you about Monica? I think that if we can't count on my father, and we can't, because I definitely don't want to involve him in all this, he has to go back to work... Anyway, I don't know what he thinks about all of this... Only Monia can help. She is resourceful and finds a way out of even the worst situations. We have to bring her here. A look of hope once again entered Svetlana's face."

"Son, we have to leave," Stożyński began the conversation.

"Dad, you know I'm not giving in this time. Further discussion is pointless. You, too, would not give in if it were about security, for mom's life..."

Antoni knew perfectly well that this was how the conversation would turn out.

"I know. I can see that you have something more serious in common. Only my mind still rejects what my eyes saw. I am trying to explain it by the fact that we ate something poisonous or got intoxicated... because, otherwise, demons..."

"They do not exist? I thought so too, but then I saw what Anatol did to me in the lake, remember my blue ankles?"

Antoni nodded.

"You have to go back to work, otherwise you will be fired and we will lose our livelihood. I'm almost there, but lest you worry too much, I thought you might..."

"Ask Monika for help?" Antoni came up with this concept.

"Yes. Do you agree?"

"Do I have any other choice?" He said exactly what came to mind.

The father packed up, hugged his son tightly, and also Svetlana. He assured him that he was only a few hours away that they could always ask for help and he would come. He looked at them and envied them this feeling, but at the same time he was afraid that it might lead them to very dangerous places...

Wojtek called aunt in the morning. He had not told her on the phone what her visit was about. Monika had led the conversation herself. She mentioned that Antek called her, that she knew about their quarrel, that she needed her presence. He felt that the consequence of her concern would be a quick arrival. So he added a few details and invited for the next weekend.

"I have one more strange question..." He continued the telephone conversation. "You don't have a friend with a small child that you would like to take with you here? Or maybe some godson or goddaughter... it's winter break..." He slyly smuggled elements of his plan.

"Where are the kids in your head from? I don't know something? Should I be afraid?" Monika panicked.

"Let's say it would be good for us to see how such a thing is handled. I'll explain everything to you on the spot. I finish before you start asking stupid questions. Bye. I'm waiting for you!" He hung up the phone with the desired effect.

Monia was shocked. So still. Antek told her about the idea of a shared apartment, which Wojtek came up with right after the holidays. Then she - aunt of good advice - advised Antoni to agree, thus expressing the strength of his trust. And now? Now they did it. Beautiful. Antek will kill her, and Ewka will throw a lightning bolt straight from the sky. She has to go there, and since she's messed up like that, at least she'll bring the baby back to cover her guilt a little. Fortunately, Monia was very popular and although she did not have children of her own, someone kept asking her to become a godmother.

The youngest goddaughter, Alicja, was fourteen months old. They loved each other. She couldn't speak yet, but she gave her free fitness - she was so fast. So Monia called Alicja's mother and offered to take the baby for a short break. Like any tired mother, Alicja's mother quickly packed the girl and sent her to her aunt.

Monika never wanted a child. First, during her studies, she did not have time. Later she felt no need. Finally, traveling appeared in her life and then the child would be a total obstacle. However, there was something about her that attracted the little ones. It seemed to her that it was probably the child she kept within herself. A child who never grew, although, as one of her goddaughters had said, she already had lines on her face. Therefore, she never refused when one of her friends gave her a child. She liked to spend time with all six godchildren.

The journey passed very calmly. Alicja repeated her words: "E! E!", Which was a manifestation of admiration for what is new and unknown. Monika, on the other hand, was wondering what sermon should be delivered to Wojtek and Svetlana. She liked this girl of extraordinary beauty and she understood Wojtek too. Who at his age would resist such charms? However, for the sake of many years of friendship with Ewa and Antek, she had to be harsh.

Therefore, when she saw the boy at the railway station in Nowogródek, she immediately adopted the appropriate face and started speech:

"I'm dissappointed! That's not what your mother taught you, and that's not what your father raised you like! To make someone a child at seventeen!" She screamed ravily, but luckily hardly anyone could understand her.

"First of all: hello Monia. Nice to see you. Yes, I'm fine, except that we need your help, me and Svetlana. What about you? Second: I don't know where you got the idea of me becoming a father. This is ridiculous and not my style at all. Third: I hope you didn't talk this nonsense to my father, because he has enough of my worries anyway," the teenager gave his defense speech.

"How's that? You didn't conceiving? What do you need Alicja for?" Monika was surprised.

"It's a very long, complicated and unbelievable story. But I guess no one will understand me like you. Only you believe in secret powers, spells, white magic and the like. I could only turn to you." Wojtek's eyes adopted the "begging" view.

"Okay, let's go for some warming tea and tell me everything in order," she replied, almost completely reassured.

The meeting in the teahouse took several hours. They drank not one but three teas. Monika did not stop, but listened carefully, absorbing every detail of the story. She knew this young boy had given her incredible confidence, and that she will bear the burden of completing the story that Wojtek gave. And the story was truly extraordinary. After all, there were demons, ghosts, a curse, drowning children. It was hard for her to take all of this for sure, but that was exactly what she assumed. I hope he has a plan, because I have no idea how I can help - she thought when Wojtek finished. Then the words were said:

"This is where our detailed strategy begins, in which you play a significant role. In fact, it's not even you, but your goddaughter. And of course, do not be afraid, the little girl is safe," he explained.

"I'm all ears."

"Olga wants a child to be able to raise it, drown it and be with it as long as possible. Of course, we're not so selfish, and we don't live in the Middle Ages, so sacrificing an innocent baby is not an option. Remember, however, that Olga is old and even as łojma, she does not have such good hearing or eyesight. So we will do this: you will go for long walks with Alice every day - so that the old woman will look at her, see that we are credible. We will say her bull that Dad has found a tourist willing to rent a cottage. After a few days, we will tell Olga that you are leaving and we need to finalize the transaction. Then you will take the baby and leave, and we, together with a beautiful doll from the supermarket, wrapped in as thick a jacket as possible, will approach Olga. I will say her to cast the spell first and Svetlana will then leave the area of Świteź Lake. When she is safe, I will hand over the doll to Olga and I will run away," he concluded.

"I do not know. It sounds a bit like a bad crime movie. And there are many understatements. First of all: will Olga agree to Svetlana to go away? Second, what if Olga asks you how to cover up the disappearance of a child. Third - what if Olga sees the baby is a doll and decides to curse you? If we do not get a satisfactory answer to this question, you can forget about my help. Svetlana is important, but your safety is my priority. Forgive any cruel words." She spoiled his mood, though not entirely.

"Take it easy. I already dispel your doubts: Olga will agree to Svetlana's escape, because she knows that living with a rebellious teenager will not give her happiness. You can see that the child is her dream. So small and innocent. If she asks us how we cover up the disappearance, I will reply as usual. Blaming the irresponsible mother and the dangerous water. The child played on the frozen lake and drowned, and the body will flow out in the spring. If Olga finds out that the baby is a doll, there will be no trouble: you must know that łojma is a demon that only has power over other demons. It may affect Svetlana's or Anatol's life, but not mine. So there is no risk. Be calm." He was convinced he had come up with the perfect plan.

Monika was less convinced. As much as she could believe the whole complicated story of Svetlana and Olga, she did not believe that this old witch could be deceived so easily. No at the moment, however, she was not able to come up with any better solution, so she agreed to Wojtek's proposal.

30

The very next day Monika dressed up Alicja and took her for the first lap around the lake. They took the stroller in case the little one got tired of an excessively long walk. The ostentatious walk by Olga's hut did not make the old woman feel anything other than satisfaction. At the same time, the young people went to visit the old woman.

"We kept our word. You have a mother with a little girl. You can take a closer look at them. They are due to leave at the end of the week. Svetlana will offer the woman to look after the baby while packing. Then you can take it. Before you get the girl, you have to drop the curse," Wojtek explained.

"Okay, my friends. I do not understand your anger. Can you not put yourself in my position? You think I'm bad to the core, and yet I just want some companionship on my way for years to come. Was it so bad with me, Svetlana?" Olga sounded extremely calm, one could even say that she was radiating sadness.

"No, I wasn't bad. But you didn't give my real mother a chance. Or maybe I would be better with her? Anyway, if you really loved me or felt attached, you'd let me go. No blackmail, no threats. I am now an adult woman and have a right to my own life. If only you would let me have one like that..." Svetlana wept bitterly.

It is not known whether it was the crying of her adopted daughter, or maybe a feeling of guilt or remorse that prompted Olga to make a decision that was surprising for young people.

"You're right. I did quite bad things to you and Anatol. If you want to live as an ordinary girl away from the lake, so be it. I'll lift the curse off you now." Said łojma.

Wojtek was surprised and definitely did not trust Olga. He did not want to agree to the witch's magical practices, but he did not even have time to express his objection. The ritual began before he could protest. Olga closed her eyes and started uttering weird words in a language he didn't understand. Standing in amazement, he thought of Svetlana. Finally the old lady calmed down and said:

"You are free, my dear. Today you will be able to leave Świteź. I will look after the mother and daughter from your cottage by myself."

She turned and was about to leave when Svetlana grabbed her hand and said:

"You've hurt enough innocent people. Please refer to the human feelings that remain in you and spare these two poor creatures. Think what you feel now as I walk away. Imagine that my mother and Anatol's mother felt the same. Think that it will be the affectionate and mother of this little Alicja. I have another solution for you. Would you agree to hear me out?" She looked imploringly at her guardian. She was afraid that Olga would hurt Monica and Alicja before they could warn them. So she had to improvise, and she got it good.

Svetlana asked Wojtek to stay outside and then had a long conversation with Olga. The boy did not know that his companion had a plan B. Anyway, the course of events was so surprising that he did not know what to expect. However, he trusted Svetlana's female intuition, after all, she had known Olga for a long time, so she probably knew her intentions. The waiting, however, turned out to be more difficult than he thought. Finally the girl left the hut.

"We will go to Minsk tomorrow morning. Three of us. It will be tough, but maybe it will work... Tell Monica to take the child immediately and leave. Olga has mood swings. Today she is on my side, tomorrow she can kill me. I do not want to risk. Especially when it comes to the safety of your relatives, okay?"

"But what's going to go? Can you speak clearer? I already feel left out enough!" Wojtek did not hide his anger.

"I offered Olga to try to get adoption. Of course, due to her age, she will have quite limited chances. However, I believe that if she tries hard, someone will give her the opportunity. After all, she is efficient, she has a lot of strength. She is only bothered by deteriorating eyesight and hearing. We have to help. After all, there are so many children, not necessarily the little ones, who need a home." Wojtek looked at her, listened and thought to himself how much happiness befell him when she stood in his way. He loved her, yes, he was convinced of it. And at that moment he loved her more than ever. She was so beautiful... inside.

The next day, as planned, they went to the orphanage. Wojtek was skeptical about the whole undertaking, as he did not believe that the procedures would allow for handing over a child to an old woman. The boy, however, thought as if he still lived in Poland. He did not know the exact situation of the country where he had spent the last six months.

During their journey, Svetlana told a teenager a short story about how several dozen people were killed in a bomb attack in Minsk in September '97. They were not mentioned, but all the inhabitants knew. She also talked about various demonstrations in which people were killed. He wasn't sure what that might have to do with them.

"Things were bad in our country. It's not like yours. Many children and teenagers have lost their loved ones and are waiting for a new home. So I am calm. There are no such procedures here. Few people want to adopt children, not mention teenagers. So many of our peers don't even remember what it means to have a loved one anymore. It will definitely succeed, it must succeed. Again, with that one sentence, she took all the anxiety from him.

It was exactly as she said. Of course, Olga could not count on a miracle. She was allowed to take care of a teenage orphan who had problems with the law. Nobody wanted to offer her help. Nobody wanted such a daughter. Olga thought it was a gift from fate. On the other hand, orphan home workers found that keeping the 15-year-old girl away from temptation could be good. In this way, Olga gained a daughter and a chance to redeem the wines of the past, and Svetlana regained her freedom.

31

"So why did you bring me here?" Monika argued.

"Don't complain, you rested, you did a good deed, or even two, for me and for Alicja's mother. Besides, you could visit me not only when I'm in trouble," Wojtek said to her.

"Since I'm here and so far I have no use for anything, let us at least spend some time together."

She looked at the photo of Wojtek and Antoni, standing on the sideboard in the living room.

"You're right, now that the worst is over, our relationship could be fixed. I've been messing with my father a bit lately. He probably thought me crazy, but he supported me nonetheless. He deserves to finish the story and time together, not necessarily in Kenya."

Monika had known Antek for a long time and she knew what should be done to placate him. Ewa often told her about his weaknesses. So she gave Wojtek the exact instructions, took the little one, said goodbye and left feeling that her mission was fulfilled.

Wojtek did everything exactly according to Monika's instructions. He called his father and asked him to come over for dinner. Svetlana at that time was invited to Olga and her new ward Katja. Their relations have been in order recently as good as never before. Wojtek asked Olga to prepare dad's favorite dish and dessert.

Antek, driving towards the lake, was struggling with his thoughts. What could have happened? Will he still have to deal with his son? Or maybe it's someone else... No, it's his only child who not only lost his mother, but also got involved in a series of strange events... but always his child. She only hopes that - as Monika said - everything has been finished, they will talk to each other, hug Wojtek and it will be like before. He must patiently wait for the development of further events and be with him, even from a distance, so that the young one knows that he will never lose his father.

"Hello Dad! Come in. We'll eat something first. Or no, first I have to tell you something. Everything is fine. Svetlana is already an ordinary girl, Olga doesn't cause any problems yet, but we have to evacuate quickly. We made it. Thank you for trusting me, for not making a fuss, for giving me a free hand..." Wojtek was excited, he spoke quickly and gestured. Antoni was happy because he had not seen his son in such a good mood for a long time. "If it's not too late... and you still have some free time... why not go skiing for the weekend? I have booked accommodation." He was counting on his old man's understanding.

"Sure we can go. Come here, son!" He brought him close and hugged him tightly, and in the end he ruffled his hair to keep the scene from looking too sentimental. "You can take Svetlana, I don't mind..."

"No. Just you and me. A man's trip," Wojtek replied firmly.

They sat down at the table together and feasted on Olga's delicacies. At the end, Wojtek told Antoni to sit on the couch and turned on the DVD. This completely sweetened father. It was a movie from their trip to the Greek island of Kos. The last three holidays together, when Ewa was already very weak. She then insisted that nothing would happen if she let go of a single chemo and take a vacation. These were the most beautiful moments in their lives. They enjoyed every sunset, every mug they encountered, and every ray of sunshine.

Wojtek is fine though, thought Antoni. They raised him well. The man stayed overnight, and the next day both men set off first for Nowogródek, and then for a trip to the mountains ordered by his son.

32

Svetlana did not know exactly what to do with her life now. It has been turned upside down in recent months. She had to gather the facts and finally decide something. First of all: she knows for sure that she does not want to live on Świteź anymore, and although she has forgiven Olga for the harm she has done, she certainly has not forgotten about them. This old woman was unhappy, and Svetlana understood her motives that pushed her to act from the past. But she could no longer pretend that they were all right. Second: she wanted to learn. What about her freedom, which she regained after many hardships, if she will not be able to enjoy it fully? In order to fulfill herself, to travel - which was always her dream - she had to educate herself, find a good job. Good, but what did that mean? What did she really want to do in life? She stared at the window for a moment and knew. She would like to help. Third: she must answer the question: who is she? Where does it come from? Where are her roots? And finally, she thought shyly, she can find her family... To answer all the questions that haunted her, she had to talk to Olga. But won't that make it worse? Or maybe the old woman will bounce again and will not want to let her go? She had to take the risk. The need to find your own identity and your own place on earth was too strong to put it to sleep.

"Hi. Have you arrived?" She started a telephone conversation. She got her first mobile phone from Wojtek for her birthday. "It's okay, but I won't be here for a while and... no, no, it has nothing to do with Olga. Wojtek, Wojtek... listen to me for a minute... I'll make up for everything after I come back... Two weeks. Well, I'm already talking. I want to look for my relatives, if they are still somewhere... No, don't come. I'll be fine... No, I don't know... I'm going to Olga tomorrow. Listen, I have to go. I'll be in touch tomorrow... no... Bye."

Why can't he understand her? Why doesn't he want her to leave? He's not possessive after all... She doesn't know if she wants him to go there with her. There, that is where? She doesn't know it herself yet. Tomorrow morning she would go to Olga.

33

"I'll never understand women. I'm with her from the very beginning. I didn't hesitate to jeopardize my relationship with my father, and now she wants to get rid of me? Does she have feelings for me at all? Or maybe she just took advantage of me? The naive Wojtuś was at hand just when she needed him. And now it's completely redundant. What a moron I am! Why did I even get involved in this?" Wojtek was sitting in a warm restaurant by the slope and he was thinking, mumbling from time to time.

Father arrived with two mugs of mulled beer.

"Something happened? You look somehow weird with that frown..."

"Nothing special. As usual, girls," the boy growled. "When are we returning?"

"Uhmm... And I told you, take her with you. I knew you couldn't stand the separation, love birds." Antek was clearly amused, which irritated the teenager even more.

"You don't even know what's going on, so maybe don't say anything. So..."

"So, my dear son, as we agreed, we come back tomorrow evening. Although, of course, if there are any extraordinarily important circumstances, we may even now pack our things into the car and drive off. Before I drink a beer." Father did not lose good humor.

"No. We will be back as planned. They don't want us there anyway..." He broke off.

Antek decided not to question his son, and even though he was a bit short of adulthood, he gave him a little mulled beer to drink. They spent the next day on the slope talking and laughing. Wojtek assumed that shouldn't try to force things. He didn't know that Svetlana had already made significant progress in her private mini-investigation.

"Good morning."

"Hello." Welcoming the women best reflected their current relationship. Cool, correct and... nothing else.

"Can I go in?" Svetlana asked timidly.

"You can always come here. Whenever you feel like it." Olga wanted to break the barrier that had built up between them.

"I'd like to talk, if possible, about my real... biological mother. Do you mind?"

"Sit down please. Would you like cocoa?" She began to bustled without waiting for an answer. As if turning her back, she wanted to hide the emotions or the shame that accompanied her, since the truth about Svetlana's past was spoken aloud.

"The newspapers wrote all kinds of rubbish. There is only one truth. Your mother, Anna, has come here to rest after a difficult childbirth and the first months of living with you. You probably wondering what about your father? Well, he didn't know about yours existence. But from the beginning, so that you understand well. Anna was nineteen when she fell madly in love with her peer in the same class. Love was consumed just before graduating from high school. Anna did not get into college, but Staś, as she spoke about him, was admitted to medicine.

"Did she talk about him? Did you talk with her?" Svetlana could not stand it and broke the old one.

"Of course. We were friends. Or not. It's a bad word. We liked each other when she came here in June." Olga looked at Svetlana, surprised to the limit. "Anyway… About the time he told her about it, she found out she was expecting a baby. She didn't want him to be with her just for that. She wasn't going to ruin his career. She took the most necessary things and left for her godmother to the other end of Poland, to Silesia. That one was then set up. She had connections, lots of money, and a soft spot for Anna. She took her in, kept her pregnancy a secret and funded an expensive house on Świteź when you were born," she interrupted the story, but Svetlana did not have enough.

"What's next? Father didn't find out about me? And grandma? Grandfather? Wasn't anyone looking for my mom? And so, aunt?" The girl asked.

"Oh, baby. Nobody ever found out. Anna said her mother wanted to visit her, but insisted that she was in college and would be coming as soon as the summer session was over. But she never came back from this vacation."

"Because you killed her, you nasty bitch!" Svetlana burst into tears. "She was so young! She had her whole life ahead of her! Or maybe they would work out?" She screamed through her tears.

"Child, calm down and let me tell the end. Your mother was not happy. As you would call it today, she was deeply depressed and had suicidal thoughts. You consider me a monster, but you don't know that I wasn't the one who caused Anna's death. True, I'm cursed and I've done a lot of wrong. However, I did not kidnap you or Anatol, and I did not hurt your parents. If you ever asked me about it, you would know... But you attributed some evil deeds to me."

"I didn't know... and I don't know if I can believe you anyway. You've cheated on me so many times, or withheld parts of the truth. Every time I leave your home, I get confused and don't know what is fiction and what is truth."

"Don't be too dramatic. Coming back to the story. One day Anna started asking me if I would like to be a mother, if you are close to me... I didn't know what she meant. The next day I found her body which floated to the edge of the lake. Before calling the police, I took you to my hut and hid you in a disused stove. They came, checked the area. They knew about the baby. There were some suspicions. That maybe Anna got rid of it earlier... But there was no evidence, no certainty. The aunt never confessed, and Anna's parents had only rudimentary information, no certainty..."

"Where was the funeral? My father was on it? Perhaps the mother had left a letter? Why did she take her own life? By me?" Svetlana did not hide her emotion after what she just heard.

"Your father was not notified, Anna's parents thought that their paths had been cut off when he started college. In a way, they were right. She did not leave the letter. And it's not your fault. Many things coincided, she was young... And then your story begins. Yours and mine..." When she finished, she rinsed the cups and sat down. There was a great deal of relief on her face.

"I'm sorry..." Only or maybe so much, said a young girl to the old woman.

They talked for a long time that evening. Svetlana then thought that the first time was really honest. They did not mind that the protégé of the old woman returned. Anyway, Svetlana became friends with her on Katja's first day at the lake. Olga answered the next questions, Svetlana was constantly wondering what she was hearing. She also learned that her original name, given by her mother, was Maria. The girl presented her plans to Olga. She wanted to travel to Poland and find her family: anyone - grandmother, aunt, or maybe... father... The old woman, like a good mother, reminded her of the ending winter holidays and the school year that was still going on, which it would be a pity not to finish.

"You're right. Since I've waited for over seventeen years, I can wait these few months as well. Meanwhile, I'll start searching on your own. So my name is Maria Lach, I am the daughter of Anna Lach and Stanisław..."

"I don't know your father's name." Olga disappointed the girl.

"Okay, but there's also Grandma Lach and the address on the note. Is this the address of my mother or aunt from Silesia?" She asked more questions.

"This is your grandparents' address. Your's mother left it on that unhappy day. I think she wanted me to notify them. Maybe she thought that when I didn't want to take care of you, I could send you back to them. However, I did not hesitate for a moment. I love you as my own child, with a love so strong that I led to your tragedy..." She thought. "Fortunately, I came to my senses in time and you managed to get everything back."

Svetlana left Olga's house in the middle of the night, when the old woman clearly ran out of strength. She was exhausted by the enormity of the information she heard, but also for the first time so calm. She fell asleep, and before going to sleep she thought about Wojtek. How unfair she was and... how much she misses him. She will tell him about it tomorrow.

34

All the way Wojtek thought about what kind of sulk he would have, how he would be silent and how cold he would be. The fact was that nothing had happened between them yet... in that sense... but they must have been close, and he hoped that things would slowly develop. At first he wondered if the waters could do these things at all, or if they had any pleasure in kissing. Now Svetlana was already a normal girl, so... nothing stood in the way. But anytime soon, no way! He doesn't know if he'll ever forgive her. He got out of the car on the run, because his father had to catch up at work and drive to his apartment.

"Thanks for everything, Dad. I'll see you Saturday, right?" Wojtek said goodbye.

"Yes, son. Thank you too. I'm glad everything is back to normal. If anything happens, call me! And remember that with girls you never know, oh, you don't know..." He slid the car window down and drove off.

"I know, I know... Drive carefully!" He said.

He turned and his plan was in ruins. She was standing on the doorstep with that voluminous hair of hers, with a mysterious look and playfully raised corners of her mouth. She was wearing a flowing pale pink dress and was barefoot.

"Won't you say hi?" She asked.

"I didn't think I'd find you here." He tried to sound stolidly.

She walked over to him and kissed him lightly on the lips, throwing her arms around his neck.

"I missed you," she added softly.

Wojtek kissed her back. Except this one was long and passionate. As if awaited by the last difficult months and quite natural - both for her and for him.

When they entered the house, she told him the sad story of her parents' love and how they had wrongly condemned Olga. She also said that she wanted to stay in school until the summer holidays and start looking.

"Let's start now. We have internet, the name and address of your grandparents. Your father is there too. We do not know the name, but we do know that he is a doctor, a graduate of some medical university. And... I would forget. How am I supposed to address you? Svetlana? Or maybe Marysia?" He smiled.

"You know, for now I'm Svetlana. When I find my family, learn my native language and feel Polish, then you will call me Marysia."

It was already late, so the search or - as Wojtek called it - googling were to start the next day. Today, it is not known whether they became even closer to each other during the last days of their separation, or because of their first quarrel, or perhaps a kiss. They fell asleep cuddled up.

35

The following months were a pain for Svetlana. On the one hand, she was looking forward to finally ending the school year and going to Poland. On the other hand, she was afraid of rejection, ridicule and subsequent disappointments that might have happened to her. She knew, however, that she was not alone, and the thought was fueling her shaky ego.

At school, they did not hide the fact that they were together. Because they were together. They lived together, cared for each other, and although they did not admit it, they knew that they had their first true love. So they held hands and caused amazement in the school corridors. They were always considered freaks. She - older than her peers, dressed as if out of a cheap fairy tale. He - introverted, rude and taking care that no one exceeds the borders of his territory. They did not seek new acquaintances, at school they focused on learning, and outside of school they did not maintain contacts with their friends. At first, this worried his father, but he thought over the matter and concluded that Wojtek had grown up and became serious with his girlfriend. And I guess that's what every parent meant. So he stopped asking about friends from school and going out together.

Wojtek and Svetlana complemented each other. Also in the scientific field. It was easy for her to learn humanistic subjects, he had no problems with science. They could always count on each other help. Until the last day of study nothing extraordinary happened in their lives. The two days in June were an exception. In the first, they found the trail..."

"Okay, let's put together our several months of work." Wojtek sat in their wooden house, where, despite many bad memories, they decided to stay until the summer holidays, in front of a large cork board with dozens of colorful cards on it. "We know that your grandmother lives with your grandfather in a town near Krakow. We established that their names were Maria and Jan Lach. We are pretty sure they are alive and well. Father probably graduated from Collegium Medicum in Krakow, because he had the closest there, but we cannot be sure. Grandma is a retired teacher, judging by the number of classes added to the community service. Grandpa has his construction company given the address. Your mum has no siblings, because your grandmother only posts photos of herself and her grandfather. She would have to add grandchildren or children... Did I miss something?"

"No, everything is correct. Just when you say all this, I get goosebumps. And I do not feel that it is about me and my relatives. They will not even like me. I'm different. I have always been. I'll never tell them about it. How am I going to get along with them?" Svetlana was full of anxiety, because the day of her meeting with her family was inevitable.

"Hey, we've been learning Polish for several months now. I tell you honestly, it's pretty good. You know you don't have a rich vocabulary, you don't have yet... but I'm really proud of you. You just have to believe in yourself, because if you don't, no one else will believe in you either..." Wojtek tried to somehow console Svetlana.

"How are we going to organize it all? Where are we gonna get the money? And what's next? What's next? I don't think I'm ready for it..." Her voice was clearly breaking, and yet she was a strong girl.

"I thought about everything. As usual, my father did not disappoint."

"We can't keep asking him for help. How will I repay him for everything he does for me?"

"Slowly, slowly. As long as I can't go to work, and I'm still a bit short of it, I don't feel bad about my father. He has money, so he helps me. I wouldn't ask him if it were to burden him in any way. This one. When it comes to travel, it's all very simple. We will travel by train to Krakow. There my father rented us a cheap hostel for a month, somewhere near a student campus and gave us pocket money for that time. And don't worry, I'm not lying to him. I had told him the whole truth. Over the weekend, I got the last details up. He promised to keep it only to himself. I trust him. We have the train on July 1st. From Krakow to Zabierzow is very close. We will be able to travel by buses. Any more doubts?" He winked at her.

"Yes. What's next?" She looked at him with huge eyes. As if he would decide her future. As if in his hands she entrusted her fate.

"I can't impose anything on you. There is a vision of a happy meeting with family in my head. And then... we can stay in Nowogródek and rent a flat close to the school, if you want, we can move to the school in Krakow so that you can be closer to your grandparents. Then we spend the weekends with my father."

"We can, we spend, we live... You talk in the plural all the time... Are you sure?"

"I do."

Svetlana did not reply the same. Not because she didn't feel it right now, because she wanted to do it all with him too. Only that much was yet to happen. And they were so young. Will nothing change between them? She couldn't know it. But she grabbed his hand and believed that his plans would come true. That they will live happily ever after. That he will finally find out who he is and how to continue living. She could not have imagined that fate prepared another complication for her.

36

The end of the school year fell on the last Friday of June. They were already packed. One would like to say - as usual with the help of Antoni - Svetlana, actually Maria received an ID card. And it was the first of the larger endeavors, and also the first step in getting to know yourself anew. Antoni hired a lawyer who helped in obtaining the evidence. Fortunately, Maria Lach was listed in the system, she had her PESEL number and address. There was never a death certificate for her. So Maria Lach received her ID card. Everything was running smoothly. By the time.

After graduating from high school, officially completing their first year of high school education, the entire class decided to organize a party. Alex, to whom his newest prey, June, seemed to be stuck (and so for several weeks), approached Svetlana and Wojtek, who were standing on the sidelines.

"Hello, lovebirds!" As always, he sounded arrogant. "There's a party coming. Will you join?"

"No, thanks, we're not interested," Wojtek answered.

"You see, tomorrow we're leaving for my family first thing in the morning. Not that we don't want to integrate." Svetlana was explaining to him again, which made Wojtek angry.

"It's not good. Because we wanted to do a party at your place, by the lake. Cool thing. Some grill, alcohol, we'll take care of everything, you would just share the place..." Alex did not give up.

"I know languages are not your forte, so I'll say in your native one: piss off!" Wojtek grabbed Svetlana tightly and went to the school pitch. "Why are you even arguing with him?" The boy did not hide his indignation. "You all have a weakness for this clown. Gosh!"

"And why are you nervous? You know how Alex is. You have to explain something to him calmly, otherwise he will not let go." The kiss lightened the situation.

In the evening, after eating dinner, they went through the documents one more time and waited for the morning full of tension. Suddenly they heard a rather intense knock on the door. Wojtek went to open it. What was his amazement when he saw a group of thirty drunk teenagers with packets of breweries under their arms. He tried to close the door, but his favorite from Germany made it difficult for him.

"Man, take it easy. Now that we've got to this mega crap, at least let us have a few brews. We also have a music and a snacks. We go in!" Alex was already inside saying that.

Svetlana only managed to carry the things upstairs and put on a dress. Guests were everywhere: on the terrace, in the kitchen, in the living room. You could hear music even at Olga's place. Drunk young students staggered near the lake. Svetlana knew this bode very badly. So she found Wojtek.

"If they go to the lake, they're gone. Anatol concluded a truce with me, but this does not apply to my guests. You know his temperament. If they violate its territory, they will die. We must get rid of them as soon as possible, or at least keep them away from Świteź." She sounded desperate.

"Well. Try to get everyone in and then we'll lock the cabin, and I'll meet you later." Each of them went the other way.

Another hour was spent collecting the cheerful company together. While Svetlana did quite well with the girls, Wojtek had to use not only verbal arguments, but also physical strength. Once they were all inside, the door was locked.

"Okay, look around you and see if someone is missing. If anyone is left outside, they are in danger. Wild animals attack at this time of the day without warning, and that's not a joke!"

Svetlana thought that Wojtek had made it right. It sounded convincing because people actually got scared. Everyone was looking for their close friends. Suddenly, June's thin voice was heard.

"I don't know where Alex is. I just went to pee and... I don't know..." June was completely pissed. Her gibberish was hard to understand. It was only clear that Alex was away from home.

Despite Wojtek's ban, who left the house, several of his friends decided to look for Alex on their own. Svetlana couldn't stop them. So she left with them. It was after midnight when Wojtek, running by the lake shore, saw an unusual sight. Anatol in all its glory, shiny and strong, was swimming in the middle of the lake, holding three dead bodies by the sleeves of his shirts... Wojtek stood paralyzed. He did not scream, did not move from his place. He could see clearly that it was too late. He had no idea what to do next.

Svetlana was wandering through the well-known places when she felt an alcoholic breath on her neck and someone's hands on her shoulders. She shivered.

"I've always liked you." It was Alex.

"Leave me." She broke away, remaining calm.

They stood staring at each other until suddenly the boy spoke:

"I can have any chick at school. Everyone but you. You are different. You have your own opinion, you are hiding some secret. Your style, your beauty... I have no words. But you chose the biggest loser and shit. What do you even see in him? What can he give you? He can't even stand up for you, he just runs away with his tail tucked up." Alex came dangerously close. "One kiss and I'll leave you alone. I just want to feel you, know how you taste... I want to be aware that I had you, at least for a while... Will you give me this pleasure?" He was pushy.

"Unfortunately not. This is against my belief. And forgive me, but I don't feel like it." Svetlana turned and wanted to leave, but Alex pulled her tight to him and was not going to give up his plans.

"It hurts! Let me go! Help! Help!" She managed to scream out before he closed her mouth with his hand and started kissing her neck as she tried to pull away.

At this point, Wojtek and another boy from their class came running. Wojtek immediately threw his fists at Alex, a fight ensued. The second boy had already called the police, terrified of what was happening at the lake.

In the end, the two of them managed to control Alex's lust. The boys took him home, badly beaten. Wojtek spat in his face and then ran to Svetlana.

"Are you OK? Didn't that motherfucker do anything to you?" He hugged her, kissed her, and checked her for any injuries.

"No. All right. But what about the others?" As usual, she showed her empathy.

"You were right. There was a tragedy. Anatol has drowned some of them and the police are on their way. I don't know about the rest.

I don't know what we'll say, we'll do." Wojtek was panicking for the first time.

Svetlana knew that now it was she who had to show her calmness and composure.

"Okay, we'll tell how it was. That they came drunk, that we wanted to leave in the morning, we have luggage. That they went to swim and had to drown. That we wanted to help them, but we didn't make it. God! Tomorrow Anatol will throw the bodies away, he always does as he enjoys the booty."

The police and ambulance arrived. Young people testified what happened. Svetlana was right. They all gave the same version of events, and the next day the bodies were found on the lakeshore. It turned into a huge media scandal. From the morning, the journalists camped under the house. Antoni, the family's lawyer, arrived. They were interrogated for the next few days, and their ticket to Poland was also lost. For now, the trip had to be postponed. The police wanted Wojtek and Svetlana at their disposal.

37

Svetlana did not give interviews. She was very assertive. When the situation calmed down a bit, a Polish woman knocked on their door - journalist. She wanted to talk to Svetlana about her life by the lake, not about the tragedy and the death of three teenagers.

Antoni and the lawyer advised her against this meeting. The girl, however, felt how much she needed to talk, to shed this burden. So eventually she sat down in front of the camera and started talking.

She told about her mother's unhappy love, about her death, and finally about life away from civilization in the company of Olga, whom she called her legal guardian to avoid unpleasantness. Finally, at the very end, she revealed:

"It was only quite recently that I found out about my past. Were it not for this unlucky evening, I would be on my way to Poland. Perhaps my grandmother, not a journalist, would have heard my story right now. Grandma Marysia, Grandpa Jan, if you watch it, know that I really want to meet you and I will do my best to find you. Dad, Stanisław, if you recognized me as a daughter... maybe we will make up for lost time," she finished with tears in her eyes.

The Warsaw reporter was so touched by the story of an almost eighteen-year-old girl from a completely different world that she promised to start all contacts in order to get her father's address, of course without interfering with his private life.

The investigation into the death of three teenagers at Lake Świteź was discontinued in mid-July. No one was charged, the act was found to be a consequence of drinking too much alcohol. Antoni came as usual for the weekend with good news.

"Lovely! I have a surprise for you! Our lawyer says you can pack and go to Krakow. I have booked your ticket for next Monday." He waved a scrap of paper in front of their nose.

Svetlana was jumping with joy. She had waited so long for this moment. She threw herself on Antoni's neck and kissed him on both cheeks. She was so grateful to this man for everything he had done for her.

"Enough, because the young will make a scene of jealousy." He laughed. When they started packing for the second time, Svetlana's phone called.

"Wojtek, pick up, because I'm in the bathroom!" The girl's muffled voice was heard.

"Yes, it's Maria Lach's phone. Please wait, I'm calling her now."

"Svetlana! Come down here. It's that journalist!" This time Wojtek was screaming out loud.

The conversation was long and kept the two men tense. Finally, Svetlana put down the phone and dropped into the chair.

"Well, say finally. What's new?" The boy asked.

"The material was broadcast on Polish television three days ago. Today, Kasia got two calls. The first one from Maria Lach from Zabierzów, who asked about mine exact address, because, as she put it, she may be related to me. Kasia did not know if she could give it to her, so she only took the phone number and said that I would contact Maria myself, if that was my will." She paused and looked as if the second message was even more unexpected.

"It's great. Your grandmother wants to establish contact with you. We will go to her on Monday, and before that we will only call and announce..." Wojtek wanted to say something else, but Svetlana interrupted.

"I think we will go to Silesia on Monday to..."

"You prefer to meet an old aunt first than your own grandparents?" The boy was interrupting her again.

"...to my father."

Nobody said anything. The men waited for Svetlana to be ready to continue the story. A moment passed and finally the girl seemed to break out of her thoughts.

"Mrs Kasia was called by a certain Stanisław Oleszczuk from Katowice. The man introduced himself as a cardiologist who looked at the material and the story told, and the name of the protagonist, i.e. mine, reminded him of some events from years ago. He asked if Kasia could give me his contact details and persuade me to talk to him."

"What are you going to do?" Antoni asked.

"What would you advise me?" You could see the loss and terror in the eyes of this beautiful girl.

"I'm not some authority on parenting.

It's also hard to put myself in your position. However, if I had to... I would first order Wojtek to call your grandparents and ask if they were ready to meet you on Monday. It is not nice to come without an announcement with such a story, especially since they are a bit older people, so their heart may not stand it. Then I would spend some time talking to them. He asked what kind of man your dad was when he was young, under what circumstances they broke up with your mother, if he could have known about her pregnancy. Only then would I call my father, but that's just my vision." He patted Svetlana on the knee and poured himself some tea.

"You're absolutely right. We will also do so. Wojtek, are you with me?" She knew the answer to that question well.

"Give me the phone." He held out his hand.

38

Svetlana's grandmother had a friendly and warm voice. This is, at least, how Wojtek perceived it. She was very happy that her granddaughter wanted to meet her. She assured that she was waiting impatiently for this moment. The whole story surprised her a lot, but there was more joy and emotion in her.

Svetlana did not hide her fear. From the moment they got on the train in Nowogródek, until the Polish border and their transfers, the girl did not release Wojtek's hand. Not much talked. The teen mentally practiced the speech she wanted to address to her grandparents, but there was always something wrong with it. She couldn't express what she felt. She didn't know the language well enough yet to name any thought or state. However, all fears were soon dispelled.

Krakow amazed Svetlana with its charm. She fell in love with it at first sight. Everything looked old here, but extremely charming. The market and pigeons, stone houses... But the people who made the greatest impression on her were: the color of the people, hurrying in different directions, different from those she knew. Unfortunately, they didn't have much time to explore. So they quickly found a connection to Zabierzów.

They stood under a small white house, surrounded by flowers and beds. Svetlana watched the dogs lounging in the sun in front of her kennel, flowers she did not know their names blooming with different colors. She admired the peace of this place just like hers by the lake. Finally, she hung her eye on the porch, which was lined with two rattan chairs and a small bookstool. Just then, the door opened and a woman stood in it.

She looked fifty. She was well-groomed and smartly dressed. She had brown, thick, short-cut hair, and a pretty fair complexion with clear lines. Svetlana thought at once that most of them had probably arisen from the news of her daughter's suicide.

A man followed her from the house. He looked much more soberly. He had gray hair, a mustache of the same color and a wrinkles. He had a serious face, but in his blue eyes Svetlana discovered gentleness and kindness.

They looked at each other: she at them, they at her. Wojtek stood to the side and felt completely redundant. However, he waited for further developments. Finally, the woman went to Svetlana and, stretching out both hands, said softly:

"Hello, baby. I don't want to impose myself, I don't expect any kind of greeting. However, if I may ask you to do so, come over to me so that I can examine you closely."

Svetlana nodded and walked over to her grandmother. After a few minutes, the next words came out:

"Just like Anna. Don't you think Janek? You have the same hair, eyes, same chin." Maria smiled alternately at Svetlana and Jan.

The girl did not feel awkward at all. Good and longing grandma's hands touched her face.

"Don't tire her anymore, Marysia. We invite you inside. You, Mr. Wojtek, too." Jan finally took the initiative.

It was obvious that the hosts were getting ready for this visit. The house, although small, looked excellent. Everything here was clean, shiny and tasteful. Each element fulfilled a specific role. Nothing was here accidentally. And there were plenty of photos. Each one featured a girl: first a tiny one, then in preschool, and finally as a teenager. Svetlana looked at this last photo longer than the others. She was surprised to see herself in the paper picture, perhaps a little changed, but herself.

"It's true, you are very much like your mother." Jan was standing behind her. "Sit down please. Would you like to ask us something? Because we have a lot of questions, but the culture requires that the guest..." The man tried to be polite, while his wife began:

"Your name is Maria, right?"

"That's what my babysitter told me, so I believe that my mother named me in your honor." Svetlana spoke softly, but slowly broke down her shame.

"Listen. You have been through a lot, you must have felt terrible in this village by the lake, far from education, contact with culture or civilization..."

"No. I missed nothing. For a long time I thought that my mother was old Olga, I was really comfortable with her. It wasn't until I found out the truth, then I missed for a real mother and her family."

"What a relief. I was afraid that you were unhappy all these years, that you might get hurt. But since you say your life has been peaceful, that's enough for me." Grandma sighed.

"Okay, now a few questions and assurances from my side," Jan spoke.

Svetlana was a little afraid of him, he was a large man with a full face and a loud low voice. The feeling lasted only for a moment.

"You will choose your own path in life. We will never interfere with your plans. We don't want you to think that the family you found will turn out to be a burden now. If you wish, you will open the door to your life a little. If not, we won't hold it against you. However, you must remember that in every situation, with every little thing, joy and sadness, you can come to us," he broke off, he was too much touched.

"In a word, dear, we are here for you. You can live with us even today, we will provide you with everything we can do and we will give you as much warmth and love as we have. You are our only dream and longed-for granddaughter. Our greatest joy in old age. If you let us enjoy you, we'll be the best family we can be..." Maria finished.

Svetlana, wiping her tears, thought that no one had ever told her so many beautiful words that ensured her good and support. She thought about how happy she could have been here these past years. How good it would be for these sincere, kind people.

39

The first day at the Lach's house was full of so many emotions that already around 9 p.m. you could clearly see tiredness both in the guests and in the household:

"Time to sleep. I have prepared a guest room for you, there are towels and everything you will need," said Maria.

"But... we have a hostel reservation for the whole month..." Wojtek informed.

"Are you crazy? We're getting our granddaughter back after almost eighteen years, and you think we're going to let her go to some shabby hotel? Well, I would not forgive you!" Grandma turned to Svetlana with mock anger.

"Well. I'll call my father and cancel everything." Wojtek was powerless against the woman's arguments.

"Are you sure we won't cause any trouble? I would not like to abuse..." Svetlana wanted to make sure that she was welcome here, although she felt it from the very first moments.

"Stop it. Go take a bath and sleep well. There are two beds in the room, but you have progressive grandparents, so..."

"Take it easy, Grandma..." She said the word aloud for the first time. It sounded so... strange, but at the same time it contained the security she had so longed for.

"Good night."

The next days in the white house passed on each other getting to know each other. Svetlana has already seen all the family souvenirs, photos and listened to a series of anecdotes related to her mother's childhood and adolescence, but she was not at all bored. She absorbed the smallest details of education, illnesses, learning to speak and first dates like a sponge. She was particularly interested in this last topic. However, she did not want to be intrusive, so she listened in peace and talked about herself, not asking embarrassing questions yet. She felt guilty about skipping a very significant part of her biography related to life in the lake. However, she did not want to unnecessarily frighten the newly met grandparents. After all, they might not believe her or consider her crazy. They could also get scared. She didn't want to destroy what they were slowly building together, which was still so fragile. Anyway, now she is only Marysia, not a wodja. She was already forgetting what it was like to return to the lake's abyss every night.

"Sorry to ask... but have you tried to contact your father?" Jan's voice was extremely uncertain.

"Oh... After talking to Wojtek's father, who has been helping me a lot, since we met, I came to the conclusion that I need to find out something about him first. So if you wouldn't mind..." She broke off.

"So he was in contact with you, right?" Grandpa asked.

"After the material was broadcast, Kasia received a call from both you and Stanisław. But I wanted to spend some time with you guys, learn as much as possible about mom... and about him."

"I understand. Of course, we'll tell you as much as we know. And we know little about Staś." He looked at his wife, who was just bringing fresh cake into the room.

"Honey, Anna was seeing Staszek from the third year of high school. Back then it was just friendship, although I knew mine. You could have guessed the boy was waiting for her permission. He followed her with his eyes, he was at her every call. A man for all seasons, as they say here," Maria began her story, holding a cup in her hand.

"My dear, Anna was also in love. If it weren't for that, he wouldn't be spending every afternoon with us. Until I complained to her that they would get bored with each other. Then she said it was just a friend," said Jan.

"Anyway, like any mother, I was right. There was a great feeling in high school. Romantic walks, trysts, holding hands and kissing on the porch began. Not that I was nosy, but they did not hide their feelings. Besides, they knew they had our consent, right?"

"Yes, it's true. We saw that they was not only hugging, but learning together. They did great. Staszek went to medicine, and Anna to the law... I mean, that's what she told us then..." Jan was slightly confused.

"We thought she was studying in Katowice, she was living with my cousin. We had no reason not to believe her. She always told us about everything. That is why it was soothing that she did not speak, that she did not come. I asked Janek to go to her, but he convinced me that we had to cut the umbilical cord."

"Yes, I wanted her to become independent, to choke on freedom. We only had one child. And as is often the case with only children, we pampered her, but we were also overprotective many times. For this simple reason, I wanted Anna to finally have some peace, but also to learn independence," he confirmed.

"Didn't you wonder that they broke up? Did they say goodbye at all?" Svetlana could not understand that the sudden departure of her mother did not surprise her parents.

"Anna said that she fell out of love, that it was not known what it would be like: he in Krakow, she in Katowice. Better to go your own way, and then you will see... She never believed in long-distance relationships, and she wanted to study in Katowice. It all seemed to make sense back then, it was logical. So we didn't try to dissuade her from these plans."

"These are exactly her words..."

"And later we found out about her death. They both looked at the floor. It took a few seconds for Grandma to take up the subject again. "About the death of her and her child. It was a shock for us. We didn't believe it was our Anna when we were called. What would she be doing in Belarus? After all, she studied in Katowice. Where did this baby come from? We were calm, because we were convinced of a mistake..." Maria took a sip of her tea.

"Until our cousin from Silesia spoke up and told us the whole tragic story. So far we don't talk to each other, even though it's been eighteen years. We never forgave her for not calling us knowing of Anna's problems. But I don't think she has forgiven herself, and it is tormenting to live in guilt." Jan was finishing the story.

Svetlana did not know if this was the right moment, but her intuition told her that it would be good to change the subject that still evoked such strong emotions in grandparents. So she risked a question:

"What was he like? He is? This Staszek that you know?" Grandma visibly perked up, as if torn from the abysstragic memories.

"Maybe I'll start with what boy he was. Well, as I mentioned, he was crazy about our daughter. It was then that we could see his devotion, patience and tolerance. Anna was not an easy character. She was pugnacious and dominant. Staszek completed her: when necessary, he was silent, when she was in need, he comforted her. He knew how to support her and tame her. That's how I remembered him from those times..."

"And I, in turn, perceive his other qualities," Jan added.

"First of all, he was very intelligent and resourceful. He had no problems at school despite working at the hospital as a volunteer. He was a good man, he was interested in the fate of others. He kept organizing some collections of clothes for the poor, food for birds in winter... This type of social worker. I did not like him as a future son-in-law only because I saw him in the future as a poor man who would give others his last shirt."

"And I immediately knew that he would achieve a lot. When he said he was going to medical school, I was sure Anna would be fine with him. Because not only a soft heart, but also a good profession... private practice. Don't think that we are materialists. But you will see when you have your child... Man wants the best..." Maria explained herself and her husband completely unnecessarily. Svetlana knew these people had no money in their heads.

"You know what's going on with him now? Do you have any contact?" There was still little news about the father, Svetlana liked more and more with each sentence.

"No family here. His parents died recently. One by one. Mother had cancer, and father... we say he died of despair, but it's supposed to be the heart. In any case, he always comes on All Souls' Day, birthdays and death anniversaries of her parents." She did not answer the granddaughter's question, but grandfather did.

"We met twice at the cemetery. First, when Anna died. We told him as much as we were told. I felt he was devastated. He didn't come to the funeral. I do not know why. The second time he prayed at her grave. I stepped up and asked just how he was doing. He replied that he had started a family. He has one son. He lives in Katowice, he is an ordinator in cardiology. He looked old and he was very tired. I saw no joy in him."

"Such a good boy. All because of our Anna!" Grandma's voice rose.

"Do not say that!" Jan did not agree with her words.

"You know I love her. But be so stupid! She could tell him, we could help with the baby. Finish studies and they would be so happy!" There was tears now.

"We've been through this a thousand times. We can't turn back time. As parents, we did everything we could. So she did, we must respect that. I've been saying this for so many years."

Jan spoke coolly and to the point.

Svetlana, who had never known her mother, felt so much for these two people now. Eighteen years have passed and they still have not dealt with this tragedy. She did not understand, like grandmother, mother's decision. There were so many solutions. She was obviously too young, and too many things suddenly fell on her mind. It had to be like that...

40

Stanisław Oleszczuk. Uncle Google has always been helpful in such matters. When Svetlana spent time with her grandparents, discovering her origin, Wojtek was sitting in a small room with a laptop. At that time, he found out that Svetlana's father was working at the Upper Silesian Medical Center, and as an intern he was on a mission for a year, somewhere in the middle of Africa. He was also a co-founder of the Maskotka Foundation, which dealt with helping children from orphanages. The network was full of articles about his social activities, thanks from the city authorities, awards and prizes.

Wojtek also found his account on a social networking site. You can see that he did not come here often, but he attached two photos: his class at the time of high school graduation and the current one - with his family. You could also find out that he likes nature movies and is interested in paranormal phenomena. If he found out that his daughter was, she is... Wojtek smiled to himself.

He prepared Svetlana for the fact that he would see his brother in a moment. As if anyone could be prepared for something like that. In any case, Wojtek did not make much of an impression. His sister was much more attractive. The girl stared at the screen and wondered how old the boy might have been, finally judging to be ten.

At the moment when she saw the family photo: smiled blonde, a happy little boy and a dad towering over them... she thought she wanted to be there with them. She wants to tell them about herself, she wants them to love her and take her in, so that everything will be normal. But is it possible? She had to find out and wanted to do it immediately.

"We're going to Katowice, grandma. I don't want to waste any more time. You are already in my life and it will not change. But I want to meet my dad, my brother..." The words flowed faster than thoughts.

"Honey, that's understandable. Tomorrow morning we will drive you to the train station and you will go to Katowice. If I can advise you, please do not take your luggage. Show yourself to him for now, talk to him, but dose yourself. Remember that there is also his wife and a boy who may feel rejected."

"That's what I'm going to do. I'll call you right away and ask if he wants to meet me at all. Or..." She looked at Wojtek.

"Yes, I'll call him. I already have practice and good results." He was smiling.

It went as smooth as the first time. The man was a busy man, but when he heard what it was about, or rather who it was about, he assured him that he would take a vacation on demand. He expected them in the morning at the train station in Katowice. He also explained that before inviting them home, he would like to talk to his daughter, preferably alone. Wojtek did not mind, he even understood this guy. He has a life, a wife, a house arranged, and suddenly he has to tell them about a past mishap. You have to show solidarity. But he wasn't going to let go Svetlana alone. He will not interfere in family affairs, but will remain in sight if she needs him. Meanwhile, need to sleep, because the bus departs at seven fifteen.

41

Everything went according to plan. Stanisław was waiting at the station with a tiny, but visible inscription: Marysia Lach. Svetlana had already seen through the bus window this tall man, who actually looked more than his thirty-seven years old. He wore denim pants, sports shoes, and a plaid shirt. He did not seem like a great doctor with a good salary and titles before his name. Kindness and uncertainty emanated from his face.

"Good morning, sir... I mean, Dad." Svetlana blushed, carefully shaking the man's hand.

"Good morning, daughter." He didn't know if he would be spurned, but he took a chance and hugged Svetlana. She gave in to it, because she too was thirsty for a fatherly tenderness that she had not known before.

"And who is that?" He directed his eyes towards Wojtek.

"He's my boyfriend, savior and best friend, Wojtek." Svetlana replied, knowing that she would build her companion up. She was right. Wojtek felt that he was not only her friend, but a kind of macho that ensures her safety. He didn't realize she saw him that way. He was undoubtedly pleased with her words.

"Let's go, there is an intimate cafe nearby. You can talk in peace." He pointed at the building in front of them.

"You know what, I'll sit down alone, search the net, and you enjoy yourself. After all, I heard this story about twenty times," he joked so that they would not feel guilty about him.

"Thank you," replied Stanisław.

Once again, Svetlana told her story. First Wojtek, then the journalist in front of the camera, then the grandparents, and finally his own father. Nothing in this story changed, the details remained the same, and the unspeakable part of the girl's fate was the same. What has changed is the audience. This one was an extremely good observer, which he owed probably to his work.

"Well. What you said, I actually knew already. However, I feel somewhere under my skin that there is something else... some dark secret or a shameful thread that you are skipping for some reason unknown to me. And please don't tell me I'm wrong, because I've had hundreds of conversations with people and I think my intuition is right." He was very convincing.

"There's something... but I don't want to talk about it..." She tried to stop the topic.

"You do not want? Are you afraid? Because if you don't want to, I understand, and we'll never go back to that. But if you would like to, but are afraid of rejection, misunderstanding, or ridicule, that's another matter. You must remember that I am your father, and nothing that would seem stupid or ridiculous or pathetic to you will not be so to me. It is for me the problem of my only daughter, which I will try to solve at all costs," he encouraged and did it effectively.

"Do you know a bit about the mythology of the Slavs?" She began, though having said these words, she had regretted it.

"And here I will amaze you. I know all non-Christian mythologies and beliefs very well. I am actually interested in such things. Anna, this is your mom, she liked it too. This is one of the things that brought us together." He did surprise her a bit.

"If so. I will not beat around the bush. However, do not ask me to elaborate on the topic because it is too difficult for me and brings about unpleasant memories." He nodded his head to accept her terms. "When Anna drowned, taking her own life in this way, old Olga took care of me. It was only years later that I discovered that she is łojma. She raised me and Anatol, whose parents she said were cruel to him. Now I know she was lying. She kidnapped, as is customary, a little boy. Wanting to keep us forever, she turned us into wodja and undine. We lived like this for several years in a lake. Then Wojtek appeared, he found the spell, he disenchanted me, Olga let me go, but before that I had to help her adopt a teenage girl. Anatol stayed in Świteź because he cannot imagine another life. I think his character highlights demonic tendencies. This is what it looks like in a nutshell. You don't believe me, do you?: She knew it would be difficult to meet her understanding.

Stanisław read about Slavic demons, especially after Anna's death this topic drew him in and allowed him to somehow reconcile with his loss. He had his suspicions about which he had not told anyone so far. After all, his beloved was obsessed with it... Now, when this girl, his daughter, comes with such a dose of new knowledge, surprising, and at the same time so fitting to all his thoughts, despite his common sense, despite all the false-similar surroundings... but he felt to believe her. But is it really possible? Are these ancient facts not only witchcraft that the idiotic behavior of people has to justify? It was so difficult to answer unequivocally.

"On the contrary. This may sound strange from the mouth of a physician, a practitioner based on the rational perception of the world... but I believe you. Healing herbs, white magic, black magic and demons. Demons, or as I prefer to call it - ghosts that wander the earth, unable to find peace after death." He continued. "And there's something else. Your mother, Anna, believed in mythology even more than I did. In fact, one could say that it completely absorbed her. Sometimes when we talked about magic, spells, I had the feeling that she was so fascinated with immortality that she would do anything to obtain it." Svetlana did not know where Stanisław's story was going.

"Are you trying to suggest something to me? Because I have that impression, but I don't quite understand what you mean..." She was confused.

"If you are speaking directly, I will too. I never believed in your mother's suicide. Anna was a person full of life, taking handfuls of it. She wanted to be always beautiful, young and enjoy the joys of the world. When I heard that she had allegedly taken her own life, I knew that there must be a bottom line... But I couldn't talk to anyone about it, and I couldn't solve the puzzle myself. Now everything is falling into place..."

"I still do not see this whole..."

"It's easy. Your mother is coming to Lake Świteź. She's tricking her aunt into paying off her vacation right there. It is not accidental. She meets old Olga, she probably gets the information from her that she is łojma. She tells her that her life is pointless, that she is pregnant and that she does not want this baby, but that she wants to be immortal. I think that at this point she feels like that, she doesn't need a child for anything, and she has the opportunity to get the greatest gift in her opinion. She knows well that the łojma will want to keep the baby, so she manipulates her. The old woman tells her how to get her dream eternal life. Anna fakes her death, in fact becoming an immortal drowned woman. Olga receives the child as her trophy, payment for a sold secret, a spell. Do you understand now?" He was clearly excited.

"But it's impossible. If mother turned into rusalka, she would have to spend the nights in the lake. I lived there for seventeen years. You think I wouldn't have met her?" Svetlana's vision of Stanisław did not fit in her head.

"After all, she could devote herself to the transformation in Świteź, and live elsewhere. Do you think that Olga, who has just got her hands on the longed-for child, would allow its mother to live in the neighborhood? After all, Anna could take you, tell the truth... Olga would certainly not risk that way," he explained.

"So what are you suggesting?"

"I suggest they have a pact. Olga was taking the baby. Anna was immortal. All she had to do was go some other place and never come back. Otherwise, probably Olga would have deprived her of immortality with the help of magic or Anatol. Do you think it's possible?"

"I think so. I've known Olga for a long time and she can get her own way. She is ruthless and, as I have had time to convince myself, still lies. So do you think I have a mom too?" A new hope entered her.

"I don't want to give you and myself unnecessary hopes. However, I am convinced that this is at least highly probable," he concluded.

"Do you want to find her?" Svetlana hoped the answer would be yes.

"I really wants. I just don't know if she wants to be found..."

Svetlana reported the conversation with her father to Wojtek. She was so excited the boy didn't recognize her. She talked about how a wonderful man Stanisław was, about the fact that he believed her... Finally she introduced the boy a hypothesis they made together. To her great surprise, Wojtek did not receive it enthusiastically.

"Don't get me wrong and don't get upset. But I don't think it is possible for your mother to abandon you to regain immortality. Anyway, even if it were so, now, after all these years, she would definitely like to meet her child or miss her parents. In any case, she would have revealed herself if she had lived."

Svetlana looked at him with angry eyes. She turned and started walking towards the station.

"Hey girl, what's the whim? You wanted to know my opinion, I presented it to you. Next time I will not speak..."

"You know what, I thought that you are the only one who understands me and that you will also be the only one to have the faith that others still lack. And here is such a disappointment! You know, it's best to go back to Nowogródek, and my dad and I will go look for my mother!" Svetlana's anger grew bigger and bigger.

"You want to get rid of me, right? I helped you with the curse, you are already a normal girl, I helped you with school, with the house, we found grandparents, father and now I am redundant. That's what you mean, right? You want to fight to get me off! I'm a moron! I will not ask or impose myself, I have my dignity. But let me tell you one thing, you are ungrateful and self-interested! Damn self-interested!" This time it was Wojtek who turned on his heel and, not knowing where he was going in this strange Silesian city, he was going ahead, not waiting for explanations of his first love.

At first, Svetlana wanted to either stop him or run after him. But then something blocked her. Wojtek was wrong. She didn't want to get rid of him. She wished he would share the happy news with her. Only he didn't understand. Or he didn't want to understand. Or was he jealous that everything was around her, her family lately? Maybe he also needed to be sometimes the center of attention? Too bad, it was not his time. If he doesn't understand that she has to take care of her own affairs now, then he doesn't love her like she thought. Maybe they spend too much time together, maybe they need a break. She wasn't going to be the first to speak.

Wojtek finally found a station and some connection with Krakow. He had left a few things with her grandparents, but he didn't care. He will go to the hostel, there may be vacancies. There he will stop and take a break from her. How much did he spend on her? He forgot about himself, his needs and dilemmas. Had she asked him why he had been so upset lately? No, because she didn't even notice, absorbed in her own affairs. Did she even know that it was another anniversary of his mother's death? Of course not, because she never asked about it. He looked ahead and saw Svetlana in a completely different light. She was a great egoist who knew how to twist him beautifully around her finger. When was the last time he was at the cinema? When did he go out with friends? Never, because of her he had no friends. It was Svetlana who felt and was different. It was she who did not want to make new friends. And he agreed to it. It was enough for him to let him know her secrets that he lived her life to be so close to this extraordinary creature. But does it make sense in the long run? What if it's not a matter of recent events at all, if that's what she is: talking and thinking only about herself? He needs to rest. He must forget about Svetlana's world for a moment and put his own in order. Make a profit and loss balance sheet after the last year. Oh… and he will not be the first one who speak up to her. She has something to apologize for.

42

"Yes, Dad, I understand perfectly well. The journey can wait. I still wanted to be with my grandparents. I can't get enough of what's happening to me lately. In two weeks, sure. No, no... take your time. Once they're ready, we'll set a date. Okay, I'm also very happy. I know, I know... only ours, don't worry, no one else will understand us anyway. Have a nice day, Dad!"

Svetlana, even talking to Stanisław on the phone, felt butterflies in her stomach. He was so close to her, although she knew so little of him. It's nothing that takes a lot of work. After all, he is an important person in the hospital and saves someone's life every day. Since she had waited so long to find her family, she would wait two more weeks. Fortunately, the vacation doesn't even come to the end so she has time. Long evenings with her grandmother, walks with her grandfather - this prospect was extremely pleasant for her.

She was aware that the return to Zabierzów would involve questions about Wojtek. They liked him, her grandmother said before they went to Katowice. She said that he was staring at her with love - my grandfather called it the Polish proverb: "He stare like a halfwit." They saw his commitment and calm. And they got to know his sad story. All this decided that Wojtek was accepted as a possible future husband. What will she tell them now? It was really just a stupid argument. They could look yourself in the eye and it would be over. But for some reason it happened otherwise. Apparently, it was supposed to be like this - she thought and threw Wojtek out of her head, now busy with something else.

"Finally! Where is Wojtek?" Grandparents were standing at the station for about half an hour, the train was delayed.

"We had an argument, he went to Krakow. I don't want to talk about it, at least not yet. Apparently our acquaintance was too intense and we need to cool down. And this answer must suffice for now. Okay?" Her tone was firm.

"Sure, baby. You better say how's your father? Do you have anything in common with each other apart from dimples in your cheeks?" Grandpa wanted to cheer her up as soon as possible.

"Wait until we get home with the story. I will make tea, bake a plum cake, I think you will like it." Grandma hugged her. "And don't laugh, but we missed you..."

"Me too. And it's not funny at all, just very, very nice..."

43

"How is he? Hmm..." Svetlana had a hard time describing her father with whom she spent only one morning. "We certainly understand each other very well. He trusts me and believes me, and I do the same for him. I have the impression that I can tell him about everything, even though he is a stranger to me."

"Did you talk about his family? Sonny?" Grandma was curious.

"Honestly, I got the feeling he didn't want to talk about it. When I mentioned his family, he suddenly became sad. Or maybe it was just my imagination. I do not know. However, he became animated as soon as I mentioned my mother. As if... he never forgot about her, and he got married only because it was right," the teenager judged. "But as I say, it's just my feelings, I can be wrong. And he didn't want me to meet his family. I mean, he said they are not ready for me to come into their lives. This surprised them, they are not prepared for it," she reported.

"I think he meant his wife more. I'm sure they didn't involve the boy. He is ten, wouldn't all this complicate his life? Would he understand it? They probably want to spare him these news for now, there will be time for everything." Svetlana not for the first time felt the deep wisdom flowing from her grandfather. Whenever something he said, it seemed to her that this was the only and unique truth, although he did not have to be right.

"Anyway, I feel there is a bond between us. Ah! Dad wants us to come my place. He would like to meet my babysitter Olga, the country where I grew up, and most of all the surroundings of Świteź." She was very bad about it, but she had to lie to them. After all, she will not say that he is going in search of her mother, who is probably a demon now. They would not understand them, even though they were wonderful people.

"You don't mind, do you? It would be in two weeks, so we still have a lot of time to ourselves..."

"It's understandable that you want to spend some time with him. We have you now, he will have you later. Anyway, we won't lose you anymore. At least I hope so." Grandma hoped that she would hear confirmation from Svetlana's mouth, and indeed, she did not have to wait long.

"Sure! You are my family. The only real one, except for my father. But it is not known with him... after all, I will not live with them. I see he can't imagine it. Or maybe it's his wife... Anyway, I'm an adult, I will probably become independent soon."

"Since we already got into this topic. If I can, I would like to ask you, would you prefer to live here with us from next school year? Don't answer now. Consider. Of course we would find the best high school, we would transfer your papers. We have a room available, and you'd like to arrange it. And we could support you financially, spiritually... But I'm not pushing. It's your decision." Maria didn't insist, but you could feel a great tension in her voice, as if she was counting on her granddaughter to answer right away that it was a great idea. This time, however, it did not happen.

"Listen both of you: I am the happiest man since I found out that I have a family. When it occur that this family is great, so much more. It's just that there is so much going on in my life that I cannot yet say how the holidays will end and where my place will be. Let me enjoy my father for now, and I promise that at the end of August we will sit down and I will tell you how I see my way forward. There is you, there is dad and there is also Wojtek. Each of you in a different place, with different expectations. And I'm somewhere in between, and I have to make sure I don't lose any of you." Grandpa Jan was looking at her and was full of pride. She was only eighteen, so much humble, calm, sensitive and reasonable.

"Then we are postponing this conversation until August," he said. "Meanwhile, what about this Wojtek?"

It was a good question. Five days had passed and he hadn't said a word to her. Nothing. No SMS, e-mail, call. She was starting to worry and felt guilty. Only those few days without him had been quite... normal. She did not wither with longing, did not cry into the pillow, and did not become depressed. So... maybe she doesn't love him at all? But why, then, is she constantly thinking about him, looking at the phone. This could not be just ordinary concern for friends. She didn't know herself.

"Wojtek... Hmmm... I don't know what to do." She looked sadly at her grandfather.

"Maybe I'll tell you something, but I don't know the details," he encouraged to confide.

So she relived the history of the station.

"I told him about meeting my father, but not everything and added that he would not understand anyway. He got angry, because he was with me all this time and somehow he accepted everything calmly. I told him to go to his Nowogródek and leave me here. He accused me that I no longer need him, so I get rid of him. I did not deny it. He's gone. I didn't stop him. That's it," she said automatically, without emotion.

"Simple." Jan smiled indulgently.

"How's that?"

"You did wrong and cruelly. So there are two options. First: if you want a boy who truly loves and supports you, then you should go to him immediately, ask him and bring him here to spend the rest of your vacation together. Of course, you have the right to spend time alone with your father, but Wojtek will understand it, just explain it to him properly. Second option: if you don't want to be with him then you have to talk to him anyway because he's a good boy and it's a pity for him to live in suspense waiting for the sign. He must be clear to know how to make his own life..." he finished.

"But do I need to know it now? He is important to me, but I don't know if I want a serious relationship to the end of life!"

"Honey, nobody expects this of you. You just need to know if you want to be with him today, share your sorrows and joys. What will be tommorow? No one knows this. Today, however, you should clear up this ridiculous situation. Do not leave unfinished matters, because tomorrow may not be..."

Jan mobilized Svetlana to act. She did not know yet what to say to Wojtek, but she was convinced that she needed to talk to him. She called and made an appointment with him for the afternoon. He will pick her up at the station and they will go for a long walk. Her heart will tell her how to pull off this conversation. Everything will work out somehow...

44

Wojtek was pleased with her phone. And while he still held a grudge, he assumed that every human being deserved a second chance. And Svetlana failed. He doesn't know where this anger comes from - is it because of the enormity of his girlfriend's guilt, or maybe because of Wojtek's great involvement in this relationship? After all, he was at her beck and call from the very beginning. He always put her needs above his own. This is probably not a mistake. Only how would a seventeen-year-old know that. His feeling was first, pure, without calculation or manipulation. He was doing exactly what he felt he should be doing at the moment. He didn't care what it looked like from the side, or if anyone thought he was a sucker and a pussy whip. What mattered was that someone gave him unlimited trust and feelings that someone needed him and that he could not disappoint him. In the end, this person made a mistake, but she is only human (now only human) and she wants to fix that mistake. These thoughts and the like ran through Wojtek's head at the moment when the entire Krakow market square was drowning in the afternoon, strong, holiday sun.

Svetlana, walking towards the boy, admired the shape of the Rotunda, the Florian Gate, and then the Cloth Hall. The latter, like St. Mary's Church, especially captivated her with their beauty. Wojtek, wanting to be a tough guy, changed the meeting place. He found that he could not to drive, pick up, because the girl has to cope. They made an appointment at the monument to Mickiewicz. Of course, she didn't know where it was, but she asked passers-by and it was easy to hit. Before she noticed Wojtek in the crowd of passers-by, tourists and shopkeepers, she was staring at the older florists, who were sitting on tiny stools, surrounded by colorful flowers. She did not know that Wojtek had bought a bouquet for her from one of them a dozen or so minutes earlier.

Finally, having made her way through a school trip caught up in a street mime, she saw a face so well known to her. And then something strange happened. For the second time in the history of this love, she felt this strange tightness in her stomach. She knew for the second time that she was blushing. Finally, her hands started sweating a second time. The first time it happened was when they met at the very beginning at Olga's house. Only now, however, she realized the strength of her feelings for this inconspicuous boy.

He stood staring at the ground, one hand in his pocket. He kept the other one behind him because he didn't want everyone to know that he was waiting for a girl. Only part of the tiny bouquet was visible. Nothing stood out. He did not have the most fashionable sunglasses or the conspicuous badges on his boots or sweatshirt. But there was something about him that made her see only him among hundreds of people. Or maybe it was not in him, but in her? He was the only one in the world because he was her.

When he saw her walking towards him, he tried to master body reflexes that revealed how much he missed her. He pretended to be looking at the ground, but he could see every detail. She tied her hair up in a ponytail and put on a fancy headband with a bow. The skirt was a mustard, knee-length, and the blouse was a mint color. She put on high-heeled shoes with a turquoise mesh on them. She looked gorgeous with a light tan and light makeup.

"Maybe I'll start with the..." she said without a tender greeting, but he interrupted her.

"Not here. Let's go for a walk, okay?" She nodded. They did not talk to each other on the way, but Wojtek did not want to intimidate her any longer and only to increase the unnecessary pressure, he grabbed her hand. It calmed her and she smiled a little. He immediately caught the movement of the corners of his mouth. Only when they reached Wawel he took a blanket out of his backpack and spread it out on the green area along the Vistula River. He also pulled out a box full of raspberries.

"Now you can tell," he encouraged.

He knew well that this would captivate her. The scenery, his nonchalance and dose of romanticism were enough to make Svetlana feel even more guilty of an unnecessary conflict.

"I'm a stupid, stupid monkey!" She shouted so loudly that a group of young people sitting next to her looked at her in surprise.

"Well, it's going to be interesting." Wojtek was bursting with laughter.

"Seriously, I want to apologize very much. I acted wrong, but that's because I would very much like Stanisław's words about my mother to be true. And you, of course, had a good sense of it and all in all good. Only that all my enthusiasm got hit from you and landed on the pavement. It was unbearable for me at that moment, you understand?" Her statements were not lacking in order, and Wojtek understood her too well.

"I understand. But I want to apologize to you for not being able to contain my emotions, I panicked and started to exaggerate your words. I should have known how emotional it was to meet your father and that you cannot think rationally about your family being or not. I should stay with you, let you cool down, and then support your every decision, because that's the role of a good partner." He was too mature for his age, but that was what impressed her about him.

"Let's not argue more about such nonsense, okay? We still have a long learning curve, but at least let us try to make our quarrels the result of some major differences of opinion. Well, now... Now you could kiss me to make it look just like in the movie." She closed her eyes and gently parted her lips, though she could hardly refrain from laughing.

He closed her mouth with a kiss, and then fed the little ones, as in Leśmian's famous eroticism. The only thing left to be settled after this exhilarating afternoon is this the question of what's next with them, with her.

"What are you going to do?" That was the first important question of the night.

"For now, I want you to come back to my grandparents with me, but also accept my decision to look for my mother. My father is taking me and I hope you will go too, to Nowogródek, and from there to Świteź. We want to talk to Olga again and find out the whole truth. If there is not the slightest doubt that the mother is dead, we will let go, and if we can grab anything, any point of attachment, we will look for her. I would like you to accompany me then. We have two weeks. Then I will decide what about the next school year. Although I have to warn you that I intend to move to Zabierzów and probably some high school in Krakow. I fell in love with this city and I am just two steps away from here to home, where they want me and where they love me. Well, that would be it for now. Unless I find... mom..."

"That makes sense. For now, let's stay on the first stage, that is, we go to Zabierzów, and then we return to Nowogródek. I will spend a few days with my father and then I will go with you. It can be like that?" He knew the answer.

"Let's go now, because it's getting dark and cold, and besides, there are people who are probably worried about me."

He covered her with his jacket and slowly they made their way to the station, and from there to Zabierzów. The grandparents sitting on the porch looked at each other knowingly when they saw them walking towards the house. Maria seemed to be saying:

"Praise God."

Two consecutive days passed in sweet doing nothing. Grandma bustled around the teenagers, offering a fruit cake, delicious muffins, ice creams. Svetlana was captivated by this atmosphere of mutual concern and she would most likely stay here forever. However, she knew that one more journey awaited her - not only in the traditional sense, but also a journey into herself. When Stanisław showed up, she was packed and ready.

"Good morning. We haven't seen each other for a long time..." he started the conversation, kissing Maria on the hand and bowing to her husband.

"This is true. However, we hope that in this situation we will see each other more often and make up for lost time." Maria tried to embolden him, he was very close to her, and she always had great affection for him.

"Staś, stay for lunch and you will leave in the afternoon, okay?"

"I'd love to, Mrs. Maria, but not today. We have a long way to go. There will be many more opportunities."

They carefully checked whether they had taken all the things they needed, and then the three of them jumped into Stanisław's big car. Wojtek was to stay in Nowogródek and visit his father, and they were going straight to Lake Świteź to talk to Olga.

It was late evening when they got there. Before parting, Wojtek gave them the keys to the wooden house, which was still in Antoni's possession for the time. Stanisław was charmed by the surroundings. He couldn't stop wonderingthat there are still places so different from those he knew, where he lived and worked. It was quiet and dark here, and only the sounds of nature could be heard. Pure wilderness. Mysterious and as if undiscovered, omitted at the stage of making the earth given by man. He insisted that Svetlana go for a night walk with him, even though he knew she was tired.

"The conversation with Olga today will not come out anyway, but if you don't mind, I would like to see a place you know so well..."

"Okay. Although, to be honest, it brings to mind not very good memories... Here is Olga's cabin. I spent my days in it. We cooked together, read books, and studied. Away from other children, away from the city, away from modern technologies. All we had was a telephone for emergency help. Here we played with Anatol as children. We were not yet enchanted then. We had a normal sandbox, toys and - it would seem - an ordinary childhood. At that time, we didn't understand what happened to our parents. Olga was a bit of a mother to us, a bit of a grandmother."

They were walking when Anatol suddenly emerged from the water. Svetlana was surprised by this meeting, but despite the difficult nature and demonicity, she missed her stepbrother.

"Where have you been? Have you come back to us? And what is this man?" He asked, his eyes telling him he was ready to jump out of the water and absorb the companion of the "sister".

"Keep calm. I only came back for a moment. And this man is my father. See, I've found my real family. And finally, after so many years... happiness. Anatol... why don't you wanna do the same? Why don't you let us help you reverse the spell and try to find your relatives? You are all alone here... Let me help you..."

She felt sorry for this beautiful boy who had been imprisoned like she years ago, and at that moment could not see himself elsewhere. She felt exactly the same, and yet she succeeded. With small steps she entered a new environment, and now she does not regret a single decision. He could too... Anatol seemed to have eased, or perhaps saddened.

"I can't even write and read well. I was not like you. I wasn't interested in science and books. I preferred to swim and play for days. What am I supposed to do now? I am much older than you. Can you imagine these laughs, mockers? So old, and he can't read. I can't use their toys, I can't sit still for more than an hour. How am I supposed to live? Who would give me something to eat? Here I may be alone, but I have power, I feel strong. I don't want to be as clumsy as a child. You have to understand and respect that. But I wish you all the best. You deserved it. If you ever were around, visit Anatol... For now, I say goodbye.

He disappeared somewhere in the abyss. Svetlana had tears in her eyes. Stanisław did not understand any of their conversation in a foreign language. But he read from the scene that it was something like saying goodbye. The girl was silent for a long time. They walked forward, the father staring and listening to the wilderness and the daughter - happy that she might be silent with him.

45

The next day, Svetlana got up early to prepare a meal for her father. She decided that if he wanted to get to know her life so much, he had to try traditional Belarusian cuisine. Fortunately, on the way, they stopped by the store, because Wojtek had left the refrigerator empty. Stanisław was awakened by crackles coming from the kitchen. He got up, made the morning restroom, and saw a sumptuous table. He had never seen such dishes before. Everything looked delicious, and as it soon turned out, so was it. He praised his daughter, helped clean up, and nodded significantly. Svetlana also wanted to have this conversation behind her.

They met Olga in her home garden, bending down and picking up some weeds. It was the first time her father had seen her, and judging from his expression, he was not thrilled with her appearance. Their luck was on their side, she was alone, so they could talk easily. She sensed someone's presence much earlier than they thought. It was she who first threw at them:

"Please, please... I can't believe you wanted to visit your old nurse. In that case, something else must bring you..." She saw the stranger, so she didn't know how much she could do or what she could say. She was careful and conservative.

"Hello. This is Stanisław Oleszczuk, my biological father. He would like to talk to you. Actually, we would like to talk to you, if that's okay with you."

"It seems to me that I have no choice, since you brought him here all the way from Poland. I just don't understand what else I would have to say to you, you have already asked me about everything, I humbly confessed my sins. What else do you want?" Olga was upset.

"He knows everything. He believes me. Only there is one more thing. He knew Anna very well. And somehow he can't believe this story of her suicide," Svetlana was extremely confident.

"The story you say? So that's how you treat my words? As stories?"

"Sorry, you deserved it yourself. As many lies as I heard from you... Do you think it pays off with trust? Unfortunately, that's not how it works. So why not save us unnecessary introductions and tell us right away what really happened to Anna." Svetlana left somewhere far away her politeness and humility.

Stanisław, who was standing aside and listening to this incomprehensible speech, knew that this way the girl would not achieve anything. So he asked the old woman to talk to him. The daughter was to act as an interpreter.

"I know that you do not know me and that you have no obligations to me. Please forgive Svetlana, but like any child, she reacts emotionally to the memory of her mother. We are adults, we know that there are various situations in life, which do not always end as we wish it." After that, Olga initially gained respect for her interlocutor and let him go on.

"Well, I knew Anna very well at the time she appeared in your territory. I know she was a crazy girl who wanted to keep her youth.

I also guess that pregnancy was definitely not on her hand. So I guess you did her a favor by taking and raising Svetlana." He took a pause in the hope of making Olga take up the subject.

"You're absolutely right. Of course, Svetlana has the right to be distrustful. Many times I withheld fragments of her mother's story from her. Sometimes I was forced to lie to protect this child. Now I tried to explain everything to her from beginning to end."

"I tried? You mean it wasn't the whole truth?" Svetlana got carried away with emotions again.

"Please, calm down and let us talk." Stanisław gave his daughter a knowing look, letting her understand that she would achieve nothing by shouting.

"I told the truth. I gave you your family address. I wanted you to find your father and grandparents right now that you are an adult. I thought that only as an adult girl you would be able to consciously decide: stay here or find your biological family. It also happened. What do you want more? You have a new home, relatives who love you..." despite everything Olga tried to explain herself to Svetlana.

"All right. You wanted happiness for Svetlana, so you directed her steps towards people she knew would give her affection. But didn't you by any chance conceal the truth about Svetlana's mother? You certainly did it for her sake, because we know that Anna did not want a child, so you protected Svetlana from disappointment and the pain associated with rejection, it is obvious. Nobody would blame you." Stanisław cleverly led the conversation, manipulating the woman.

"You're a wise man. Okay, if that's what you want... I'll add the last piece of the story. The part so far, including Anna's suicidal thoughts and depression, is real. As Mr. Stanisław says, Anna did not want to have a child. Not then. She dreamed of studying, living together with her beloved, and here such a thing happened to her. I was afraid that she might hurt herself. And she did. Just not as I presented it to you. Anna found a book on magic and demons from me. She asked what must be done to turn into a rusalka. I never told her that I was łojma myself. She asked, so I answered. It never crossed my mind that she would try it. With me, she never spoke of immortality or keeping youth by force. When I told you that the next day after our conversation about motherhood, I found her changed and called the police... I was telling almost the truth." Olga was tired. "We had to arrange a fake funeral and such a things, but it worked."

"Please, let's get it over with. Finally, tell me everything so I don't have to go back to it again." Svetlana had a pleading expression on her face right now.

"I met your mother this morning. All she said was that she was no longer a mere mortal. I knew what she meant. So I just asked what would happen to the child. She stated that she has never felt a connection with you and that she will leave you here. I did not try to dissuade her from this idea because she would not be a good mother at this point in her life. Second, she had the prospect of returning to the lake every night."

"But where did she move? Where was she or is she?" Svetlana was getting more and more excited.

"All I know is that she wanted to change her whereabouts. It's difficult, given the lifestyle she chose, but possible. I saw her making a map of water bodies near the places she wanted to visit. However, eighteen years passed. I can't even guess where Anna is right now." Svetlana did not know if this time the old woman was trying to deceive her or hide something again. But she had no choice, so once again she believed her words.

Stanisław interrupted the conversation:

"Has Anna not appeared with you all these years? She did not want to meet her daughter or return to being an ordinary woman?" He asked factual questions.

"Young man, Anna will never be able to be an ordinary woman again. Svetlana and Anatol were transformed without their knowledge. Therefore, it was their right to decide for themselves. In nature, everything makes sense. Anna made a conscious decision. Nature will never allow her to return to the old order of things again. Answering yours earlier questions: I got a letter once, I even have it somewhere in the cupboard. In it, she asked if Marysia was okay. Only that. She asked to write back quickly to the address provided. I wrote back in one sentence, because I was afraid that she would want to take my child from me. It was about a year after the transformation. After that, there was no more contact attempt. I swear."

The story sounded plausible, but you could expect anything from Olga. Stanisław, who believed that he knew people, believed in this version of events. This, however, did not satisfy him.

"Fine. Now I only have one more request. You knew her, you talked for a long time... Where do you think we could look for her?" The man never lost hope of meeting the love from years ago and the mother of his child.

"We have about twenty lakes in Belarus. If I were you, I would delete the large ones or those located near towns and cities from the list. We demons have it that we don't like crowds and unnecessary onlookers, especially since sometimes our appearance changes imperceptibly. We live best in a remote area. So Anna would not choose Lake Cno, there is a hiking trail right next to it. It can also be assumed that she would reject Dryświaty, which is where the power plant and lots of people huddle around it. The same goes for

Lake Łukoml. Narocz and Sielachy are resorts where whole families with children rest, so they out. Sparysz was drained."

"Then which lakes should we explore, assuming that Anna stayed in Belarus?" Asked Stanisław.

"She definitely stayed in Belarus. I think she wanted to learn more about what she had become. And only here are there people who could explain it to her exactly. I believe she found another old łojma to be her confidante and guide through the demon world. As for the lakes, I think you should go in the following order: Szo, Ikaźni, Lake Głębokie, Kromań, Drywiaty, Bohiń, Nieszczerdo. And don't ask why. This is what my intuition tells me. This is what I would do to stay calm and relatively anonymous."

They thanked the woman and left. She couldn't tell them more. Svetlana wasn't sure if it was worth looking for her mother, because she didn't trust Olga. Stanisław, in turn, was filled with new energy and he felt that for the first time in a very long time he had a specific goal that could lead him to what he missed so much - to complete happiness.

46

Wojtek joined his companions the next day. Only then the three of them sat down and begin a serious conversation about the future. The conclusions were obvious: Svetlana and Wojtek were ending their holidays. The girl did not want to stop studying, because she had already wasted a lot of time. Besides, she thought the search would expose her to further disappointments, so she preferred to abandon them. Wojtek had the same opinion. He thought his girlfriend had been through enough. Anyway, she found people who loved her, so it should be enough for her. He did not believe Olga's stories. Stanisław was the most enthusiastic of the three, but he was a rational man and knew that education was essential. After hearing his daughter he said:

"I think you should go back to school. I will take a longer vacation and visit lakeside towns and villages. I should be in a few months. Let's not expect anything special, but... I can't let go... not now... when I know when I heard it..." There was too much emotion in him right now. He couldn't make a sentence. In his head, he was already planning every detail of the trip, writing down the most necessary items, and wondering how he would deal with the language barrier.

"Well. If you are both here, I can make an official announcement of what I have decided regarding my future. I've been thinking a lot this weekend. That is all that is happening right now is new and surprising for me. I need time to learn it - give it to myself, to get used to the fact that I am Polish with Polish grandparents, Polish father and surname. I have to transform into Marysia Lach, and it will not be easy. However, I want to cut myself off from what reminds me of an unhappy childhood and start over. But quite so, right from the start."

She was looking at Wojtek, and her eyes had that strange expression. As if they wanted to justify what he was about to say. The boy knew that look and knew it was bad news. He didn't interrupt her, though, ready for anything. "Tomorrow I am going back to Zabierzów. I will live with my grandparents and move to the Krakow high school. I will start my second grade as Maria Lach, whose father lives with a new family in Katowice after my mother's death. I will get education, meet new places and people. I must finally open up. With you, Dad, I'll be seeing on the weekends if you wish. As for your family, decide for yourself if you want us to get to know each other. I don't care. Of course, I look forward to hearing from you during your trip around Belarus." She did not mention Wojtek a word.

"Forgive me for asking. Where is my place in this story?" He couldn't stand it, but he was extremely calm.

"You've done a lot for me. In all our adventures, I have gone from hating to loving you. You are great: wise, responsible, mature, and you have a soft heart. But today I have to find myself. And I want to do it alone. If you let me, I wish keep us in touch. However, it will be better for you to stay with your dad in Nowogródek. I believe our paths will cross yet. Except this is not the time. I thank you for everything." She wanted to kiss him and hug him, but he pulled away and covered face with his hand.

He had neither anger nor sadness in him. He only felt the immense void that was left after her departure. Because even though she was standing next to him, he felt she was gone. He couldn't resent her. Yet something stung inside him. He decided to act like a man.

"It was nice to meet you, Svetlana. Last year was the most special of my life for me. I will never forget you. However, I can't imagine how I could talk to you or write to you knowing that you are no longer mine. I couldn't take it. Maybe our paths will cross one day. If not, you must know that you have been the love of my life. Now don't say anything else." His words did not reflect what he felt at the moment. He always believed that you only love one time. His parents were the proof. Another Stanisław, who, despite starting a family, was still thinking about Anna. And that was the only thing that made a black cloud gather over his forehead. He would never love anyone like that again. He will always have HER in front of his eyes.

"We're going to the station. I am going back to Krakow and my father is going back to Braslaw." She turned and walked away. From afar, she shouted: "I believe that we will meet. It just has to pass some time. This is not a goodbye, so I will only say: see you later."

He didn't even have time to answer. He stood like a pillar of salt and stared at the receding figure. The same one that fascinated him then by the lake. It was as foreign to him now as it was on that first moonlit night...

Return to the lake

1

Marry returned to the dorm after class was over. On the way back, she passed places she had gotten to know well over the last few years. She looked at them with great sentiment. She bought two chocolate potatoes in her favorite confectionery, which has almost become an everyday tradition. She found that in her fifth year she had much more free time than she had in the previous years. Before that, she struggled to combine full-time studies with work in a cafe that served as a bar in the evenings. With her tongue hanging out, she covered the route from UP to Szewska street, where her "source of income" was, on foot, sometimes by bicycle, and at other times by tram. Now she could easily work overtime. The only reason she wasn't doing it was because she had to concentrate on writing her master's thesis. It can't be as hard as everyone says. I'll just sit down, collect some books and that's it! - she thought. She was going to deal with writing until December and spend the summer semester lazing around and looking for a job, the one she dreamed of. And starting the other degree course. Her promoter was sympathetic to the plans, he knew her student well, he knew that she was ambitious and conscientious. He wished her many successes and supported her development. She finally got to her dormitory. Inside it was warm and clean as always. It is the only such dormitory. The elevator quickly took her to the fourth floor. She turned the key in the lock of room four hundred and fourteen.

She looked at this room with sentiment. Before they hit here, they went through hell. First year - an old house where heating bills kept her awake at night. Three roommates, one of whom brought another man home every night. Kitchen and bathroom, probably before the war. But it was there that she met Kaśka. Her Kaśka. A soul mate, a best friend, a cure for all evil. Second year - a small apartment in a block, right next to the university. Beautiful, renovated, with a terrace. The only trouble is the walk-through room and another roommate from hell. Bad smell, long hair in the drain and mold on food in the refrigerator - it was her calling card. And she found this boy... What was his name? Leon. Every day they had to listen to their quarrels, endure his nightly trips to the refrigerator in search of something to eat. Nightmare. Finally it worked! In their third year, they got a place in a dormitory. Both. Only two of them in one room. And what! Fortunately, the boy from the local government - Marcin - had a weakness for Marysia... It was also successful in the next and finally the last, fifth year.

A large window with a bright roller blind, white walls, which they always decorated for Christmas with Christmas lights and a chain, and during the year they hung pictures of their loved ones on them and from time to time a calendar with divine men. The table was already slightly upholstered on one side, but still nice and practical, the wardrobe was repaired more than once by the kind Mr. Landek - porter and conservator. She remembered how Kaśka tried to fill the printer with ink and everything was black there: blinds, walls, furniture. Also Kaśka herself. First, she was terribly angry with her, and then they just laughed. Their two laptops sat on a long desk that ran across the room. Some pens, two swivel chairs. The shelves could be immediately divided between the two owners. One - with ironed napkins, jewelry boxes and dozens of books. The second one, which had everything: powder, hairpins, perfume, a pencil and a square with a vase. Perfect reflection of their different characters. Miss in order and miss in a mess. Two perfectly joining halves.

Marysia sat down on the bed and began to remember each Christmas Eve, where guests would bring shop ravioli and instant borscht. Yet there was something magical about them. They shared the wafer, they were always dressed in festive clothes and she knew that everyone in this group wishes her well, everyone cares for her. All parties, the St. Andrew's and birthday parties. Fortune telling, pouring wax, talking until morning, hectoliters of drunk and liters of wine poured out. Pizza cartons with baked mayonnaise, successfully replacing the most exquisite dishes. Her hard drive had a problem holding all the photos documenting the last five years.

There was also a tiny bathroom in the same room. The same one in which Kaśka conducted her longish nighttime conversations with an ex-boyfriend. The same one that no one ever wanted to clean and in which Kaśka cried so many times, hiding it from the whole world. The closet they threw their clothes out before each event, creating one-of-a-kind stylizations. It will be hard for her to leave this place in less than nine months...

Kaśka was of course an inseparable element of the four hundred and fourteen room. Lovely, though she didn't realize it. Short, a bit heavier than Marysia, with beautiful eyes and thick, long hair. She didn't seem friendly at first, but that was because of her distrust. She has created a kind of protective armor.

"Dudess! I think you are overwhelmed! Why do you want to write a MA thesis now? Can't we take another semester of slack and then get down to business?"

Yes, Kaśka was the complete opposite of Marysia. She did everything at the last minute, she did not finish the projects she started. She was a mess and a night owl. However, Marysia did not pay attention to her shortcomings. She loved her like a sister for her sensitivity, kindness, trust, sometimes bordering on naivety, for her big heart, clumsiness and smile. Perhaps it was the differences in characters that made them get along so well that it was their fifth year together. Marysia tried to remember a bigger quarrel with Kaśka. And... she couldn't. Don't think there were such. Of course, there were misunderstandings, silent hours, sulks. However, they are always short-lived and have a happy ending.

"I promise you that I will only write while you learn your formulas and equations. I do not intend to suborder my master's degree all my life, I have friends and work. But I prefer to start earlier and finish earlier," she explained. "You know me anyway. I have already done some research, I have ordered books in Jagiellonka, if I press myself, it will not take so long."

Kaśka envied Maria this order. And not only that. She envied her quick metabolism, the ease of establishing contacts and several admirers. Moreover, in her eyes, Marysia was very talented, clever, witty and very sociable. In a word - ideal. Of course, Kaśka was not aware of her secrets and not a very pleasant past.

Maria like Maria - she didn't even notice those flirty looks, the ease with which her studies came, and the groups of loyal friends she easily won over at the end of her first year. She was too modest, and life constantly taught her humility.

It has changed over the years. It's a fact. Starting with her external appearance: she lightened her hair, began to buy fashionable clothes and cosmetics. However, she did not take money from her grandparents. They paid for her dormitory, her father sent a certain amount every month, which she spent on food, photocopying and books. For everything else, she paid with the money she earned. In her character, her attitude towards people has changed. She became more trusting, friendly and open during her studies. In high school, she still had a problem with that. Now she felt that she could finally breathe deeply, because she had suppressed her fear and complexes. But most of all, she knows who she is, she knew her origin and place on earth.

"Actually, why don't you still have a man?" Kaśka started their daily chat. There were already two mugs of coffee on a small table by the window, and next to it favorite chocolate potatoes. "Look, there's Piotrek from the fifth floor. Cool, handsome, maybe a bit too smart, but generally it will get away with it. There is also Jarek from AGH, who, in turn, could be more confident, but he is a good man and how does he look at you... And my favorite - Michał..."

"If you must know, then Piotrek and Jarek have no chance. They are ordinary colleagues. Piotrek... I don't know what he really is. Everything is hidden under the mask of a macho. Anyway, my intuition tells me that he is a womanizer and he would betray me. We also see each other once a week when we accidentally cook something together in the kitchen. I don't even know if I have anything to talk to him about." Marysia smiled and Kaśka burst out laughing.

"You're crazy! You're always looking for a hole in something. It's good that this time you didn't give an unfashionable shirt or dirty shoes as a reason for rejection!" Friend did not stop laughing, even when Marysia threw a pillow at her.

"I don't feel butterflies in my stomach when I see him, don't you understand?"

"And Jarek? This one is also not bad. I would like to go out with him myself, but only when I throw my greatest love - chocolate wafers!" The girls definitely had a good mood.

"Jarek, Jarek. We met him twice by accident. So much. I didn't even think about him in those terms. Anyway, it wouldn't be love with any of them..."

"How do you know? Have you experienced one already, to know how to differentiate it from mere infatuation?"

They talked every day for so many years. However, Kaśka never managed to get an answer to this question. Marry always put her off, refused to talk about her past, as if something unpleasant had happened to her. Kaśka felt, however, that the closer to the end of her studies, the more Marysia opened up, therefore she tried to pursue the topic as soon as an opportunity arose.

"Yes, I loved someone very much and I know how I feel when love comes. I'm just afraid that I'll never know it again, that the feeling was so strong it burned me out. I don't know, maybe I'm talking nonsense, because I was seventeen then... but there is something to it. There is no need to talk about true love, you don't have to analyze it, you don't have to ask yourself questions... You just know that it has entered your heart. You don't think about it, you only feel it. It cannot be explained otherwise."

"Okay, and Michał? You didn't say anything about him..." Kaśka didn't stop.

"Michał is great. I like him. If there is such a thing as a beauty type that somehow suits us, then he is my type: tall, blonde, bright eyes. He has a great figure. Moreover, he is close to me. We study together, both of us are interested in history, we spend a lot of time together and I know that I can trust him and count on him. You know he has been with me all this time. When I was taking my exams for studies, at each session, he helped me find a job, supported us financially when we didn't want to tell our family about something. Anyway, I can see that I am important to him. But we have had more than one conversation on this subject. I explain to him that I am not able to declare myself yet and just be with someone."

"Only that studies are about to end and he will probably want to know what he is standing on. He will not wait for you forever. Well, unless he will... Besides, Marry, he's just a guy... and you guys don't even kiss?" Kaśka knew that she was crossing the thin line between the usual friendly conversation and inquisitive questioning. However, she was aware that even if she offended Marysia, she would forgive her anyway.

For the first time in a long time, Marysia felt embarrassed, although she was only Kaśka. She was ashamed that her roommate might find her some kind of non-touch or excessively prudish. However, it's true, since Wojtek's time... she hasn't let anyone touch her.

"Yes, you're right. We've actually been dating for three months. Nobody actually sees it because we don't act like a real couple. There has been a breakthrough recently, just don't be too much happy, because I grabbed his hand and kissed his cheek goodbye." Marysia knew that Kaśka would laugh at her.

"On the cheek? How old are you? Twenty four or fifteen? Sorry, Marry, but at this age, a guy is looking for more!"

"I'm not ready. I still have someone else on my mind..." Her voice was filled with sadness. "That's why I never want to talk about it and come back to it. When I don't think I'm really happy."

So many years have passed, but for her the most beautiful memories were still those of the holidays at the lake in his company. Now, a long time had passed, she didn't think about what was bad, she remembered only the good times. When he was with her, when she woke up, he organized books, ID cards, and school for her. When he lied to her father for her, sacrificed time, friends... everything. Their first meeting when she was such a dragon. She smiled to herself.

"Hey, I don't want to be nosy and it's none of my business, but you're a virgin?" Kaśka knew that this question must be asked one day, although she could have guessed the answer.

Marysia did not mind talking about sex, initiation and such things, especially with her closest friend. Even so, she felt like a freak.

"You know. And it's not about religious reasons or anything like that. I simply loved, and maybe still love someone with whom I was too short, too early... And now I can't, and that's it."

"Listen. Why bother so much? Can't you just find him? Call and confess your love? You know, it will be like on a romantic comedy." Kaśka stood on the bed and started to act out a cut-scene. "It's raining, you learn that he will be standing on the bridge at the specified time. You go against him, you are wet but happy. He spots you and starts running towards you, then we have a passionate kiss, a night spent in his embrace, and they all live happily ever after." Friend, as usual, simplified the matter.

"It's not so simple. I also associate unpleasant memories with him. Anyway, he certainly already has someone and is happy. Apparently it was supposed to be this way. End of period. And we will see with Michał, I will probably get involved in this relationship and give him a chance. It just takes a while. Besides, you know the adage: "If he loves, he will wait.""

2

Marysia graduated from high school with commendation. Admittedly, science subjects were not her forte, but her grandparents invested in tutors and even mathematics went quite smoothly. She had discovered in her second grade that she was most interested in the history of the country that was her homeland and about which she knew so little. Of course, she urged her grandfather to tell her about wars, uprisings and the constitution, but with time his knowledge was no longer sufficient for her. She was constantly reading history books, various types of magazines and she knew for sure that she wanted to connect her future with this direction. At one point, she even felt that the story probably no longer had any major secrets from her. This allowed her to feel at home in Poland, at home. Finally.

So no one was surprised that after graduating from high school she applied for history. She competed at the University of Silesia, Jagiellonian University and Pedagogical University. However, she wanted to stay in Krakow, and since she was thinking about working as a teacher or lecturer, she finally chose the third one. The grandparents insisted that she stay with them in Zabierzów, because - despite the fact that three years had passed together - they still could not enjoy the presence of their granddaughter. However, Marysia preferred to try to live on her own, relieving this couple of beloved people. Of course, there was also the father... Yes, the father.

Stanisław Oleszczuk, starting his search for his first love and the mother of his child, he assumed that in a few months he would be able to discover the truth lying somewhere at the bottom of the lake. However, each Belarusian reservoir hid so many secrets, so many people had to be met and talked about that, as a result, it had been on the way for three years. It had an impact on his family and professional life. The wife filed a divorce petition with the court, there was one hearing and that's it. There was still his thirteen-year-old son at the moment. It was only because of him that he would interrupt his search from time to time, spending a week or two with him. He also temporarily abandoned his duties as a practicing cardiologist, finding a good replacement. Finding the truth, or rather Anna, became his obsession...

Marysia often talked to her father, but she was terrified of what he had done with his life. She has already come to terms with the fact that her mother has simply passed away. He continued to live with illusions, plunging into successive expeditions and hopes. Requests and threats did not help. He closed everything in one sentence: "I will not rest until I find her or her grave". Marysia was tired of the fact that she was the only one who shared the secret of the chief physician, but she knew that she had to stand by him. Even when it became necessary to think up more fairy tales told to grandparents or people she meet. She explained Stanisław's expeditions with a newly discovered travel passion, professional fatigue and the need to relieve himself, and finally the crisis in his marriage and escape from problems. Thanks to this, she gained relative calm.

As for her father - Marysia finally won a place in the dormitory, because in addition to taking advantage of her friend's friendliness, she checked in with Stanisław to add more distances. Her grandparents always gave her something when they came to visit or when she was spending the weekend in Zabierzów. Additionally, her grandmother would not let her out without a bag full of various delicacies, which Kaśka enjoyed the most. She was in such good contact with her father that she did not feel his lack too much.

"Wow! How many steamed pancakes and dumplings. There are also delicious mushroom croquettes!" Kaśka always looked at a new delivery. She, in turn, brought pancakes, cabbage rolls and many, many other delicacies.

Katarzyna lived in the Kielce region. Due to the fact that her family was not very wealthy and the girl devoted a whole lot of time to study and did not work, she rarely went home to save money. The return ticket was quite expensive. Anyway, Marysia, from the very beginning, or actually from the moment she liked Kaśka for good, shared everything with her - with reciprocity.

Marry did not stay in touch with her half-brother because his mother did not want him to. So she felt like an only child, which is why it came naturally to her to treat Kasia like a sister. This one was a good straight girl who tried to pass the exam sessions. She liked going to the mountains, playing the guitar and had a "memory for numbers" - as she talked about herself. That is why she chose mathematics as the direction of her post-secondary education. Frankly speaking, Marysia did not see her as a future teacher, because she experienced every lesson she taught too much, not to mention the monthly internships at a nearby school. If it were to be like that every day... But she wished her friend the best, motivating and supporting when it was needed. Already in the first year, Marysia made friends with several people from her group. Among them were Michał, Szczepan, Marta and Agnieszka. They ate lunch together in the university canteen, together they prepared exam notes, spent time together in the library and finally partying together in the dormitory or in Krakow clubs. Each of them was different. Michał came from a good home, which in their language meant that his parents earned a lot of money, had a beautiful house with a garden, and did not spare their son cash. They supported him, always offered help and good advice. This disturbed Marysia a bit. That, or maybe the fact that Michał was a bit spoiled, and therefore not very independent. However, he was an honest and good-natured boy. Szczepan had a difficult childhood - he was an orphan, he had no family support. He had to think about what he would prepare for dinner or where he would get the money for the rent. The pension he received from his parents was very low. He was perhaps the best man in their pack. You could always count on him, he listened, comforted and radiated warmth and goodness. Marysia adored his benevolent and kind look smile and blonde hair. She was always ready to help him. Fortunately, he was optimistic and smiled at everything, though he often felt helpless or not good enough. The girls tried at all costs to raise his self-esteem and cure him of his complexes. Efficiently.

Marta was crazy. She was a year younger than them because her parents sent her to school earlier. And rightly so, because the girl was incredibly talented and intelligent. What others did for hours, she read once and could recite flawlessly in class or in an exam. In addition, she had so much energy that she infected everyone around her. She had a slightly exotic beauty, original style and always attracted the attention of the opposite sex. Although they were all pretty, she was the one who was always the center of attention, she was the one who left with a pocket full of obtained phone numbers and she ignored all the flirty looks. She was free, like a bird, and when she felt like she would admit a man for a moment or two. But it was pure entertainment. Nothing more.

When Marysia was in a bad mood, she always called Marta. Kaśka analyzed everything with her and the conversation ended with the depression of both girls. In such situations, Marta would take Marry for a beer and get her drunk, making her laugh at the same time. This method has proven effective.

There was also Agnieszka - short, with a beautiful, lush hairs, shapely, full of humor, an extremely hardworking girl. She came from a small town, but she was always the best dressed, her clothes the most ironed, and she was most prepared for classes. They didn't like her right away. She looked cool and aloof. However, when they allowed her to come closer, their eyes saw her true face - a good, caring friend, always at service.

Together they formed an almost explosive mixture, but left to themselves, away from their loved ones, they could always rely on each other. Marysia felt that they were her second family. It was only thanks to them that she got better after parting ways with Wojtek. During her high school days, she only lived in the past. It was they who let her take her mind away from those memories, and in their company she no longer had to think about what had happened to her. Of course, no one knew about anything. She began to write a new chapter of her life, page after page, not wanting to return to the earlier, long closed. She was not going to turn back, but to walk forward with her head held high. This is how they got to know her and this is what they had in their hearts.

"It's Thursday, the academic year has not yet started for good, and we, students of the teaching specialization, have just finished the long, exhausting, depressing apprenticeship in high schools, so we could easily go somewhere today..." began Marta, the initiator of all events.

"Couldn't we use those cheap theater tickets instead of going to the party? We keep promising ourselves that instead of having a beer, we'll go see some ambitious play." Agnieszka tried to find an alternative to the weekly trips to the pub.

"You can go to the theater on cloudy and depressive days. Today we're going for a beer and dancing!" Szczepan decided for everyone. "As long as it is bright, the sun is shining, let's enjoy life!"

"Look, I'm out today. I would like to go to Jagiellonian University and borrow the rest of the books I need. Once I have everything with me, it will be easier for me to start writing." Marysia spoiled everyone's mood by reminding them of the necessity to collect materials for master's thesis.

"Certainly not today! My dear, we have seen four times during the summer holidays, and in a moment they will start harassing us, because November will past fast. Today we go and that's it!" Marta's legs were starting to dance.

"She is right! Anyway, I did not go to college to study books." Agnieszka laughed and the rest of the company echoed her.

"Marry, don't be wimp! Take Kaśka and come to Basztowa at 10 PM. Ok? You will make your way to Jagiellonka earlier, borrow what you need and take care of the study on another day. Win-win situation, isn't it?" Marta wanted to make sure.

"Well. Although it does not suit me at all. I'm in neither mood nor outfit..." She tried to complain yet, but everyone turned their backs on her and started planning where they would go today. Marry missed them. Loud, laughing, optimistic about the future. And this is the last such year. She knew that one day she would have to finish her studies and grow up. However, she did not think that this time would pass so quickly. She felt neither ready nor willing to start work, let alone start a family. And yet she will not be forever young and attractive 24-year-old, in a moment she will become invisible to the male part of the population, because it will be replaced by newer models. If it were still wodja... No, she tossed the thought out and never came back to her.

After returning to the dormitory, Marysia found Kaśka tired of studying for another test for several hours and staring out the window at the opposite couple, hugging each other on the bed. Their dormitory, and the one opposite, were divided into a hotel and a student part. Various things were happening in the hotel part. Colleague from the lower floors often came to Marysia and Kaśka to delight their eyes with the sight of a naked female body or a sexual act.

"The charms of the dormitory," said Marysia without much surprise. The scene was repeated regularly.

"Hey, they rent from the fifth and up, don't they? But we are unlucky, just at the height of our room, some guys are always playing with the ladies..." commented Kaśka, although she did not look scandalized, but rather interested in the spectacle.

"You'll be glad to tell you something right now." Maria made the face of a mother disappointed with her child, Kaśka knew her well.

"It's party! Finally! I thought history had completely forgotten about pleasures. Everyone will be there?" Kaśka was already heading towards the common wardrobe to choose some outfit for the evening.

"Everyone will be there. It's already six o'clock, and I haven't even had lunch. Well, but image is more important, so throw everything we have in the middle." The procedure was always the same. Kaśka put her hand in the wardrobe and all the clothes landed on the soft carpet. It doesn't matter if one was a size thirty-six and the other a size forty. You could always make a nice and quite original combination out of it.

After choosing an outfit, the girls did each other's makeup and hairstyles. Maria loved giving her stylizations names. So there was: a breeze of the Orient, a familiar cheer and the like. Marysia had a flair for this, unlike Kaśka, who always stood awkwardly in front of the mirror, waiting for her friend to approve the choice or possibly to improve her beauty a bit with make-up.

Finally, when they were ready, Marry, as was her custom, began to groan.

"Why are we even going? As usual, instead of one we drink three beers, as usual there will be no nice men, as usual we will be back in the morning, not in two hours and I will sleep at the monograph lecture... I will know nothing, will be tired and lying to my grandparents again that I will not come for the weekend, because I got poisoned with a kebab. Eventually they will guess..."

Every party for five years has ended the same for Marry. In the first year, Kaśka was scandalized by actions of history students. She did not drink alcohol, did not dye her hair, and wore modest clothes in dark colors. It was Marysia's friends that got her a little bit get rolling. Reluctantly at first, then with great pleasure she accompanied them in subsequent meetings. After each event they shared, Marysia said a sentence that was already known to everyone when she looked at Kaśka, who was sleeping in the tram: "I created a monster". Meanwhile, the monster was making more arguments to get Marry moving.

"But that today we will meet some fantastic men, we will not drink too much, but culturally, and I promise that we will come back no later than two o'clock, because in the morning I have a test and I have to pass it."

"You know we always say that?" Marysia gave up, and Kaśka nodded her head and was already closing the door, pushing out her roommate.

3

Wojtek winced as he passed the Pedagogical Dormitory. He might be cool and brand new, but it didn't look like a decent male student house. All glass, with a quiet elevator and a beautiful reception. He wasn't partying there. Once he only went to visit a friend, but it felt like a hospital, not a dormitory. Tightly closed doors, few people in the corridors and this silence... Something he could dream about at home. Finally, his beautiful temporary "house" was emerging from behind other buildings. It was nothing that he once found a cockroach here, it was nothing that the door was so thin that you could hear your neighbor's every word. But there was an atmosphere here. Full muse all day long, breweries in the kitchen and all the guys around. No need to clean up, worry about calling the manager. He remembered New Year's Eve well, when suddenly a wild crowd had gathered in his room and someone with great fantasy took a fire extinguisher from the corridor and emptied it onto the floor of the room. He remembered his first-year roommates making their own alcohol. He also could not forget what the consequences of consuming it were - during the game they were watching, they were drinking cheap drink with their friends at the call and one of them lost his eyesight for a moment. Dormitory. Total play. He will miss it if he manages to defend his thesis. He had nothing yet - no ideas or materials. He reported some subject to the thesis advisor, but it was not fully thought out.

In general, he chose AGH to impress his father and follow in his footsteps. In fact, he dreamed of Economic University, because he was thinking about starting his own company in the future. But you can have an engineer and do that too, and the father is so proud to have found a worthy successor. He told him so much about this university, about its achievements, adventures, and escapades. Wojtek did not regret that he listened to him. It's been a good five years.

Coming out of the elevator, he already knew that Jarek was in the room. He could hear the sounds of his favorite music. From dinner, as usual, nothing happened, because neither he nor his roommate had been to the family house recently. There must be some Chinese soups left. Wojtek and Jarek's room resembled a small hut after a tsunami. The boys' clothes were hung literally everywhere - on the bunk bed, on the open door of a falling wardrobe, on the edge of the table and on the key of a small cupboard. There was ketchup on the table and a red plastic board with buttered sandwiches on it. There are two computers with huge speakers by the desks, cobwebs and dust in the corners of the room. Fortunately, none of them were allergic.

"How did it go?" Wojtek shouted to drown out the music.

"No revelation, but forward!" Jarek turned off the playing box. "You remember my friend from hometown? Marta. She was with us at annual higher education students' holiday in the first year and probably at another party, some housewarming party. Then somehow the contact broke off, because she found a group of friends. So short with curly hair."

"It seems familiar to me. What are you getting at?" Wojtek suspected Jarek of evil intentions to match him. After all, he had a girl, but Jarek kept telling him that she was not the one, and suggested other girls.

"Well, today she called and asked what I was doing. They go somewhere with chicks from her group and she asked if I could get some buddies."

"I do not believe. The chick calls you after four years and you are immediately at her call. Do you know what it means to be assertive? Such a skill for real men! Those who suffer alone later." Wojtek was looking for something to eat and at the same time making fun of his friend.

"Man, not everyone has a girlfriend like in the underwear catalog and scientist IQ. Be human and come with me to this party." He stared pleadingly. "Perhaps I would also like someone to wash my jerky, cook a broth, hug to young breast and console me in moments of doubt." Jarek was infected with good humor.

This is true. Everyone envied Wojtek his Paula and their shared history. When Svetlana left him and walked away without any qualms, he thought that he would never make a life for himself. For several months he could not find a place for himself. He didn't know if this was depression, but he couldn't eat, he didn't sleep at night, he stared at the TV for hours and didn't care. He was reminded of the time after his mother died. Second year of high school would be a nightmare, especially in Alex company and after that nasty lake accident. It would have been if it weren't for her. Paula didn't care at all when he had Svetlana next to him. However, when they started their second year of studies, she took care of him, offered him help in writing essays, and then he saw how beautiful and wise she was. She was about five feet seven inches and had long blonde hair. That's why everyone said she looks like a model. Anyway, she could be. She changed the way Wojtek was dressed, persuaded him to go to the gym and - as his classmates said - made him a real sweetie. She pulled him out, maybe even pulled him out of his apathy and melancholy. And since she had put so much trouble into this development, she did not intend to leave him after graduation to another woman. She changed her interests from the humanities to the sciences and chose the AGH University of Science and Technology in Krakow as her dream university. They lived not far apart, so she had Wojtek under constant control. Besides, she liked to pay him visits, which Jarek called raids of the Supreme Chamber of Control. Though she couldn't complain about chance, and she really had nothing to complain about, she still felt as if he wasn't quite sure if he was in the right relationship. It seemed to her that she loved him more, that she was more trying and involved. Now that they had survived together for over six years, she wanted to drag her lover to the altar.

Wojtek did not know if he loved her. Of course he pronounced the words automatically, but did he really feel it? She was so different from his first love. Confident, sometimes even arrogant. She had never scruples, she had been pursuing her goal. I guess that's why nobody liked her. But for him she was good, caring, loving. Only his father kept saying that she didn't suit him. He considered her vain and ruthless. Maybe he was right, but these disadvantages could become advantages. He knew that he and his children, if they ever had them, she would defend them like a lion. And that she was vain - not her fault that everyone admired her. When she was alone with him, he could see the true self of Paula. And he even liked it. The father was satisfied with this relationship for one reason only. He knew his son wasn't having casual sex, but he had a permanent partner. And it must be admit that Paula was amazing in the bed..."

"What are you thinking about? About this party?" Jarek asked, seeing his colleague staring at the floor and seemingly absent.

"What do you think about Paula?" Wojtek was now completely different.

"Well, she's a great chick. In addition, she has a scholarship, is smart and you can see that she cares. I'm the only one who doesn't like her, but that's not the most important thing. And why do you ask?"

"You see, she starts talking more and more about what will happen when we graduate. She's talking about herself, of course. That she would conduct audits, that she would earn a lot of money, but that if a child appeared, she would quit her job for a while. That she would like to start planning a wedding before defending her master's thesis, because now the dates are very long. That she chose us to live somewhere near Krakow, not too expensive. That we would take a loan in half, and that half would be covered by her parents, and my dad would buy the equipment... She would like to have a dress from some Polish designer, and I would like a suit from some... ah, I don't remember the name. And that he knows the guy from the real estate, so then we could change the apartment into a larger apartment, and of course arrange it in a modern style, only white and black..." Wojtek wanted to continue, but he saw Jarek's uncertain face.

"Wait a moment... Are these your plans or Paula's plans? I thought you wanted to do an internship in Nowogródek with your father and then start a business. I don't know anything about your paternal intentions. An apartment near Krakow? Have you ever said that you dreamed of a home? That you would like to build it with your father, that you dream of a garden, trees, a barbecue and a dog in a large kennel?" Jarek seemed confused.

"That's the problem. She is already trying on wedding dresses, and I don't even know if I want to spend the rest of my life with her. You see... I still... I don't feel what I used to..." Wojtek didn't like to come back to this topic, but now it was rather necessary.

"I've told you so many times to call her or go. It's just like two steps away. But no, you insisted like a donkey. If you don't feel Paula is the one, then stop it before the girl collapses. Or else, try to find Svetlana and see if you really have anything else in common. If not, you will know that you can plan your next life with your current girlfriend." Wojtek was surprised that people used to call Jarek wicked loser or meatball. Maybe he was slow, but he could listen and advise. He was undoubtedly his best friend. All these difficult years. And maybe he's right now too.

But what would he tell her? Maybe she has a husband or a child... She probably doesn't want to see him, because she would have given a sign. Anyway, she dumped him, hurt him, ripped his hearts out - apparently with other insides, because now he feels empty as an empty shell. He hated her for it, and his father also felt grievance for her. Because simply in the world - you don't act like that. This way you don't get back your kindness and affection. No! He won't look for her.

"No. If she wanted to, she would find me. Apparently she is happy with someone else. I'll tell Paula that I agree to everything. She just has to wait for the proposal, because first I want to close things at the university."

"You will suffer for your pride. You will see. And who do you think you will do to spite? Me? Svetlana? Only yourself, man. And this is not a decision about a new pair of shoes..."

Jarek did not take his eyes off the computer, but Wojtek heard him very clearly. "What about my request? Will you come with me? Only without Paula, or I'll be feeling stupid, okay?"

"I'll go, but if she asks where I will be, I'll tell her. She might come later, when you will have fun with Marta. Okay?"

"Okay. Thanks. I will not play with Marta. First of all, she's not that girl, secondly I care. I would like to impress her, because she always sees only in me a buddy. And I liked her since elementary school..." Jarek once again talked about the girl of his dreams.

Wojtek, meanwhile, wondered what he should do with his life. Soon it will be time to make decisions that will affect his future. Only he had no idea which way or with whom to go.

4

"Listen? Another party with friends? You know I don't like it. Where will you be? How do you not know yet? In that case, let's make an agreement that when you take a place, you will write me a text message... If I feel like it... I do not promise. I don't understand why we can't go on a double date... Then they'd get to know each other better with us... All right. Bye."

Paula was furious. Wojtek always informed her about his out at the last minute. She always had a pre-made schedule for her boyfriend. She didn't like anyone, even him, changing her plans at the last minute. She was going to spend the evening with her lover tonight, and now... of course she would have to go to some stupid place to see if he was okay. And to pretend that he likes Jarek. The clap who couldn't do anything, always staring at the computer. Well. She loves Wojtek and has to forgive him for these shortcomings. Anyway, the studies are ending and she will have him all to herself. For sure, contact with Jarek will break, and if it doesn't happen naturally, she will take care of it. Jarek doesn't like her, you can feel it. But how could someone like her, someone who buys clothes at a market, has no idea who Dior is, and he probably chose the hairstyle from the Four Tank-Men and a Dog TV series. He is always silent when he sees her. He won't say a word. Although she sees delight in his eyes.

It was almost eight o'clock so she started to get ready, because two hours is very little time to amaze everyone. And Paula liked it when the whole room's eyes were on her. Wojtek's girl was very slim, she could hardly find clothes for herself, because she was wearing a size thirty-four, but her bust did not fit very well. Everyone thought fake tits was another gift from her daddy. Paula did not care about these comments, she knew very well that this was what nature had given her. A smile, yes, made by a specialist. The veneers gave the perfect effect. Hair-style - hair extensions in the most expensive salon, but in the end the basis was her own. The rest is the result of heavy exercise in the gym with a personal trainer, plus a solarium and designer clothing stores.

In the house she had two wardrobes, a styling room with a few mirrors and all the necessary equipment. When, at her express request, they moved from Belarus to Krakow, her father made sure that she also got a large bathroom next to the bedroom. She was a spoiled only child, but she knew well that she would do well in life without her father. She gained a profession, hard work and several connections. She had what was called a charm to it - if only she tried, because she generally hated being polite to people. Now she only had to finalize her relationship with Wojtek. He was reluctant, but her mother explained to her that it had been so with men for a long time - it was difficult to convince them to marry. So she did not care about his doubts and did everything to convince him that in fact, he really wants to spend the rest of his life with her. The stares and slaver over her of other men at the sight of her made this task much easier.

Today she's going to be wearing that glamorous sequin gold dress. It highlights her tan and slightly bleached hair ends. She will go alone. There is no point in making yourself unnecessary competition. She would wait until midnight. Then Wojtek will be a little drunk and that's when all those morons from Pedagogical Univeristy will want to pick him up. They wouldn't have had the courage to do it earlier, Wojtek is definitely not their league. By the way, she couldn't understand how you could go to teacher school and earn a lifetime of two thousand a month? How would she pay the rent after such studies, visits to a beautician, hairdresser, manicurist, expensive dresses and shoes? Well, it's not a competition, but God helps those who help themselves - as her late grandmother used to say.

5

"Shall we get a beer before we leave? You know, to courage." Jarek was very shy.

It was the biggest obstacle in finding him a girl. He was tall, had dark hair and eyes, he did great in college, you could say he is gallant. However, in dealing with girls he became clumsy and closed. He couldn't break, take the first step. Wojtek tried to match him up throughout his studies. Unsuccessfully. All the girls finally decided that he was a good boy, but you can't pull him out of a sentence halfway through the date and wait for a kiss goodbye because he can't get together for a quarter of an hour. He didn't get drunk, but he seemed to feel better knowing that alcohol would relax him a bit.

"Sure. You're buying because you are crazy about the date!" Wojtek made fun of his friend, but he felt sorry for him that he had to go through it all from the very beginning. Getting to know, getting nervous, waiting for the news, longing... He had it already in his relationship behind him. Those monkeyshines, games, flirting... Although at the moment he realized that with Paula he had never reworked some of this package. He neither waited nor missed, nor tried too hard..."

"So?" Wojtek did not know what the question was. "Do I look good?" Jarek repeated.

"Look, in my fancy shirt, and from the best stylist in town - Paula, you must look... nice. But I don't know how much of my perfume you poured on yourself because I can barely breathe in your company." Wojtek did not blame him, but only wanted to tease. "Seriously, you will have no equal, especially when you give your famous hip movement on the dance floor." The boy started to laugh and Jarek hit him in his arm.

"We're leaving. Remember that there will be some of Marta's friends there, so you could be nice."

"And you, remember that I will be getting married soon and will live near Krakow with four children."

The boys were in a great mood, although Wojtek was on happy too much at meeting some history teachers who, desperate in their fifth year, are looking for a husband. He liked Marta because she was cool and didn't want anything obliging. At the party that Jarek mentioned, she even flirt with Wojtek, but he knew about the feelings of the roommate, so he dismissed the girl. He was afraid it might be the same today, but he was going to go out quickly and leave them alone. Maybe his roommate will get together and play a real macho. It would be good because he's a nice guy and he deserved happiness like nobody else.

"Where are they? Do we have to wait for them here?" Agnieszka was pissed, because the November air and her skimpy dress did not create a very good relationship. Anyway, she had a tendency to catch a cold for any reason, and the sun was long gone and it was getting unpleasantly chilly.

"Maybe we'll do this: I'll go with the girls to a pub, and you wait for your macho from AGH, okay?" Szczepan did not want to wait for latecomers. He admitted silently to himself that he didn't like these boys. Not that he was jealous, because he treated the girls as sisters, not as potential candidates for a wife, but in these losers he sensed the mania of grandeur and... the superiority with which they looked at him. The fact that he wanted to be a teacher made him worse? He was a social activist and an idealist. Well, it will somehow survive the meeting with great engineers. Although this one was even okay, just a little reticent.

"What about Marry?" Marta asked.

"Marry will arrive in an hour, because Kaśka remembered that she was supposed to give her notes to her friend. They just texted me," Aga explained.

"Okay, go. I'll come with the guys."

"You will come out for a desperate, who is extremely interested in their company... But that's just what I'm saying," Szczepan added.

Marta did not care about Jarek at all, but recently she was hitting assholes only, so she thought that for a change it is worth meeting this good-natured man and believing in men again. It will be difficult, but she also has to settle down someday. She couldn't imagine herself being a wife or mother, much less a classic hausfrau.

She dreamed of long journeys, exotic lovers... stop! She had to go down to the ground and Jarek was supposed to help her.

When the cheerful crowd was walking away, Marta noticed two boys in the distance. One is a well-known Jarek, a friend from primary school, who was in love with her. He was nice and calm. But she liked the latter. Divine... hair, eyes, silhouette. She failed once, but maybe today... But isn't he out of her reach? Until now, it had seemed to her that "such" guys could only be seen in color magazines. Yes, she definitely has to let go. She is a strong six, he is, without a doubt, a ten. Nevertheless, she quickly straightened her hair and smiled at them.

6

"How long are we going to stay here?" Marysia was irritated because they were only supposed to take the notes to her friend Kaśka, and it turned out that there was a party going on in the dormitory. She didn't seem to be going out.

"Let's stay until midnight and then join the historians, okay? Please, the boy I told you about is here... It's only two hours... The party on the market square is just going to start..." Maria couldn't refuse her, so she took a bottle of beer and sat somewhere in the corner.

It was crazy. The music was so loud she couldn't hear her thoughts. She only watched cheerful people running around her and others in costumes and makeup. It's good that in her dormitory, parties are held behind closed doors to rooms or in the kitchen at best, without disturbing others. Otherwise, she wouldn't have graduated from college, at least not with that average grade. Kaśka placed herself on the kitchen windowsill in the company of the boy she mentioned earlier. And Marysia began to remember again... The lakeside house, his soft hair and smile. So long had passed, but the images in her head were still alive. She dreamed that he would stand in the doorway and as if nothing had happened, he shook her hand. She thought about it so hard that she did not notice the row that took place in the kitchen and Kaśka, who waved her hands in front of her eyes and pulled her downstairs.

"You mean we're leaving?" Torn from the world of her innermost dreams, Marysia was slowly returning to reality.

"Are you even listening to me? I'm telling you that asshole offered me a quickie! What a clown! And I thought he cared about me! Sucker!"

"I told you to arrange the notes and go, but nobody ever listens to me..."

"I'm not listening to the talk now. Water over the dam. Don't say anything to me yet, let's go to the historians."

"As you wish, you are so touchy." Marysia hugged Kaśka and immediately all the tension disappears.

"Glad to have you, you know?" Kaśka whispered. "Even such the wisest and always perfect know-all lady!"

7

When Marta entered the club with her friends, Agnieszka was the most happy. It is true that she knew that her friend was interested in the higher one, but the smaller one was also not bad. In recent years, she has met many boys: at the university, in dormitories, at annual higher education students' holiday or at work. However, neither could meet her exorbitant expectations. Now she has realized that most of her friends in the year are in a stable relationship, are engaged or even married, and she is single. Perhaps it is not worth looking for a prince charming, but looking around and letting someone at least talk to you?

"I ordered a round of kamikaze. Let's drink for new acquaintances!" She winked at Jarek and picked up a glass with a blue drink.

"But I would rather drink for refreshing the older ones..." Jarek, in turn, eloquently looked at Marta's side.

"Let's drink for this and for this!" Marta was in an excellent mood, although she did not notice Wojtek's interest. He kept looking at his watch and the entrance. As if he was waiting for someone, or as if the company bored him completely. In doing so, he affirmed a rule that had been known for years, saying that unbelievably handsome men are either busy or not possibly a vain.

"Let's go dancing!" Agnieszka pulled Szczepan, Marta joined them and Jarek immediately ran after her.

Wojtek was bored. Not because he didn't like these people. He simply had completely different things on his mind now that were a little overwhelming. He drank a few beers but did not take an active part in their conversations, and he did not go on the dance floor. Confusion - that phrase best reflected his state of mind. It was close to midnight, and he knew Paula would be here in a moment. She always did. For five years she had been telling a story that she was playing with friends, but decided to check him out. It hadn't bothered him before, but in the perspective of living together... He realized that Paula was simply possessive. Not jealous, because jealousy is natural, and she transcends all limits. Checking his phone was the order of the day. He had to excuse himself for each female surname. Even when the hotline woman called, Paula resented him for flirting with her, and he wasn't doing it. He was laughing when a girl on the tram smiled, he knew that Paula was about to writhe around him, she would grab his hand, and if it was a pub, she would probably sit on his lap. At first it was even nice, now only irritating and tiring. If she comes in and I feel what I always had when I saw Svetlana, I will propose here. If not... I guess I'll have to have an honest conversation with her..., he thought.

He glanced for the hundredth time that evening at the entrance to the disco. She was there. She was giving her bolero to the cloakroom. Her arrival did not pass unnoticed by any of the men in the room.

She backcombed her hair and made a fashionable braid over her left shoulder, she was wearing a shimmering, short dress that beautifully displayed her long tanned legs. The teeth were so white. She waved to Wojtek, who nodded at her. When she went to see him, he already knew what he should do.

"Hi. You look like a million dollars," he began. She loved it when he stroked her. She was used to compliments - not only from her boyfriend.

"You know, my group and I were partying nearby. But I missed you so much that I decided to see what you were doing." He knew the fake well, all too well.

"Look, we need to talk about the future..." He tried to get it over with.

"In this place and right now?" She was surprised, but she thought that maybe this was the moment, so she decided not to be too fussy.

"Yes, because I think you deserve honesty. Maybe I was in a rush to confess, for which I apologize..." Wojtek started his speech.

Paula knew what he was up to. She looked down at her right hand, and on it - in spite of anger - she was wearing a golden, large ring that matched her evening creation. Fortunately, the nails - made the day before at the beautician's - looked phenomenal. After all, she will have to take a photo with the phone and immediately post it on Facebook so that everyone could share her joy. She listened to her boyfriend, but the hand she hid under the table to quickly get rid of the tinsel.

This was not how she imagined the engagement. Her friends talked about romantic dinners and weekend trips. One boy even took one to the Eiffel Tower and asked for a hand there. What am I going to tell them? That he did it at a disco? No sense. I will have to organize a trip on the weekend, preferably to Barcelona or Rome... I will say that he did it then... she made more plans in her mind.

"Like I said... you deserve the best. You are amazing. The combination of beauty and intellect... I could always count on you, you are a support..."

"Oh, Paula..." Jarek and the rest of the group got to the table, tired of dancing on the dance floor.

Paula was furious and didn't even try to hide it. These losers were going to spoil their moment. She couldn't let that happen.

"Hi! I am Agnieszka, this is Szczepan, Marta, and you already know Jarek..." Aga wanted to be nice, but met with a chilling look.

"Excuse me, but you interrupted something... could you go?" She muttered through her teeth, trying to fake a smile for a moment.

"No, no, sit down. We will go anyway. Excuse me, Paula didn't mean to be rude." It wasn't the first time he had to apologize for her, explain her... especially to his father. She was sometimes so cruel and insolent...

Wojtek's explaining did not change the group's opinion. They considered this girl conceited and mean. Who does that? Could you go? She wasn't even invited... Embarrassment - nobody said anything, but you could easily read their thoughts, running along the same track.

"It was nice. Have fun! Jarek, see you in the dormitory. Just don't go too far, brother!" Wojtek said goodbye.

Paula only took her little box that served as a purse, moved her head as if she was throwing away her hair (tied together today), and left without saying goodbye.

"Gosh! Such a cool guy with such a bitch!" Agnieszka started commenting on the situation.

"Yes. She's quite... hmmm.... original. But with Wojtek, when they are alone, she behaves completely different than you had the opportunity to see, which is why the guy is confused. He is going to propose to her." Jarek tried to repel the attack.

"What???" Marta was devastated. "Such a girl? I understand that she has a great body, but I guess you are looking inside, at least a bit... please, tell me that it is..."

"You can't put us in one sack. For many, such Paula is an ideal. Because you must know that she is not a dumb blonde. She really is all there, she is learning great. Coming back to the guys, most of us prefer an average girl who is sensitive, good, has a lot of warmth... right, Szczepan?" These words of Jarek made Marta see him in a slightly different light than before.

"As you can see, Wojtek does not need this heat too much." Marta made a strange face, waved her hand and said that this evening would be successful after all. Otherwise, Marry will kill her.

The discussion flourished when Marry joined the group of friends, and a few moments later Kaśka, returning from toilet. Their expressions showed that there were complications along the way.

"Hi! Finally! What stopped you? This is my friend Jarek." Marta greeted the latecomers first.

"Hi. Nice to meet you, Jarek, I've heard a little about you."

Marysia sent a knowing look at the boy, irritating Marta. "Guys, what I have to endure because of this Kaśka! First, instead of giving away the notes, we ended up at some birthday party in the dormitory, then a drunk first-year student started to approach me, Kaśka had a heartbreak, and now we could not catch any night-bus, so we walked from the town to here..."

"Marysia reported the course of the evening."

"At least you missed the impossibly irritating scene."

"This time Szczepan took up the story. "Hot chick came to spy on her boyfriend, who is Jarek's roomie, she made a scene for us that we were sitting at our own table, and then she left, turning on her heel... Do you feel it?"

"You have a nice roommate, since he chose such a woman." Marysia was catching up with drinking, not to impress someone, she just wanted to warm up after a long walk on a chilly night.

"I'm sorry, Wojtek is really fine. Only he has a rich biography and he seems to be a little lost..."

Upon hearing the name Wojtek, Mary almost choked on a kamikaze drink. Szczepan patted her back. She did not fail to comment on this:

"Apparently all Wojtek's have it! But enough about that, let's go dancing!"

And this time she was right. She returned to the dorm just before five. She only managed to bathe and eat breakfast. The lecture began at seven-thirty. They all looked like phantoms, but the professor was used to it. Szczepan had to leave the room several times and go to the toilet. The girls were knowingly glancing at each other and giggling.

8

When Wojtek and Paula left the premises, the boy decided to take the girl to him. Jarek will have some more space, so the room will definitely be empty. Paula preferred them to talk in Planty, but he stuck to his version. They finally got to the dormitory. The receptionist kept saying that if this lady is going to stay overnight she has to pay a fee. Wojtek denied this with the same stubbornness, which surprised the girl a bit. She imagined that once he proposed to her, they would love each other long and passionately... Eventually the receptionist backed down, adding that she would keep an eye on them.

"What was I saying?" It was getting harder and harder, especially since they stayed a deux.

"The fact that I am amazing and deserve the best... You don't forget such compliments." Paula's bad temper left and she focused fully on her boyfriend. She knew that she would tell about this moment many more times in her long and happy life. So she wanted to remember everything carefully, with the smallest details.

"That's why I let you go..." He thought that would do the trick.

Paula did not react to these words immediately. For a moment she thought she had misheard, so she decided to ask:

"What do you mean that you let me go?"

"I will not give you happiness, because I am not happy with you. I thought it would come eventually. That I will stop dwelling on the past because you will give me everything I need. Five years have passed and I don't feel anything. I like spending time with you, we're fine, we understand each other... but I don't love you. I won't spend my life with you just because it's comfortable. You deserve a fiery feeling, and I won't give you that..."

For the first time in her life, Paula was completely shaky. For the first time in her life, she also didn't know what to say. So she sat on Jarek's dirty sheets and stared at the floor. Finally, she decided to speak out on this issue that would ultimately decide her future.

"You're not gonna do this to me. I put too much heart into this relationship. I picked you up after she left you. I gave your life meaning. I pulled you out of the dimple. Thanks to me you went to college, thanks to me you function somehow. Without me you will go back to square one and life will slip through your fingers." She was composed and tried to use good arguments to influence the change of the boy's decision. But her voice was trembling.

"Paula, it's over. I don't know if I will feel sorry for myself or become a monk or an old bachelor. And honestly speaking, I'm not interested in that right now. But I know that I certainly do not want to be your husband and I do not see our future together. No apartment, no kids. I wanted to, I tried to digest it all, see with your eyes, I did everything to make it work. I wasn't going to let you down. It fails... I can't... I don't want..."

The last words slowly turned into a scream. He wandered around the room and made gestures. "I'll call you a cab. If you ever want to talk, call me. I will help you always if I can. Just get rid of your illusions. We will not be together. Never. I'm sorry." He sat down next to her and closed her hands in his. He kissed them gently as well, but it was a gesture... of friend.

Paula, realizing that she would not be able to do anything, lost her temper. She went off the deep end. She tore her hands from his embrace, punched him with all her strength in the face, and then screamed at the top of his throat:

"I do not want your help, I will not call you again! Also, don't count on my grief and tears! You won't see them! In your place, I have at least a dozen guys who would do anything for me! Only you are loss! And thank you, I won't take a taxi! I will take a walk to cool down from a donation of nonsense and crap I heard! You've wasted six years of my life! And I wish someone would waste six of yours! Also remember that any harm we do comes back to us. So I foretell you a long, unhappy, single life! Goodbye! You're an asshole! I will mail your things or cut them to pieces!"

That's why he didn't take her for a walk, he knew she was going to give him a gigantic scene. How well he knew this girl. She remained completely calm, but only for a moment. Although she was almost crying, she didn't shed a single tear. She is very strong... Relief - that was all he felt now.

He got rid of the big problem that kept him awake at night in the last months. Even if he is left alone... he prefers it than to being with someone by force. He lay down and fell asleep. He dreamed of a beautiful fairy-tale scenery. Well known to him. A lake shining in the sun, a wooden house and a girl combing her long hair. He ran to her, and when he had her at hand, he touched her shoulder, she turned to see... Paula. Awake, he glanced at his watch. He overslept the first exercises.

9

"Jarek is nice though..." Marta was in better shape than the others. Only she ate the entire dinner in the canteen. Szczepan, Agnieszka and Maria only ordered broth. "I think we will do one more group meeting, I will encourage him there, and then I count on a date..."

"Sounds nice. But why suddenly such an interest in a guy you have known all your life and so far has not impressed you?" Szczepan used to be sarcastic. Or maybe it's not sarcasm, but sperm solidarity. He, too, was once treated like a toy. He was a nice buddy, so you could hang out with him for a while and then throw him in a corner and find he was just a friend after all. So far, he has been going through a breakup with Nikola, although it's been six months now.

"You see, sometimes people pass other entire lives, only to finally one day discover that they have something more in common..." Marta tried to sound romantic.

"I would rather say that at a certain age a woman realizes that her life is about to expire and therefore she sees a man she despised as someone more, because she knows that perhaps no one else will be interested in her..." This time Szczepan exaggerated.

"It's rude. I go out before I say something nasty and have an argument. In that case, I'm setting us up with Jarek and his friends for Saturday. Except for Szczepan, if that's how he should approach it. Everyone is in Krakow, is anyone going home?" The company nodded in agreement as a sign that they would not miss the evening when a new feeling was to be born. In fact, they wanted her to leave, so that they could fight the giant hangover in peace and quiet.

"Only when this girl from Wojtek is coming, I will not come. Everyone despises me all week anyway: lecturers, ladies from the dean's office, the dormitory manager and even the lady from the bakery. I don't need to feel like zero on the weekend. Besides, she introduces me to complexes and picks up all the guys, because although she is taken, she is dripping with sex..." Agnieszka also wanted to hunt a guy, because Szczepan's words, although painful, were true after all.

"Okay, let me make a point that she should be gone. See you then," said Marta as she was leaving.

"You are angry?" Szczepan did not like conflicts.

"No, you idiot!" She smiled at him.

10

"Hi Michał. She's taking a shower because we were supposed to run as usual, but only one of us lasted more than fifteen minutes." Kaśka invited the guest inside.

Michał might have been less than a meter and ninety. Blond with short, spiky hair with pale green eyes. He was not fat, but rather muscular, but with little Marysia he looked like a bodyguard. No disco bully, nothing like that. Muscular, masculine. This is how Kaśka saw him. And always elegant. Today he was wearing tight jeans that made his ass look quite nice. Shirt with a double collar with a fine check pattern, emphasizing his eyes. A stylish watch completed the whole thing.

Marysia left the bathroom and saw a boy sitting on her bed. He measured her from the feet to the top of her head, she was embarrassed.

"I'm getting dressed and drying my hair. Wait for a while."

"All my life I've been waiting for you..."

As usual, she didn't know if he was serious or if he joked. Though she felt that even if it was a joke, there was a bit of truth in it. He was sitting there, and yet she felt nothing. Nothing. A man from the reception desk or a neighbor of four hundred and thirteen might as well have appeared in his place. The impression would be the same. It couldn't be love.

"I'm ready. Maybe we'll go to Błonia?" She suggested, because she could see Kaśka's ears sticking out from behind the book. "In this room, as you can see, there is no privacy!" She winked at her friend.

After a while, they walked among hundreds of people of their age, but also old men walking their dogs or roller skaters devoted to their activity adoringly. Błonia had it to themselves. Regardless of the season or the weather, crowds of people gathered. Maria knew the history of this place well. This great meadow belonged first to the nuns, who later turned it into a tenement house and gave it to the city. The area was neglected and turned into a huge swamp where people who died in times of epidemics were left behind. It was not until the beginning of the 20th century that order was laid here, and Krakow sports clubs were established.

"Listen... How is it with us?" Michał started quite inconveniently, but he was tired of it for a long time and finally he wanted to throw it out of himself.

"I was gonna ask you what you mean, but I'm not going to pretend to be stupid." Marysia knew that this conversation had to come sooner or later. She hoped it would be "later".

"As of today, I cannot answer you," she continued. "I realize that this answer is not very self-fulfilling. You graduate and want to know where you stand, it's obvious. But I don't know..." she was telling the truth.

"Fine. You may not know, some say you never know 100%... There is still a long time until the end of the academic year. Let's make an agreement that you will spend these months reaching the final decision. I do not hide my feelings. I've never even tried. I think you...

I'm in love and I'd like this relationship to develop... even if it will take a long time. I just need to know that I locate my feelings well..."

"You're very important to me. Really. In fact, I let you in as close as anyone else. Well, except..."

"Wojtek, I know..."

"Time will tell. And of course I agree. I'll tell you as soon as I'm sure..." She felt guilty. After all, she had nothing to accuse Michał of. He was with her, he looked after her. He did not lack grace, intelligence and sensitivity. He could be her husband, the father of the children. He could... but he wasn't... he wasn't... Wojtek... Only that nobody would be Wojtek. It's funny, because Wojtek had so many flaws. He was nervous, jealous, he had his moods. And what? Now she knew that it was not true that all love was the first.

"I'll go now. You seem to have to think." He tried to kiss her lips. In fact, it worked, but he felt as if it was forced and unnecessary for Maria.

He was right. She liked him but he wasn't physically attracted to her. He was polite, that is, boring and predictable. He cared for her, so she didn't have to try at all. He was sensitive, meaning not very masculine. What's wrong with her?

11

"I'm leaving. It seems that Marta has a feeling for me..." Jarek, refined and elegant, headed towards the door. "Hey, you don't look your best. All in all, it's been a one-day since you got rid of the "problem," and you're still somehow discomposed. Shouldn't you rather rejoice?" He was trying to make his glum roommate laugh.

"Thanks for your concern, but I guess that's how I experience parting with girls. Sitting and thinking. Although this is not the my dream. All in all, maybe I would go with you? I will drown my sorrows in alcohol. But I'm smelly and have nothing clean to wear."

"Sure, come on. But you've got some," he looked at his watch, "five minutes."

Wojtek took the fastest shower in his life. He poured into the perfume he had on hand. He grabbed one of the T-shirts lying on the chair... not very fresh, and... he was ready.

"I don't think I will be good looking today." He laughed. "Finally, I just want to go out somewhere and have a beer. I'm not going to pick up anyone. I'm telling you this so you don't try to match me up with those girls! I don't have the mood, man..."

"You know, whenever you don't intend, you get an opportunity... That's life," Jarek instructed as he entered the elevator. "But take it easy, nothing by force. I'll be busy with Marta."

12

"Well. We are all, so let's repeat the plan." Marta gathered all her group in the pub an hour before Jarek's arrival. They went to her favorite club. The girl loved Latin atmosphere. She was a great salsa dancer, which she intended to teach the boy. And her comrades liked mohito and capirihnia, so they did not protest. "First we sit together, then we all dance together, but when I come to the table, you suddenly leave us alone, okay?" She repeated her brilliant plan for the hundredth time.

"Every detail is well thought out. Masterpiece!" Szczepan mocked his friend.

"You better not speak up today! The plan may be simple, but you'll see how effective it will be. Jarek said he would try to get Wojtek out. If any of you were so kind and took him to the dance floor when I will be alone with my object, I would be grateful..."

"I am rather unsuitable, recently he totally blew me off," reminded Agnieszka.

"Marry? I can count on you?" Marta expected someone to support her in her actions.

"Remember that I'm here and I can hear you." Michał was also with them, and he did not like Marta's plan. Fortunately, Marry had scoffed it a bit too.

"Uh... yeah. Of course I will throw my hair over and raise my skirt, and then I will tease and coquette..." she joked. Michał threatened with his finger.

"Has anyone noticed that this is important to me? You can never be counted on! You must always make fun of everything. Lodge of scoffers!" Marta was irritated.

"Gosh! I'll take him to the bar, we'll order some drinks. Relax, you will have your Jareczek to yourself." 0Marysia did not like the nervousness that Marta introduced many times, so she wanted to cut the topic as soon as possible.

"They go, they go... Only calmly..." Marta, sitting in front of the entrance, saw Jarek and Wojtek.

The roommates entered the pub, gave their jackets to the coatroom and ordered a beer. Then they sat down at the girls' and Szczepan's table. They greeted everyone. And then it started."

"Don't we know each other?" Wojtek's heart was beating very hard, but he did not quite believe what he saw. "Because you remind me a lot of someone..."

"Hi, Wojtek..." she only managed to choke out, because the words stayed in her throat.

The friends stared at the two people who didn't say anything to each other, but were looking at every part of their bodies to each other, as if they hadn't seen each other for a long time. Michał was watching the scene particularly closely. He felt clearly uneasy, but he didn't want to interfere. At least not yet.

"Can you let us in? Because it's starting to get weird..." Marta was irritated with what they were doing. Her plan is coming to fall.

But they were silent. Wojtek gave Marysia's hand and asked to dance, because he knew that the others would not understand anything anyway. They weren't playing a slow song, but it it didn't matter. Wojtek hugged Marysia to him. After a moment of incredible tension, Marry tilted the head that had been resting on his shoulder until then.

"Will we get out of here?" she suggested.

"I was supposed to ask you about it..." At these words, she took the initiative and grabbed Wojtek by the hand and dragged him to the exit.

The boy only thought that he could shave himself and find some clean clothes. Jarek was right. The best thing comes when you least expect it. Marysia did not think at all. Neither about what will happen next, nor about the friend she has failed, about Michał sitting at the table.

"What are they doing? They ignored us and left us without saying goodbye?" Agnieszka was indignant. "Hey, that's not how it is done, really!"

"And I think I know what's going on..." Jarek didn't want to explain anything. Wojtek's look spoke for itself. It must have been love from years ago. "But I won't tell you anything, even if you torture me."

"Jarek, is this the boy she was connected with as a teenager?" Marta whispered in the boy's ear so that Michał would not hear

Only that Michał did not have to hear or ask anyone about opinion. He knew it was "this" Wojtek. She had never looked at anyone that way, and had never seen her act as spontaneously as she was right now. He was furious with himself, because it was enough for him to convince her to an exhibition today or to buy cinema tickets... She didn't want to go here anyway. But as always, he wanted to be fair to his friends from the year and not disappoint Marta. Well, he got an award. He already knew he had lost her. He hated this guy. He'd love to punch him with all his might, but that's not his style.

"I don't know, but this is a girl that Wojtek loves more than his life since high school..." Jarek replied and both with Marta knew what they had witnessed a moment ago.

The people quickly forgot about this bizarre situation, in fact, as soon as they played a hit of this fall, they all went to the dance floor and the topic died a natural death. Only Michał drank one beer after another and waited for his girlfriend anyway. He felt humiliated and devastated. However, he deeply believed, or maybe he was lying to himself that Marysia would eventually come back and explain everything to him somehow for the sake of all these years together. By mere respect for him. Finally, around four in the morning, completely drunk, he decided to leave the pub. As the last of their pack.

13

After leaving the place, Maria and Wojtek were not as bold as they were in the face of many people and loud music. They stood facing each other and looked at each other for a long time. The thought flashed through the girl's head that he had someone... that friends mentioned the last party... divine and conceited... was it like that? And she grabbed his hand, embarrassing... she doesn't act like that normally. What possessed her at all? But that's Wojtek. Her Wojtek...

Wojtek, in turn, did not allow himself to think that Svetlana - Marysia may be in a relationship. He considered himself the biggest lucky guy in the world at the moment, and he wasn't going to waste this opportunity. It was he who spoke first:

"You look wonderful. I didn't think you could be more beautiful than then... and yet... You are already a real woman..." He wanted to continue, but Marysia interrupted. She realized that he must have become a Casanova, since having a girlfriend, or even a fiancée, and he would give her such compliments here. It stopped the amorous fire.

"You know, it's already late. I'll go home..." She said it a little against herself, but she didn't want to be another easy prey for him. And he looked like someone who could have any girl. He grew into a man. He had a trendy hairstyle and was well dressed. Probably because of that cocky divine girl..

It better to withdraw than suffer later, like then...

"What happened? Are you kidding me?! Such a meeting and you just want to leave me? Again? No, I won't let it happen... Not this time." He was determined. The woman of his life stood before him. He knew that he would not let go, and if he had to, he would fight for her: with her boyfriend, with her and with whom else it would be necessary.

"Well. We are adults, and we always told each other everything directly. Wojtek, I know... I know you have someone... and I... I don't break relationships. I'm not that kind of girl..."

Wojtek smiled and was completely calm. It was just Paula. Not about him.

"Your friend has out-of-date data. Me and Paula are in the past. I broke up about a week ago because she wanted to build the future together, and I... I only live in the past. I can't get away from it, from the memories, from these days, from our days, from adventures, make... You may consider me a fool or a messed-up romantic. Except that I never forgot you. You're in my head all the time. You drill my thoughts. Each girl is just a pale imitation for me, and it doesn't grow up to your heels. I can, of course, be satisfied with a substitute, but for what? Svetlana... or actually Marysia... I want you and only you. Understand? You are the love of my life. Either you or no one else," he said in amok. He couldn't himself, though he wasn't gushing out on a daily basis.

But now he felt that the opportunity will not repeat itself. It's his to be or not to be. Everything had to be said, closed so as not to regret anything. He wanted to know that he had done everything he could to get her back.

"If all this is true, why didn't you find me?" Maria was extremely touched, but the whole situation seemed unreal to her. She felt as if she were in a strange somnambulic trance, not knowing if she was more awake or dreamed.

"You think I didn't think about it every day when I woke up? Except, as we both remember, you didn't want me to disturb you in finding yourself... You put it like that, right? And you know that I do not impose myself. Anyway, I knew we were destined for each other and we would finally meet. It had to be like that..." Wojtek at that moment had the answer to everything.

Maria stood in front of him and various emotions were accumulating in her - from indescribable joy, through surprise and amazement, agitation to panic fear.

"You will not say anything?" Wojtek was surprised by the silent attitude of Marysia. He would love to pounce on her and kiss her, but life is not a romantic comedy.

"What should I say? Everything seems simple to you. You are after broke up, you meet your old love and you think that it will work out on its own." The girl was a rationalist. Of course, she was glad that she met Wojtek and she would like everything to be as it used to be. But they were not seventeen years old anymore, they had to face the consequences of their decisions.

"But what's going to work out? Let's just give ourselves a second chance. So much. If you want it..."

"There is also Michał." This one sentence was enough to deprive Wojtek of a good mood and an optimistic look into the future. Now he knew that he had a real rival, maybe better than he, maybe love for him would be stronger..."

"Who is Michał?"

"It's a hard question. In fact, if I had known the answer, I would probably have had a wedding ring on my right hand." This remark stuck into Wojtek's heart like a dagger. "Michał is a cure for all evil, a comforter, a friend, an arm to cry. He is a support..."

"That's enough! You are doing that on purpose?" Wojtek was furious, but he tried to control his emotions. "You love him?"

"No."

"You love me?" He risked a lot, but also had a lot to lose at the moment. He had to know. If she doesn't love him, he will leave. He would leave her here... and be tormented for the rest of his life.

"Yes."

"Yes?" He couldn't believe what he had just heard. His eyebrows rose as did the corners of his mouth. His eyes began to sparkle and for a moment he looked like a little child who had just talked a parent over for another ice cream.

Mary, on the other hand, stammered out through her tears:

"I love you. I have always loved. It was only so hard for me with it all. I didn't tell you about it then, but I was so lost... I didn't know if I was Marysia or Svetlana. Is my house on the Świteź, where I spent my whole life... or in Zabierzów, where people are close, but still strange to me. I was struggling with my thoughts... Olga raised me, and now I am leaving her, repaying her in such a way... I felt like an abandoned child of Anna... I thought every minute since I found out about her, why did she leave me? I felt Belarusian, and I should feel Polish... It took me a long time to get inside myself and find my identity. I'm sorry... sorry."

Wojtek wanted to hug her, but he still didn't know if he could. He only put his arm around her and set her down on the nearest wall, slowly letting her calm down.

"Now you know who you are?" Wojtek noticed that she is finally calm... not like a moment ago.

"Yes." Marysia blew her nose and said firmly, "My name is Maria Lach, for friends Marry. I currently live in Krakow, but my family home is in Zabierzów. There are two of the most important people in my life. I am Polish, a student of Polish history. I am going to learn it and then teach it to others." It sounded confident and proud.

"And your father? Do you have any contact? I hear you didn't take his name." He was trying to be gentle.

"Yes. You see... the father sacrificed everything, I say it without the slightest exaggeration, he is still looking for Anna... His family didn't understand why he was doing it, so he is now divorced. I feel sorry for his wife, such a story happened to her. And my stepbrother, whom I have never met and probably never will. Stanisław must love my mother very much. That's why I don't want to be with Michał, because it would be like with my father. Reason is not the best advisor in choosing a partner for life.

"How many lakes are left to check?"

"There is Nieszczerdo left. It is the last one. Yesterday he called that he was staying with some granny. I'm glad it's over. This trip completely consumed him... I don't know if he will have anything else to come back to. I have no idea how he explained it at work... He should finally forget... You can't live like that, you can't."

"And you see, I do not agree. If Anna is the most important person he has met on his way, then he should look for her... She must be somewhere... And if he would be really happy only with her... Anyway, I understand him... Even if he finds her grave, he will be able to forget. Make a new life, otherwise I can't see it."

"I didn't know you were such a romantic..." Marry smiled and thought about how lucky she was to be here with him. "I'm so cold..." It's been a long time since they sat down on the wall.

"You're right. So... are we going to me or to you? Because we haven't finished our conversation yet..." He covered her with his jacket as he said it.

"Don't play games with me, Mr. Stożyński! Not to me, not to you. I know a quiet and 24/7 cafe not far from here. We'll be warm there, no one will interfere... and I don't have to worry that you will fling yourself at me." Marysia smiled.

And she was quite right. Wojtek was so tempted to fling himself at her. She would probably forgive him, but he didn't want to risk it. Anyway, he has just found out that the longer you wait for something, the better it tastes.

14

Wojtek and Maria spent the whole night in the cafe. By the time it started to dawn, they knew why they chose these and not other study destinations, marveled at the fact that they lived next to each other in dormitories, and had failed to meet for the past four years. Marysia told about her grandparents - about how they arranged her room together, how they experienced her father's divorce. Wojtek, in turn, mentioned that his dad met someone, but in the end it didn't work out, he talked about the nightmarish years in high school without her... about Alex's transformation from an idiot teenager into a perfectly normal guy. Finally, as they gathered to leave, the boy asked:

"Do you have any news from Świteź? You don't know how Olga and Anatol are doing?"

"No, I don't have any news, and how would I get it? Honestly... it's weird... but sometimes I miss them. I even thought that maybe in the winter session I will visit them... only for a few days... You see, there are moments when I feel a void, although it seemed to me that I closed this chapter. You think I'm crazy?" Marysia expected criticism from him.

"It's perfectly normal. This is your babysitter. And your... sort of... brother... If you want, we'll go together. I am going to visit my father, who somehow settles down in Belarus and carries out project after project."

"We'll see. I don't want to plan anything. So far, I'm glad you showed up. You're going to complicate my life a little now... but thanks to you I also got some answers to important questions..." She intrigued him and although she wanted to end it, he did not let her.

"Now that you've started... what are you going to do?"

"At the beginning I have to talk to Michał, give him his freedom, because now I am sure that I have nothing but great sympathy for him. Secondly, I would like to pass my exams on first terms, in some subjects I can do it soon, because I want to defend my thesis earlier, and the lecturers are even understanding. Finally, I have to visit my father. I feel that he will go crazy there without contact with someone he knows or loved. I have to explain to him that it's time to stop and go home."

"I still do not see one important thread here..." Wojtek said it half-jokingly, half seriously, but he expected the answer as seriously as possible.

"Ah, this thread..." Marry teased him like the good old days. "Well, if you say it's fate, let's see what comes out of our meetings. You can invite me on a second date..."

He said nothing, just settled the bill and led her to the dormitory.

15

The November weather did not surprise anyone. Marysia and Kaśka's window was dirty with stains. None of the girls had time to do the cleaning. Although time would probably be there, it was worse with willingness. Marysia wanted to earn as much as possible for the trip to her father, so she took all possible night shifts in the pub. Kaśka also worked, so their room looked like a mess. Wojtek suffered the most. Although he was currently doing an internship at one of the banks to facilitate his future start, he always found time for Marysia. She, unfortunately, couldn't find as much of it as she wanted. And he would like to spend every minute of the day with her. He felt that he had lost so many of those minutes already. Their meetings were usually held at Marysia's workplace. Wojtek sat at the bar and between one client and another he could exchange a word with his beloved. But just knowing that she was close that she wanted to have him with her, gave him enough joy.

Their dates were neither stressful for both of them, nor were they full of that strange tension when people were just getting to know each other. They didn't need the introductory stage to get used to each other again. After that one single night conversation, they knew that they were again the same couple who lived together, talked about everything and spent passionate moments surrounded by calamus. However, they were much more mature.

Wojtek, at some cold evening, asked her somewhere between Bagatela and Plac Inwalidów:

"You want to defend your thesis in March... Why the rush?"

"I would like to start another studies. I am hungry for knowledge that has been denied me for many years. There are still so many things that interest me... Well, but first I have to take care of my father. I want to be with him as long as it takes to get his affairs in order. And I am going to find a job and continue my education extramural."

"Where do you want to live after graduation?"

"Do you have any interesting proposition?" She stuck her hand in his pocket because she didn't take the gloves with her.

"It was supposed to be a surprise for some time... but since we have already started... I spend all the holidays since I started my studies at work. And not one that requires heavy thinking, where you are paid for your time with an appropriate certificate. Father wants to teach me to respect money, as he says. That is why I have been kneading biceps at a construction site in Belarus for four years, in three summer months. And so it turned out that a good sum was collected from this work, for which I bought a small apartment in Krakow, although judging by the travel time to the center, actually outside..."

"I'm impressed. I thought that these muscles were the effect of the gym, and here such a news... And I would live in this apartment... as who?" She was not sure if she wanted Wojtek to answer this question. She was afraid, and on the other hand, she wanted to hear the declaration.

"If you work on yourself a little more, and buy some curtains or decorations for your apartment... maybe even as... Mrs. Stożyńska."

They smiled and kissed each other as they turned into the alley leading from the Pedagogical University to the student campus. They were joking today, but both realized at the same time that, although indirectly, they had promised each other a life together. There was no longer any need for confessions or additional questions. They wanted to spend the rest of the days together. She only had to defend her thesis, find a job, throw the tenants from Wojtek's apartment and bring Stanisław back.

Marysia did not fully believe what had happened to her during the last month. Until recently, she did not know what to do with her emotional life, and suddenly she loves, she is loved, someone wants to marry her and that's not all, she too wants it the most in the world. The girls weren't such enthusiasts. Every conversation for some time has been something like this:

"We thought, and this is the opinion of all of us, aha and Szczepan, that you are more responsible and organized," Kaśka always started, but Aga and Marta nodded their heads.

"If you were with him, but you broke up anyway, maybe it would take a little longer to think about going back and going back like that. After all, you skipped a good few stages of acquaintance. You don't get married just like that!" For the first time Kaśka did not understand the decision of her roommate.

"I don't often have the opportunity to admit Katarzyna is right, but however, this time I really agree with her," added Szczepan.

"Marry, take your time. I know that with Michał was not exactly this, but gosh... you are already like a couple. Maybe you will think about it..." Marta did not want to spoil her friend's mood, but she was worried about her.

"I can really see that you have revive. That you are so happy now. And good. Just think it all calmly and answer the question, is it not only temporary, like then in high school..." Aga commented.

Marysia was not interested in this at all. She listened to the voice of her heart. Nothing else mattered now. She knew they cared for her, but if they only knew about the spell, about Olga, about all this, they would understand for sure. But now they must trust her.

16

"Dad? What are you saying? I can hardly hear you! I'm fine. Yes, I'll have a few days, but not too much. I could talk to the thesis advisor... For a week or two? Hmm... I'm writing a thesis... Well... don't be nervous. Why the rush... What you mean that you find? But are you sure? In the cottage by the castle? One, yeah? I will come... at least for a while... maximum until Christmas... but I don't know if I will make it... okay. I'll buy a ticket for Friday. Połock, and then Nieszczerdo. Well. Be careful..."

They met in front of her college. It was cold so they decided to move to the college cafeteria on the corner. On the way, she did not want to say anything to Wojtek. After they sat down with the sour rye soup and dumplings at the small table, she began:

"I talked to my father. He was in some kind of amok... He ordered me to come as soon as possible..." Marysia was not delighted and you could feel it, even when you didn't know her very well.

"Now? In the middle of the term? How are you gonna do it? And why at this point?" Wojtek was apprehensive, he knew how hard the girl works for her success.

"I have already talked to the thesis advisor and I will simply miss a few meetings, and I will pass the exams instead of first date in the session, in February. Father claims that he found mother..." She broke off and she watched her boyfriend's reaction closely.

She didn't know what to think about all this herself. Maybe father had completely went haywire, the distance, the loneliness, and the obsessive desire to find Anna had done their job. What if he's right? Somehow she couldn't let the thought come to her mind.

"Did he tell you how he found her?" Wojtek remembered the situation from years ago. It was about her mother too. But then he said too much. He didn't want to do it a second time in his life. Once the reaction to the news of the discovery of his mother had ended his acquaintance with Marysia. So he chose his words so as not to offend her by accident.

"He just said that he rented a room with an old woman who lived just outside the Castle of the Nieszczerdo, near the lake. It is she who claims to have seen the woman from the photo he showed her. Not only that, the granny is convinced that the she lives in the lake, because there is no other house there..." Although it was about her mother, when she said these words, Marysia felt that chills were going through every part of her body. On the one hand, she wanted so much for Stanisław's confession to be true, on the other, she did not want to expose herself to unnecessary disappointments and another painful news.

Wojtek knew he had to show her the way...

"Then you must go. If that's a false lead, you'll be back after a few days. If something turns out to be the case, I know you can handle the exams later. If you didn't listen to your father now, you would always feel remorse and feel that maybe you missed meeting with Mother."

This is another thing that captivated her about this new, older Wojtek. Support and wise advice he was throwing out. And that this time he said what she expected so much.

"Do you want me to come with you?"

"Yes, but only for a few days. One of us has to take care of education and apprenticeship so that the Stożyńskis and the Stożyński's children have something to eat. She turned it into a joke, but she didn't really want him to subordinate his affairs to her confused life again. She will go there, she will probably find nothing and they will come back together.

"If that's how you put it, I won't argue. We will visit the fathers, if you need me, I will travel from Nowogrodek to Połock and find this lake. If not, I'll be back and meet you afterwards. Okay? When are we starting?"

17

They only took a few sweaters, two pairs of pants, and warm jackets. They expected that when they set off on Thursday evening, they would be back in Krakow on Monday at the latest. Marysia's grandparents were not delighted with the idea, but they did not know the real cause. Anyway, explaining that the father needed support finally convinced them. It was perhaps not the noblest of them, but recently they have slightly changed their attitude towards Stanisław. It seemed to them that he completely ceased to care for Marysia. He left and suddenly contact with him seemed to have broken off. After all, he and Marysia had so much to catch up with, to discuss. This girl really needed his support, while he escaped. And that thing now. Is she supposed to support him? After all, Marysia is finishing her studies soon, she will have to think about a job, an apartment, maybe getting married. Did Stanisław meet Michał at all? They couldn't remember, but probably not. And now it is he who needs the support, destroying her plan that she has devised so carefully. They were not delighted about it. And Wojtek also appeared. Marysia's father found out about it by phone.

Meanwhile, Stanisław, in all his takeover of Anna's case, thought that this good boy was so much in love with his daughter. Almost like he in Anna. Except that that story ended tragically. He didn't want to experience it for the second time with Marysia.

What if Wojtek wants to take revenge on her? What if he just wants to pay her back for the harm she has done to him? He was afraid of this return, but he had to trust her and observe everything from a proper distance. He knew his daughter - she grew up to be a responsible and thoughtful young woman. She will definitely be fine this time.

"Just take care of yourself and let Wojtek look after you. And don't sit there too long because you're on the run-up to finish your thesis!" Grandma shouted to lovers leaving by train.

"Don't worry, I'll make sure that she comes back to writing as soon as possible!" The last word did not seem to reach the Lachs.

Jan gave Maria his arm and they headed towards their white house. The story of Marysia's return to Wojtek made her grandmother extremely happy. The woman accepted it like another page of a beautiful romance that happens so rarely in our life. Grandpa did not fail to have a lengthy conversation with... Marysia. He didn't have to with the boy. He knew every detail of their separation from years ago, and they talked about it with their granddaughter more than once. He wanted to hear from her that she was confident in her feelings so as not to hurt two men at the same time - Michał and Wojtek. He was, however, calm, as he watched from the side how Marysia underwent a great transformation. How she gets to know herself, her roots, and with what enthusiasm she asks him about the smallest details of the history of the country in which she lives and the family she has found.

Waving goodbye to her, he was waving not that insecure and lost teenager who was several years ago in the same place and with the same boyfriend in front of their white house. He waved a confident and well-behaved woman who was about to start a family and start an adult life. He smiled.

18

The journey was quick. They constantly talked about what could happen and what Marysia should prepare for. They remembered Olga's spells, disenchantment. They also wondered if Stanisław could persuade Anna to come back. But what return? If she chose the life of the rusalka herself, she would always return to the bottom of the lake. Would Stanisław settle down for her in a total remote area? Would he suspend his job? These and similar questions prevented the two young people from getting bored while traveling by train. Marysia took an active part in the conversation, but somewhere inside her only thought was that she really didn't want to go back there. She was afraid to go back to the things she had closed long ago. To places that were associated with pain and disappointment. Finally, she did not want to come back, because she was afraid that somehow Belarus would consume her again and would not let her go... After all, as Wojtek said, there was a void somewhere inside her.

The moment came when Marysia changed into another wagon, going to Połock. From there, her father picked her up, fearing that nothing bad would happen to her daughter on the way.

As she left the wagon, she noticed a silhouette of someone who looked like Stanisław. As she came closer, she barely recognized the figure of her father. He was unshaven and his hair was shoulder length and very greasy. He was wearing a coat and gloves and worn shoes.

She was ashamed of, but she thought for a moment that he looked like a tramp. This thought was replaced in a moment by concern and guilt... If she were here, she could take care of him... And he was left to fend for himself...

"I'm so glad to see you! I missed so much..." He threw himself on her neck as if he were a child. A tear ran down his cheek. "My dear, my daughter. Sorry for seeing each other so rarely... You probably think I'm crazy, but you'll see for yourself... I'm taking you to Polina first. You have to meet her. Then you will judge with your objective and more rational eye whether what she says has any sense... You will understand it better than me... because she herself... you know..."

"I know. Let's go," she agreed, although she didn't want to go back to what was already far behind her. She was afraid that the awakened memories would not be forgotten for a long time and would confuse her, so orderly for several years, life.

19

The landscape of Lake Nieszczerdo and its immediate surroundings did not differ much from what Marysia was so well known. Świteź, however, was mainly surrounded by meadows and thickets, while the place where they found themselves resembled a great forest, with a huge blue eye in its center. The tall trees and the water pouring in small streams into the forest and the great protruding tree roots scared Mary a little. She remembered clearly that Olga was afraid of the demons living in similar places. This great forest, the sounds of which only convinced the girl about the existence of creatures inhabiting it, caused the heart to beat faster. The lake itself attracted no less attention. Compared to Świteź, which was small and could be circumnavigated very quickly, the Nieszczerdo looked enormous, beyond human sight. You could hide here for years and remain unnoticed, she thought. There was also something sinister about the lake. Świteź seemed transparent, blue, innocent... Here, all you could see was its distorted reflection emerging from navy blue, almost black water. If someone bent too much... Anatol would have a lot to do here. One hand movement and no trace, no movement on the surface of this dark lake. Polina's hut was slightly larger than Olga's, but just as simple in its construction and equipment. Maria wanted to know if the old woman was łojma, but her first impression did not indicate that.

Previously, she lived with her husband in one room, the other - equipped with a bed and a small table with a chair - was intended to receive guests or tourists who had gone astray somewhere nearby. The husband died last year and she was left alone then. She was over seventy but seemed to be a very cheerful and resourceful person. Polina's house overlooked the ruins of a nearby castle.

"Few of the holidaymakers who come here know that this beautiful building is almost five hundred years old. It was built by the dangerous Tsar Ivan, when he fought a war with Poland. It was supposed to be an expression of his power and proof of the final takeover of the Połock land by the Russians." Polina, noticing Maria staring at the ruins, felt obliged to explain her history of the place where they were located.

"I'm interested in history, that's true. But I'm more curious about where you know my mother from?" The girl didn't want to waste any time. And although she had no intention of doing so, the sentence she had just said sounded rather rude.

"Your dad showed me a picture of a woman. At first, I didn't recognize her face. But when he stopped at my place and started to tell her story... something crossed my head. We had our little ritual with my husband." She sat down on the chair, handed Marysia a cup of tea, and slowly told her story.

"Every evening while the days were still warm, we followed our regular route through the forest. We tried to always return home before dark so as not to expose ourselves to forest demons."

"Forest demons? I have not heard of such." Marysia pretended she had no idea what she was talking about. She was well aware that the water wraiths could not be the only such creatures, and she remembered stories told by Olga, but she wanted to know as many details as possible.

"Yes my dear. If you meet a lesawik, you must make him laugh quickly in order to survive. There are also błędnica and somewhat nicer dobrochoczy. But I don't want to bore you right now, much less scare you. Anyway, one day we were leaving the forest when it was already very dark. That's when I saw her..."

"Who? You mean my mother? Since it was already after dark, and you are not the youngest... you could be wrong..." Marysia did not believe that finding her mother would be so real.

"Child, for the first time in my life I saw a beautiful woman who almost walks, not swims, on the lake. It was definitely a demon. Of course, I didn't see the color of her eyes or the shape of her mouth, but she had hair like your mother's and such a sad look that is remembered..."

"Have you only seen her once? And when exactly was that?" The girl asked, still not accepting that the woman's words might turn out to be true.

"The first time I saw wodja two years ago, but after my husband's death, I used to continue my walks in the forest and several times I happened to meet her right next to the lake or heading towards it."

She smiled but avoided talking. So I didn't ask any questions. I was afraid to get into her black books. You never know if there is some undine around in the company of wodja, and there is no joke with them..." She broke off. Marysia knew this all too well. "We last saw each other last week. Then I looked at her closely... It was the woman in the photo... And the strangest thing... though the photo was taken over twenty years ago, the woman hasn't changed at all. I would say that she is your sister rather than your mother... It reassured me that it was wojda."

The told story shocked Marysia. And although she promised herself not let anyone interfere in her newly regained life a few years ago, it seemed inevitable now. She hasn't missed her mother lately. She had a grandmother, a father and a grandfather. There was also Wojtek. She didn't even know what it was like to have a mother, so she couldn't miss that feeling. But she wasn't going to lie to herself - she wanted to meet her, talk to her get her support... Sometimes she watched programs about adopted children and felt a bit like them. They had wonderful foster families, new parents who raised them in love, but the thought that there was someone out there who would answer the most difficult questions was too strong to abandon it.

And with this most important question, both in adopted children and in Marysia, there was - why did you leave me? What did I do that made you leave me and walk away?

She turned to her father.

"How do you want to meet her? Or maybe you have already met? What are you gonna tell her? Do you believe she will want to talk to you? It's been so many years... Is she even herself?"

"I didn't want to do anything without your participation. Anyway, I've only been here for a few days. I'm going to go to the lake before dark and wait. To tell her everything that I have accumulated over the years. If she won't listen to me, I'll go away. However, I must be sure that I have tried..."

She knew exactly what he was talking about. His plan was trivial, and actually the only one that came to her mind. They will meet, turn a few sentences into three, and it will be what will be. Nothing by force. She is already an adult woman and since she has been coping without her mother in the last, most difficult years, she will do well now. She just wants to know the truth and her motivation.

20

The following days were very similar to each other. Wake up, breakfast, a walk in the forest and wait for Anna in the evening. The weekend passed, after which Marysia was to return home, but her mother did not show up. The girl began to consider Polina a cheat who - thirsting for companionship - wanted to keep them a little longer. Anyway, she liked Nieszczerdo. Though it initially frightened her, she now thought of it as a bottomless well with many secrets. It was reminiscent of the times when it was impossible to live without a lake. She disgusted that Svetlana, who lured defenseless men into the water, but - although she did not tell anyone about it - she would like to feel this enormous physical strength, the power to decide the fate of others. It was something that could not be put into words. Wojtek. She had to call him, not think about stupid things.

"Drive. No, I don't have to, but I want to. Don't think it's the father's influence. Yes, I spoke to her and she is convinced. A few more days, two weeks at the most. Absolutely. We will meet in Krakow. I promise. Yes, I know... Me too... I love you. Do not worry. Bye."

Wojtek was returning to Krakow alone. He was afraid that if he left her here, he might lose her again for some unknown reason. However, he did not want to meddle in their family affairs.

21

It was Tuesday. Exactly two days after Wojtek's departure. She lurked with her father again after dark on the edge of the forest, right by the lake. The moon has reached its fullness. There were a lot of stars in the sky, and somewhere in the distance they heard the voices of forest creatures, it is not known what origin. The landscape was beautiful. Marysia pondered for a moment the power of nature around them. How many secrets was she still hiding from them? How many creatures do people still do not know, living in the belief that they are the only creatures on the earth? And yet there was this great vault above it, in the distance you could see the cultivated fields, now sleeping and gathering strength for the hot summer. There were also meadows, swamps, peat bogs... If a demon lived in each of these places, it could turn out that people constitute only a small part of the population. She listened to the silence she missed so much in the dormitory, in the buzz of the university, in the laughter of her peers. Now she was one of them, but she only felt really free in nature.

They were both here today. Resigned and doubting. And then the bad streak was broken. In the all-encompassing darkness, they suddenly saw a figure moving in a fluid motion from one end of the lake towards its center. She was walking, or maybe she was swimming right next to them, but she didn't notice that anyone was watching her.

Completely ordinary, but she got mysterious shine. She was smiling to herself. She looked like... Marysia couldn't find a comparison until she finally found it. She looked like she was in love. She had dark, long hair - just like her. She was slim and - as Stanisław whispered - "nothing has changed". As it soon turned out, she did not smile to herself, but to the beautiful young man who met her from the other end of the forest. Marysia was impressed by the boy's beauty. He could be no more than twenty-five, dark complexion, dark-haired, with almost black eyes. He looked a bit like Latin or person of mixed race... He had a flawless complexion and fine stubble that made him manly. Dressed quite simply - in a T-shirt and cotton pants, he gave the impression that he was not from that era. Eventually, at the edge of the lake, they hailed each other passionately and then walked away, kissing constantly and never tearing away from each other.

Marysia's father was almost sure.

"All clear. Your mother fell victim to Latawiec... For Mary, the spoken words had no good explanation. Latawiec? She did not know if she understood it well, although the Polish language had no secrets for her anymore.

"What Latawiec? And why a victim? She looks incredibly happy. She just fell in love. She has the right to do so, so many years have passed... And the guy, sorry, I don't want to upset you, he's unearthly..."

"Just to know, unearthly. A very good word. Let's get out of here before they see us.

I'll explain everything to you if Polina confirms my assumptions. We won't do anything today, we have to prepare ourselves thoroughly for the next meeting." Father sounded somehow strange, but you felt that new strength had entered him. He, too, had that weird expression on Anna's face. It was the face of someone in love.

Marysia did not want to leave. He had to grasp her arm so hard it almost hurt her. And she just wanted to lie there for a while longer and enjoy the view of this beautiful woman who was indeed very much like her. Eventually, she succumbed to her father and, deeply disappointed, returned to the cabin by the lake.

22

They returned in the middle of the night, Polina was asleep. So they lay down, but Marysia could not sleep. She drifted around the room like a shadow until she finally decided to get some air. She sat down on the front steps, it was cold. She exhaled through her mouth, forming a cloud of vapor. If it were still wojda, now she would have to rest at the bottom of the lake. What her father said puzzled her. He had to talk to Polina and hence this today's hypothesis. Anyway, he always said that he was interested in the demonology of the Slavs. Suddenly the girl heard something like a creak. She looked around and shouted:

"Is anyone here?"

But no one answered. Despite the fact that Polina's hut was several hundred meters from the forest, Marry, frightened, decided to go back inside. In the morning, they all sat together at the kitchen table. Polina was not as good a cook as Olga, but she did her best to make her guests feel at home. For breakfast they served draniki with sour cream, kvass with mint, and for dessert, jelly made of frozen forest berries. The guests ate the prepared meal culturally, thanked, they wanted to start a series of questions that torment them. Marysia started washing the dishes, and Stanisław presented his theories, quickly finding support from Polina. Then he started flipping through the book he carried everywhere with him, while the woman told Marysia story of a demon called latawiec, because the girl apparently didn't understand anything.

"You see, as I said, in places close to nature there are always a lot of demons. Latawiec is one of them."

"Okay, I know that. How can we be sure that we are dealing with this particular demon? What is the danger for people on his part? Because every demon threatens them to some extent. How do you even become Latawiec? What powers are gained then?" Marysia could not contain her curiosity, especially since it was about her mother. And she realized that now that she was only human, it would be difficult for them to fight someone much stronger.

"When a man died young and suddenly, he could turn into Latawiec with the proper rite. As with the rusalka it was eating a lobelia, with Latawiec it was grabbing something that was sticking out of the sky. It was believed that latawiec was shooting stars. Of course, you had to know the right spell, which, when uttered at the time of death, gave you a chance of transformation."

"I don't understand how you can grab something from the sky? What would that be?" Marysia wanted to know the details so as not to be surprised when developing the action plan.

"It could have been a branch from a tall tree, a spider's web hanging from a high, which is easy to find in the forest, especially in autumn. Some say that the dying person could also have caught the bird... There are many beliefs. I pass on to you my grandmother's words.

To be sure and clear, you would have to ask Latawiec."

"Well, and what happened to such boys after death?"

"They are very interesting demons. Usually they find married or already occupied women nearby. They cast a spell on them, but it is not easy to resist them, because they have an extraordinary beauty.

Once they lure their victim, she has no chance. It is said to be losing her mind and senses. Until someone brings her out of this state, she will be surrendered to her bridegroom..." Polina finished the story, looking at the worried faces of her listeners. She knew, but did not tell them that they would have to fight a difficult fight for Anna's soul. But she knew someone who might have given them, ways to win this fight.

"How do we get her back?" Stanisław was eager for action. He had spent so much time searching for his first and, as he admitted in one of his sincere conversations with his daughter, his only love, that he was not going to waste any more time.

"I know little. My grandmother always said: carry garlic with you so that Latawiec does not carry you. Except that Anna is already in the possession of the demon. You guys have to carry the plant in order not to succumb, but what will help... I have no idea. We can only consult a book of spells. There is one woman who they call the witch. She lives half an hour away. I'll go her tomorrow first thing in the morning and I'll try to bring you a book or any necessary tips."

"We will be very grateful to you, Polina. We have to get Ania back. Especially if she loses years here without her will and knowledge." Hope entered Stanisław.

Marysia was not such an optimist. She couldn't sleep. Another sleepless night in this place at the end of the world. She left the house again with a cup of warm milk. She didn't want to wake anyone up.

So what if she met her mother today if she couldn't have a word with her? So what if she might see her tomorrow when she is under the influence of a demon and won't even recognize her? Or maybe she will know and in a moment forget? She doesn't know how it works, but it hurts her immensely. Later, she wondered what it would be like to have a mother who looked like a twin sister. Will she break down and be able to speak to someone so young as to her mother? Will she have a chance at all? It was all more confusing than Marysia had thought before. At one point, she felt the strange feeling that she was being watched again. She did not want to draw attention to herself, but she tried to see her pursuer. She strained her eyes to see a pair of eyes at the edge of the forest, under a tree. Shiny, bright, penetrating. She did not take her eyes off them, trying to identify their owner. She failed, and the eyes vanished from sight. Was it Latawiec? And she didn't take any garlic with her! No!

The last thing she needed to share her mother's fate. It would kill her father. She went into the kitchen, peeled a clove of garlic and smeared it on the backs of her hands, knees and forehead. Only then she felt relief and a relative sense of security.

Wojtek called and woke her from sleep, which she actually fell into only in the morning. She didn't tell him about the newest discovery. She felt it would be better if they tested their hypotheses to be true. Besides, she didn't want him coming here now. He was supposed to study, give tests and think about the future. Their common future. During the telephone conversation, she sounded quite natural, so she did not arouse the boy's suspicions.

It was already eight o'clock. Polina went to visit her friend, Stanisław was still asleep. Marysia decided to collect her thoughts. She took garlic with her, as Polina had told her to. The forest looked mysterious at this time, but not sinister. That is why she directed her gaze there, and then her feet.

She walked slowly and lazily, studying the unfamiliar plants and listening to the birds sing. During the day everything looked different. Beautiful, innocent and inviting. The trees were tall, the fog was about half of them. You could see winter was approaching.

Gray and dim green dominated. There is nothing left of the colorful autumn leaves and the smell of mushrooms. Suddenly, looking up, instead of straight ahead, the girl screamed and fell into a ditch covered with earth. She got scared because the ditch turned out to be quite deep. Before she felt severe pain in her right leg, she remembered some books, maybe from The Knights of the Cross, that bears were caught in such traps. And then she realized that not only she would not get out of here any time soon, but she might also expect some not very pleasant company. She was scared.

After some time passed and the first post-traumatic shock, Marysia realized that the pain in her leg was probably bone fracture. It was too persistent for dislocation, and there was no sign of a sprain. Anyway, she's not a doctor. In addition, she did not take the phone with her, but probably would not have mobile phone coverage here. All she had to do was sit and wait for rescue. This one came only hours after the incident.

23

It was already quite light, the day was sunny. The sun fell into the forest through the cracks in the crowns of trees, which had already thinned before winter. The imprisoned girl thought about how much work she had left, and how little time she had left. She is stuck in a ditch in the middle of the forest, instead of copying excerpts from articles and reading history books. And now she will be using crutches. Peak of dreams. Below, all she could see were worms and roots. So she looked up once more and was surprised to see a beautiful, big deer. She didn't scare it, and even though she was staring at him intensely, it didn't take its eyes off her. How did she know those eyes? She already knew it was it who watched her at night. She told it her story:

"Yes, I know... I'm an idiot. Well, that's how it is swinging in the clouds. But don't be afraid. My father will start to worry and will come to my rescue in the company of Polina, who knows the local forests like her own pocket. Anyway, I didn't get very far, so they'll find me very soon. Right? And by the way, you are beautiful... and I think you have rabies, since you are not afraid to come so close to people..." She broke off, because the deer disappeared.

Marysia continued to devote herself to her monologue, it encouraged her in this rather uncomfortable situation. Suddenly someone grunted eloquently above her head.

She immediately thought that it was the father who expressed his displeasure. She was wrong. The sun dazzled her, but she noticed a huge man with red hair and freckled skin. He had big hands and a friendly expression on his face. He looks like he was made to save women in trouble, she thought. Then it occurred to her that she might be dealing with another latawiec, so she gripped a clove of garlic tightly in her hand. She felt the sticky juice on the back of her hand. Finally, a low but warm voice broke the awkward silence:

"Miss please." He held out a long stick to grab onto it. She wrapped herself around it, which looked rather clunky. The man brought her to the surface with one stroke of his hand. His strength and dexterity amazed her. It was as if he grew up in the woods and worked hard, physically, of course. Or... there was another possibility.

"Thank you, sir. I don't know what I would have done if it hadn't been for..."

He didn't let her finish that awkward thank you.

"...If it wasn't for the deer. It brought me here. I am a forester. So you can say that I am created to save such beautiful women in forest trouble." When he said these words, she felt at least strange. It was as if he was reading her mind. "And please do not call me sir. I think we are of a similar age. Of course, you look much more attractive than me, but it's normal for women..." He smiled and Marysia seemed that he winked. There was something fascinating about him.

On the one hand, the appearance and strength of a man, on the other hand, carelessness of a boy. She didn't even try to lie to herself. The woodsman caught her eye.

By the way, I'm lucky with cool guys, she thought.

"Now an unpleasant thing. Leg..."

"You think it's broken? It hurts a lot, but I don't know anything about it. My father is a doctor..."

"No. Looks like a twist. You're in luck because I'm also a pretty self-educated osteopath. Don't worry, I won't hurt you and you will surely be relieved."

"You intend to..." Marysia did not manage to finish her sentence once again, when her new acquaintance made her foot take a natural position with one move. "Ouch!" She gave vent to her emotions.

"You're welcome... I don't remember your name..."

"Marysia... ouch... And... yes... thank you... although it was not pleasant..."

"Marysia, the time is coming for pleasure..." He stretched out his big hands and the girl was already drowning in his arms.

She blushed and felt extremely uncomfortable. Not because a stranger carried her out of nowhere or why, but because she liked it very much...

24

It seemed to her that she had spent several hours in his arms, and yet it was only a dozen or so minutes. He did not take her to Polina's house, but to his hut deep in the forest. It's strange because she wasn't afraid at all. She didn't know the man, the forest was full of demons, yet she felt safe and - for some reason - she trusted this giant. Yes, he was very strong, she could see his muscles flexing under his shirt as he carried it in his arms. His face was sun-drenched, with numerous freckles, even though the Queen of Winter was almost there. A few scars on his hands - probably from hard work. It's impossible to hide... the forester is handsome in his own way... - she thought, staring at him.

"I see that you are not embarrassed at all?" He said.

"What?" She had no idea he noticed.

"Oh, Marysia, is it nice to look at a shy boy who is very confused by this behavior, especially when his perpetrator is such a beautiful young woman..."

Marysia blushed again and hid her embarrassment by turning her face away.

"You didn't tell me your name," she tried to change the subject, as she felt the man intimidate her more and more.

"Leszek. Lesław. Lech. You can choose your own language version."

"Don't you feel lonely being here alone, away from civilization?" She couldn't stop her curiosity.

"And how do you know that I don't bring another beautiful girl here every day to save her life and then expect a decent thanks?" It was impossible to read from his gaze whether he was joking or serious.

Marysia was concerned about it. Only then this seemingly reasonable girl thought about it. Polina warned her about the demons. Probably he is one of them. Not enough for the father to remove a spell from the mother and now from her. She was stupid... What if he hurt her?

"I'm sorry, I think I'll... just leave..." She tried to get up when she felt a piercing pain in her leg.

"Marysia, I was joking... Don't be afraid, please... And wait, I have to immobilize your leg. I just wanted to make you something to eat first, after all, you spent some time without a meal. Look, I'm not a monster. I've never hurt anyone, and neither will you. Please believe me, I am completely harmless." He seemed worried, it calmed her down.

They entered Leszek's forester's lodge. It was a combination of his office and home. She was away from the hustle and bustle of civilization, in the middle of the forest. Marysia felt very relaxed here. Peace and quiet, contact with nature, a perfect place to rest, she thought.

It was certainly possible to forget about the problems of everyday life here. The cottage was wooden, painted with dark orange stain. Through the window you could see the feeders for animals, prepared in advance for winter. Inside, it was dim, only the crackle of logs burning in the fireplace could be heard. There was a large couch in front of the fireplace and a small wooden table.

The girl sat on it, but she turned her back to the heat and watched the man bustle about the kitchen. It was all one whole. The kitchen, desk and corner by the fireplace, cleverly separated, created a romantic and warm atmosphere. The lack of a woman's hand was not visible there at all. No trace of dust, scattered clothes - as it happened in the house on Świteź, when she moved in with Wojtek. Everything had its place here, the house was modestly, but tastefully furnished. Warm carpets, paintings depicting nature, although not in her style at all, made an impression on Maria. After a while, the sound of cracking wood began to emanate from the tiled stove, and the water placed on it began to boil. Soon they ate a delicious soup. On the eye of Marysia - mushroom soup.

"How did you get here?" Marry asked question after question, feeling an irresistible urge to get to know him better. It was close, as if it were at hand. Dressed in a green shirt with the sleeves rolled up and similar pants. She did not know if it was his private clothes or the uniform required for work in this position.

"Hmm... I haven't really talked to anyone about it. But also another thing

So the interlocutors are missing. But to the point: about four years ago, my buddies and I came here for camping. I was twenty-one at the time and had just finished my undergraduate studies in forestry. We were partying hard, but only with men, if you know what I mean..." He winked, but he seemed very saddened. "Well, I had this stupid idea. Climb the highest tree and watch the setting sun from it... I know what you think, spare me..." Marysia did think about him in terms of a brainless man. It only surprised her that this was the third time he had known exactly about it.

"I was totally drunk. I fell. Oh, the end of the story. My buddies left, I stayed." He paused, but you could feel the enormous bitterness in his voice.

"You fell from the tallest tree and didn't kill yourself?" He glared at Maria at that question. But he did not answer.

"We eat soup together, right?"

"Yes." Marysia felt shivers down her spine. Polina's words about demons lurking everywhere began to pierce her ears once again.

Is Leszek one of them? Would he stay here if he was about to finish his studies? How is it possible that he wasn't paralyzed? Why does he live here alone when he was outgoing? She was confused. She was afraid, but he fascinated her. She knew she should, but she couldn't walk away.

Only then she realized that he was watching her, leaning against the wall as if he knew again what she thinks about. As if he was trying to x-ray her.

"You're smart. And it so rarely goes hand in hand with such unusual beauty. You know, I see a girl similar to you here..." He changed the subject to distract her and to lull her vigilance. And it achieved the intended effect. Her heart began to beat faster. She knew well who Leszek was talking about. She didn't interrupt him, wanting to get as much information as possible. "One guy wrapped her around his little finger. Shame to see. When she arrived here, she was confident, brave, and determined. Now he made her a brain mush and she was subjected to him... You know what I'm talking about, right?" He didn't have to ask, he had known the answer a long time ago.

"I know. Look... I don't have time for games. You see, I am also determined and I know perfectly well what I want and why I am here. So I will come to the point. The woman is my mother and also wojda. The man you're talking about is probably Latawiec. I just don't know who you are... but I hope you can tell me. If not, I'll find out for myself. Nothing will surprise me, so don't worry. I'm not some random girl you're saving. What I have been through in my life, I could give to a few people. So out of respect for me, sit down and say everything you know. If you want, ask. I have nothing to hide." It hasn't been a long time since she made such a bold speech.

As she was saying this, with great passion and force, Leszek approached her dangerously close, hammering her into the wall. There was no way out for her.

Except she doesn't want to go nowhere. To Leszek, she seemed resolute and defenseless at the same time. He looked deep into her eyes and kissed her. Gently and yet passionately. She didn't break the kiss, but didn't embrace him, as if submitting to his will. He broke off first. He went for the chair, leaving her against the wall feeling unsatisfied. He pulled out two glasses and poured red wine into them.

"Sorry, I couldn't help myself, and I had to close your mouth somehow."

Only this? Marysia was amazed. What is he thinking? She should hit him! No, she should have turned him away. Why didn't she do it?

"Coming back to the topic... when a young boy dies in the forest, he can turn into Latawiec, but also... As I fell from the tree, I knew I would not survive. However, I had a gift from Polina with me. She knew me well then, she knew that I was crazy, that I like to balance on the border. One day she handed me a package and said that in the moment of an imminent threat to my life, I should put its contents in my mouth. I did so too. When my buddies left, convinced that I was dead... when the whole family said goodbye to my body deposited at Polina's place, I began my new life..."

She listened eagerly. A tear ran down her cheek. How well she understood this boy. After all, she was past what he did.

"I miss the city very much, for my friends. For carefree. For girls, parties, studying... life..." He banged his fist on the table.

She walked up to him from behind and grabbed his hand. He turned and hugged her to his big chest. She did not break away. Why didn't she break out? Why had she let him kiss her? It was at this point that she thought about Wojtek for the first time. Just for a moment.

"You see... not only this woman is wojda. I was one too, so I understand perfectly well what you are talking about. If it comforts you... there are spells, spells that can help people like you and me. I am the best example of this. I am already an ordinary girl. It was successful. You just have to look for... I have a friend, a babysitter... Olga," she tried to say everything at once, which made her gibberish barely understandable.

"Nothing can be done!" He threw her away and sat down in the chair. "Don't you understand? I myself decided that I wanted to be that troll! You should know that independent, informed decisions cannot be reversed!" He was angry. "The leg is gimped. Here you have crutches, makeshifters, but it's not far to Polina's house. Go!" He was pointing his finger at the door without even looking at her.

"If that's what you want..." she whispered innocently, hoping it would move him. She was not wrong.

"I do not want this. Only it is all so painful. And you are too great to be here with me. I know you'll be gone soon, everybody's gone after they know my story. And I don't want to suffer. I don't want to be alone here. ...Go before... I can't stand another disappointment, another failure..."

He was so powerful, and he acted like a little boy right now, who needs to be comforted immediately.

She approached him once again. He knelt in front of her and began kissing the back of her hand. She pulled his head against her thighs. It was at this point that she realized that she had once again complicated her life.

25

She explained to her father for a long time why she was so irresponsible and set out on her own deep into the forest. She explained that Leshy is a really good demon, but only Polina's support calmed Stanisław. Then all four of them sat down at the wooden table again and decided to analyze the situation. Leshek began:

"Every day before dawn I see Anna walking towards Latawiec. It looks as if she emerged after the night and wanted to spend every spare moment of the day with him." He did not realize how much these words hurt Stanisław.

"However, it should be remembered that she is kind of passive, so it is not she, but a secret force that drives her into his embrace." Stanisław felt that this boy was reading his mind.

"Latawiec is strong? I mean stronger than you?" Asked Marysia, who was trying to come up with a plan in her head to wig out her mother.

"Hard to say. Each of us has our strengths. It is impossible to say for sure which of us is stronger. We haven't got in our way so far. Latawiec most often takes the form of a black bird, rules the wind, whirlwinds. He can also cause a storm, but he risks a lot here, he can die from it. Some people believe it's the devil himself..." The last sentence clearly neglected the audience.

"Look, you don't owe us any debt, rather I owe it to you. You saved my child, you immobilized her leg you fed her." Stanisław looked significantly towards his daughter. "But I don't have much room for maneuver, so I have to ask, would you please help us?" He sounded almost desperate, though you could feel he had a hard time involving a boy he had just met in his most personal affairs.

"I am aware of that," Leshy muttered mysteriously. "I just don't see why I should endanger all my animals, plants, Polina. You must realize that making such a decision will be devastating."

"I will be forever grateful to you," added Maria.

And I'll do whatever you want - she thought.

"Let's say I will help you..."

"Then let's figure out how we can get Anna back. Then we will consider how to get her out of Latawiec's spell. For now, I'd like to work out how we'll get her out of the lake so that he doesn't notice it and let us go as far away as possible. Any suggestions?" Nothing is left of the madness his daughter attributed to Stanisław on her way to Belarus. He seemed to be the factual, sober doctor she had met at the moment. Just a little unreal situation.

"I think there's only one way out." Leszek looked at Polina and Polina nodded as if she knew exactly what he will say. "I have to challenge him to a duel, informing that only one of us is the master of the surrounding area," continued Leszek. "Such a duel is the only way to get rid of him and save Anna."

"Is it dangerous?" You could hear worry and anxiety in Marysia's voice.

"What do you think? For one of us it will surely be. I have a whole forest behind me. All animals, forest creatures, trees, shrubs - are on my side. He rules over what is in the air. Clouds, wind, rains

- are at his service. If we choose neutral terrain, the advantage is on his side. Only the forest will give me refuge."

"That doesn't sound good." Marysia tried to make her father decide to exclude Leszek from the whole undertaking. She didn't want to endanger him. He, however, did not give up.

"I know perfectly well, but we have no other choice. So how do you want to play it and what can we do to help you?" Stanisław was excited and deeply moved.

"Tomorrow I will tell him that we have to fight a fight for the domination of this piece of nature. I'll make an appointment with him on the lake shore. When we start, you need to intercept Anna and go with her as far as possible from here. It is best to go to Świteź, so that she can reach the lake before midnight. You, sir, you will look after her, and Marysia, together with her łojma guardian, will have to find a way to free her from his influence. Otherwise he will find you..."

"What about you? The girl asked."

"If anything happens to me, Polina will be nearby. If I die... well, maybe it's even better. I am not made to live alone. I'm drying up here. If I win, you will have more time, because Latawiec will not stand in your way."

"What do you want in return?" Stanisław asked, fearing what he might hear.

"I'm only interested in one little thing." He smiled. "If I undertake this, Marysia will spend a month with me on any date she chooses. Of course, I promise to keep her safe, take care of her comfort and well-being. And... of course I won't do anything she doesn't want. Polina can assure you that I cannot force people to make decisions."

"I do not like it." Stanisław was confused. Why is this boy trying to ensnare his daughter? Or is he going to cast a spell on her? Maria's voice broke him out of his thoughts.

"Agreed. I'll be here as soon as I pass my exams. I won't have a full month, but I can keep you company for about three weeks." She accepted the conditions set by the young demon quite readily. "It's a small price to pay for such a sacrifice," she added.

"And you don't even need additional negotiations... I'm pleasantly surprised." Marysia saw the gleam in his eye easily. And for the second time she thought about Wojtek. This time she paused over him a little longer. She had promised him that they would live together and that they would spend the rest of their days together.

"And Wojtek? Have you thought about him for a moment? Did you look at the phone from yesterday? Do you know how many times he called? In the end I picked up because he was ready to come here!" Stanisław easily saw his daughter's goo-goo eyes and was surprised that this sensible girl allows herself to be manipulated by any boy, that is, a demon.

Leshy stared at her, air escaping from his nostrils. He looked like an enraged beast.

"Who is Wojtek?" He asked with relative composure. Marysia did not know how to summarize their tangled history. Fortunately, Stanisław took over again.

"Wojtek is her fiance, boyfriend. He saved her, set her free, took care of her... now everything is fine. You don't want to destroy it, do you?" He looked at the young man eloquently.

He did not answer. What if I just want to? I want her to be mine. She is so innocent and stubborn and beautiful at the same time, he thought.

"You agree to my terms, or should I go back to the forest?" Leshy suddenly grew impatient and angry.

"Dad, it's only a month... Remember what... who we're fighting for..." She knew that with these words she would soften the old man.

Marysia felt terrible. She knew well that what she feels about Wojtek is sincere and true. She was going to spend her whole life with him. What's wrong with her having a month-long bachelorette party during which she will have a good time? Of course, she will not be able to cross any border, she could do nothing that would make Wojtek sad.

She will usually bring joy to this lonely boy who, like she in the past, has no support and no soul mate here. It is not a sin, it will not disappoint his boyfriend. But probably she's already done it today. And what does that show? Certainly not about the power of love. Anyway, she is only human, she makes mistakes. She cannot be twenty-four hours a day, seven days a week, an exemplary student, granddaughter, daughter, and girlfriend. She was disturbed by what she thought about and the hardness with which she did it.

"Well. You'll talk to him tomorrow. We are waiting for news from Polina. Everything will be clear the day after tomorrow. And let fate be favorable to us..."

26

They met in the morning. At dawn, actually. At his place. Marysia went there with a certain degree of uncertainty, but also excitement. He wanted to spend a whole month with her. But why? The nature of the romantic told her that in this way he would want to convince her, seduce her, make her stay with him. Common sense, however, shouted that it was some kind of trick. After all, Leszek is a specter, a demon and... he may be preparing an ambush. She had been through enough. And yet there was something like that... - She tried to dismiss those intrusive and inappropriate thoughts.

The phone rang when she was at the edge of the forest, here she still caught coverage sometimes. On the one hand, she really wanted to answer, on the other, she was blushing at the thought that she had failed Wojtek in this way. Ultimately, however, believing that anxiety would bring him here, as her father had suggested, she got the phone.

"Hi... Yes. At best... It's a long story. I'll tell you everything after I return. I know, but I'm staying a little longer, because... there is a chance that my mother is still here. There is no need for you to come. A few days... no more. No... Wojtek, I can't hear anything! Hello? Nobody's hitting me. I'm sure. Wojtuś, don't come. Let one of us take care of his own affairs. Yes? Oh, thank you. I... I... you too... Kisses."

Was she sure she was saying these words honestly? Is it possible that you love someone when you get attracted to another person so easily? A moron. I will explain everything to leshy. She will certainly understand and give her freedom. He is a wise man. It means being.

"Who did you talk to?" He surprised her a dozen or so meters from the hut.

"How is it you heard it? I've been quite a long way..." She felt that strange tightness in her stomach against him again.

"Didn't Polina tell you? You didn't ask her about me at all? I cannot believe that such a curious young lady did not try to find information about me in other sources."

"What didn't she say?" It is true, Marysia realized that she believed the few words he said and did not even try to verify it.

"I can assume the form of animals. The most common choice is deer. It's such a noble animal... Sometimes I hear something clearly from a distance. And when I try very hard, I can even hear the unsaid..."

So that's it... That's why the animal was watching her with such attention then. It was him... and... he read her mind. That's too much.

"No, she didn't tell me that. I don't think anything can surprise me anymore. Listen... I came to ask you... but you probably know what..."

"Save it. I take back what I said. The animal came out of me again. Sometimes I feel like this.... wild lust... don't get me wrong... such intense feelings, as if multiplied, intensified... And ... sometimes I manage to read my mind in such a state, but only when

I focus very, very hard. This is such a warning for the future." He was laughing like a child.

"This strong feeling... do you feel that way with me? Is it good or bad? Would you like to hurt me?" She was scared, and yet she followed him all the way to the bench in front of the house.

"No, you don't have to worry. I don't want to scare you... I feel strange in your presence. I won't say what I want to do with you because it's indecent..."

She felt immense embarrassment. Suddenly her cheeks grew hot, her hands began to sweat, and she started to play with her ring. No, there was no sign of her confusion. Leszek wanted to somehow save her from this situation.

"Anyway, it's just positive feelings. And I would never do anything to hurt you. The end." He seemed as flustered as she was. There was also a sense of resignation radiating from him. "You love him?" He asked.

"Wojtek? Yes. I think so." She blushed.

"Do you think or feel? These are two different things. Love is the heart, thinking is the mind."

"My life is a series of failures. Wojtek is the only constant. And now that we've met years later, I know it's meant for me. It couldn't be a coincidence. I do not hide that I like you very much. There is something like that in you... but there will be nothing between us. My heart is taken. I am happy with someone else. Please respect that," when saying these words, she didn't know if they were coming from her heart or from her head.

"Then there was no topic. You are a great girl, good luck to you. And if you didn't work out..."

"Stop it!" They started laughing and thus relieved all the tension that had built up between them in the last few minutes. He was definitely a kindred soul to her. She didn't feel so good in anyone's company. Of course, except for Wojtek and Kaśka.

27

It was a beautiful morning, dawn after the day it was held conversation of two demons. Latawiec was amazed at the word of leshy. Although he did not like anyone, he did not think it was a shame that someone ruled the forest and the animals until not tries to invade his living space. He wondered where did this idea suddenly come from? However, it was not long before he accepted a challenge. He could not have done otherwise to don't look like a coward. They agreed on the edge of the forest that one and the other could use his strengths. They were not going to fight to the death. The fight was to end by one side is not going to defeat. However, this is a clash of two stubborn, proud and tough demons, so it was possible assume that the duel will at least close to death...

Marysia had a long conversation with Wojtek. It wasn't easy. The boy resented her for not waiting for him. That she had deprived him of an opportunity to support her. That he was disfellowshipped once again. "If something happens to you, I will never forgive myself and you!" he said in the phone. He was supposed to get on the nearest train and ride to her. They both knew that he would not make for the duel, but Marysia did not try to stop him. She got her way too many times.

"Hello. How do I look?" Leshy, dressed in camouflage pants and a black T-shirt, looked nothing like a demon.

He looked like a young cadet on his first day of service. Masking outfit, face painted with paints. She remembered action movies with Rambo. For a moment it was even funny. Just for a moment.

"You look like you're gonna wait for the enemy," she trailed off. "I'm scared... I'm very scared. That something bad will happen to her, to you... and yet you..."

"Shhh..." He hugged her, keeping her from screaming. "I'll do anything to keep your mom safe."

Something disturbing interrupted the scene. Marysia felt a cold, piercing wind on her back. She knew another demon had arrived. She went to the shore of the lake, where her father was waiting for her in full readiness. They had an old water bike at their disposal, which was to be used to intercept Anna. The motorboat would be too loud, it would get the attention of Latawiec.

Everything happened very quickly, at least for Marysia and Stanisław. When Latawiec flew over the lake, dense, navy blue clouds were gathering above it. The lake turned even darker, it was almost black. It was hard to see anything. Marysia stared at the sky and realized that the demon did not have the form of a human then, but as if it were clouds or a whirlpool of the air, it was difficult for her to describe it. It was pouring down rain, there were also flashes and gusty winds... Suddenly all the water from the lake rose, creating a wave several meters high, resembling a tsunami.

Everything happened so quickly that the participants of the event had not taken any action.

In the meantime, Leshy managed to take the form of a falcon and fly away, but all the animals standing at the edge of the forest, as well as Stanisław and Marysia waiting for Anka, were flooded with great water.

Latawiec had lost so much strength that it had to take its human form for a moment. Then the advantage was gained by leshy, who escaped the powerful wave. It is true that the sight in front of him broke his heart. The bodies of his forest companions are scattered around the area, trees and shrubs devoid of needle and leaf remains. And right next to the lake, the girl who has been so important to him lately. He gathered all his strength, accumulated anger, and struck Latawiec. He, however, at the last moment simply disappeared in the form of zephyr, because that was all he could do at the moment. In a moment both men were facing each other again. Leshy whistled and from the distant part of the forest a pulsating sound was heard... Suddenly there appeared crowds of boars, turns, and finally bears advancing towards Latawiec. Latawiec, clearly weakened, tried to defeat the animals with lightning bolts from the blue. However, only a few of them were hit. The only thing left for him to do was to hide in the water, which could hardly be called a lake after what was left of it. The animals stood on the banks of the gigantic puddle. Some have decided to exceed it. Leshy, confident of his victory, whistled a second time. Then a flock of various birds appeared over the head of Latawiec. It started pecking at his head, eyes and limbs until one could hear the words coming from the demon's mouth: "I give up!"

At that moment, lightning struck - the only weapon from which Latawiec could die like one who fights with the sword and dies by the sword. This rule was also valid here. A huge bolt of lightning hit the head, exploding the skull.

Leshy made a sound which made all the animals unanimously retreat towards the forest. He walked over to the demon's body. It looked like stone. Then the leshy's face changed. How much strength in his legs, he began to run towards Marysia and Stanisław. Fortunately, the tide only covered them for a moment. They were alive. They were breathing. Unfortunately, the roots and pieces of wood did their job. Both were badly bruised, Marysia's hair was covered with blood. Leshy took them to his lodge. He asked Polina for the right potions and began to nurture her father and daughter with full dedication.

"Hang in there, baby, you'll be fine. I just don't know about your mother... But we'll deal with that later... In the evening, Wojtek finally came to the old woman's hut. Having learned the whole truth, he must have beaten the record in the hundredth race, reaching the forester's lodge. There was a view not very nice to his heart.

"What were you even thinking, man? Get off her!" Wojtek did not mince words when he saw Marysia, half-naked, asleep and a boy leaning over her with a fresh bandage.

Leshy gave him a sinister look that Wojtek felt as a great pain in the frontal part of his skull. He almost doubled up.

"You're at my house, on my property. Here is your fiancée, whom I am helping to regain strength, so that she can be happy with you. So sit down and let me do my job, or leave before the animal comes out of me."

Wojtek got up. His anger drained away when Leshy made a place for him next to Marysia, who had just regained consciousness and spat out a little water. She was very confused about it.

"Wojtek? Where is Leszek? How did it end?" She muttered.

"Take it easy. Actually... I don't know... Could you... come over here?" The boy turned towards his potential rival. It annoyed him that he would not be her hero at the moment. He was furious that he couldn't answer the most important questions. However, he wanted his beloved to calm down a little.

"Marysia, you are at my house. After the wave flooded you, you passed out. As you can see, I am alive and well. Latawiec is no longer here. Your father should wake up any minute, he's here with us, but he had three broken ribs and a concussion I think. He's recovering." His calmness had a very positive effect on the girl.

"That's good. And... what... what about her?" There was nothing in her eyes but hope.

The harder it was for the demon to utter these words:

"I did not see her. She was not near the lake or the forest. Honestly, I didn't look around carefully. The most important thing was to save you and your father. As soon as Stanisław wakes up, we will go looking for Anna. It's only a few hours, we have plenty of time until evening, so don't worry. Now just lie down and rest. You have everyone you love with you...

Wojtek listened attentively and patiently, although the two of them, with their last passages, clearly did not need him. However, he decided to act. He was no longer the same boy who turned on his heel at the unexpected sound of goodbye and let fate rule his life.

"Look. Let Leszek stay here and look after your father. Meanwhile, I will take a flashlight and try to find Anna."

"Don't get me wrong, but I know this forest. There are many traps I have set, and many fallen trees after the duel. I'm not going to have you on my conscience. We will move as soon as Stanisław wakes up."

Wojtek did not want to agree, but Marysia looked at him with pleading eyes. He was afraid she would not survive if something else happened to him. That's why reason took over.

"Well. Let's do other thing. I will run for Polina, let her look after our wounded, and the two of us will go looking for Marysia's mother. It can be like that? They will be safe and we will gain time, she may need help now."

"So be it." Leshy started getting the equipment needed to break through the devastated forest. Marysia fell asleep. Polina soon reached the forester's lodge and wishing good night, said goodbye to the guys.

28

Afternoon and evening were far from peaceful. First, just after midnight, Polina was awakened by Stanisław's cough and groaning. The woman reacted immediately. She explained the situation to him. She forbade leaving the bed, pointing to the stiffened ribs. It was not easy, because the man broke away and wanted to take an active part in the search operation. Fortunately, the pain turned out to be too intense and kept him in bed. Then they heard the scream of Maria, who had apparently dreamed of the latest events. Polina helped her change soaked shirt and lulled her to sleep. This is what the night in the cabin looked like. Meanwhile, two young, determined men tried to fulfill the last dream of a girl who captured their hearts.

"Anna must be here somewhere in the woods. There is no lake now. We've got about four hours to find her and find a body of water nearby. I don't know if we can..."

Wojtek was terrified, he did not want to be the one who would have to convey bad news to Marysia and at the same time the one who had let her down.

Leszek had a completely different attitude.

"Don't fall apart. Let's find her first, then we'll worry about the rest. Or maybe she has been swimming in a creek a long time ago?"

The men had been looking for a few hours. There was little time until midnight, and Anna was nowhere to be seen.

Leshy finally decided to use his power. Why so late? He wanted to win this competition honestly and put Wojtek in his place? He failed. At one point he whistled twice and the chirping of birds heard over their heads. The demon stared up at the sky as if making contact with them. The birds flew away.

"The birds did not fly to warm countries for the winter? How did you do that?" Wojtek did not know all the supernatural abilities of his new friend.

"Stop! We have to wait a while. When they arrive, we'll know where to look."

"You could have done it all this time and only now did you decide to take this step? You're a loser, really! You could save her mother, but rose with honor? I do not believe!"

"Wojtek was furious and highly ironic. He did not notice that the expression on Leszek's face had changed.

The demon attacked the boy, starting a fight. Fortunately, aerial allies flew in, interrupting it. Otherwise Wojtek would not have come out alive.

"You are lucky," threw leshy, getting up from his knees and spitting next to Wojtek lying on the ground. "They found her. It's a long way from here, it must have been following the wave thrown by Latawiec. It's an hour until midnight, we don't stand a chance."

Wojtek never knew what to do in crisis situations. He envied his father's ability to react quickly. He hoped that when he grew up, the same would come, but it didn't. Or maybe he was wrong?

"Listen, let's run to Anna as soon as possible. I know we won't be able to save her. However, we must do something else..." Stożyński suggested.

"What do you mean?" Leszek did not really know what his companion meant.

"We have to get her to Maria. So that they could have that one important conversation. Otherwise she won't forgive me. Do you think we can do this?" Wojtek did not have time to hold a grudge, be angry or sulk. This time he had to go beyond his ego.

"Go to Marysia, wake her up, see what state she is and prepare for what may happen. Come on! Anna and I will join you in a moment." Leshy didn't want to waste any more time talking.

"But how can you..." Wojtek did not finish this sentence, because instead of a boy next to him he saw a beautiful deer. He didn't have to ask any more questions. With strength in his legs, he ran towards the lodge.

29

Marysia was still weak, but she hadn't suffered any major injuries, so she felt better every hour. Stanisław was in worse condition, so he lay there and complained that he entrusted these two young men with the life of the most important person to him. The most important, except maybe his daughter. They said little, stared out the window, except that all they could see was the darkness. Though the sky had brightened somewhat after the recent storm, it was still near midnight. Marysia was slowly losing faith in regaining her mother.

This young woman's thoughts circled in three orbits. First of all - what about Anna? Will she see her again? Will they be able to exchange a few words? What about Wojtek? Will he be disappointed? Disenchanted? Or maybe he didn't notice anything? And finally Leszek... She felt so sorry for him. But she couldn't help and hated the feeling of helplessness. The deliberations were interrupted by the sound of branches breaking, coming from the front porch. It was Wojtek who tried to cover the last part of his route.

Before he could say something, he stood for a few moments with his hands on his knees and his head down so he could catch his breath again. Finally he sat down and began reporting the course of events in a rather chaotic manner.

"But how? After all, Anna is immortal! When he takes her out from under that tree, she'll regain her strength and everything will be well!" Stanisław could not believe that this was how it was supposed to end.

"Dad..." Marysia was well aware that Wojtek was right. At that moment she realized that she will not get to know her mother. She also wanted to prepare her father for this, though she couldn't find words that were good enough.

"Dad, it doesn't work that way. The rusalka remains immortal only when she returns to the lake for each night. Sometimes there are exceptions, but Anna has been transformed following the same ritual as me and based on the knowledge of the same person, so... it's the only condition to remain immortal. There are probably several, if not several dozen kilometers to the nearest lake, and about twenty-five minutes until midnight. You have to accept it."

Stanisław did not answer anything, only turned to the other side, so that the tears that had begun to flow unknowingly down his cheeks would go unnoticed by his companions. He wanted to howl in pain, but he had to be strong, be strong for his daughter who was about to lose her mother.

Suddenly, leshy with Anna in his arms appeared at the threshold. She was breathing heavily, as if the gasped air was not soothing. Marysia remembered this nasty feeling and at that moment she felt it with her mother. Anna was put in the bed where her daughter was resting a moment ago. Stanisław, with Wojtek's help, somehow managed to move so that all three of them were very close to each other. Leszek gave a sign to Wojtek and they both left with Polina's cabin.

"Stasiu?! It's you?! I really die, since I have such hallucinations..." Anna whispered, because talking was becoming more and more difficult for her. "No, it's definitely not you. Although the eyes... you have the eyes of Staś..."

"You're not hallucinating. Where should I start? What to say? We have so little time! Now that we're finally here together..." He was holding back his tears.

"And who are you?" She turned towards Marysia. Marysia did not know what to say.

"I am your daughter, the same one that you got bored very quickly, abandoned years ago and left alone to the prey of that old witch!" This was not the reaction the girl expected from herself, but the emotions prevailed. This was what she had wanted to shout to her all these past years.

"Marysia... You're so lovely... I don't expect you to forgive me. I don't think I've ever forgiven myself, so how could I expect that from you?" She paused to take a deep breath.

"Why did you do that? How could you? Do you know what harm she has done me? Anyway, you can't know. You were never with me!" Marysia was sobbing. Anna wanted to grab her hand, but the girl quickly pushed her away.

"You're not likely to like the answer. I was young and stupid. I had things on my mind other than the child and its upbringing. If this is any consolation, I regretted my decision every day, and the rusalka's life is torment."

Marysia did not want to go on arguing on all matters from the past at the moment, there was no more time to talk about how well she knew what this torment was - which was Anna's fault.

"I do not remember the last years at all... As if something had possessed me, I feel as if I had woken up from a dream, and at the same time as if I fell into this dream..." Stanisław knew well what his beloved meant. "The most important thing is that you found each other and that we had this one moment for the three of us. Staś... I have never stopped loving you and thinking about you. Daughter, every day I wanted to come back for you, but I was afraid to turn your life upside down, I had no right to do so... Be... for yourself... support...." She quietly passed on, closing her eyes and taking her last breath.

Stanisław and Marysia were sitting motionless. He nestled in the body of his beloved, she was staring at one point. What had just happened could not reach them. The men waiting outside listened patiently to see if anyone would ask them in. Finally, Marysia came out in front of the forester's lodge.

"Leszek, you have to take Anna's body and bury it somewhere in the forest. My father has fallen apart so badly that he won't let her go. I have neither the strength nor the desire to fight him. This is the only correct solution." Marysia spoke coolly and to the point.

"Done." He put a hand on her shoulder, expressing that she could count on him.

Wojtek ran up to the girl and hugged her. They said nothing. Finally she started:

"I think I'm heartless. I do not feel anything. No emptiness, no pain... just relief. That she regretted, that she hadn't been well without me... I'm cruel, huh?"

"No. I guess that's normal. She is a stranger. How are you supposed to behave? Everything will be fine..."

The sounds of an argument came from the cabin. It was Stanisław who did not want to say goodbye to Anna's body. Leshy eventually used force and did what Marysia asked him to do.

"I will go with you. We will prepare the grave. And you go to your father. You will come to say goodbye to her when you will be ready, and to your father when he will fully restore. Okay?" Wojtek took two shovels and followed the leshy. He kissed her forehead.

Marysia nodded and went back inside. The following night brought nothing but sorrow and tears. Wojtek and leshy erected a grave, made a cross out of two thin sticks, and on it they placed a plate with the name, surname and dates of birth and death. Marysia joined them in the middle of the night. Even though it was already very cold, they spent several hours there. At that time, Polina prepared an infusion for Stanisław from setwall, known as valerian. She combined its herb with hops, lemon balm and maypop - thus gaining a powerful sleeping aid. This was the only way they could alleviate Stanisław's suffering and stop him from leaving the hut.

Only in the morning, when he could get up on his own and the first emotions subsided, leshy helped him move to a known place. They left him there alone, and as they walked away, one could hear the man's quiet monologue.

30

"You took everything?" Wojtek made sure that they would not come back here for a long time.

"I had nothing else. Dad... are you ready?" Marysia looked at Stanisław with care and love.

"Yes. I'm ready to come home, to live. Though I don't know how to put it all back together. I don't have the strength for it..." It was clear that he had to go through all the stages of grief before he could really start over. After a while he turned to Polina and Leszek: "Thank you for everything. For your help, for your support, for the risk you took by inviting us to your homes. If it weren't for you, I would never know the truth. Although I will never forgive myself... that it was because of me... that she could still live as... because it was me, after all..." His voice kept breaking.

"If not for you, she would still be dull under the charm of Latawiec. If it weren't for you, Marysia would never have known the answers to her questions. If it weren't for you, Anna wouldn't have met her daughter. All thanks to you. I wish you health and peace." Leshy shook his hand for goodbye.

Wojtek noticed with what admiration Marysia looks at the demon. He doubted the strength and constancy of her feelings more and more. However, this was neither the place nor the time to engage in this serious conversation.

"Goodbye, Leszek. Thank you for everything." She kissed him on the cheek.

Leshy pulled her close to him to whisper in her ear:

"If you only wanted... I am here." Fortunately, the blush on her cheek was invisible for Wojtek.

They didn't talk much to each other on the way back. Stanisław fell asleep right after entering the compartment. Marysia stared at the window. Wojtek was irritated, but he knew that he had no right now, with Stanisław, to express his emotions.

"What's up with you?" And yet the conversation had to come sooner or later.

"Why are you asking?"

"I don't understand..." Marysia understood well. Stanisław fell asleep from fatigue, physical pain and the most acute, internal. So the young people could continue the conversation without witnesses.

"What was that supposed to be with this guy? You have feelings for him, right? I saw you looking at him and that kiss for goodbye... I must admit... meaningful scene..."

"You have nothing to worry about. He stays there, I am coming back to Krakow with you."

"And you really think that such an answer will make me happy? I will tell you how I hear it. Be glad that he lives so far away, because if he was closer, I probably would like to stay with him... I guess I deserve honesty, right?

And not for such a round-the-clock. Do you have feelings for him?".

Marysia let herself be provoked, or maybe she wanted to expel the remorse that tormented her.

"All right, all right. I admit: mea culpa. He saved me from trouble and I liked him. Cool guy, that's it. It even crossed my mind that I could stay there with him because he is very lonely. But in the end, I thought about what WE went through together, what binds US together, and threw all those thoughts away, letting him know that I only love you."

"Ok. Everything's fine. Except I want to marry you. I have to be sure that in five, ten, or twenty years your feelings won't change. And if just any gorilla can charm you within two days, how does that bode for the future?! Do you even know what you want?" At this moment, Wojtek thought about Paula for the first time in a long time. She had many flaws, but he could always be sure of her. She would never cheat on him, never hurt him. She only have eyes for him."

"You know, maybe the come back was too fast, maybe we were too impulsive. Let's give ourselves a few days to think. I will focus on writing a thesis. Too much of this."

"You're always on the run. Always. Whatever the problem arises, you turn tail. You're like a guy! Apparently, we enter the cave, when there are complications, we cannot face them, and here you are! Anyway, if you prefer... Let's give ourselves another few days. For now."

Wojtek went to the corridor because at the next stop he got out. Stanisław and Marysia left the train shortly after him. The girl's father wanted to check in the hospital where his friend was the head of surgery, if his ribs were all right and if he had other injuries, because he still felt sore and uncomfortable.

31

"How's that? Again? It was just a big come back, and now a few days off?" Jarek did not believe what he heard.

Wojtek returned from the trip furious, overwhelmed full of regret. He was unpacking his clothes, or rather throwing them, trying to relieve his aggression.

"Man, I need a drink. Not one."

"I'm out today. I have a date with my girlfriend Marta." You could see that he was completely and happily in love.

"So I'll drink with the flies."

"You have to forgive me..."

Wojtek did so as planned. He bought a pack of beers and devoted himself to contemplating the essence of male-female relationships, unhappy love, and the cruelty of the fair sex. The considerations spanned for a good few hours as the pile of crushed empty cans grew and grew. Then she showed up. She entered there like to her place. She saw Wojtek's body hanging from the stool. She looked around and gathered a few things into a lovely golden box. Then she removed the black heels with a pink bow and moved Wojtek onto the bed. He opened his eyes as she hung over him.

"What are you doing?" Paula was a little surprised by this passionate kiss he gave her.

"You'd love me all our long live together, Paula, wouldn't you?" He mumbled.

"Yes, you idiot! I would love you, I would love you. But you chose other one." Even though their breakup was still very fresh, Paula had a great weakness for him and she didn't know how to hold a grudge for long.

"Stay with me today." He kissed her again. Paula did not need to be repeated twice. She deluded that maybe it will change something else. That when he sees her devotion, he will come to the conclusion that no one will be like her. And if not, there's a chance the other woman won't forgive him and... anyway, he'll come back to her. So she took off her short black-and-pink dress, exposing her perfect breasts, flat stomach, tanned and firm body in lace, black and pink underwear, and started kissing this half-alive object of her feelings.

Marysia thought how great a moron she was. Any woolly-back from the forest who delayed helping her mother just to show how macho he was, turned her head. Maybe there is something wrong with her? Maybe after all these experiences she needs the help of a specialist? After all, who is normal and sane? She meets the guy of her dreams that she has been thinking about all the time for the past few years, and then she kisses the red-haired forester! She did not sleep all night, but neither the unfavorable appearance nor the classes at her thesis advisor could dissuade her from her decision. She had quite a lot of money left aside, so she jumped on the way to the ATM and another place. When she rode the elevator to the eighth floor of Wojtek's dormitory, she was extremely proud of herself.

She just needs to get rid of Jarek, but it shouldn't be too hard. She loved this amusing romantic. When she entered the room, she saw Wojtek sleeping. Jarek was gone. He looked so vulnerable and beautiful. He was not wearing a T-shirt.

"Wojtek, wake up." She shook him gently and felt the alcohol odor. "Oh, someone had a nice party. Yes, I know, it's my fault. Wojtek, I have something important to tell you..." She shook a little harder and only then the boy woke up.

"Hi... What are you... what are you doing here?" He was a bit confused.

"What? I wanted to apologize to you for everything. Moreover, I am sure that I love you more than life that I only want to spend it with you, give birth to beautiful blonde babies for you and grow old by your side. In other words," and here she took out a gold wedding ring," would you agree to be my husband?" Wojtek smiled and wanted to pull her into bed immediately, when the door opened and on the threshold, in the same black-and-pink underwear that he vaguely remembered, stood fresh, fragrant and perfect Paula, who slowly clapped three times in hands.

"Bravo! Bravo! Bravo! Really touching. But are you sure you want to give birth to, as it went, blonde babies to a guy who, in a relationship with you, has passionate sex all night long with his ex-girlfriend?" by saying these words, Paula knew that she was losing Wojtek, she only wanted one thing, that this cunning slut Svetlana, or Marysia, didn't have him either.

"Excuse me, Wojtek, could you pass me my dress, which is under the covers?" She made her way to the desk where her high heels lay. She put on yesterday's outfit, winked at Wojtek, blew a kiss and as she left she said: "You have my number, sweetheart. When this good girl goes away crying, call a real woman! Bye."

Looking at this scene, Marysia felt as if she had left her body and stood next to it. Wojtek jumped out of bed, grabbed her hand, but she broke away and only said:

"Goodbye."

"I was drunk! I don't even know what happened! Or maybe nothing happened! You know she's manipulative! Marry!" He shouted to the departing elevator.

But she couldn't hear him anymore. She didn't want to hear and listen. So though. All her plans and dreams are gone! How could he do this to her? Of course, in revenge for Leszek. Only there was nothing between them! And he slept with that skinny floozy! He couldn't hurt her more... She turned out to be a moron! She spent the last money on a wedding ring, which she will admire now... When she burst into her room, Kaśka did not even have to guess who it was about.

"Well... well! Your version is as always heavily colored and exaggerated. Now let me tell you how it could have been..."

"I know how it was. I am neither stupid nor blind..." Marusia was walking around the room and did not let Kaśka come to a word.

"Okay! But nevertheless, I insist that I may introduce your vision of events. Ok?"

"OK but..."

"Shut up for a moment! And listen to me!" Kasia was not patient, so not all of them augured her career as a teacher.

"Sorry, go ahead."

"You could smell alcohol from Wojtek, right?" Kasia started her mathematical investigation. Her analytical mind turned out to be indispensable in many situations.

"Exactly."

"Next to Wojtek's bed there were piles of empty beer cans, right?"

"Yes."

"When you tried to wake Wojtek, he was almost unconscious, right?"

"Truth."

"Historians, historians... cause - effect. Well. Wojtek got drunk as a lord yesterday. He drank about twelve beers. Even if it took all afternoon and evening, it's a big dose. Girl came to get her knick-knacks, and he was lying drunk. She got into his bed because we know she is his psychophane, and in the morning she told him that they had sex. Oh, the whole story."

"Sure. Everything is so simple for you. Or maybe it was as I see it. Devastated Wojtuś gets drunk, the bitch comes to get her stuff he complains that I turned out to be hypocritical and untrustworthy. She comforts him, kiss and kiss and they end up in bed.

And in the morning I caught him at it! Especially since... well... how to say... he may miss it... because we... never did..." Marysia was embarrassed.

"Still? Nothing? Okay, I don't comment. It is an individual matter for everyone. But going back to the explanation of the mystery, you Sherlock, everything is correct, there is only one small "but"..." Kaśka was so pleased with herself that Marysia wanted to kill her. It was about her future, not some math puzzles.

"Whoever drinks a glass of wine can be a sex god in the evening. Unfortunately, all studies clearly show that when men drink slightly more alcohol, they become unable to have normal sexual intercourse as it causes erectile dysfunction. Simply put, Wojtek couldn't cheat on you with Paula. If he was unresponsive to stimuli, his little friend was even more so."

"Maybe... maybe... you're right. I don't know anything about this completely. But that doesn't change anything. If a guy drinks so much that he can't remember who's in his bed, then something's wrong!"

"Marry, I don't want to be mean, but Wojtek doesn't drink much every day. Unless he has a good reason. And we know who brought it to him. Don't try to put all this on him now, it's kind of unfair, don't you think?" Kaśka always tried to remain objective.

"We both failed. I don't know what now." Marysia was depressed and didn't really know who should take the first step and ease the situation.

"Fate is on your side. I would leave it to it. Besides, Wojtek will definitely take the initiative. Write your thesis calmly and you will see that there will be no trace of this great drama in a moment."

"Maybe you're right. But when I remember this sight and her triumphant expression, I feel like vomiting! Write a thesis calmly? Kaśka, are you crazy?"

"Only peace will save us... Sit down to the computer and write your thesis."

"So I will. At least I will try, because my thoughts still circulate in the dormitory several hundred meters away from us. Thanks, Kasiula!" She cuddled up to her friend. Without her, life would be so difficult.

32

Wojtek has not sobered up so quickly. It was a few moments before he realized what had actually happened in this dirty, dingy room. He took a quick shower and drove straight to Paula's apartment. On the tram, he only glanced at his right hand and the wedding ring that were there. For a moment, when he didn't think how he would undo it all, he felt full of happiness. Marry proposed to him. She wants to grow old with him... Now he only has to beg the madwoman somehow to help him... Fortunately, he knew Paula for a long time and he knew what would soften her the most. He bought a bouquet of tea roses, her favorite marzipan-stuffed chocolates, and a beautiful white gold bracelet. There was no other way out. He knocked on her apartment and the girl told him to come in. He hit the record button and stepped inside.

The tenement house on Bracka looked old and neglected from the outside, but the apartment inside was, without the slightest exaggeration, luxurious. He knew it very well, almost like his own. He spent more time here than at home. All rooms had white walls. The kitchen with a dining-room, the largest in the whole flat, built-up with white, glossy cabinets, with a crystal chandelier, black accessories and a large white table with only a narrow vase with one violet gerbera on it. As always sterile clean. She wasn't here. He went into the living room.

Here, in turn, white mixed with red a sofa and a small tread on a white, low bench. Little furniture - only a TV cabinet and a glass display case. Paula didn't even look at him.

"Hi." Nobody answered. "I might start. I wanted to apologize you. Not for yesterday, for everything. You were the best thing that happened to me after Svetlana left. You are the most beautiful woman I have ever met in my life. I have never seen a woman so ambitious in pursuing her goals. I am sure that you will be very happy and that you will achieve great success in life. I never wanted to hurt you or make you suffer. Being with you felt like life made sense. There was a void there, but it wasn't your fault at all. You were the perfect girl. There is something wrong with me. Please, accept this little thing from me for an apology. This breakup did not turn out the way I wanted. I didn't have time to say and do everything. I'm sorry, be happy, love."

"Wojtek put a bracelet, flowers and chocolates on the bench, leaned over the girl sitting motionless on the couch and kissed the top of her head. He was heading towards the front door when he heard:

"Wojtek!" She looked him straight in the eye. "I was lying. We didn't get sex yesterday. Nothing happened. You kissed me, but while I was hoping for more, you just fell asleep. You started something you couldn't finish. I was about to leave, but pathetic as it was, I wanted for a moment to feel as if we were a couple again.. Sorry for that scene in the morning, but I still love you and can't handle it..."

"You're welcome. I was going through the same. I believe you can handle it, you are very strong. Like I said, you have a friend in me."

"If you want, I'll explain it all to her. Now go on before I fall apart."

"Goodbye."

33

He rushed to the dorm. Marry should forgive him! He has evidence! But will it be so easy for him? Nothing is easy with this girl. But that's probably also why he cares about her so much. The conversation between Marysia and Wojtek in the dormitory was quite short. Neither of them wanted to waste any more time in unnecessary arguments. Wojtek played the recording from the phone in which Paula confessed to lying. Moreover, Marysia also felt guilty.

"If it hadn't been for my behavior, you probably wouldn't have gotten drunk alone and given this... didn't let your ex jump into bed. I don't want to go back to it anymore." The girl threw her arms around his neck and wanted to kiss him.

"Wait," he interrupted her. "Did what you said this morning... Did you mean it?"

"Of course. I will not hide that my thoughts, so far, are saturated with the image of my mother... and I can't focus on anything else, I constantly see her beautiful face and I think we could..."

"You couldn't... it wouldn't have happened... you know it yourself."

"I know... but you must give me time to live my own mourning. I am defending my MA thesis in March. The advisor set the date for me on the seventh. And then... then choose a wedding dress, invitations and all other bridal stuff. Do you agree?"

She seemed to be happy, but Wojtek saw that it was only a fixed smile. The loss of her mother was too recent.

"I agree. We will live happily ever after. I promise."

Mary spent all her free time reading, analyzing, writing, summing up and drawing conclusions until Christmas Eve. She had to quit her job in a pub, otherwise she wouldn't have had a chance to deal with the winter exam session and defense on the dates she had planned for a long time. Wojtek was very understanding and helpful. They spent time together mostly in the evenings, when Marry was tired of writing, and on their way to the college or library.

It was the first such holiday. The white hut in Zabierzów was even whiter because it was covered with soft and fresh powder. Even the Christmas trees only protruded from selected branches. It was quiet and dark. She had been helping in the kitchen since morning. After all, there were only two of them - with Grandma - to feed all the guys gathered. For the Christmas Eve came Stanisław - still moody, but making the best of a bad bargain, Antoni Stożyński - who, despite the passage of time, was still living alone, of course Wojtek and grandfather Jan.

"Your father seems absent... for a month now. Is there anything we should know?" Grandma started the conversation while they were cooking the carp.

"I don't know, his trip. I think he wanted to discover something new... something groundbreaking in natural medicine... some herb... at least he failed. Better not to bring this topic up with him. But he's better now, at least I got him out of there. And he went back to work, it absorbs him completely. Maybe it's just plain fatigue."

Grandma was not a nosy one, so she broke off the inconvenient topic.

"Wojtek is also somewhat uncomfortable... You have no idea about that either?" She looked at her exceptionally beautiful granddaughter today quite meaningfully.

"All in good time, Grandma. I would advise you to take a look at the fish, as soon we will only have 11 dishes to eat." Indeed, the carp was already baked.

The grandparents' lounge looked fabulous. A white tablecloth was spread over the big table, with a red runner on it and a few golden candlesticks. The crockery was the color of snow and gold. Baby Jesus was lying in a stable on a hay, with a wafer next to him. In the corner of the room stood a huge fragrant pine tree, tastefully decorated with openwork angels, wooden stars and large red baubles. There were gifts under the tree. Lots of gifts. They all looked dressily and very elegant. Men in suits, grandfather with a bow tie, others in ties. Stanisław did not resemble dosser from the train station anymore to Marysia but was again a respected cardiologist. She also looked today exceptionally.

In a red knee-length dress with a black collar and a storm of curls - she could pose for any Christmas issue of a women's magazine.

Until now, Marysia did not believe in God. Olga gave her no choice. She was a demon, a ghost, someone with no right to ever go to paradise. Now, since she lived with her grandparents, she has caught up. She received the Sacrament, Confirmation. She felt that the truths of faith were close to her, and in difficult times she found solace in prayer. These holidays were special because it was the first time that she spent with all the people important to her. There was only one missing... She still couldn't come to terms with her passing.

After praying, eating delicious dishes prepared by my grandmother - among them dumplings with cabbage and mushrooms, red borscht with dumplings, peas with beans, white borscht with mushrooms, fried carp, soup with carp heads, challah with honey - Wojtek started his speech:

"Since we are all here today, I would like to announce that Maria and I got engaged and are planning to get married this year. Of course, I will not do anything without the consent of Mr. Oleszczuk and the Lachs. So I ask you a question: will you give me your daughter and granddaughter as a wife?" He was very nervous, he could barely pronounce the next sentences. It was unnoticeable to those here but Marry could see the hardship it took. She herself was just as nervous as he.

Grandma cried and they were tears of happiness. Grandfather announced that he had always been an ally of this relationship. When Stanisław finally realized what had just happened, he replied:

"I couldn't have asked for a better son-in-law. You helped my daughter when I didn't know about her existence yet, you forgave her when she was lost for a moment, and finally fate let you find herself. I would be a fool and a cruel man to get in the way of this feeling. Welcome to the family, son!" The men patted each other on the back.

"And I a better daughter-in-law. Marysia, I am very happy, for my part I can promise you that I will help you as much as I can. What more can I say? I wish you happiness, perseverance and the love that I experienced myself. You don't need anything else," added Antoni.

They spent the rest of the Christmas Eve setting dates, guest lists, dishes and other purely wedding matters. The fathers decided that they would cover the cost of the wedding in half, as the family was not very numerous on both sides. Grandparents offered to arrange an afters at their home. Grandma had already spread before them a vision of erecting a huge gazebo in the garden and breaking the floorboards for a dance floor. Marysia and Stanisław forgot for a moment about Anna's death - amidst the bustle and talks about flower arrangements, the flavors of the cake and the best inn in the area.

34

Marry and Wojtek informed a group of their closest friends about the engagement just before the end of the calendar year. Exactly at the meeting where they planned how they will spend New Year's Eve. Their annual several-day trips have become a tradition. They were already in Krościenko on the Dunajec, in Szczawnica, in Kościelisko and Gdynia. Fun has always been combined with sports and sightseeing. This time, however, the bride and groom welcomed the New Year's Eve - admittedly in a permanent line-up: Marry and Wojtek, Jarek and Marta, Agnieszka, Kasia and Szczepan - but in the dormitory. They agreed that they were broke. In the dormitory, all the parties mixed together to create a gigantic rush of young people. There was a lot of laughter, dancing and memories - because this is their last student New Year's Eve after all.

"Unless someone will fail in the final exam," threatened Marta.

The entire team was already getting ready for the Stożyńskis wedding. It was decided who would go with whom, when the bachelorette party would take place and whether the stripper should be blond or brown-haired. Wojtek only jerked his finger jokingly, staring at Marry as in a picture. About a few minutes after midnight, Marysia felt unwell. She took a deep breath in her mouth as if she missed it so much, she doubled over.

"What's happening? Does anything hurt you?" Wojtek asked anxiously in his voice.

"I don't know, very strange, but kind of a familiar feeling... As if I couldn't catch my breath... Get me out of here..."

The boy took Marysia in his arms and carried her to her, now empty room.

"It's a little better. But it was like when I was... you know..."

"I know. Only you're not anymore. You are human, so you need to be examined as a normal human. In the hospital. As far as I know, you have a father who works in one. Tomorrow is the New Year, but the day after tomorrow we are going to Katowice. Have all the research done for you. You have to be in good shape, you have an exciting year ahead of you."

"Normally I would have protested, but your arguments are so convincing... Aaaaaaa..." She said nothing more. She began to choke and roll her eyes.

Wojtek did not know what to do. The attack lasted about ten minutes, it seemed that Marysia was losing consciousness and regaining consciousness.

"We're going to the emergency room. Now. There is nothing to wait for," he was saying to her, but she was hanging from his hands and she did not answer, even though she was conscious at the moment.

Marysia lost consciousness several times within a quarter of an hour. When the air didn't reach her lungs, she saw strange images. There was a mother in each of them. She warned her of something, nodded her head, and finally, with the frightening darkness in the background, summoned her to her.

She did not look as she remembered her then, her eyes red and her fingernails long... She was afraid of her like that.

35

Stanisław made a few calls and on New Year's Eve, apart from him, Wojtek and grandparents, there were also the best doctors from Lesser Poland. She had all the possible tests done, exhausted with hundreds of questions, but nothing disturbing was found.

"Everything's back to normal so far. There is no indication for keeping you in the hospital. Plunger, fumes, tobacco smoke - maybe it all made you feel unwell. If symptoms reappear please report. The results are correct, Staszek has seen himself there is no reason to be afraid." Doctor Nowak presented the condition of the patient.

"Yes, I saw. Everything looks good. Just what it was... Oh nothing, we're taking you out of here. I'll take two days off and watch you a little. You will not come back to the dorm for sure, we will bring you a laptop and you will work at your grandparent's place. And I'll keep an eye on you."

Nothing strange happened during the two days spent with my father, nor during the next two days in the dormitory. January passed quietly. Marysia passed all the exams of the seminar session, she almost finished writing her master's thesis only minor corrections remained. They were going to go to Wojtek's father for the weekend and to the slope with him. Marysia was packing her things.

"I would like to go with you..." Kaśka complained, sitting under the covers. And by browsing the list of materials that she had yet to obtain and were necessary to create her own thesis.

"Nothing hard. Take out your backpack and off we go. You have food and accommodation for free, you just need some cash for the slope and a ticket." For some time, Marysia tried to devote as much time as possible to her roommate, she enjoyed them because she was about to part ways.

"And who will go to work for me? I didn't get a replacement... Anyway, this will be a romantic getaway for you, and I would just... Marry?! Marry?!" Marysia slumped to the floor, began to wheeze as if the air was not getting into her lungs, and suddenly she lost consciousness. Kaśka immediately called an ambulance, the ambulance took the girl to the hospital where she had been staying recently.

The situation repeated itself. All tests were performed again. However, the results were not as good as last time. After many medical discussions, a series of bizarre examinations, the reason for this has not yet been discovered. After two days of observation, Marysia felt better and left the hospital at her own request. The situation with the dormitory did not repeat until March.

36

Maria did not have time to repeat the tests after the last incident, although her father, grandparents and Wojtek insisted. The day has finally come. She got up very early, just after five. Kaśka was snoring on the next bed. Her stomach clenched, but she knew it all too well. This meant that today she was facing an important exam. She ironed a white blouse and black skirt. She looked at the haversack but knew she wouldn't swallow anything today. At least not before noon. Because by noon it will probably be over. At half past nine, Kaśka's alarm clock rang, she jumped to her feet, put on a random blouse and left the dorm with Marry.

"We are all here, do not be afraid... because... we want to find out what it looks like..." Szczepan joked to loosen the future master's degree a bit.

"You think I don't know that?" Marysia was only slightly excited. "When am I supposed to give them chocolates? And you know, this book for my thesis advisor that I found in the antique shop."

"Well, I told you. If they ask you questions, then they ask you to leave so they can consult. Then we will prepare chocolates and a book for you, and you will give it to them after announcing the result." Kaśka found out from her older colleagues how the whole procedure works.

"Unless they say that it wasn't good enough to give you this academic title." Szczepan did not give up.

"We invite you in." The professor stuck his head out of the office, putting an end to any further teasing by his colleagues.

Wojtek was twice as nervous. He wrote an important exam for Marysia, who was to enter the supervisor's office once, and for himself, which he was allowed to take at a later date. Due to his girlfriend's recent weakness, he spent his time studying medical textbooks instead of engineering textbooks. Fortunately, the doctor turned out to be understanding and allowed him to pass at a later date. He was less afraid of Marysia, he knew that she would do well. He only wished he would be late with congratulations and a bouquet of roses. Well, life is not a romantic comedy after all...

Szczepan, Marta, Agnieszka and Kaśka stood at the door and listened. It's been a long time, but their friend was a talker, so no wonder. Suddenly the door opened, and they saw a macabre sight. Two professors were kneeling over Marysia's body. A third was opening a window and trying to draft.

"Move away from the door, give your friend a little air..." one of them said. "The ambulance is on its way..."

"She defended thesis?" Szczepan asked this inappropriate question at the moment and got an answer.

"Yes, she got five, but then she started to choke... Isn't she an asthmatic? Don't you have any of her inhalers?"

The promoter asked.

"Unfortunately, it is not asthma or allergy. This is not the first time... but she has never been unconscious for so long..." explained Kaśka.

The ambulance arrived in no time. Marysia was connected to a respirator to allow breathing. However, she remained unconscious. The girl's friends took her personal belongings, called Stanisław and Wojtek, who, after a written - not very well in his opinion - exam, joined them in the hospital.

"Perhaps in her childhood, she experienced some trauma, an infectious disease or something else that can now be felt," said Dr. Nowak. The same one who dealt with Marysia the last and penultimate time. Wojtek stood aside and listened to the specialists' exchange. "I don't see any other option. We really tested your daughter for all her medical conditions. You know that!"

"You know our history. I don't know, I just don't know! We would have to go to Belarus to see Maria's babysitter to find out something. What is the situation like? Just be honest with me, this is my only daughter..."

"I don't want to be smart, but you should probably do it. It means going to that babysitter and doing an interview. Staszek, have you seen these results... Life parameters are incorrect... we cannot find the source, and it is getting worse every hour... If her condition continues to worsen..."

"You don't have to finish." Oleszczuk knew very well that Marysia is in bad condition....

He just didn't know why or how he could change it.

"I'll go." Wojtek could not sit idly any longer. He saw his fiancée change minute by minute. He had to act. "You have to stay here to supervise everything, you have friends, you are a doctor yourself... I won't do anything here. Oh yeah, at least I'll find out something... maybe we'll find a solution... You say we don't have much time..."

"All right, son. Go. Just watch out for yourself, because in emotions people sometimes do stupid things. Everything right. If you don't know something, call us if you can find coverage there. If you were in trouble..."

"I won't be in trouble. Don't worry. I think that, in fact, Olga also cares about Svetlana that is Marysia. And she'll help if she knows how to do it."

"And your studies? I don't want you to neglect anything. Marysia will not forgive me." Stanisław felt that he could not send this good boy on a lonely journey to the demons' habitat, on the other hand, he had no other choice.

"If I don't go, Marysia may not speak to you at all."

This last sentence was left without comment. Stanisław Oleszczuk nodded, embraced his future son-in-law and wished him luck. Marysia's condition was critical. The cause was not found, and there was less and less research to be done.

37

"Yes, Dad. I'll be there in a few hours. I bought a ticket for the next train. Will you grab me? Well, I'm saying it. She's dying, Dad! This is not some joke! Okay. Someone lives in this cabin by the lake now? You don't know... ok. Anyway, I'm going to do it in one day. Well, we'll do that at most. I'm going to pick up a few things and go on the train. See you soon."

Antoni was devastated. Will his family be haunted by bad luck forever? Until recently, he believed that Ewa was watching over them, that she would not let Wojtek come across anything bad. And now? He didn't know anymore...

Wojtek was confused and filled with anger. Why not others? Why is it the fate that keeps throwing obstacles to their feet? How much peace have they had? A few months? If not a spell, searching for a family, a missing mother, demons, it's now a disease... How long will they have to go through before they start a peaceful married life? Will it be given to them at all? He pushed that last thought away. What if Olga doesn't want to talk to him after all? Or if she has no idea what it might be? What will he do then? Will he sit helpless next to Marysia's bed and watch her go?

He reached Nowogrodek late in the evening, but he insisted that he wanted to go to Świteź today.

Antoni knew the whole truth about Marysia and her past, he knew very well that it was the lake brought nothing but worries and troubles, it was not for nothing that Svetlana wanted to leave this area as soon as possible. So he agreed to an evening visit, but only in his presence.

"You can't come with me. This woman is distrustful when she sees you, she won't say anything. Our whole plan is going to fail," he tried to talk father out of it. "You can come with me, but I will enter Olga's hut alone. Otherwise it won't work. Compromise? And there is nothing else. There is no more. You have to trust me, and it is not worth returning to what was." Wojtek did not have time to argue about details, let alone initiate his father in all the dark matters of the past.

"Well. Compromise."

"Well, show me what your four-wheeled wonder can do." They reached Świteź before midnight. It was in Olga's cabinit's dark already. Wojtek knew that it was not nice to visit this time, but it was an exceptional situation. So he decided to knock on her door. Nobody replied. Wojtek decided to go inside.

"Olga? You are here? It's me, Wojtek! I need your help!" He shouted from the threshold.

No one answered, so he switched on the lamp on the table and went to the room next to the kitchen, but Olga was nowhere to be found. He had completely ignored such an option. He sat down, resigned, on the kitchen stool and was overwhelmed with discouragement. What now? His gaze drifted over the furniture one by one, to a bookshelf until it finally hit a window.

Behind him, in the moonlight, a beautiful, even fairy-tale landscape was visible. Spring wasn't coming to life yet, but it wasn't so cold anymore. There was a remnant of snow on the lake, from under which grass and brush were slowly emerging. The lake glowed alternately blue and white. Wojtek was scared when the clock struck midnight. Then the silence was broken with a male cry. The boy looked at the water again. He was not mistaken in his guesses. It was Anatol.

"Dad, come in and rummage in Olga's things. I know it's not nice, but we don't know what happened to the old woman, and maybe here we can find answers to the questions that haunt us." He wanted to pull Antoni from the lake. He seemed very convincing.

"What should I look for?" Father asked.

"First, any information about Svetlana, some research, medical history, balance sheets... I don't know, anything related to her health, past illnesses."

"And then?"

"And then... well, you can laugh, but Olga is a herbalist, medicine woman, and believes in the healing power of herbs and some... rituals." He was looking for a good word that would replace witchcraft, łojma, spells sorcery. "Such a thick book, right over here, look for something there about unconscious people and how to help them. You will make it?"

"Excuse me, what are you going to do?"

"I will walk around, but only close here. Maybe the woman has fainted, maybe she's lying somewhere and needs help. Just a while and I'm coming back to you. Okay?" He wanted to make sure that his father did not follow him and interrupt his dialogue with Anatol.

Antoni muttered something under his breath, excited about his new mission. Now Wojtek only had to face this bully with whom he had already had a real problem. Fortunately, Anatol was alone. He emerged from the water with his bare, muscular torso, exactly as Wojtek remembered him from their first meeting. He was afraid that it might become an easy prey for the water demon, but he had to take the risk.

"Anatol! Anatol! Do you remember me?" He screamed to call him to the shore of Świteź.

"You're loveer of my sister... I remember, and I can see well thanks to the slide from you. What are you doing here? Are you with Svetlana?"

"No. Svetlana is very sick. Doctors can't help her. That's why I need to talk to Olga immediately. She is hers, is our only hope. I didn't find her in the hut, can you tell me where to find her?" Anatol was the only one who could help him. If he didn't know what happened to the łojma, no one else would answer that question.

"Łojma ran out of food..." Undine did not notice the seriousness of the situation, as if Svetlana's fate did not interest him at all. He continued across the lake and answered Wojtek casually. "I don't feel sorry for her, Svetlana...

Who resigns from immortality, she owes herself..."

"How did her food end? She went shopping?" The boy did not comment on the last sentence, nor did he understand what the food for Olga was about.

"Oh, stupid, stupid... Did you think that Olga eats all the things she did for you? After all, this is a strong and long-lived demon! Olga must add to her food what ensures her immortality and relative strength."

"What's this?" Wojtek hoped that something that could be found nearby and that the old woman would return to her home in no time.

"The herb is called goody. You won't find it this time of year, and the old woman's stocks are exhausted. So she decided to visit another łojma and ask for support. Oh, the whole story."

"Where does the other one live? Or else, when Olga comes home?" Wojtek was irritated by undine's disrespectful approach, but he couldn't show it to him.

"The other one lives in the bushes next to the Szo." It was easy for Anatol.

"Where it is? Far away from here?" Wojtek asked desperately.

"How should I know? Goodbye! Time for dinner..." He dived and never came out again.

Wojtek was left alone with his doubts. He didn't even know if he understood the name of the lake correctly. How would he look for Olga in some vast area? He has to ask his father for advice.

38

After a quick study of the map, it turned out that Lake Szo is less than four hundred kilometers from Świteź. The road alone would take over five hours, and finding Olga another dozen or so. So they decided to return to their father's apartment in Nowogródek for the rest of the night, and to the lake until the very morning.

"I haven't found anything to be a clue. Only in this one book there is such a strange picture... I took a picture with my phone, we will study it at home. The language is probably some Old Belarusian, I don't understand anything..." he told his son about the results of his search.

The picture from the secret book of spells showed a girl, she was dressed in a white dress and a white wreath. Wojtek did not know if it was about the fact that the spell had power only in spring, or something else entirely. There was another girl nearby - the same as the other one, which was lying on the ground and held by the throat. There was also a third one, walking on the lake - exactly like Marysia when she was getting this strange attack and before, when she was wodja. There were two flowers or herbs in between these drawings and some text he couldn't read.

He woke up extremely early, left his father a card and went alone. He sat for several hours in front of the łojma's house, but she did not come. Finally, after the afternoon, he saw the silhouette he knew.

Huge breasts dangling almost knee, hair on arms and legs... Olga was not in the best mood, judging by her external appearance. It didn't bode well.

"What are you doing here? You better have a good reason. I'm not in the mood for social visits." Sweat poured from her forehead, even though it was cold. At close range she looked very weak and tired.

"All right? You do not look the best..." Wojtek wanted to buy the old woman's favors first.

"No! It's not okay. Because of all your affairs, I forgot to stock up on goody in the woods and now I'm going to starve here!" The woman was clearly agitated. For a moment, Wojtek was afraid she would hurt him.

"Where can you get it? I will help you if you help me. We'll find this goody. But first I have to go..."

"No. I can't do anything for you until I get my weed. The łojma living on Lake Szo is not there. I don't know who might have them. But I know that if I do not eat goody today or tomorrow at the latest, I am done."

Wojtek was furious, but he tried to look at the situation with a sober eye. He remembered about Polina, who was after all a herbalist and healer like Olga. It's a few hours from here. So he had to hurry up.

"Dad, I know you're angry. Yes, I took your car. Look, the old woman has forced me to do a favor. I'm going to Polina. You know... the one where Marysia stayed with her father recently... Yeah, yeah. I'll be there in the evening or at night.

I don't know how long it will take. Don't worry, everything is under control. Go easy to work. Ok. Bye!" He ended the telephone conversation and rushed to the next place.

Wojtek has set the navigation to Nieszczerdo. Polina was the last resort. He just quietly hoped that he would not meet him. He didn't need this one yet to want to go to Marysia. And even if he hadn't told him anything, the man might have read it in his mind. But he wasn't going to focus on him. He will take the weed and come back.

In the afternoon he got there. Nothing has changed since the last time. The torn trees were only folded in one place, instead of the lake - a small wet spot, surrounded by grasses and bushes. The light was on in Polina's hut. He briefly outlined the purpose of the visit, and his whole body showed impatience and haste, so Polina quickly rushed to her cupboard with herbs and took out a large bag.

"I collect the goody in case some łojma wants to hurt me or drive me from the lake. For half my life I was afraid that one of them would deprive me of my home, so every spring I stocked up this herb so that I could use it as a bargaining chip. Now that there is no lake, I am safe. You can go ahead and take the entire bag."

"Thank you. You're saving my life. Actually, it saves Olga's life, and maybe most of all Marysia's." Wojtek hugged the old woman and was about to head towards the exit, when he heard behind his back:

"What about her?" Obviously, the voice was of leshy.

Wojtek could not hide anything anymore. He didn't even try.

He confessed to the demon everything as if in confession.

"I don't know how I can help. Polina? Could I? I'll do everything."

"Leszek, I don't know spells, only the power of herbs. Everything is in your hands. She alone knows what can be done in this situation."

"In that case, maybe we will have to scare her or use force..." Leszek wanted to be of some use at all costs.

"Come on. All she wants is that weed. If it weren't for you, I'd be on my way. So if you let..." Wojtek hoped that he would finally leave this place.

"Go. Save her."

39

He met Olga the next day. He was terribly tired. For two days behind the wheel. There and back. He tried not to think about how hungry he was and how much he was thirsty. At Polina's, he only managed to get himself a piece of cake. He did not even have the opportunity to call Stanisław and ask how Marysia was feeling. Even though he did not have a hands-free set and it was forbidden to do so, he picked up the phone:

"How's that? But what does it mean? You got her back? God... that's lucky. I will be with you in a dozen or so hours, she must hold out, there is no other choice. Well. I do what I can. I know."

The news of Marysia's collapse and her temporary loss polished Wojtek off. While he had been overcoming fatigue, more kilometers and increasing obstacles, now he felt a need for everything and the accumulated adrenaline probably disappeared for a moment. Does it all make sense? What can Olga come up with, since dozens of doctors do not find the source of the problem? Will he make it in time? If not, will he be able to live with this awareness? After all, he did not even say goodbye to her. He tried hard to remember their last conversation. He called in the morning to give her a kick in the ass on the phone, to make her laugh a bit and distract her from the exam for a moment. Did he say he loves her? He couldn't remember it. His only consolation was that she was certainly knew about it.

He knows it now, too, and he certainly won't give up without a fight. So he'll pull himself together and be a man.

The meeting with Olga was different than before. The woman looked terrible. Her body began to wrinkle strangely, her nails so long they seemed to weigh on the hands that hung loosely from the back of the rocking chair. The old woman made sounds that made Wojtek feel goose bumps. He finally stopped staring at her and said:

"Relax, I've got a sack of it. Enough for you for the next months... just tell me what to do with it..."

She pointed to a mug with a tiled stove on the sideboard. The boy put water in and poured a teaspoon of herb into the cup. Then he served the hot drink to Olga and it was unbelievable how she began to change before his eyes. The nails seemed to be absorbed into the hands. The hair has become a bit fluffier and healthy. The skin was much less wrinkled. Olga got up from her chair, stretched as if awakened from a deep sleep.

"I have fulfilled my task. Now it's time for you." He believed deeply that Olga hadn't used him by trick, but she could really help him.

"Did I understand correctly? For several months, Marysia has started to choke for no reason. She's losing strength. Now she can't function by itself without the machinery, right? Has anything strange happened in her life recently?"

– Before these attacks began...

"She was with her father in Belarus. This one, as you know, was looking for Anna. Then there was a duel of a leshy and latawiec, Marysia was under the water for a moment, then she recovered, we buried Anna, we came back..." he tried to sort out the recent events, which were really a lot for a few months.

"Wait, wait... Did you say you bury Anna? How's that possible? After all, she was immortal? What the best of you guys did..." Olga looked at him as if he were a fool and kept shaking her head. Finally, she spoke again, "Legends say that the rusalka's child, no matter if she is human or a demon, dies with her. The next months pass and Marysia's condition will continue to deteriorate. There isn't much time."

"I do not understand. How it's possible? And how do you know how much time is left." Wojtek did not want to accept what he had just heard.

"Boy, I won't answer questions I don't know the answer to. Legends passed down from generation to generation said that a child died for as many months as a rusalka died for hours." She looked questioningly at Wojtek.

"We found Anna at night, but her torments lasted several hours. Maybe three, four. She died in November, so... Mary is going to die in March? It's March already! What can we do? Come on! Think of something!" Panic seized him.

"There is a spell in the book of spells that helps dying girls. However, there are certain requirements and there are some consequences. Interested?"

The boy nodded, though the answer was obvious. Olga took out a large book, so well known to Wojtek. She searched for a long time, read, thought said something under her breath. She also checked the condition of her herbarium and finally spoke to Wojtek.

"Svetlana must turn into Mavka, which is your Lady Midday. I don't know if she will decide to take such a step. Mavka lives underground during the winter. Only in April does it come to the surface and settle down somewhere near the cornfields. It remains on the ground only until harvest time..."

"No! There must be another way! We want to live a normal life, start a family. I am fed up with this nightmare..."

"Then I won't help. I'm sorry. Drive and say goodbye to her." Olga closed the book and began to bustle around the house. There was no trace of fatigue on her face or body, no trace of the deadly threat that had just threatened her.

Wojtek was desperate. Why did he have to fall in love with her? Why did fate put her in his way? There are so many girls... hundreds, thousands, millions, and he met Svetlana. He didn't want any other, so he decided to act.

"What does it take to become a Lady Midday?" It wasn't a perfect plan, it didn't really make him happy, but he had to do something.

"Is Svetlana clean?" Olga asked.

"I do not understand?"

"Are you... or she with someone... you know... is Svetlana a virgin?"

Wojtek was first indignant at the old woman, then he thought that it was probably a necessary condition to turn into this particular demon, and finally realized that he had no idea. Nothing happened with him. Not then in high school, nor now. In fact, he wondered why. There were a few occasions, but Marysia always found an excuse. Maybe she wasn't sure about his feelings, or maybe she wanted to wait until the wedding. After all, in recent times, faith has become important to her. Exactly... faith... after all, she will not agree to turn into a demon. Use magic again. Black magic.

"I don't know. I think so, she is a virgin. Are there any other conditions to be met?"

"You need to take the chickweed, vetch and leucanthemum infusion with you. I'll have it ready. I'll write the spell text for you on a piece of paper. Let Marysia, when she wakes up, drink the brew and say the words from the sheet. Then she will turn into Lady Midday. Is that clear to you?"

"Yes. Prepare these herbs quickly and tell me about Lady Midday."

Olga started taking out her paper bags with dried plants and at the same time told:

"Lady Midday appear on summer days. They are very harmful and dangerous demons. Anyway, rusalkas are like that, but as you can see, everything can be overcome."

Olga slowly and solemnly poured boiling water over every plant separately, then rinsed its flowers, peeled them from unnecessary leaves and put them into a large vessel with holes at the bottom. "Headaches, strokes, fainting while working in the field - it's all their doing. On the other hand, when they become angry, they can even lead a person to death. Like any demon, the Lady Midday has additional powers. For example, it can take the form of a fog. My great-great-grandmother used to say that when the grains are undulating like the sea, it is a sign that Mavka is moving between them."

Wojtek listened and felt more and more dilemmas. Wouldn't it be better to let doctors do what is theirs? Will it not be worse for her to live like this? Maybe not to propose such a solution at all? What if she got angry with him? He had done something inappropriate once, and how did it end for them? The rush of thoughts flooding his head was interrupted by a quiet wailing, or maybe Olga's singing:

The sun rocks the earth,
clouds were wiped from the sky.
Whereas I can hear in silence
grain is falling from the ears.
Women's calves turn white
in tucked up skirts.
The earth bursts with hope
Lady Midday is born.
The birds in her braids are sleeping,
when the sun-broken earth,
like this will from God
walks her way somewhere.
Nobody will know about it
Where is she going, where she came from
Whose hard lives
She lifts on carrying pole
She goes on still further
She will stop somewhere for a moment
Woman is burning a candle there
Peasant dying there
The birds in her braids are sleeping,
when the sun-broken earth
like this will from God
walks her way somewhere

She will come to me when summer
In how many years I do not know
She will come standing in front of the hut
She will say: It's time for you
The children will take the earth
I will do so for now
And on a fragrant Sunday
I will follow Lady Midday
I will follow Lady Midday
I will go with Lady Midday... [1]

Everything became clear. Wojtek thanked Olga when he was taking a bottle with a freshly prepared infusion from her. A piece of paper with text that had been copied from a magic book was sticking out of his pocket. He went to his father, give him the car.

"You've been away for a long time. You look terrible," Antoni began.

"Dad, can we go to Krakow as soon as possible? I have herbs that can help Marysia overcome her disease."

"Okay, son, I'm getting ready. I'm glad you found something. You have to try everything. Did you call Staszek? Marysia's condition unchanged?" Father asked as they set out.

"No, nothing has changed. She's still unconscious. Doctors throw up their's hands. They even called the United States to consult this case with a professor, but it didn't help," Wojtek calmly explained, while inside he was boiling with nerves. He couldn't even

---

[1] K. Grześkowiak, *At noon.*

tell him the truth. Stanisław. Yes, he will make a decision. He knows everything, he knows it, and he is her father. So if Marry hadn't woken up, then… he, he would take it upon himself.

They gained the hospital after a long and exhausting journey. They saw two car accidents and they almost skidded. Wojtek was extremely tired, but he did not fall asleep even for a moment. Adrenaline didn't allow him to do that. He didn't remember when he had anything to drink or eat in his mouth. They were already on their way to the hospital parking lot. Suddenly blood run from his nose and… it was the last thing he remembered.

He woke up in a hospital bed with a drip and cannula in his vein. His father explained to him that he had to dehydrate his body in the last few days. He did not really agree to idle lying down, especially since his beloved was several rooms next door. Antoni explained to him, however, that Marysia's condition had not changed. It has not changed for the better.

"Doctors say it's an agonizing phase. Life parameters weaker and weaker, Marysia does not even breathe herself. Wojtek… I don't want to be a bad prophet, but… I think… you should say goodbye to her… just in case…"

Wojtek did not answer anything. He didn't even wait for the liquid to drip into his vein, tore the tube out and ran towards the girl's room. He turned around halfway to take with him the items needed to perform the rite. He saw her first. Lying in a white shirt, hooked up to these strange devices, tubes sticking out of her hands, a mask that supplies oxygen to her face. Pale, with greasy hair. Her eyes were closed and her hands were so thin. She didn't look like the girl he had met by the lake, but like her husk. Tired, weak, she was breathing slowly only thanks to machines. He cuddled up to her, kissed her forehead, and ran his finger down her cheek. It was his Marry after all. His future wife.

"We need to talk. And quickly," he turned to Stanisław, who was lying next to Maria's bed.

He then explained the situation to the man. Said everything he learned from Olga.

Stanisław listened, but seemed to be absent. Wojtek noticed that he had aged terribly. Compared to his father... but that wasn't the most important thing now. He had the impression that Stanisław could not hear him. And he counted so much on his opinion, advice, decision...

"I don't think boy we can do this to her, not a second time... She'll never forgive us. I'd rather let..." He broke off.

He broke off because something unexpected happened. The apparatus to which Marysia was connected began to make a strange noise. Unvaried and poignant. Wojtek knew it from medical films and series. Suddenly, three doctors, several nurses, were next to him. He and Stanisław were pushed away from the bed. An action to save her life has begun. The boy was looking at the scene that was taking place right in front of his eyes, and yet he did not fully participate in it. He felt like a spectator of a melodrama, he couldn't move. Stanisław was held by two gorillas, he was struggling and shouting something deep, but Wojtek could not make out the words.

It seemed to the young Stożyński that it lasted forever, but the scene lasted only a few dozen seconds, maybe a few minutes. Doctors unlinked the girl from the apparatus, removed the tubes and needles and began to leave the room. Wojtek understood what had just happened. Then he broke through them, poured a drink from babysitter down Marysia's throat, and desperately began to read the words on the cards in Russian.

Stanisław was looking at him, and his eyes showed the last ray of hope. Doctors walked away and nodded, believing the despair had driven the boy crazy.

They were left alone. She and he. He stayed by her side for several dozen minutes. It bothered him that nothing was changing, nothing was happening. After all, when Olga drank the decoction of the goody, the reaction was immediate. Maybe he gave her the fluid too late? When he was about to leave, Stanisław and him became witnesses of something unexpected. Marysia suddenly opened her eyes. She inhaled with all her strength, choked on it, and let it out again. Then her appearance changed. The face, still pale, grew a little sterner and the beauty even more expressive. He had the impression that the hair was browner, and so were the eyes, and her lips were redder, like blood... He wanted to say something, Stanisław came closer... to the right, and began to spin around its axis. Both men stared at her in amazement. She spun faster and faster, it was difficult for them to still see the shape of her body. Eventually... she disappeared... instead of her all they saw was a gray-blue, almost transparent cloud. This one was dispersed, or maybe it was simply no longer visible to them.

Wojtek then remembered Olga's words about the supernatural powers of Lady Midday. He knew that there was no more wodja, no Svetlana, or even Marysia.

Once she grew strong, he knew he would have to map the fields nearby cultivars and begin in them, as Stanisław once did, to search for his beloved Mavka, his Lady Midday.

EPILOGUE

***

Wojtek stood on the porch. Today he was starting a long-awaited holiday leave by him and his family. The smell of grain wafted around him, a warm summer breeze blowing his blond hair, cut here and there with gray threads. So much is said about ghost villages in the Lublin region, about depopulating this region of Poland. About unemployment, the lack of prospects. He found refuge here. His place on earth. Did he choose this piece of land quite by accident, as he convinced himself? "You're finally here." The woman with the short hair threw her arms around his neck and smiled heartily. "We have to speak." Her voice was soft but firm.

The man in his thirties seemed tired. It was not, however, fatigue with the travel he had made, with the contracts he had concluded in recent weeks, or even with his company's financial problems. There was more with the frowning and absent gaze. He kissed the woman in denim overalls on the forehead.

"You painted again..."

She became confused and began to clumsily wash the paint off her forehead and cheeks, looking for the stains almost blindly. She looked like a little girl and would be turning thirty-third in a month.

"You promised you would talk to her more. Do you know, that I can't be home as often as I can, and our daughter... well, she is what she is, and she really needs company." He looked at her rebukingly. Then his gaze wandered a little further. There, near the cornfields, a little girl was sitting in a huge sandbox. Wojtek's face softened, he involuntarily tilted his head to the side and smiled under his breath.

"When Matilda falls asleep, we'll talk calmly." The painter entered the house, leaving him alone.

Today was hot, no wonder, after all, it's the beginning of August. Wojtek took off his tie and put it next to the large flowerpot standing on the left side of the white door. He sat down on the stairs and soaked up the scents in the air. Their small white house with orange roofs blended perfectly into the local landscape.

What did he love this place for? For the proximity of the eastern border, for the influence of the East and the West, visible to the naked eye- especially in large cities - the heritage of various religious groups. What particularly captivated him, he had at his fingertips. The traditional rural landscape, the silence, the proximity of soothingly rustling farmlands and their small farm buildings, which his wife turned into a prospering agritourism villa.

By the way, his - pragmatics - has always been astonished by the fact that a house, a cowshed and a brick barn find so much interest among townspeople. However, he did not interfere, he did not judge.

Janka used to say that she needs something of her own, and if it was something that made her happy, he was happy too. The extra money in the shared budget was also useful.

"Daddy! Daddy! You are here!" He didn't see the silhouette, he heard only Mati's childish voice.

"I am, angel. I was looking forward to you. Are you playing the catcher in the grain again?" He no longer looked like a tired 50-year-old. His eyes regained their glow, his figure seemed less hunched, and a sincere smile distracted from the first gray hair.

"I have so much to tell you." Five-year-old Matylda was a copy of her mother. Short-cut mouse-colored hair, expressive blue eyes and dimples in both cheeks made Wojtek repeated ad nauseam in her presence: "You can't fool your genes". In addition, she was extremely independent, smart and - which was more of a curse than an advantage - painfully honest and oversensitive.

When he had finished tickling her, tugging her, and enjoying her careless and contagious childish laughter, the little obedient wandered into the bathroom, where her bath was waiting for her.

Wojtek was not going to send any e-mails today or answer the phone. The last two weeks had been filled with nothing but work, now he would devote time to his women for a change.

There were five rooms in their house. Three at the top were occupied by summerers, the ones at the bottom belonged to them, to Stożyńskis.

Judging by the complete silence, the guests were not at home. Or maybe they were, but at the moment they were enjoying the charms of the August evening. The interiors were arranged and renovated by Janka. The rooms were alike. Wooden, with doors, bolts and wardrobes that have been preserved for many years. Restored by local handymen, they aroused the admiration of laymen and antiques experts. She named the rooms after the colors that dominated each of them, but also the herbs that she passionately cultivated in her home garden. And so, guests could choose a lavender suite, consisting of two rooms and a bathroom, a rosemary suite in a soothing green shade, with a huge double bed and a double wardrobe, and a mint room - the smallest, but extremely romantic and cozy. Usually they recorded full occupancy between May and September. Janka was constantly working on a marketing strategy that would provide them with year-round profits. She wanted to take a chance on families with children. Not only because such families traveled more and more and expected all amenities for their children, but also because Matylda, who was mainly among adults, would finally have company.

***

The suitcase was unpacked, it was finally possible to breathe a little. In the small kitchen, on the counter by the window, lemonade waited for him in the warm months, and in the hallway, the smell of baking cake spread. This was another advantage of the villa and his wife. Her pastries were known all over the area, so the strangers often visited their restaurant, even if they did not stay longer. Whenever he poured lemonade into a glass, he thought about how he and Janina had met. It was the first time he had the opportunity to taste the drink she prepared. Then, however, he was simply doused with it.

It was in what he called the era of denial for his own use. The era of pushing HER out of memory, of being thrown out of his head, of being taken out of his heart. The era in which he had regular conversations with a psychiatrist and fathers: HER and his own. Their position was extremely unanimous. He remembers this time as a blur - by the way, what a correct comparison in this situation. He was then taking a number of psychotropics, which allowed him to get out of bed and not spend the next decade of his life hidden in the fields and meadows. He remembers a few sentences uttered by Oleszczuk and his father: "You cannot, you should not look for her. It is futile. She forgot. You won't be happy with her." When the psychiatrist assured all the boy's relatives that he had gone through all stages of mourning and was ready to start a new life, Stożyński senior was to help him bounce back and set up a company.

Then Nina appeared. She did not like being called Janina or Janina, although he liked this traditional version of her name the most. But... Nina forcefully pulled him out of the embrace of melancholy.

The first order of the young Wojtek's company: construction of a cable-stayed suspended bridge with a length of one hundred and eighty meters. A simple matter. And yet. Ecologists appeared, claiming that the actions of Wojtek's company and the city would lead to enormous losses for the environment, as the bridge was to run over Bird Island. He did not listen to the details of the shouts or the slogan of the banners, because his eyes were drawn to a young and extremely militant ecologist, who he would most likely chain to a bed in his bedroom instead of a tree...

On the one hand, it was a pity to withdraw. On the other hand, he wanted to win the favor of the mysterious Nina. He was in no mood to form a relationship, he was thinking rather of getting away from the past. However, life wrote a completely different scenario.

***

"She fell asleep. She's been just lying down and falling asleep lately. She does not listen to even one fairy tale fully. But no wonder, she is active from early morning until late evening, staying in the yard." Janina sat down next to him, and earlier she put water for tea.

She loved her traditional kitchen. It was identical to her grandmother who died years ago. A tiled stove in the corner, all the furniture in traditional wood and the most important element - a huge table, which was to invite all household members and guests. Dried herbs hung over the stove, and a mortar, pepper mill, and coffee grinder stood on the tiled shelf. She hung short curtains on the windows, because she loved it when the sun's rays were reflected in the restored cupboard in the morning. She wiped the table top with the cloth, took the remnants of rhubarb infusion from the cup and sat down next to her husband - her great love.

"I like this place. He wasn't looking at her, but somewhere in the distance, into the horizon."

The sky was orange and red. Even he, this pragmatist by birth, skeptic by experience, and ignorant, appreciated the fact that he could live here. By the way, Nina sacrificed a lot of friendship in the name of this love.

He was so different from her companions with his mathematical approach, engineering precision, eating meat and carving trees anywhere. They both had to compromise, but the feeling that brought them together was so strong that it wasn't much of a problem.

***

Nina cared for her surroundings. Initially, she was considered positive in the village, but still crazy. She didn't eat meat, she disgusted with preservatives, didn't dye her hair, didn't paint her nails, and was constantly creating something. The first room they renovated after coming here was her studio. What was missing there? A painter, a sculptor, and a stained-glass artist would find themselves here. Nina put on fireclay ceramics. In short, she made angels and other figurines, which she then decorated beautifully and put up for sale. She would not have made a living on what she was making in her additional "business," but her spouse's company prospered so well that she could afford an original passion.

Anyway, the contribution of a woman to their home budget was considerable. The renovated villa: ecological, natural and quiet attracted people from all over Poland and abroad, mainly with its cuisine. Janka called it slow food, which Wojtek only understood when they hired a cook and debated together the menu and products that they would obtain only from befriended, certified farmers, the seasonal menu and eggs from the hens they were to start breeding.

Initially, Wojtek did not believe that someone could be attracted by a deserted region full of roadside shrines, but poor in shops and attractions straight from the metropolis.

Quickly, it was clear that he was wrong, and the area was full of cereal fields, bicycle routes and old churches it brought in hominess longing corporate rats, yobbos, eco-freaks and fit-mothers with their children.

***

"Matylda is still talking to her imaginary friend." His wife threw him out of the deliberations.

"I told you, it's nothing wrong. I read on the Internet that..."

"I do not believe! Your online diagnoses really are not a determinant for me. Maybe you should go to a psychologist with her?"

"Don't dramatize. You know that Jarek's wife works at the school. We spoke on the phone recently and..." He didn't have time to finish.

"You still have contact with those people?" Janka was surprised and her expression changed. The eyes got bigger, the eyebrows went up in surprise. "I thought it was a closed topic and we will not come back to it.

Janka got to know only a part of her husband's story. She had no idea about Svetlana, about the lake, about Anna, about Stanisław, and about the collapse. She only knew that Wojtek had lost his beloved girlfriend that he had risk one's health, that he could not stop thinking about her for a long time. She wanted to believe that the demons of the past would not get him anymore, and the easiest way was to break with them by going as far as possible. She did not realize that demons could really exist and catch a human when they least expected it.

"Nina. Jarek is like a brother to me. The fact that I talk to him does not mean that I am tearing up some old wounds and nothing will change.

Anyway, I will not continue. You know me. It's just you and Matylda. Nothing else matters to me."

She hugged him. She breathed a sigh of relief.

"What did that friend say?" She asked, though her voice showed no interest in the answer.

"Well, children in a certain period of development invite an invisible friend to their lives. You know that she has contact with her peers so rarely. Only when the guests show up, and besides, she is an only child and probably feels lonely. Even more so there is nothing to worry about."

The woman moved away, got up, and went to the door. Wojtek had to re-analyze his statement to find the reason for this behavior.

"Nina, that's not what I meant..." He broke off, because he knew perfectly well what the end of this conversation would be if he continued.

The subject of children... No, the subject of the second child was a taboo subject in this house. Janka dreamed of a huge family. When they first entered their new home, she joked that they had to fill every room with offspring and that they could get down to work even now. Some time after this confession, she was already pregnant for the first time. As it turned out- the last one. During delivery, the cervix and its body were damaged. The diagnosis was the same for all the gynecologists visited in the following months - secondary non-fertility. Recommendations: enjoy having one child you want, because every fourth couple in this country was not so lucky.

Wojtek agreed with the statement of their doctor who supervised the first pregnancy that it was not the end of the world. They had Mati. Their beloved one, go-getting, delightful little girl. However, Nina had to accept the actual state of affairs for a long time. She was visiting, to Wojtek's fury, herbalists, female friends, and shamans who were constantly prescribing new potions and elixirs to work a miracle. Wojtek never told her that out loud, but he was afraid. He was terribly afraid. His first love, the greatest and the only one, was doomed to a tragic fate because of the closeness of such types of women. He was afraid that he would not survive what happened to him a second time. He was afraid because now it was not just about him, but about his beloved little creature. He successively knocked her out of her mind about visits to natural medicine specialists and asked her to respect his and the child's peace. Eventually, they managed to sweep the topic of the second pregnancy under the carpet. The man, however, was not sure if Nina was still looking for a medicine behind his back, which made him shiver.

"From tomorrow on, I'm all hers. I will spend every second of my day trying to talk about this friend." He extended his hand to his wife.

She walked over to him, put her legs around him and started kissing him. They looked like two teenagers who, not paying attention to the world around, indulge themselves.

***

Mati got up first. She ran to the kitchen, climbed onto a small stool, and put on the water for tea. Then she left the house, ran to the barn, that is, to their restaurant, which was built in the former barn. She greeted Mr. Jurek, surveyed the mezzanine with the library, the bread oven and the suspended wooden bar. She ran her little finger across the tops of side by side tables and ran outside.

She breathed a little breast. She looked at the lavender-scented herbarium, at the swings moved by the summer wind, at the flower part of the garden, situated in a less sunny place. She said that you can never get bored here, you can only be a little lonely. Though since her friend showed up, the latter didn't bother her anymore. She glanced at the white socks. A red spot appeared on them. She lifted a finger and put it to her nose. The blood is running out. She reached for a handkerchief, rolled it up, and put it in both holes.

"Do we have any visitors?" Wojtek was still in bed, while Nina was putting on a T-shirt and shorts in a hurry. He studied his wife for a moment. Her figure was the same as before pregnancy. Slim, without sides, stretch marks, only a few scars, it reminded of the birth of a toddler. Small breasts that nourished his tiny daughter, a little dried,

they were the most beautiful in the world for him.

"I'll tell you later. Yes, we're fully booked. Old people are in lavender, in love in mint and a family with a child in rosemary."

"A child of Matylda's age? Will she have a peer even in the evening?" Wojtek was overjoyed, because the holiday had begun perfectly.

"No, the boy is ten. He is unlikely to be interested in anything that is outside of virtual reality. Well... o tempora, o mores..."

"What?" Wojtek was not good at Latin.

"Google it." She winked at him and disappeared through the door.

***

It will be his day with his daughter. He will take her wherever she dreams. There will be ice cream, unhealthy snacks, and lots of fun. Of course, they won't mention what they did to Janka. Although no, Mati with her honesty...

He found her in a restaurant kitchen. She stood on a stool next to Jerzy and served him more spices. She was white as a wall. Her nose was dusted with flour or powder, she looked lovely. He had always felt that people got too excited of their children. Hundreds of photos on your phone, dozens of anecdotes, bragging about achievements. When he was still a teenager, he was terribly irritated by family gatherings where this type of situation occurred. Now that he was a father himself, he knew that certain behaviors were extremely difficult to escape. He believed that he was completely non-objective and completely in love with his baby girl.

"Baby, it's your lucky day! Your great dad will fulfill your wishes today. Come on, try me out... What do you fancy, young lady?"

"I don't know," the girl muttered, not taking her eyes off her duties.

"What? I make you such an offer, and all you can say is: I don't know? My miss, I thought you had more ideas. I'm disappointed." Wojtek pretended to break down, kneel in a corner and almost flood with tears.

"Oh, Dad. Don't be silly. We can do anything, just..."

"Just together... I know, sweetie. You are so smart..." he anticipated the thought of his offspring.

"As long as we can make it by noon and be back in the house," finished Matylda, indignant.

Wojtek felt a slight twinge in his heart. After all, his little daughter, a little girl he had rarely seen since the beginning of summer, was crazy about him, counting down the seconds to the meeting, and wouldn't waste a single minute with her daddy. What happened to his baby? He decided to pursue the topic.

"It's already nine o'clock. What are we gonna do in three hours? Do you have a gunslinger duel right noon that you absolutely must come back here? Or maybe there is something else?" He tried to cover his confusion and disappointment with a joke.

Matylda put down the herbs, wiped her hands on a kitchen cloth, and said goodbye to Jerzy. Then she took her father's hand, led him to the porch, and began the conversation all over again.

"Dad, mom probably told you I had a new friend." She was so focused and serious that he could hardly see her as a five-year-old child. Unfortunately, the topic of the invisible friend kept coming back and it had to be dealt with. But he didn't know how to react or what to say.

"Yes, she did. So it's a girl? Will you tell me about her?"

He tried to get as much information as possible to get used to the topic.

"It's not a girl, it's a woman, Dad. She is older than me and very pretty. I can't tell you more, otherwise she wouldn't want to meet me anymore," she told about her friend, all the time looking towards the fields.

Wojtek did not expect such an answer. And while he had not been very stressed about his daughter's friend, it was at this point that he felt uneasy. Older? A very pretty woman comes at noon to play with his daughter? In what? And why?

"Hmmm... Since you are friends, I would like to get to know her very much or learn something more about her. I guess that's normal since I'm your dad, right?" He did not give up.

"She says no one needs to know about her because she could be in trouble then. Anyway, I've already said too much. She'll be mad at me." Matylda looked a little sad.

Wojtek tried to gather the information he heard into one whole, which he liked less and less.

"So your older friend is in some trouble, she comes to you at noon and nobody can see you? Maybe it's some bad girl? Maybe she persuades you to something? Mom has ever seen her?" It was more and more difficult for him to hide negative emotions from the little one.

"Daddy, why are you mad at me?" Matylda moved away from her father.

"No, no, honey. Excuse me. I didn't want to spoil your mood. Maybe let's not talk about it anymore, but ride our bikes to the forest, we'll be back at noon." He felt it would be the best solution. At least for now. He did not intend to encircle the five-year-old as it would be counterproductive. Anyway, he had a plan. He will observe his daughter's meeting with a secret friend.

***

Nina was just finishing a yoghurt cake with fruit, so there was a lovely smell in the house. He lured the elders who had been staying in the villa for two days. They no longer had the strength or the desire to travel further routes. Their dream was simply to enjoy the view, the smell of home cooking and the closeness to nature.

"Did you sleep well?" The owner asked.

"Thank you, excellent," replied the gray-haired old woman, about seventy years old. She was dressed in an elegant floral dress almost to the ground, made of thin material.

Her husband was standing next to her. An old man in polo shirt and trousers with a clearly marked crease.

"My dear, you have a wonderful daughter." The old woman was talking to Janina, but she was looking at the receding figure of a girl dressed in a helmet and knee pads.

"It is true. She is very mature for her age. Sometimes she surprises me and disarms me with her wisdom." Nina was proud.

"Don't be offended, but it bothers me that on the worst of the heat, you let her be in the open sun. It's an extremely hot August, isn't it? And she is hanging out for hours with this woman just then. This is her governess, cousin?" The old woman took another sip of tea and took out a fan with a colorful bird.

"With what woman?" Nina immediately quit washing dishes soiled during baking and sat down next to her temporary tenant.

"I thought it was her teacher. Dear child, why are you so pale? You do not know her?" The old woman became worried.

No. Nina didn't know any woman Matylda could talk to. There was no farm nearby, they had no relatives or friends here. Few neighbors but all busy. She was terrified. She had no idea who her child was spending time with. And yet she always prided herself on the fact that she had her daughter at hand, that she spends all the time at home, that she accompanies her in household duties. And yet. She missed something, missed something didn't notice. What kind of mother is she?

"Please tell me more. It could be unsafe. I had no idea about anything." She hoped for a moment that maybe old woman had made a mistake or that she had changed the facts a bit.

The old woman did not satisfy her curiosity. She only added that around noon, a child always wanders towards the cornfields with a blanket and a bottle of water. That, admittedly, she is wearing a hat and she is smeared with filter cream on the porch. However, she spends the next two hours at the edge of the fields and is accompanied by a young woman. The old woman doesn't know how old she may be, what exactly she looks like, because both distance and age do their job. But someone had been with the little one every day since they came here.

***

The bike trip was a bull's eye. Finally they had time for each other, they were just the two of them. The last months have been spent trying to save the company, the number of orders has drastically decreased over the quarter. As a result, Wojtek spent most of his time in the office looking for solutions, establishing new contacts and creating a marketing strategy. He had the impression that his daughter had grown up, that she was even more mature, which was probably an exaggeration, but well, sometimes parents do not look at their children objectively. There was no doubt that her statements were quite coherent and thoughtful. Sometimes her way of thinking surprised Wojtek, and her ideas and reflections had nothing to do with her age. He thought it was due to the company of adults, and he couldn't tell if it was an advantage or a disadvantage.

They were on their way home when suddenly several police patrols passed. Somewhat confused, they sped up. What they found definitely disturbed the peaceful landscape.

"What's that supposed to mean?" Wojtek did not hide his horror when he abandoned his bicycle at the gate and ran up to Nina.

Mati has already thrown herself on her mother's neck, a bit scared.

"It's a nightmare. Mati, will you go play to the lavender to Mrs. Wanda and Mr. Alfred?" Nina needed a few minutes to be alone with her husband.

"All right, Mommy. But I didn't do anything wrong, right?"

The baby was still a little confused.

"No, of course not, honey." Nina kissed her cheek and led her upstairs.

Now policemen with hounds were walking around their house. A dozen or so people were rummaging in the crops, some were near the forest, and others were searching their property.

"Will you tell me what the hell is going on here?" Wojtek suspected that his wife discovered what he had discovered, but he preferred to make sure.

"Ms. Stefania, you know our vacationer, said that for several days she had been watching Matylda taking her blanket around noon and going to the edge of the field, and then talking for several hours with an older woman. It is not known who she is and what her intentions are. God, what if she's some kidnapper or psychopath? What kind of woman starts a relationship with a small child secretly? What if she did something to her?" Nina burst into tears.

Her husband hugged her tightly and said nothing. He only looked into the distance and seemed to be analyzing the facts he had just discovered.

"Sorry, lady and gentleman, we need to talk to the baby." One of the officers interrupted the scene. "If we're going to help, we need to know who to look for. I suggest that one of my people go with you. We'll try to do it my way."

Nina had to control her emotions first.

In her head hundreds of thoughts circulated. Of course, like a mother, she couldn't make a sober picture of the situation right now. The worst and macabre visions pierced her mind minute by minute. But she knew that she must, she just has to cooperate with the police.

"Mati, come on, let's do some scratch and talk." A police psychologist sat in the corner of the room, while Wojtek suggested that the child play. Meanwhile, Nina brought the lemonade and joined her family, trying to make a frown mocking smile.

"You know, when I was away, you met your friend. This relation has been going on for several days, right?" Wojtek inconveniently started the conversation with the little one.

Matylda was not stupid and knew perfectly well that she must have done something wrong, since mommy was crying, daddy looked different than usual, and their yard was occupied by white and blue cars and men in uniform. So it was not easy for her to answer her father's question.

"Mati, you see, we always tell each other everything. That's our contract, right?" Wojtek changed his tone to a bit more firm, but still gentle.

"Yes, Daddy, but I don't want anything bad to happen." Matylda finally filled the room with words.

"Of course, honey. None of us want that. Only gentlemen came here to us, because someone is looking for your friend and very much wants to meet her. I mean, we think it's about your friend, but we don't know much about her.

Would you help us? Because if it's her, then the one looking for her would be very happy to meet."

"Who's that?" Matylda believed.

"It's her dad. He had been looking for her for a long time and he missed her, you know how I do when we say goodbye for a long time. So this dad loves her very much, he would like to finally find her, hug her and take her home." The first nerves were gone, and Wojtek's voice was becoming more and more certain. He hated lying to her, but now he couldn't find a better solution.

"It would even be correct. My friend said there were definitely a few people looking for her. But she doesn't want to meet them anymore, because it won't change anything anyway." Matilda sold the first information to the police and parents.

"Or maybe it will. If these loved ones were already here, if she had seen them, maybe she would have decided otherwise?"

"I do not know. Maybe. She says that she will always be alone and that she enjoys sitting and talking together," she continued.

"Well, how do you spend your time? Are you just talking or maybe you are playing something?" Wojtek was reluctantly heading in the direction that his dark thoughts were directing him.

"At the beginning, in May, we just got to know each other. And now we walk together in our field, we draw and tell stories." Mati watched the policeman sitting in the corner, who was peeking at her and writing something constantly in his notebook. "Oh. And she keeps asking such funny riddles." Mati smiled, but nobody reciprocated her reaction, so she grew serious again.

"How's it in May, honey? You got it wrong, it is August now."

"Daddy, I know. A friend of mine had moved here in May. Our friendship has lasted for several months. Only I went to kindergarten before and we couldn't always meet. And now, on vacation, we spend time together every day." This last statement touched everyone present. Nina walked over to the window and started whipping.

"Okay, let's scratch it now. Take the card, I'll take mine. I told you sometimes about my old friend Jarek. I'll draw him for you because you've never met. He has big black eyes like a deer, you'd like them. You draw me your friend, did you say what her name is?" Wojtek looked at the card.

"She doesn't have a name. She says she doesn't know her name anymore." Matylda talked and drew.

A crazy woman, Nina thought.

The white sheet was slowly filling up with colors, dominated by white and yellow. Even from the child's indistinct drawing, it was easy to decipher certain details. The woman had long, slightly disheveled blonde hair, a white shirt down to her thigh, and a white face. She was holding a wooden pole in her hand.

"She takes her dogs with her sometimes." The girl drew the animals as best she could.

Wojtek, whose elements of the puzzle slowly began to form a coherent whole, turned pale and red alternately. Nina, watching him closely, asked them to leave for a moment, leaving her daughter in the company of Mrs. Wanda and the psychologist.

"Would you like to explain something to me?" She tugged hard on his sleeve. "Do you know anything about this madwoman?"

"What to explain?" Wojtek did not pay attention to her. He was absent.

"Your whole life "before me", "before us", does it have anything to do with what is happening in our yard, with our daughter?" The woman's voice grew louder, turning into a scream at the end of the sentence. "Answer me! Answer me finally! It's about my baby!" Not only was she screaming, she was hitting her husband's chest.

Wojtek had neither the strength nor the desire to go back to the past once again. He closed this chapter once and for all, although in the light of today's events it seemed that "forever" in this case does not exist. He was definitely not going to tell Janka the story now, but he knew he had to say something to reassure the innocent woman.

"I don't know if you will understand. I don't even know if you'll believe me if I tell you who our daughter is talking to. This is really the least important. The most important thing is to prevent another meeting. I have reason to believe that, despite what the sources say,

Matylda is safe, but I am not sure for 100%." He was saying something, but it sounded so enigmatic that Nina became more and more irritated.

"Tell me straight. Short. Explain. I'm not an idiot, but maybe I will understand," she insisted.

"Short? Fine. You know I was in love. Well, my ex-girlfriend's name was Svetlana and she lived by Lake Świteź in Belarus. She was a demon - rusalka, or if you prefer to follow Mickiewicz - Świtezianka. Then I helped her reverse the spell and she became an ordinary woman. Then our paths parted. Fate, chance wanted us to meet again. The feeling revived, or maybe it never really went out. We planned a wedding and got engaged. Suddenly Marysia felt worse, I will not go into the details of the story about her mother, so as not to complicate things, until she finally collapsed. Then I turned her into another demon - Lady Midday. Of course, thanks to the support of charlatans, whose help you used so eagerly in the past. I believe she found me here and is seeing our baby. I just don't know what her intentions are." Wojtek recited these few sentences as if he had learned them by heart. His face and body showed no signs of emotion. He stared into the distance as if looking for answers to questions that haunted him in the setting sun.

At first Nina was silent. She sat down on the stairs and put her head in her hands. Indeed, she did not understand much of what he said. She couldn't believe that this pragmatist, an engineer can believe in supernatural beings. She is different. She has always been interested in white magic, herbal medicine and natural medicine. She was close to the foundations of Buddhism and Hinduism. She was convinced that man has at least several incarnations and is reborn over and over again, and that his soul wanders. But he? Wojtek? Her Wojtek? "Funny, isn't it?" He still couldn't meet her eyes.

"Not at all. Rather terrible." She tapped him on the shoulder and went to the room upstairs to look after her little daughter.

***

When the police cars left the villa, Matylda went to sleep, and the vacationers stopped asking embarrassing questions, the two spouses decided to come up with a plan of action.

"First, tell me everything you know about this demon. My guess is that when Marysia turned into it, you kept looking for her and read what you called sources?" Nina did not have time to fully process the information she acquired today. She just took it for granted and decided to go a step further just to keep her family safe.

"Yes and no. I mean like this: I've read hundreds of books about this demon, but no, I wasn't looking for HER."

"May I ask why? If I understood correctly, she was love of life, destiny and so on. Why then?" They were talking quite calmly, sitting on the wooden swing in front of the stable, but slightly away from the entrance so that no one could hear them.

"You see, I know someone who has devoted his entire life to recovering his beloved, also a demon. I also know what life this person led, what losses it suffered and how it ended. I'm not, I wasn't ready for this. I was hoping to finally be free from the past, that she would never find me. I considered Marysia dead, I went through all stages of mourning.

I got to know you and thought finally it will be beautiful that it will finally be normal." He finally met her eyes.

"Why can't it never be like this? Why, when people are happy for a moment, does something have to disturb their peace?" Nina's questions were rhetorical. "Who is the Lady Midday and what can she do to our child? And the key question is, how are we supposed to protect our family?"

"What can I tell you? She looks just like Mati drew. She is the soul of a woman who died just before or during her marriage. And that's all the information that is consistent in every region of the country. Then the problems begin. Some believe that she is killing farmers. Others say she only causes a stroke and faints in the field. Oh, I forgot, you don't have to worry that much, because Lady Midday only comes in summer and disappears in autumn. Let's hope it turns out for good. There is still a lot of information about her..." Nina saw that Wojtek was cutting the topic because he did not want to tell her something that she did not want to hear.

"Tell me, I want to know everything. And do not be afraid, I will not fall apart, this is about my little daughter, I am as fighting as ever." It's true, despite the enormity of what Nina experiences today, perhaps due to the adrenaline rush, she felt she had the strength to overcome all the obstacles she encountered, including the demon.

"Well. Lady Midday hate children," he said in one breath. Despite his wife's declaration, he noticed that the sentence shocked her. However, he decided to continue.

"She kidnaps them and carry them in bags or… bury them alive in the ground."

He watched her reaction carefully, but it was different from what he had expected.

"Hmm... I think in my naivety that if this Maria wanted to kidnap, let alone bury Matylda alive, she had hundreds of opportunities to do so. After all, our child claims that they have been seeing for several months. Don't you think it's a bit weird and inconsistent with what you're saying?"

"I know. I already thought about it. Because you see, when SHE was a rusalka, it was also not exactly like that, let's call it stereotypical. And then she fell in love with me and - how to explain it - this human part began to dominate the demonic one. I think it is similar this time. Maybe the original intention was to hurt Mati, but maybe there's a fight somewhere in the middle." Wojtek tried to sound specific and logical, although it was difficult.

"What's the plan?" Janka already had her own, but her husband was an expert in extreme situations, so she preferred to get to know his version first.

"I have to talk to her. Nina, you don't even know how much I don't want it. But I have to. I hope to find out what she's doing here and ask her to leave us alone."

"Good," she said only that one word, but there was everything in the melody of her voice: fear of losing a loved one who would see his first and greatest love, fear of losing a child, which they might not be able to protect when confronted with the power of nature in the form of a demon, finally regret to Wojtek that he brought them such a fate.

She told him to go to sleep next to Matylda because she needed to think a moment longer. Instead, she started her computer and entered the search term: Lady Midday. She learned much more than her husband wanted to tell her.

She finally fell asleep. The images that ran through her head resembled Munch's paintings on the one hand and Van Gogh's on the other. Harvest, flowers, stuffiness, black dogs, old women with twisted faces, orgies of naked girls with farm hands. She woke up drenched in sweat after a few dozen hours. Matylda was standing next to her, smiling and ready to play. When asked where daddy was, she replied that he had gone to talk to someone.

"Mati, we need to talk." Nina knew the girl wouldn't like what she heard now.

"I know. I guess you don't like my friend." The daughter was really smart.

"It's not that we don't like her. We're concerned that she's much older than you, and you shouldn't be spending that much time together. We'll find you a friend your age. Don't worry, it is vacation, daddy's off, we'll be spending a lot of time now, okay?" She stroked the baby's head.

"I'll be sad if I can't see her anymore. I could entrust her with every secret, tell about everything that happened to me and what I didn't like." Matilda was offended in a childlike way, she folded her arms and formed herself horseshoe mouth.

Nina felt a pang in her heart. Wojtek always accused her of being too involved in running a guesthouse and his own passion - art, and paying the child too little attention. Perhaps he was right. Maybe Matylda was looking for support from a stranger, because it was she who had failed as a mother. But she loved her more than her life, engaged her in everyday matters encouraged her to help with chores. Only normal human conversation was apparently missing. What could she, a five-year-old girl, tell this woman? Did she talk about her and Wojtek? Was she complaining about her? Nina involuntarily fell into a rather somber mood.

"Please, tell me more about this girl. Anything. Do you know anything about her? Was she just listening to your stories?" Nina wanted to know the enemy.

"She didn't say much. She was just very sad, but I couldn't comfort her. The first time she came, she looked at me strangely. I was even scared for a moment. Not anymore after that. She asked what dad's name was, where he works, what we do in our spare time. She also asked about you. How did you meet, is this your family home. Such things." Matylda was playing with her doll.

"You told her everything?" At that moment Nina was dominated by one feeling: jealousy.

"No, I don't know. Some things I told, others I didn't." She continued the doll's care.

"Ok, dear. Have fun for a while, because you remember that you have to go to that policeman this afternoon?"

"Yes, but I'm a little scared. Don't you guys want to do something bad to my friend?" Matylda looked worried again.

"No, baby. We want to help her get back to where she came from so that she won't be so sad anymore." Nina was bending the truth.

***

Wojtek spent several hours lying on a blanket. For him - an active person who was constantly in motion, it was a rather boring job. So he decided to comb the fields of cereals, and walk around the area. He was hoping to finally meet HER. At first, he put the whole script in his head, as if what was about to happen was a scene or just a film shot that had to be played out in the world, and then returned home and forgotten. Why then did he feel this strange tightness in his stomach? Why was his hands sweating so much? Was it just sweating because of the August temperature? What would he tell her? Apart from the accusations and reproaches, of course? How would this meeting end? Or maybe it isn't SHE at all. Maybe she's some freak, a loner. The latter, however, was unlikely.

"Daddy! Daddy!" A small figure ran towards him with a bottle of water under her arm. "She's not coming anymore. It's already after three o'clock. She always comes only for an hour or two and disappears," Matylda explained to her father.

"Well. I'll try to talk to her tomorrow." Wojtek breathed a sigh of relief despite everything.

"We have to go, remember?" The daughter admonished.

"I would almost forget. Let's go." Indeed, lost in the events of the past, he forgot about the appointment visit.

The police station was almost empty. Few employees in their offices, in the corridor, not a single person. Their neighborhood was extremely peaceful. Not much happened. Therefore, when Nina reported the suspicion that there was a threat, the commander immediately took appropriate steps, supporting himself with support from nearby towns. Today they were to go to Lublin together with Matylda and the commandant to create a memory portrait of the suspicious woman who harassed their underage daughter. Only today was it possible to arrange a meeting with the staff aspirant, who was one of the twenty specialists in the country dealing with this activity. After less than an hour, they arrived at their destination.

Wojtek already knew that it was all pointless, that it was not about a criminal, but about HER. However, the mechanism did move, or maybe somewhere in his heart he still hoped he was wrong. He wanted so badly to be wrong.

"Hello, young lady." The policeman shook hands with Matylda and took out a lollipop from the other. The girl smiled immediately. "We will draw today, but we have the best tools for that in Poland. You've never seen one like this before. Will you sit down?" He invited the girl to the table. "Look, we have different smileys here. First you choose the head, then the hair, eyes, lips and the best - coloring at the end. Shall we play together? It's a bit like a computer game, you will have a lot to tell your peers at kindergarten."

Wojtek was no longer surprised that this man is one of the most sought-after sketchbooks in the country. He was a great psychologist. His daughter was already involved in the fun and judging by her behavior, she managed to relax, which was so important in the whole process.

"It will be your own drawing. I will not interfere, I will only show you what shapes you have to choose from. Then we'll print it and you can take it home. Choose the person you would like to have with you. Mom and Dad are always there, but I heard you have a new friend who is lonely. We will help you find her family, and you will be able to have her drawing always with you. What do you think?" The experienced policeman continued.

"I like this idea. Can we draw now?" Matylda eagerly took action.

While the girl was browsing the tools available in the computer program, Wojtek was looking at the forensic laboratory, which did not look like that. There were many flowers here. The walls were green in color. There was soothing relaxing music in the background. Matylda got warm cocoa. There was a red light outside so that nobody would disturb you.

The five-year-old was willing to cooperate. She gladly answered questions and corrected the still-created portrait. Wojtek did not interfere, he sat on the chair and waited.

"End!" The little girl exclaimed. "She looks exactly like my friend. Everything is correct!" Matylda did not fully understand the situation and she was glad that it was fun and in addition everyone is proud of her.

"Bravo, skinny girl!" The policeman came a little closer to Wojtek, and Matylda was waiting for the finished portrait to be printed.

"We will send the photo to all units. We will also show them in the local media," whispered the policeman in the ear of Wojtek, who only then looked at the computer monitor. He almost passed out from the sensation. All doubts were dispelled. It was SHE. Marysia. The way he remembered her. The way he loved her. It did not escape the policeman's attention.

"Do you know her? Do you have any information that might help with the investigation?" He asked.

"No, I can't help," he muttered, and thought that there was nothing here for the police's efforts. "Goodbye."

"We will keep you updated..." Wojtek was not listening. He knew he had to solve the problem himself. But could it even be possible? And what could he, a mere mortal, do in this situation? He didn't know.

***

Nina was finishing the telephone conversation with Wojtek.

"So you're staying? For sure? Okay, but watch her. I know, I know, come back in the morning. No. Ok. Me too."

She was worried about her daughter and husband. She spent the entire evening accompanying the vacationers not to think too much about what had happened to them. Finally, tired, she fell asleep on the kitchen couch. The next day, however, she decided to take matters into her own hands. At most, he will fail. As it neared noon, she headed towards the farmland and... who knows why... she took a thick stick with her. Minutes passed, hours passed, but no one showed up. The heat was taking its toll, so the resigned woman, instead of creating dialogues in her head, which she probably won't be able to do anyway, finally returned home. She felt as if get a weight off her mind. In a moment her relatives arrived. Matylda insisted on going to see her friend.

"Child, I told you that you can't see her anymore!"

Nina was very irritated by her daughter's stubbornness. "We talked about it."

"You know, maybe tomorrow. Today, after all, it's already a few hours in the afternoon," Wojtek unexpectedly interjected, which made his wife angry. After all, they were establishing a common strategy.

No meetings, the child as far as possible from the farmland and full control.

"Mati, can you go to Jerzy? He said only you can spice the perfect risotto." She tried to hide the irritation. Once they were alone, she no longer had to control herself. "What are these ideas?" She said.

"Do not panic. Let me explain. Now we are sure. The girl in the portrait is Marysia, or actually I don't know who it is, but we are definitely dealing with a demon. I think we need to send Matilda to one more meeting. I'll hide somewhere nearby and then try to talk to Marysia."

"Wojtek, do you think this Lady Midday is stupid?" Nina didn't like her husband's plan.

"I know. Sounds naive, right? Only I can't think of anything better. Any suggestions?"

"Nothing. Well, maybe one. I will take Matylda to my parents. Or maybe we can fly together for an overdue vacation. The summerers are here for a while longer, and I'm willing to give them money to get out of here."

"Are you sure this will solve the problem? Because I have the impression that if we don't talk to HER, the situation will repeat itself every year. I'm not going to live in constant anxiety, fear for a baby. What if she really wants to kidnap Mati? Maybe she feels sorry for me that I changed her? Maybe she is looking for revenge?"

Wojtek was walking around the room, brushing his hair with his hands.

He was probably not intended to panic his wife, but this is exactly what he achieved.

"What are we gonna do now?" Nina burst into tears. While in the morning she had the impression that her motherly love was a cure for all evil and would protect her daughter from all the evil in the world, now she lost all hope.

"I do not know honey. I don't know..." Wojtek felt so helpless for the last time when Marysia was about to collapse. "We certainly cannot run away, because there is no escape from her."

***

The days passed peacefully. At high noon, Matylda was heading in the known direction. Right behind her, however, was followed by an escort in the form of mom and dad. Instead of a carefree vacation, the three of them felt a strange tension. The summer vacationers left the villa, some - because the planned stay had ended, others - because of strange events, the police and the arrest warrants hanging around.

The end of summer was beautiful. Warm, but not too hot. They loved this place the most at that time. Wojtek got up early in the morning, when the forest fragments were still plunged in twilight, but the sun's rays were already shining with their delicate light on their ridge. The deciduous and coniferous forest presented all shades of green, but slowly began to show colors. After waking up, Wojtek liked to take a walk around the property. It gave him a relative sense of security, but he also enjoyed the still dormant buildings. He looked at his surroundings with sentiment. He would be devastated if, for whatever reason, someone told him to leave it. How much heart he put into creating this atmospheric restaurant. How much did it cost him and his wife to arrange the garden, create a herbarium, a flower part, and even a wooden playground with a huge sandbox, zip-line and a monkey grove, which this season was abandoned in anticipation of its little one lady.

Even the hen pen he had been so opposed to at first, which had been completely out of the way, now seemed to him to be an integral part of the place. Atmospheric, with soul, with history, and above all - their own.

The most beautiful memories of a man were born here. Here he came with a clean slate, completely changed, silent and humble. Here his love for his wife flourished, and then for what he had received the most precious - for his daughter. He couldn't just give it up. It would break his heart.

Since then, on the day of the police arrival, Lady Midday has not come. Maybe two or three warm weeks left. The Stożyński family used every moment to squeeze out the summer like a lemon. So there were hiking, cycling trips, swimming in the pool, reading books together, joking around and laughing from time to time. Nothing has changed in this regard. The three of them stood behind each other by the wall, even stronger than before, and even more than before, celebrated each moment together.

The only thing that changed a lot was Matylda. Not immediately. Gradually.

"Honey, why are you sad again?" The mother could not calmly watch this lively and energetic child becoming more and more lethargic and gloomy day by day. However, she explained this with the disappearance of a secret friend.

"I'm not sad, mom. I've told you this many times. I just feel tired." The child has been acting differently than usual for some time.

"Are you okay, Mati?" Wojtek looked at his daughters' legs, they were emaciated and battered. No wonder, because the last few days were full of activities. The face, on the other hand, was almost completely white, and yet the sun was shining strongly, and they did not apply sunscreen on it regularly.

"I'm a bit faint, but it's probably hot." The little girl was picking the ground with a stick.

"Have a drink. And let's go inside, mother decided."

"When was the last time we did her tests?" The conversation took place between the parents. Supposedly Matylda was present, but she still relied on the bed, staring at the ceiling and communicating little.

"I am ashamed to admit it, but probably for her two-year birthday. Do you think there's something wrong with her? Do you think..." She didn't finish, but the adults understood each other without words anyway.

"No, no, let's not go crazy. Maybe she is anemic? We don't pay much attention to her diet. Especially recently. Constant trips, some bread for the road, soup. In kindergarten, at least she ate regularly, and then she always ate, asking Jerzy in the kitchen."

"Or she has a heat stroke." Nina knew that she was not keeping an eye on the baby, and this season she was spending way too much time in the sun at times when she should avoid it.

"Yeah, maybe it's a stroke." He caught it. "It would even make sense. Mati, do you have any other problems? You have a headache? You, little one, never complain about anything."

Wojtek was sincerely concerned.

"Sometimes I get a little pulsing like this right here." She pointed to her temples.

***

Matylda has always been an exceptional child. Nina did not know what colic are, she did not have to complain about the rebellion of a two-year-old, even tearing a child out of an idyllic village picture and handing her over to foreign kindergarten teachers at the age of three did not result in hysteria or regret. Their daughter was cheerful, compatible, creative and companionable. She did not make scenes, did not roll on the ground, she only cried when she was very afraid of something, but even that she did so quietly so as not to cause trouble. Often Nina wondered why she deserved for such a peaceful and joyful motherhood. Her husband's voice broke her out of her contemplation and making pauses in honor of her daughter.

"Anything else that might bother us?"

"Oh, and that blood!" Nina remembered. "It's true that several times I blamed it on fatigue and lack of sleep. Changes in the rhythm of the day. It's definitely anemia."

"Blood? From nose?" Wojtek was angry that he was finding out about something as the last one, and his wife-artist is excessively relaxed.

"Yes, her nose bled several times. Nothing big. It happens sometimes." Nina felt the scolding look on herself.

"Well. There is no point in discussing this. Make an appointment with her pediatrician tomorrow. Let him do research, prescribe some iron. And, my lady, from tomorrow we take care of the food. Vitamins, vegetables, fruits, meat. You have everything here in abundance. I'm going to talk to Jerzy right away and have him make you a little fat."

"All right, Papa. Maybe I'll have a little more strength, because I don't feel like doing anything lately." She turned over to get a better view of the clouds moving across the sky.

***

Wojtek was a model father in the eyes of Matylda's pediatrician. Exemplary dad - this is how he used to talk about him, when he had regular check-ups right after the baby was born, he asked how to wash the baby's belly button, how many units of vitamin K should be administered, how often should the baby defecate, where to start expanding the diet baby. The doctor also made a quick, not to say rash, assessment of Nina. Gray, drab, extravagant. Rather little concerned with the fate of the child. Like many who met a couple, the question crossed her mind: what does a man do with such a woman?

They have not visited the pediatrician's office very often for several years. Matylda was ill two or three times a year when they enrolled her in kindergarten, but she got immunized quickly, she took an expensive probiotic and the problems were over.

"So we have headaches and blood from nose. Please help the child undress, I will listen to her and watch her more closely," the doctor commanded. "By the way, you could check back a bit more, not only when you are already worried about something. Basic tests performed at least once a year give at least a minimal overview of the health condition," she said, listening to the girl's beating heart. "What's that?" She glanced at Matylda's legs and arms.

"Bruises. Simply," replied Janka, confirming the doctor in the belief that her attitude towards upbringing is extremely loose, and even disrespectful.

"Just bruises? Are you aware of the fact that bruises appear due to a shortage of blood platelets responsible for clotting?" She did not hide her irritation.

"And here we don't have a bruise or two, just forearms and legs covered with them."

"I didn't think... I thought it was a bicycle, climbing, running... like in kids." Nina was slouching more and more, and if she could collapse into the ground, it would probably be the moment when she would use this skill.

"Has there been any elevated temperature? Osteoarticular pain?" The doctor directed more questions towards Wojtek.

"Mati, answer the doctor," the man encouraged.

"I don't know, I guess normal, sometimes my legs hurt." The girl looked bored.

"She had no temperature. Well, maybe a few times, when she's just blown away from kindergarten. Probably a virus, I killed it with the right drug, and since there were no other symptoms, I did not make an appointment," Nina explained again.

"There is no point in asking. Symptoms can mean anything and everything. I don't like enlarged lymph nodes, but Matylda may be having some kind of infection. The throat looks fine, the ears are clean and auscultation also without reservations. I am writing you a referral for basic research, which will give a broader view of the situation."

She leaned down at her desk and began printing the referral and prescriptions.

When they said goodbye to the doctor and got into the car, Nina gave vent to negative emotions.

"How I hate her. She always considered me a bad mother and didn't even try to hide it. It is embarrassing and unprofessional. But you, you are the Daddy of the Year!"

Wojtek smiled, probably for the first time in several days.

"Don't overdo it. That's the way she is, but you don't choose a doctor who is nice for your child, but one who makes a good diagnosis, right?"

"True, true. She has the best opinions in the region, and she's the deputy head of paediatrics, so I'll eat her rude remarks and stupid comments somehow."

"Get some sleep tomorrow, and I'll go with Mati for research. In fact, she could tell us anything. No hypothesis was put forward. And maybe better. We will be sure when the results come."

***

The next morning, Wojtek dragged his semiconscious daughter out of bed, helped her dress, and took her to the laboratory. He hated such places. Ubiquitous white, the smell of disinfectants wafting in the air. Corridors full of sad people waiting for specialists. He was grateful that diseases had been bypassing his family so far. He reviewed the referral: peripheral blood count with a manual smear. Fortunately, Matylda was brave, because the sight of a nurse piercing his child's vein was almost unbearable for Wojtek. He hated the days of her earlier vaccinations and her tears shed over it, and those wide eyes when the needle was inserted into her body.

"Okay, now it's ice cream time." He wanted her to forget the morning events as soon as possible.

"You know what mom says about it?" Matylda was smiling broadly and her dimples on either side of her mouth looked delightful.

"Of course, but there are exceptions to the rule. And today we will make an exception." Wojtek was in a good mood.

He spent the last days with his daughter and wife. He felt relaxed, though he still had the events of the past weeks in the back of his head.

But he was becoming more and more convinced that the Lady Midday had arrived, she had found out what she wanted to know, she assured that Wojtek is happy and she decided to leave him alone.

This scenario was also passed on to Nina and - surprisingly - she probably gained peace of mind. Now it was only necessary to take care of the kid, nourish her, so that she would be prepared not only mentally but also physically for the new kindergarten year.

***

"When will be results?" Nina welcomed her family. "And what's on your face, my lady? These are probably not traces of sugar-filled ice cream, which bring nothing with them except a humus bug..."

"Don't scare her..." Wojtek interjected. "Ice cream eaten on special occasions has not hurt anyone yet." He winked at his daughter, and Matylda smiled. "And the results will be today, tomorrow, and in two days at the latest. I'll download it online and they'll send it to the doctor. Then we will make an appointment."

"Well. What are we going to do with this beautiful day started with ice cream?" Nina was also in an excellent mood. "How about Zamość? We've been living here for six years and we're still at home."

"I'm sorry! First, Lublin, second Kazimierz Dolny, third Kozłówka and also Janowiec. Little for you, woman?" Wojtek's tone was playful. Matylda liked it when her parents teased each other.

"Little, man. And good, I agree. We have already got to know a part of the region, but Zamość has still not been discovered by us."

"Is there anything fun for kids?" Matylda was afraid that this was another trip that would bore her. It is true that parents did everything to make her stay at the Janowiec castle and Lublin cathedrals more attractive, but for her, they were just ordinary walls."

"Of course! First, we will visit the Zamość zoo. What do you think?" Mother knew exactly how Mati reacts to animals. She remembered her daughter's delight when the chickens were brought. As she cared for them, she made sure that they did not lack food or water. That's why she thought she would bribe Matylda with this very offer.

"Zoo? Really? It's wonderful! I'm going to change into a clean blouse and take some old bread from Jerzy."

They haven't seen her so lively for a long time. "Listen? What did you say?" Nina was proud of herself.

"Nothing," said Wojtek.

She hit him on the head with a pillow and went to prepare provisions. Matylda loved excursions, and most of them were a backpack with treats.

***

Zamość, not without reason called the architectural pearl of the Borderlands, delighted them at first sight. They decided to move zoo to the bottom of the list - much to Matylda's chagrin. They promised, however, that they would tell her a number of interesting legends related to the city, when they would visit its charming places. They started their tour from the Town Hall and the Great Market Square with its characteristic colorful tenement houses. Nina insisted that they enter the Zamość Museum, but lost the vote 1:2. However, she did not give up at the entrance to the synagogue and put it on her own. She also insisted on spending at least a few minutes in the cathedral and visiting each of the nine chapels. Her companions were less and less amused. Ultimately, they ended up in a zoo. To Matylda's enormous joy, it turned out that the garden was still growing, and recently hippos, zebras and giraffes have arrived. Of course, this resolute five-year-old girl accosted whoever she could to ask her questions and get comprehensive answers. For parents, it was a moment of relaxation, especially since the zoo employees showed angelic patience.

"Daughter, if you love nature so much, maybe we would go to Roztocze?" Wojtek asked a bit ironically. He planned this attraction of the region, but saw that the child was shuffling, breathless.

"What's this?" Asked Matylda, although Nina realized that she was already very tired. In fact, even a little too much..."

"You do not know? Child, what kind of world do you live in? Roztocze is a wild land, to which man has not been allowed for years, so it was inhabited by all strange creatures, from fairies, through elves and dwarfs..." the words he just said can be extremely true. Except that instead of fairies and elves, the dark forests of Roztocze might have been inhabited by latawiec, leshy, and other demons he knew a little less about.

"Okay, but I'm already very sleepy and tired. I'll take a nap in the car." Matylda was pale and her lips were dry. Indeed, as soon as she got into the vehicle, she fell asleep. Wojtek was glad that the child got tired of an interesting trip. Nina was slightly less optimistic at the moment.

"Maybe we needlessly tire her so? After all, she is probably anemic, and she has less strength."

"Don't overdo it. We took long breaks at the zoo, and we walked around Square very quickly. I had just had a glimpse of the architecture of the Padua of the North and you guys have already taken me to the zoo."

"I will not comment on it out of politeness." Nina knew that Wojtek was giving way to Matylda much more often than she was.

"I'm kidding. We will go alone one day, like our daughter already will recognize that time spent with elderly people is time wasted."

"Why are we going to Roztocze? She's had enough."

"We will get off for a while, wet our feet in the river... like in love." He wasn't looking at her, just at the road. But he knew she was blushing.

***

They drove up to the less frequented part of the Czartowe Pole reserve. They wanted a little peace and time for themselves, without onlookers and passers-by. They pulled out a blanket and stared at the waterfall. Embraced, they didn't say much, they were enjoying the time together. Their daughter was still asleep, carried on the blanket, so they decided not to disturb her. Unexpectedly, something or someone broke into this postcard frame.

"Did you see that?" Nina jumped to her feet, scared.

"They were dogs?"

"Dogs? Big black dogs with horrible eyes! Where did they get here? We'd better go." Nina got into the car and closed the door. She adjusted Matylda's blanket resting on her emaciated legs and waited for Wojtek.

Meanwhile, the man looked around as if searching for the continuation of the scene he had just watched. And he lived to see it. It was like a blink, a split second, but it was definitely there. A beauty in a see-through white thigh-length shirt, long blonde hair that ends at the height of shapely breasts. Chasing the pack of evil dogs. Did she notice him? Probably not. Though his heart was beating like crazy, he decided to wait a moment so as not to let know anything by his face. He got into the car. He did not say bout her to Janka.

***

After returning home, Wojtek was absent. He performed all activities mechanically. However, the whole day trip took its toll on all three, so his girls did not notice the man's strange behavior. Matylda was asleep all the time. Her father carried her to her crib and sat down beside it. He studied her room. She wasn't like other girls her age - dressed head to toe in pink, with one and the same favorite story, and pierced ears. His baby girl was different. She had the walls painted yellow so that even in winter she would have a little sun at her fingertips, she preferred books over piles of stuffed animals and dolls. She had loads of them. She slowly put the letters into sentences, and reading was a lot of fun. She was not satisfied with the first reader. When they entered the bookstore, she looked at the covers for a long time, asked to tell what the story was about. Yes, books dominated this little room - they occupied a large bookcase in the center. Apart from it, there were also: a wooden bed, a table and a chair, and a wardrobe. Matylda also chose lamps in the shape of clouds, stars and the moon. Wojtek looked at his daughter with delight known only to her parents. Everything about her was perfect. He didn't even notice when he was overwhelmed by sleep.

***

"Someone's vacation is over!" The smell of bacon fried eggs wafted through the kitchen. Nina was a master at preparing scrambled eggs.

"And so I extended it by two days. Anyway, September is about to begin, Mati will return to kindergarten, you will have lovers of autumn landscapes in the guesthouse. Well, and someone has to earn for this house." Wojtek smiled and kissed his wife on the cheek. But he still thought about yesterday's picture.

"Your phone has vibrated maybe three times already."

"It begins. It's not even nine o'clock yet, but clients are ready to attack." He looked at the cell phone and was surprised.

"Mati's doctor. Since when do doctors themselves call patients?" He asked a question that chilled the blood in both of them.

"Call back." Nina wiped her hands on a cloth, threw the wooden spoon into the sink and biting her nails, was standing next to her husband's head.

"Hello? Yes, it's me. I understand. But could you please say more? I understand. Well. Which one? We will be. Of course." He put down the phone.

"What happened?" Nina's heart was pounding like crazy.

"I do not know anything. She wouldn't say. Only today we are to come for a consultation. I call my office to say they can cope without me. Wake up and dress Mati," He issued the instructions.

Nina woke Matylda, they went downstairs. The little girl did not want breakfast, and for some time she would rather not eat at all. They thought the heat affected her as it did adults, and there was no need to worry.

Two mothers with children were sitting in front of the doctor's office. They sat down next to it, but were silent. Matylda was playing with the rag doll she had taken with her, making eye contact with the other little companions of misery. Her parents, on the other hand, stared at the floor. Nina was biting her nails again. The patient was leaving the office with his mother, who was finishing a conversation with the doctor. The latter, noticing the Stożyński, immediately asked them to come to her.

"Take a seat. Matylda, would you agree to go over to Mrs. Krysia, the one who always weighs and measures you? She has prepared blocks, puzzles and would like to play with you. Meanwhile, I will be right next to your parents. Ok?" The doctor was composed and her voice was grateful and calm.

"Ok." Matylda was an open child and she never had any problems with entering into new relations. Although she preferred to be sure that her parents would be somewhere close.

"So it's bad if we can't talk in front of her." Nina's eyes slowly filled with tears.

"Stop it," Wojtek silenced her. "Doctor, what did the tests show? Just bluntly and please, in understandable language."

"Of course. To begin with, I will say that Mrs. Krysia takes Matylda's blood for re-examination in a moment. The results I received and consulted with the oncologist..."

"With the oncologist?" Nina couldn't keep her emotions in check. "She has cancer?" She was choking on tears.

"Janka, stop it. Calm down." Wojtek wanted to hear everything the doctor had to say.

"So, the results I got are surprising for me and the oncologists. They show that Matylda suffers from AML, i.e. acute myeloid leukemia..."

"I don't believe! I don't want to listen to that! This isn't really happening." Nina got up from her chair and started pacing nervously around the doctor's room. Wojtek also could no longer control himself. He hugged his wife and after a while convinced her that they must listen to the rest.

"Dear Mr. and Mrs. Stożyński, acute myeloid leukemia is a disease that occurs most often in the elderly, in their sixties. In its course, white blood cells are changed, which - generally speaking - displace healthy cells and lead to disease symptoms."

"What's the chance it's a mistake?" Wojtek hugged his wife in the arms, who did not hear the doctor's further words.

"Big, I think. We do not agree with the age of the patient, moreover, this cancer is rare, even in adults, and usually affects men. Only the symptoms and blood parameters agree. However, the tests should be repeated immediately. Maybe it's a mistake." The doctor tried to calm down the parents.

"When will the new results be?" Nina wiped her nose with a handkerchief.

"Today. I'll see to it myself. As soon as I receive them, I will notify you immediately."

"Ok. Let it be that way."

"For now I don't want to tell you anything more. I have to be sure," she added.

"If it's this disease, can we cure it?" Nina wanted to leave this room, confident that even in the case of the worst diagnosis, she would be able to help her child.

"There are different options. Allograft, that is, from a foreign donor, and pharmacotherapy."

"Tell me, can she die? Could it be too late for all this?" Nina was hysterical.

"Mrs. Stożyńska, I can't say that..."

"Answer me!" The woman was furious.

"Untreated acute myeloid leukemia can be fatal in days." The doctor lost her patience.

There was silence. Nina stopped crying. She took her things and left the office. Wojtek had hundreds of questions that have now flown from his head. He stared at one point and couldn't move.

"Mr. Stożyński..." The doctor tried to rehabilitate herself. "Here's the address. Please report today and call me. This is a clinic with a hematology department. It is necessary to perform a bone marrow biopsy.

It will enable us to finally confirm or exclude the occurrence of the disease. Mr. Stożyński?"

"Did you write it down for me? Thank you. Of course, we're going there already." Wojtek did not look at her. He took the piece of paper and left. His wife was waiting outside, and Mati was playing with blocks in the nurse's room.

"Go home. I'm taking her to another exam. After this we will be clear. For now, let's try not to break down. Maybe it's some terrible mistake," he was uttering words that sounded artificial. Probably because he himself was not convinced of their validity. But he felt he had to say something.

"I'm her mom. I am going with you. I'll pull myself together right now," she says dryly.

As they headed for the clinic, Matylda sensed a tension, but thought her parents had argued, which had happened more than once, so she didn't care much about it. She hummed a song and waved her doll to the melody. Nina did not take her eyes off the cell phone. Wojtek did not even have to ask her what she was looking for online. As you know, the Internet is not always a good advisor. Nina was clutching her quivering lips again and again, but she was holding back her crying in time. She did not want to arouse any suspicions in her daughter.

***

Hematology Clinic. Wojtek thought it was just a sad place. Like walls with pictures from fairy tales, like pastel and warm colors, but still the children sitting here, probably like their daughter, were now waiting for the sentence.

"Unfortunately, we still have difficulties with the treatment of acute myeloid leukemia." Nina heard fragments of Wojtek's conversation with the doctor. At that time, she was sitting by Matylda, who was taking marrow from the area of the breastbone. "We will determine the changes in the chromosomes of these cells, then we will look at genetic mutations," the doctor continued.

Nina was in the office, but she felt as if her spirit had left her body. She couldn't explain it. Only some fragments of reality reached her. For a moment she even thought that she was mad, that she had lost her sanity. It didn't matter to her.

"...yes, mainly a graft, but I immediately realize that it is not always possible to find a donor. Anyway, we will take all decisions and further steps only after examining the cells."

Matylda woke up. Tired but smiling.

"Can we go home now?" Asked her mother. "Mommy?" She repeated.

"Honey, mom is not feeling well. We can go home. We will eat something delicious and read this new book about the legend of the Far East.".

Wojtek wanted to fall asleep already, to wake up the next day. Let it be tomorrow. Tomorrow they will wake up with a fresh mind, tomorrow they will find a solution. Tomorrow... what if there is no tomorrow at all?

"I'm ready." Matylda was standing with her little rucksack at the door of the clinic, Nina was there with her.

They went to bed extraordinarily early. They were all exhausted. Nobody had the strength to browse the Internet anymore, nobody wanted to talk or even be together. Each of them took time to get used to the situation. And even five-year-old Matylda was already a sensible and perceptive girl that she knew - she was sick. Probably seriously, since mommy is acting so weird and daddy doesn't say anything. Will she die? If so, where will she end up? And will she meet mum and dad there? She fell asleep.

***

As soon as the results were obtained, the Stożyńskis were notified that they would convene a medical council. Matylda stayed with Nina's parents, who, having learned about the situation and the condition of their daughter, unable to take any action, came to the Lublin region. Wojtek and Nina were sitting in the corridor as stressed as before the most important exam. He was nervously glancing at his watch, she was biting what was left of her fingernails. Things were going so fast that they both felt like in a movie, as if the script provided for a fast-paced action, and the characters, i.e. themselves, played only assigned roles. They still hoped the movie would have a happy ending.

"We invite you inside." The senior doctor made a gesture indicating empty seats in the left corner of the room.

There were five doctors. Three men, a woman Wojtek did not know, and their doctor. Everyone seems to be over fifty. Their expressions showed no emotion. Not only that, one carefully noted something, the other seemed to be answering the SMS. For them it was another patient, another business meeting. For Wojtek and Nina it was to be or not to be their family.

"Mr. and Mrs. Stożyński, let me start with the fact that the blood tests showed exactly the same as the original ones. So the hi-thesis about error and the substitution of results has been refuted.

As for the puncture and its results, well... leukemia cells at this stage infiltrate the child's internal organs and lymph nodes. As you have noticed, the patient's weight has decreased, and the liver and spleen are enlarged. Finally, unwanted cells slowly take hold of the entire bone marrow and grow beyond that."

The patient's weight... She has a name. Matylda. His Matylda. Wojtek was outraged by the behavior of this official.

"Doctor, as always, can it be clearer?" Wojtek looked imploringly at his daughter's pediatrician. For the first time since they met, she looked deep into his eyes, and the look was different than before.

"Mr. and Mrs. Stożyński, Matylda is in the final stage of her disease. Important organs... the organs necessary for her further life become ineffective successively... We cannot help her anymore..."

For the first time in days, Nina spoke. And the way she took it, she was probably heard throughout the hospital. Complaints, insults, curses caused most of the body to leave the room. The three of them stayed with a doctor they knew.

"What should we do now?" Wojtek did not have any plan. He simply didn't know what they would do after they left this room.

"You should talk to her, prepare for worse well-being, use up all overdue leaves and spend as much time as possible with the three of you. If you are a believer, it's time to bring a priest to her.

If you need anything, I am at your disposal." She lived a hand on his shoulder and headed for the exit.

"Doctor? Is it our fault?" He asked the last question, which made the air thicker.

"This type of leukemia affects children out of one hundred percent of cases. Children between the ages of two and five. It is recommended that you have basic blood tests at least once a year and be monitored, constantly monitored. Let's not look for the guilty. Goodbye."

Nina threw a few bitter words as she was leaving. Wojtek held her tight, because he was afraid that it might lead to misconduct.

"Or maybe you will stop challenging and insulting everyone around you and look at yourself?" He screamed.

"The quack in the skirt called me a nasty mother, she blamed me for Mati to die!" Nina crouched in the corner of the room.

"This quack made us understand that she had to be examined and her symptoms should not be underestimated. How many times had she said she had a pain behind her ears but had no fever, so we didn't react? How many times has she had a bruise on her body and we told her to be more careful when running? How many times has her nose bled and you haven't even told me?" He roared.

"Well. So, it's my fault. Blameless yourself. Daddy of the year you come home and do not live in! Maybe the baby needed more attention instead of this decaying company! Do you blame me for not noticing something? And you? You? What do you notice? Do you know the names of her classmates? Do you know what her favorite color is? You remember the names her three rag dolls? So, get the fuck off me!" Nina ran out of the room.

***

They spent the next few days launching all possible contacts to reach the most evoked professors specializing in the treatment of acute leukemia. Wojtek's father had a few doctor friends, from his high school days. So they called, scanned the results, answered all the detailed questions, and even drove Matylda around Poland. In the end, it always ended with the same statement - save your child from these trips, don't waste time on further visits, try to come to terms with the situation, maybe seek help from a psychologist...

They didn't want to make up. They wanted to fight, they wanted to save their beloved child. They talked coolly, in an official tone, and only on topics related to the child. One evening, Wojtek, sitting on the porch, when everyone in the house was asleep, began to analyze the situation again. Life had taught him, however, that there is not always a way out, and if there is, it is extremely brutal. However, this last sentence made him think more and more intensively about an unconventional solution. After all, he had already gone through it once, after all, Marysia was also supposed to die, and yet she is alive, and yet she wanders in the woods. Maybe... just how to do it... and is there enough time... and can he know how...

He hastily put on a thin jacket and boots, got in the car and started riding. He had no doubts where he should go. It was cool and dark, but he didn't make a mistake. He had been here quite recently. He did not know if he would meet HER, if she would like to talk to him, or if she was still here at all, after all summer was ending... He got out of the car and walked over to where they had recently encountered black dogs, or at least he hoped it was here.

"Marysia! Marry! Svetlana!" He shouted as loud as he could. "Marysia! I need your help! I beg you! She will die! Only she was left with me!" Nobody replied. He tried a few more times. He looked around, looked and listened, but there was no one. He sat down on an overturned tree and stared blankly at the humming waterfall. He didn't know where it had come from or when it happened, but when he turned his head, she was standing by a nearby tree.

"Marysia? He got up and tried to approach her, but she reached out and showed him her hand to stay where he was."

"I know about everything. What do you expect from me? That I will give her a fate that you have prepared for me?" She spoke softly, almost in a whisper, and her voice did not sound like the one he knew so well.

"I couldn't lose you..."

"You lost me anyway, and maybe I would have peace? Maybe I would be calm for a moment?"

"What if not? If your soul was tormented? I thought it would be better... I thought maybe we could make it..."

"There was no chance of that. Another transformation that cannot be reversed.

A demon that wanders forever, aimlessly and without place on earth. Anyway, let's not talk about it." Her voice was full of regret and resentment.

"And yet you found me? Why? I can't believe you wanted to kidnap my baby or bury her alive. I can't believe you are killing farmers... I will never believe it, I know you."

"Or maybe that's just what you think? You think transformation doesn't make change? You think I don't have to fight myself every time I see a man nearby? You think since I was a gentle and sensitive woman, now I have scruples as a Lady Midday? You have no idea how much it all costs me. How much effort and pain for the human element to overcome the instinct given by nature!"

"We have to help her, Mary. I don't care how. This is my baby. I want to have her with me, even in the worst form." Wojtek wrung his hands.

"And how can you be sure that Matylda will be strong enough not to choose the demonic nature and decide to turn off humanity? Then you will lose her anyway. If she died in illness, her innocent soul would go to heaven, if there is one at all. Lady Midday tried to dissuade him from the obvious decision she had already made.

"Why did you come back? Why did you find me?" He returned to the previous thread.

"I knew Matylda was sick. As the Lady Midday I am constantly in motion, always elsewhere. I feel sick, then I have an advantage over the victim. Such a "gift". The girl's illness brought me to Roztocze.

Then I found out it's your baby. I decided to prepare her. We talked a lot, but I forbade her to mention it to anyone."

"Since when did you know? You purposely forbid her from speaking so that we wouldn't have time to help her? You wanted revenge? Did you want to feel my pain? Bravo! Really! Bravo!"

"Don't you dare talk to me like that. I can disappear anytime and leave you." Lady Midday's eyes darkened.

"Stay! Please." Wojtek was crying.

"When I arrived, there was nothing else to do. The child was poisoned from the inside, I could smell a putrid smell that you cannot smell. Her organs were completely saturated with it. I'll spare you the details."

"We can turn her. Just as? Come up with something, please." He wasn't looking at her. He spoke as if he were not entirely convinced of his point. He was acting like a madman.

"I do not have too much time. After harvest. With the first chill, I will blow in the wind to return another summer."

"So let's do it today, tomorrow..."

"You think it's that simple?" The female figure was more and more irritated, while the man was more and more indifferent and powerless.

"I don't know. I don't know anything anymore."

"I knew you would come here, that you would ask me for it. I was preparing for this. If we are to do this, it must be made Godling.

Then you will keep her almost unchanged form: a child. She will still want to prank, still cheerful, innocent and timid. You live in a perfect place. Godling love peace, tranquility and farmhouses. They are hardworking, helpful.

"Will we live like we used to?" Wojtek was suddenly animated, but in saying this he was showing naivety, not to say infantilism.

"Like we used to? Nothing will be the same. Matylda will not grow up. She will always be five years old. Besides, she will only come out from time to time, so you will have to hide her from the world. It will be your secret forever. Are you ready for it? Is your wife ready for this? Did you even ask her what she thought about it?"

"No. I don't know if she would have agreed. Probably not."

"I'm not going to do anything without her permission, and also without Matylda's permission. You must all be aware of the consequences. I am absolutely against it, but if you will, I will help. You don't have much time. If you decide to change your baby, we'll meet at the same time tomorrow. It's a bad decision, Wojtek. This is all you need to know. Goodbye."

She wanted to turn away.

"Marysia?" Wojtek just wanted to ask one more question - "Don't you feel anything anymore? Did you know how to just forget about it all?"

"I'll never forget. I know one thing, it's good to see you happy. It is enough for me to see my father's pain go through hell a second time. It's better this way, Wojtek.

It's better this way." She disappeared in a flash.

"Marysia?! Marry?" The man was running around the branch, but he couldn't find her anywhere. So he sat down and wept again. During the last few days he had to keep up appearances to get his wife out of bed, not to show weakness in front of his daughter. Now, when his companions were only trees and birds, he could finally vent all the emotions accumulated in his head and heart. "I've never come to terms with your departure. I will never stop loving you, Marry. But it's better this way. Let's just fix Matylda..." he groaned.

He didn't come home until morning.

***

"Where were you? I thought you did something to yourself? I'm going crazy!" For the first time in a long time, Nina spoke without nerves, but with only an audible concern in her tone.

"Leave me alone, and I'll have nothing left," she finished.

"We need to talk. Time is short. Come on, let's get away a bit from home so that no one can hear." He grabbed her hand and they walked towards the forest.

As he introduced her to the purpose and details of the night's meeting, Nina couldn't speak. Not only did she only recently learn about the existence of demons, but now would she turn her child into one of them? It was beyond her comprehension. Besides, she wouldn't do it to a child. She rejected this option before Wojtek really managed to bring it closer to her.

"It's the only solution to have her with us. You know perfectly well that we will no longer be parents. Can you live like this? Will you be able to live without her? I don't." Wojtek tried to convince his wife to his extreme plan. "And those little creatures, those protective spirits that Marysia mentioned..."

"No. I will not be able to. However, I will also not be able to see my child, who is always five years old, looking in the future at her infirm parents, at their death... Who will help her understand this then? Who will stay with her?

They will chase away her, and she will be alone. And with her becoming a five-year-old, she won't even understand why this is all happening. Wojtek, have you thought about it at all? Are you running amok?" Nina, whom he suspected of losing her senses, was now clearly speaking and was more of a pragmatist than he had been all his life.

"Maybe you're right." He was angry with himself. Indeed, his selfishness outweighed his common sense. "But she would be with us, the three of us could hide on the sidelines here, live like hermits..." Once again he did not have time to finish his thoughts.

"I'm sure I'm right. Since we cannot help her, then at least let her go quietly and not expose her to further suffering. Will you promise me you'll drop this topic?" Nina wanted to be sure that Wojtek's whim would be forgotten. She had enough revelation for a few weeks. The latter, however, seemed completely ridiculous.

"On one condition." He looked deep into her eyes.

"Matilda will speak for herself."

"And as if you want to explain to a five-year-old girl that you will turn her into a demon, and then we will get older and older until we finally leave her. I do not agree." Nina was stern. In her opinion, her husband has completely lost his common sense.

"I'm not going to explain it to her. We'll leave it to Lady Midday, her friend. Since they have such a great contact with each other... besides, Marysia is impartial, indeed, she even agrees with you. She will present her the situation and we will see what Matylda will answer her.

Can it be like this?" Wojtek wanted to get it over with, gain acceptance from his wife and accept what fate would bring.

"Lady Midday agrees with me? And yet she knows best what kind of life it is, what sacrifices, how much suffering and pain it is. So be it then. I don't know what's right and what's wrong. I am completely lost and I cannot really see the situation soberly anymore. Perhaps indeed a third party should decide. For the sake of the little one. Our little one." Nina burst into tears again.

***

There was a nervous atmosphere in the house, but hardly noticeable by the little girl who lay on the couch by the open kitchen, book in hand. She was very weak, pale, with two white gauze pads sticking out of her nose.

"Mati. We have a surprise for you," Wojtek began. "Would you like to meet your long-lost friend?" He watched the child's reaction closely. Nothing pleased her so long ago. She hurriedly kicked off the blanket covering her skinny legs and was ready to leave.

"Of course, Papa, I missed her so much." Matylda regained her old gleam in her eye.

"She moved, but recently I met her on the waterfall, which someone did not see because she fell asleep in the car like a baby." Wojtek tried to loosen the atmosphere even more.

"Oh, Dad, why didn't you wake me up? You know how much I care about her!" Matylda was getting more and more excited, which caused mixed feelings in her mother.

"Well. Let us not overdo these emotions. Get in the car."

Matylda sat down in her car seat. Nina watched her in the mirror. She no longer looked like she had at the beginning of summer vacation.

She wasn't the same girl anymore. Most of all, she has changed outwardly. She lost weight, although she was very small before. Her gums were swollen, and her skin and conjunctiva were pale white. Numerous ecchymoses and bruises appeared on her tiny body. Her behavior has also changed. She was weakened, constantly tired, she did not feel like having fun or outings, and even less so to meet her grandparents, friends or strangers in general. She asked only her parents to be with her. Of course, Nina's parents spent a dozen or so days with them, Mr. Stożyński came by, who broke his heart at the sight of his granddaughter and could not come to terms with the fact that Wojtek, who lost his mother, is now about to lose his only child. As his state of mind was contagious to Matylda, they both asked him to come back together. So only the three of them remained. Mati constantly complained about the pain in her legs, often also in her arms, so they usually took turns feeding her, and when she wanted to spend time in the garden, Wojtek carried her there in his arms. Fortunately, she was not feverish, she was warm and, in addition, she did not come into contact with other people than her parents, despite the reduced immunity, infections did not attack her, as the doctors had announced.

***

They got there. Terrifying and mysterious. Nina remembered the pack of black demon dogs. Her retinue. At that moment, she thought that this was the stupidest thing she could talk Wojtek into. That their child might have fallen victim to this demon, that they did not really know the intentions of the Lady Midday, which could be false and wish them ill.

They got out of the car, it was very late. Matylda did not fall asleep from adrenaline. Wojtek covered her with a warm blanket and went outside.

"We are here! We are waiting for you!" He called as he did last time.

There is darkness all around, the trees rustling all around and the waterfall, barely visible, but only audible by the visitors.

Nina was afraid of this meeting for so many reasons that she even stopped remembering it.

"Marysia! Are you here?" Wojtek's voice sounded more and more desperate. "Come on show yourself finally! Can't you see that she's almost asleep?"

"Honey, lie down and sleep. If your friend shows up, this time I'll wake you up right away. I promise."

"All right, Mommy. Just do not forget." Matylda put her head against the glass and after a while she was sleeping soundly.

Wojtek shouted a few more times.

Then he spoke in a normal tone, as if accepting the fact that the Lady Midday will not come.

When Nina woke up, it was light. At first she had no idea where she was. She quickly remembered: night, transformation, Lady Midday. She looked around. Matylda was still sleeping in the car seat at the back, Wojtek was sitting motionless by the fallen tree limb, but his eyes were wide open.

"What happened? I fell asleep, I'm sorry! Wojtek?" Nina was shaking her husband furiously.

"She didn't show up. She just deceived us in the world. She probably thought transformation was a bad thing, she made it clear right away. But why did she tell me to bring her here? Or maybe she was here, but she chickened out? She did not want to take such responsibility..." Wojtek thought aloud.

"Apparently it was supposed to be like that, although... I must admit that I was slowly getting used to your proposal. Maybe it would really be better if we didn't have to watch her fade away, experience a funeral, cover her bodies..."

"Hush, hush… it's okay." Wojtek hugged his wife in his arms. He loved her more than anything. Both of them. The last weeks and days have been difficult for them, but it is still his Janka. Same. He knew he had to provide her with maximum support in the coming days. "We're going home. Mati needs medication and something to eat."

***

They arrived around noon. Wojtek bent over backwards to please his daughter. He mentioned the funniest names of dishes that he could think of, and which her mother, the cook, would later prepare. Mati, however, did not want anything at all.

"Oh, please, daughter. For daddy. Just a few bites. Please, please, please…"

In the office he could be the president of people in charge, at home he could shave his legs and turn into a princess if his only child asked him to.

Matilda sat down on the couch. She became serious.

"Do you know that I love you very much?" These words in this situation made the eyes of both parents wet, who immediately abandoned all their activities and hurried to the end of the couch.

"I'm very sick. I know because I don't want to play or laugh anymore and sometimes I don't even have the strength to breathe. I am already very tired. And everything hurts." Adults know that they should be tough, that they shouldn't get fall apart in front of her. But now this task seemed quite impossible.

"Can you take me to the blanket now? There, by the cereals? I will look at the grove for a moment, at our house…" She lacked the strength to go on.

Nina did not have the strength to answer, luckily Wojtek took up the baton.

"Sure, baby. Daddy will pick you up and sit with you. Maybe the three of us can sit?"

"No, Daddy. I would like to be alone. Just don't get angry," she broke off.

"No. Everyone just needs to be alone with themselves sometimes. Do you want to take something with you? A doll?"

"No. I don't need anything."

Nina kissed her baby girl's forehead and both cheeks. Of course, she put on her hat, because the sun was still warm enough. Wojtek threw a blanket over his shoulders and he took Matylda in his arms. He put her in the place she showed him, put a pillow specially purchased for her under her back, kissed her and assured her that she was being watched by her mother from the window, and as soon as she raised her hand, they would run for her.

"Daddy, don't worry about me. Everything is ok."

She smiled fondly.

Wojtek did not know where this child was so optimistic and cheerful that she could share a few adults, Admittedly, she had been receiving painkillers, and so far had not been plagued by additional illnesses, but she was so weak and tired. He admired her.

Nina was standing on the porch with a cup of tea. She hugged her husband and they both stared at their perfect creation. And their child was already watching the almost autumn landscape. Nina resembled Chełmoński's Babie Lato a little.

Typical rural landscape, a pasture and a girl lying on it carelessly. A bit lazy, a bit dreamy, united with nature. In the background, the blue of a calm sky...

Suddenly, to her immense surprise, the woman observed what she initially assumed to be hallucinations. There was a black dog in Chełmoński's painting, but now she saw him also here, several meters in front of her.

"Wojtek, do I have any dreams, is there a dog there?" She wanted to make sure and dispel the fear that she was losing her mind.

"Yes. I can see him too, though dimly."

There was something else. Matylda picked up a thick stick from the ground, leaned on it and stood up. Nina broke free from Wojtek's embrace, but Wojtek held her firmly with his hand.

"Wait, please."

She eased the resistance and waited obediently, though her heart was racing. Suddenly, out of nowhere, a female figure emerged. Nina saw her for the first time. She was standing still. A tall young woman in a flowing white tunic. Her face was raw and pale like Matylda's. Nina remembered a fragment of the description of the demon found on the web after their first conversation about the demon with Wojtek. Indeed, it was a virgin of delightful beauty.

She walked over to Matylda and took her hand. Nina doesn't see very well from a distance, but neither of them seemed to be talking. Matylda only turned towards the house, waved her hand at her parents, and turned back towards the horizon.

Nina was ready to run towards them, but Wojtek again grasped her hand tightly. She stayed with him.

They were still standing on the porch, watching the landscape change. Nina felt like Karolina Friedrich from the painting The Woman in the Window. Light outside, she - like the heroine of a painting - interested in the view in front of her. No, not interested, rather delighted with the figure of a young woman with blonde hair and a child staring at her. It all seemed tender, tender against the lighted sky. They were heading towards the huge sheaf of grain together, all the time holding hands, while she nervously squeezed the hand of her lover. After all, they could no longer see them...

Summer was over. Their waiting for the worst has also ended. That was the last time they saw Matylda...